Kai Nez is pathetic. At least that's what his mother tells him after blaming him for his father's death from a diabetic coma. He's the poor part native, part white gay guy the bullies picked on in their small-town high school, on the outskirts of Phoenix, Arizona. The crush he has on the football quarterback—homecoming king Conner Mitchell—will always be that, a crush. And he's fine with it. Until Conner corners Kai at his graduation party and gives Kai something to fantasize about, then disappears. Years later, Kai is bar tending at a local restaurant. He's happy where he's at and he's good at his job. Then Conner Mitchell shows up at the restaurant and bulldozes back into Kai's life. At the same time, weird things start happening in the duplex he shares with his best friend. Haunted house things.

Conner Mitchell lives the good life, born into wealth, perfect student, perfect athlete and dating the perfect girl. But perfection is over-rated and short lived. After college and landing a lucrative job as a pharmaceutical rep, he breaks up with his girlfriend, moves back to the small town he grew up in, and finds Kai again. The brief moment they shared at his graduation party has always haunted him. And now Kai is dealing with a different kind of haunting and needs his help.

Kai is skeptical and fearful of both ghosts and Conner's intentions. Conner isn't going to let this chance pass him by. It's time to show Kai who he really is and prove to Kai he's not pathetic. He's perfect.

The unauthorized reproduction or distribution of this copyrighted work is illegal. Criminal copyright infringement, including infringement without monetary gain, is investigated by the FBI and is punishable by up to 5 years in federal prison and a fine of $250,000.

This book is a work of fiction. Names, characters, places, and incidents either are products of the author's imagination or are used fictitiously. Any resemblance to actual events or locales or persons, living or dead, is entirely coincidental.

The Haunting Crush
Copyright © 2021 Christie Gordon
ISBN: 978-1-4874-3381-9
Cover art by Martine Jardin

All rights reserved. Except for use in any review, the reproduction or utilization of this work in whole or in part in any form by any electronic, mechanical or other means, now known or hereafter invented, is forbidden without the written permission of the publisher.

Published by eXtasy Books Inc

Look for us online at:
www.eXtasybooks.com

The Haunting Crush

By

Christie Gordon

Dedication

To the Ghost Adventures team, part of my inspiration for writing this novel, along with my sons and their friends, who are always an inspiration.

Chapter One

Kai stepped through open sliding-glass pocket doors onto a flagstone patio and stopped, scanning over the other teenagers in t-shirts, ripped jeans, and shorts, hovering around a beer pong table.

A blond boy threw the ping pong ball into a triangle of red Solo cups, hitting his target. Beer splashed out of a cup and the throng cheered, some with hands raised.

Kai's attention turned to Bryce, who stood beside him, his brown hair cut around his face and swept to one side, his large blue eyes fixating on the game. He sipped beer from a clear, plastic cup.

"Pretty nice place Conner lives in, right?" Kai swung his long hair over his shoulder.

Bryce gave him a sly smile. "These entitled kids have it all. I mean, look at this fucking place." He waved his arms. "It's got to be at least eight thousand square feet. Crestview is fucking lit. Fountain Hills' finest. Even better than Firerock Country Club."

Kai nodded, taking in the Grecian columns between arches of stucco and red draperies hanging down and tied to each one. Out beyond the immense patio lay a manicured lawn with palm trees rising up around a rectangular pool with a hot tub attached in the middle. A few teenagers splashed about in the turquoise water. As he drank his beer from his clear plastic cup, he looked out over the expanse of natural desert hills beyond an iron fence, saguaro cacti rising up with what looked like their arms raised. The nearest neighbor had to be acres away. "Anyway, it was cool Conner invited us to his graduation party, right?

"Good thing you're his chem lab partner." Bryce gulped some beer and chuckled, peering at him. "You got some good taste, man. Too bad he's not gay." He smirked at Kai.

"Can't have it all, I guess." Kai let his smile fade and stared at his beer. Conner Mitchell, football quarterback, homecoming king, biggest crush of his life. Nothing would ever come of it, but at least they'd become friends at school. All because he was good at chemistry and Conner wanted his help.

"Bro, I've been thinking." Bryce gave him a wide grin.

"Oh, no. What now?" Kai shook his head and leaned against the edge of the door jamb, stuffing a hand inside the front pocket of his gray, board shorts.

"So, you know how they say some Asians are bananas? You know, yellow on the outside and white on the inside?"

"Yeah . . . Do I really want to hear this?" Kai released a puff of air.

"Well, you're an apple. You know, red on the outside and white on the inside." Bryce erupted in a belly laugh.

Kai lowered his brows and grinned at the same time. "The fuck? What's wrong with you? My skin is not red. It's barely even brown."

"But you're native. That's makes you red, right? And you act white, get it?" Bryce slapped his arm.

"You're fucking crazy. Natives are not red. I'm only like one quarter Navajo anyway. My dad was half." Kai frowned. At least that's what his CDIB card said. If only his father were alive, then maybe his mother wouldn't hate him so much. He drew a deep inhale. Time to change the subject. "I need to take a piss."

"Sure, man." Bryce looked him over and wrinkled his brows. "You're not mad at me, right?" He touched his arm. "I didn't mean to make you think about your dad."

Bryce meant well. He just wanted to make me laugh. "No, I'm not mad." Kai flashed a forced smile at him. "I'll be right back." He walked off through a large family room with modern leather furnishings and high ceilings, attached to a kitchen with alder wood cabinets and high-end, stainless-steel appliances.

Paige stepped to him and swung her dirty-blonde hair behind her shoulders, her red bikini showing off all her curves. "Hi, Kai. Glad you could make it." She held a glass of red wine.

"Hi, Paige. Can you tell me where the bathroom is?" She gave off a bad vibe. He wrinkled his nose. He was never really sure what it was exactly that bothered him so much about her. *Maybe because she's Conner's girlfriend?* He smirked. Maybe.

"Oh, I think all the ones on this floor are taken. There's one upstairs, next to the office." She pointed up to an open balcony hovering over the room with a black iron railing and bookshelves lining the walls.

He looked up. "How do I get there?" This house was immense.

She pointed to a hallway, behind a wet bar. "Did you see that stairway by the front door? That goes up there."

"Yep, thanks." He sipped his beer and strode over tan travertine flooring, under the balcony and through a hallway, then up a flight of circular stairs with green Berber carpeting. At the top of the stairs he found an open set of tall double doors leading into an office covered in dark wood, then an open single door and closed single door beyond it. He could barely make out a tile counter behind the middle door. "Must be that one." He walked into it, flicked the light on, shut the door, and locked it.

He turned and scanned over a bathroom with a travertine tile counter, gold fixtures, and deep-red towels. He gulped the rest of his beer down, then threw the cup into a gold waste basket. "Nice." After using the toilet, he scrubbed soap over his hands from the white ceramic dispenser, then examined himself in the mirror—his straight, brown hair parted off-center, falling down the sides of his face just past his broad shoulders, the large, almond-shaped brown eyes under curved brows, the smallish nose, and full lips. His skin wasn't red. Bryce was an idiot. It was definitely darker than his white friends', but not as dark as the Pima on the rez.

He shut off the water at the sink and dried his hands, looking over the white NASA graphic t-shirt covering his chest. With all these rich kids in town, the Goodwill here always had great stuff. He smirked. Maybe this shirt came from a kid at this party. *I wonder if they'd notice?*

He should have graduated this year with Conner. He thinned his lips and hung the towel on the rack, folding it to match the others. Maybe if he hadn't spent that year in foster care after his dad died ... He whispered, "Oh well." He sighed, opened the door, and stepped out.

Conner stood in the hallway, wearing black swim trunks, looking him up and down, his muscled chest bare. He licked his lips. "Kai."

His breath caught. "C-Conner?" He took in Conner's chiseled male-model looks, the ice-blue slightly narrowed eyes resting under straight dark brows angled up at the outer edge, the pointed nose, the generous lips with a bit of pout, the longer wavy brown hair on top of his head parted on the side and draped over his forehead. His angled jaw held a sprinkling of stubble. He stood a good four inches taller than Kai's five-foot ten frame. He drew a deep breath and focused on the inch-long scar running over Conner's cheek, under his left eye. The sack Conner took that day was scary. It had looked like Conner might have lost his eye.

"What are you doing up here?" Conner came in close, his bare chest brushing against Kai's.

Kai knit his brows. "Um, just had to use the bathroom. Paige told me they were full downstairs."

Conner raked his teeth over his lower lip, then threw Kai's arms over his head, crushing him in a deep kiss, tossing his back against the wall, thrusting his hips into Kai's.

Kai widened his eyes. *Holy fuck.* He opened his mouth, allowing Conner's exploring tongue inside. He tasted of beer and pizza and everything he'd always wanted. *How the fuck is this happening?*

Conner seized him by the waist and shoved him through the third door.

The back of Kai's legs struck something hard, throwing him off balance. He fell to his back on a bed and bounced. The door slammed shut. The room went dark.

Conner came down over him, devouring him with open-mouthed kisses, grinding his hard cock on Kai's hip, groaning. "Fuck, this is okay, right?" Seduction and desperation laced his voice.

Kai stole a deep breath, fighting to keep up with his demanding mouth. "Y-yeah." He kissed him with more intensity, sensation building in his swollen cock with each thrust of Conner's hips.

Conner roamed his hands down Kai's body, found his hands, and lifted them up over his head, holding them down. He shifted his hips to thrust against Kai's thigh, gliding his hard cock over him through his shorts. The thrusts became erratic. "Fuck, I'm close. Are you close?"

Jesus, is he going to come? Kai drove his hips harder, faster against Conner's, sliding his solid cock against his groin, letting delicious pressure and friction pulse through him. He wound a leg around Conner's, frantic for more. His peak teased him. "A-almost."

Conner pushed frenzied thrusts against him, kissing with urgency, letting out groan after groan. His body shuddered and his head reared back, his face tensed, and he released one gasp after another.

He's coming. As an intense sensation engulfed Kai's cock, he drove harder, letting wave after wave of orgasm spurt seed into his boxer briefs, moaning with each one.

As it calmed, Conner lay over him, panting. "Shit, I'm sorry." He rolled to his back.

Kai laid on the bed, staring up through the dark, the only light weaving in through shades drawn across the window next to the bed. "I-I don't know what to say."

Conner rose up and stood from the bed. "Don't tell anyone. Okay?"

Kai lifted up on his elbows, squinting at him. "Sure." What the hell was going on? How did he feel about this, never mind Conner? He swallowed hard and pursed his lips.

"Y-you know where the bathroom is. Maybe I'll see you downstairs." Conner glanced at him, drawing his brows together, then opened the door and left, shutting it with a soft click.

Kai fell to the bed with a sigh. "What the fuck?" He lifted his forearm to rest over his eyes. How many times had he imagined doing something like that with him? At least a hundred. He raised a corner of his mouth. But now it had happened, and he felt . . . empty. Fucking alone. He never in a million years thought Conner had any interest in him, or any interest in guys at all. Why would he do that? Because Conner knew he was gay? Everyone knew it at school. It wasn't a secret. That must be it.

He rolled to his side with a huff. He should get cleaned up and go home. The last thing he wanted to see was Paige hanging on Conner all night. *Not now. Fuck that.*

He rose from the bed and walked into the bathroom, cleaned up with a washcloth, then strode out, trotted down the stairs, through the hallway and found Bryce, still standing on the patio. "Hey."

He grinned at Kai. "What took you so long?"

Kai shifted his weight and scowled. "You'll never fucking guess."

Bryce looked behind Kai and lifted his chin. "Hey, Conner."

Conner brushed up behind Kai. "Hey." He glanced at Kai, frowned, then walked off to the beer pong table.

An ache built in Kai's chest. This was fucked up. He pressed his lips together. He didn't want to feel something real for Conner. He shouldn't feel something. There was no way what happened was going to turn into anything. He was a crush and a fantasy, and nothing was going to change that. "Let's go home."

"What? Why? The party's just getting started." Bryce lifted his brows.

"You stay. I'll go." He went to leave.

Bryce grabbed his arm. "No, I'll take you home. It's five or six miles, it's hot out, and you won't have any water."

"I can run that in forty-five minutes easy, but okay. Let's go." The run would have helped to clear his mind, but Bryce was right about the water. He hung his head, then glanced at the beer pong table.

Paige had her arms draped around Conner's bare chest, smiling, leaning her well-endowed body against his.

As Conner gulped beer from a cup, he wound his arm around her shoulders.

Tears stung Kai's eyes. That was the Conner he knew. Not the one from upstairs. Not the one who kissed him until they both came. That Conner didn't exist. Why should it? Who was he? Just some poor-ass gay, not really white, not really native fucker. With a wince, he shut his eyes tight and blinked the tears back.

"Fuck, Kai, are you okay? What the hell happened?" Bryce grabbed his arm, creasing his forehead.

"Nothing. Just take me home." Kai bit his lip and headed for the front door with Bryce following, swerving through laughing, drinking teenagers. Should he tell Bryce, or keep Conner's secret? Bryce had a big mouth, so telling Bryce might let it slip out. *So what.* Conner was graduating in a few days. What would it matter?

Kai came to a large set of wooden double doors with an ornate iron handle, opened it, then stepped out into an entryway paved in more travertine. A lion head fountain rested on the wall, dripping water out of its mouth into a basin. This place was over the top.

Bryce shut the door behind them. "You going to tell me what's going on now?"

Should he tell Bryce? Maybe part of it. He needed to think on that. He furrowed his brows and walked down a set of cement steps. Desert landscaping, lit up from the ground, surrounded them—tall saguaros, ocotillo, and mesquite trees. As he reached the long winding driveway, he looked out at the street toward their car. A few javelina snorted and stopped to look back at him. "Shit." He pointed.

"What?" Bryce peered down the driveway. "Fucking javelina? How are we going to get to our car?"

Kai frowned. Just what he needed. "Guess we'll have to wait it out. They'll leave soon enough."

Bryce walked to the side of the driveway and picked up a landscaping rock. He drew his hand back.

Kai went to him and seized his arm. "What the fuck? You want to get attacked?" *Idiot.*

Bryce frowned at him. "Yeah, guess you're right." He threw the rock into the landscape.

With a sigh, Kai sat down on the warm cement of the driveway and wrapped his arms around drawn up knees. "Just wait. They'll leave."

Bryce sat next to him, crossing his legs. "So, tell me what

happened."

Kai drew a deep breath. Maybe Bryce could help make some sense of it, because right now, it made no sense at all. "Fucking Conner kissed me."

"The fuck?" Bryce widened his eyes. "You've got to be shitting me." He snickered. "Are you sure you didn't hit your head or some shit?"

Kai narrowed his eyes at him and tensed his jaw. "Come on, I'm serious." He rocked once. "He, well, he caught me outside the bathroom upstairs." *Damn, it was awesome though, really.* He relaxed his shoulders, letting a faint smile work his lips. "He pinned me up against the wall and kissed me. Like, a lot." *No need to mention the rest of it.* The memory flashed through his mind. Lust tingled up his spine. He licked his lips.

"Fucking Conner made out with you upstairs? With his girlfriend at the beer pong table?" Bryce dropped his jaw open.

"Yeah," Kai said. "He told me not to tell anyone, though. So, don't say anything."

"You think he might be questioning and tried you out because you're gay?"

"Probably." Kai huffed. *Of course. That settles that.* Bryce had come to the same conclusion he had, so it was the most logical answer. "Yeah, that's probably all it was." It was time to put Conner back where he belonged, in daydreams and fantasies.

Bryce glanced at the bottom of the driveway. "Hey, the pigs are gone. Let's go."

Kai released a short laugh. "They're not pigs. They're peccaries." He stood up and brushed off his behind.

"Yeah, whatever. They look like hairy pigs." With a laugh, Bryce rose up and walked down the driveway.

Kai sat in the passenger seat of Bryce's old Honda Accord,

picking at a worn spot in the gray cloth seat, his arm resting on the open window frame. It was already hot at night, and it wasn't even June. "Dude, if you don't get the AC fixed in this car, the summer's going to be brutal."

"Yeah, whatever. When are you going to get a car?" Bryce glanced at Kai and smirked.

"After I get some money saved." He looked out at the spray of cactus and rock beds speeding by the car under the streetlights. "After high school I can finally work full time. Janice said they'll make me a bartender at The Fountain Bar and Grill if I stay there."

"Yeah? Cool, man. They do pretty well. I was thinking of trying that place out." Bryce pulled the car into a drive and came up on the side of the street. "The Village. Home sweet home." He pushed the shifter into Park.

Kai looked out over sets of plain square stucco buildings, the living quarters on top and open carports underneath, all with flat roofs and cream paint, nothing bigger than a two bedroom. Everything was different here, no fancy columns, no natural desert. It was as if they put the plainest buildings they could think of out in the desert and then surrounded them with pine trees, oaks, and palm trees to cover them up. He opened the car door. It groaned in protest. "You need to oil these hinges or something."

Bryce stepped out of the car and shut the door with a thud. "Whatever. At least it runs." He turned toward the buildings. "Hey, is that your sister over there?" He pointed.

Kai surveyed the area around his building and frowned. "Yeah." *Something's up.*

May sat on the tar drive under the building, her knees drawn up and picking at something unseen in the asphalt. Her long brown hair fell over the shoulders of her white sleeveless shirt and flipflops covered her feet.

"Shit, that's not good." Kai walked toward her.

"You need help, man?" Bryce followed him.

He held his palm out to Bryce. "No. Mom probably had a spell again. Just go back to the party."

"You sure?" Bryce knit his brows together.

"Yeah. It's not like I haven't dealt with this a million times already." He pursed his lips. He never knew when his mother would go off. One minute she'd be fine, and the next it was like a bomb exploded and everyone around her was a target. "See you later. Let me know if anything interesting happens."

"Sure." Bryce got back in his car and started up the engine.

Kai stepped to his sister and narrowed his eyes, placing his hands on his hips. He didn't like the look of this. "May."

She peeked up at him with her big brown eyes, glistening in the dark. "What are you doing home so early? I thought you were looking forward to the big fancy grad party?"

He tensed his lips. She didn't need to know the details of what happened. "Just didn't feel right staying." He sat next to her, crossing his legs on the pavement. "So, Mom—"

"She's fucking insane." She huffed and focused on him. "I cannot wait to graduate in three years and get the fuck out of here."

It was exactly what he'd thought. "What was it this time?" He drew a deep breath.

"Does it matter? The God damned pizza she ordered for dinner had onions. She hates onions. You'd think someone took a shit on her food." She scowled.

He released a quick laugh. "Maybe someone should."

She snickered and dropped her legs down, resting on her hands behind her. "I'm not sure you should go in there just yet." As her attention turned to him, her smile waned.

He let loose a puff of air and placed his elbows on his knees. "I'm just going to go to bed. It's been sort of a shit night and I'm tired."

"Oh, what happened? Want to talk about it?" She lifted her

brows.

He gave his head a quick shake. "No."

She narrowed her eyes. "Did someone bully you at the party? Maybe one of those asshole jocks?"

He flashed his eyes at her. "No." He wasn't sure he'd call what happened bullying, or the jock who did it an asshole.

She made a frustrated noise. "Fine." She glanced at the building behind her. "But if you go in there now, don't say I didn't warn you."

"Yeah." He rose up from the pavement and brushed his hands together. "Don't stay out here too long." He glanced toward the wash beyond the masonry stucco wall, at the scraggly mesquite and palo verde trees mixed with tall, broad-leafed cottonwoods. "At some point all the addicts are going to come crawling out of Saguaro Woods. You should be inside before that happens."

She let loose a long exhale. "I know."

With a sigh, he went to the door inside the carport and opened it, walked up the steps and out into the main room. Everything was dark. He scanned the area. Where was she? Maybe she'd gone to bed already.

"Kai."

He startled. No such luck. "Y-yeah?" He flicked on the light at the wall and took in the worn green couch the cushions with permanent dents, the oval oak coffee and end tables, the white ceramic lamps with maroon shades, all from the local Goodwill. He assessed his mother, her dark hair cut just above the shoulder, parted on the side, her age showing in the hint of jowls and wrinkles around her eyes and mouth, her blue eyes gazing back at him. She was the only one in the family with blue eyes. The only one not native at all. Her brown t-shirt with kittens on the front didn't quite fit her mood. He twitched a corner of his mouth.

"Kai, why is your sister outside? Tell her to come in. It's

not safe out there." She glowered, then lifted a red, plastic glass and twirled it, the ice making clinking noises.

Shit, she's drinking. He stared at the floor and frowned. "I-I tried, Mom, but she wants to stay out there a little longer."

"What the fuck is wrong with you?" She slammed the glass on the coffee table, the contents splashing out, and stood up, her body menacing, even with her thin frame. She stalked toward him. "I told you to get her. Do what you're fucking told for once!"

He cowered and grimaced. "I-I just want to go to bed, Mom. Okay?" He stole a peek at her.

Her face relaxed. She came close and whispered in his ear, "You're so fucking pathetic. You know that? Just like your father."

Her favorite jab. It still hurt. Tears stung his eyes and he gulped hard. May was right. He should have stayed in the driveway with her. Mom was on a rampage. He bit his lip and stepped toward his room.

She seized his arm. "Don't you walk away from me. Not when I'm talking to you." The words spat out of her mouth. She sneered at him, studying his face.

He peered down the hallway. If only he could get to his bedroom, then he could lock her out. His lower lip trembled. Her alcohol-laced breath shivered over his cheek.

"You crying now? Is that what queers do? Cry at every little thing?"

He winced and yanked his arm free. He didn't need this shit tonight of all nights. "Leave me the fuck alone." He blinked, and a tear raced down his cheek. As he strode to the hallway, he swiped his face and rubbed his eyes. He couldn't let her get to him like that.

He walked into his bedroom, slammed the door shut, then locked it. Would she try to open it? He tiptoed backward, fixating on the doorknob, holding his breath. Maybe he'd get lucky. But would that mean she'd go after May in the driveway now? He wrinkled his brow. She usually knew better than to do this outside. Child Protective Services wouldn't hold back if someone called them again.

His mind flashed to a tattered, bare house, no electricity, and no running water. His father lay limp on a linoleum floor, a water bucket fallen sideways by his head. A puddle of water all around him. He remembered screaming, then his mother blaming him. How could he possibly have known that his father hadn't taken his insulin that day? How could a five-year-old kid be responsible for that? He shook the memory away. She was fucking insane. Maybe they'd be better off if they'd stayed in foster care.

It's quiet. Why? Did she go back to her drink on the couch? He released a long sigh. "Shit." As he slumped his shoulders, he made his way to his twin bed, one of two mattresses on the floor, with a few brown blankets thrown on top, and sat down, resting his elbows on his knees and his face in his hands. That was close. It could have been so much worse. He gulped hard and lay down on the bed, looking up at the popcorn in the ceiling. "What a fucking night."

He rolled to his side, pulling his legs part way up and sliding a hand under his pillow. Hopefully, mom would fall asleep before May came back in. If not, he'd have to deal with her all over again. May . . . He smirked. She was supposed to have a Navajo name like him, but the idiots at the hospital fucked it up and put May on her birth certificate instead of Mai. Figured. She didn't look native one bit. Not like him. No one ever asked her where she came from or what her ethnicity was. *No one ever asked her if she was adopted.*

He nuzzled into the pillow and shut his eyes. He should sleep. Tomorrow he would have to study for finals. He popped his eyes open and whispered, "Shit, Conner." He would have to see him in chem class on Monday. That would be awkward. Would things be the same between them, or was their friendship, whatever friendship they had, ruined? He wasn't going to solve it tonight. He closed his eyes.

Kai raced past a burnt-orange brick building with letters in cream, reading *Fountain Hills High School* over a metal awning painted in turquoise. His black backpack bounced on his back as he ran. As he approached a turquoise iron fence, he slowed and strode through the open gate, over cement walkways with natural desert all around, scrubby bushes, short mesquites, and palo verde trees dominating the area. The cactus had been removed. Didn't need some teenager falling and getting a body full of needles. Other teenagers milled about, laughing, and talking, stuffing Pop Tarts and Nutra-Grain bars in their mouths, drinking Gatorades.

Sweat beaded on his brow. The morning sun was already warm, and the run didn't help. As he walked under a metal awning to a brick building with the letter *C* over the door, he stopped and looked down at his maroon Volcom t-shirt, black shorts, and worn black Vans sneakers, the holes at the pinky toes taunting him. Maybe he could find a new pair at Goodwill this week. He lifted the corner of his mouth. That was the least of his worries.

His heart pounded. It was time for the chemistry final. Time to see Conner. A bump lurched him forward and he took a step. He twisted his head to see Lucas, Conner's *friend*.

"You going in there or what?" Lucas, his blond bangs falling over blue eyes, freckles rolling over his nose and cheeks, sneered at him, then held up his fist. "Get out of my way, gay boy."

Fucker. "Uh, yeah." Kai cringed, then opened a glass door rimmed in turquoise metal, stepped inside, and strolled down the hallway to the chem lab. He didn't need another beating by that asshole. As he approached the door, he wiped his hands on his shorts, took a deep breath, then walked inside.

Kai scanned over the room, taking in the black-topped lab tables with wooden drawers running down the middle underneath, his gaze resting on the table he shared with Conner. It was empty. His classmates filled the other tables and chairs. Cabinets lined the walls all around. Conner must be late. He went to the table and took a seat on a metal stool, then slid a yellow mechanical pencil out of his backpack. He chewed his lower lip and focused on Mr. Lewis.

Mr. Lewis sat behind a desk, looking the room over, his dark glasses resting low in his nose, his gray hair cut short.

"Okay everyone, let's get started." Mr. Lewis walked around the room, handing out stacks of stapled, type-written papers. "Remember, keep your eyes on your own work. I catch anyone cheating and you're done."

Conner burst into the room, panting. His white gym shirt pulled tight across strong shoulders, and his black gym shorts exposed the thick muscles in his thighs. As he took a quick look around, he walked to the seat next to Kai and sat down.

He stifled a grin and focused on the test sitting in front of him. "You're late."

"Yeah." Conner opened his gray backpack and pulled out a green, mechanical pencil. He leaned close to Kai. "Keep it open so I can see."

He whispered, "If you get caught, you're going to fail the test."

"Yeah, whatever." Conner wrinkled his brow, hung his head, and wrapped his arms around his test.

He peeked at Conner. A flash of Conner gasping in pleasure rippled through his mind. Heat lit up his groin. He shouldn't think about that now. But damn if he hadn't thought about it all weekend. He almost hadn't been able to study. He bit the nail on his thumb, then perused the test, flipping through the pages. This would be a piece of cake. And when this was over, he was going to talk to Conner.

Kai brought his finished test to Mr. Lewis' desk and set it in a wire basket.
"Have a good summer, Kai and I'll see you next year." Mr. Lewis smiled at him.
"Yeah, thanks. You, too." As he walked out of the room, he stole a peek at Conner, still hunched over his test, his fingers working over a calculator. He stepped through the doorway, placed his backpack on the floor and propped his back against the wall. His next test was in an hour, so he had plenty of time to talk. How would Conner react? So far, everything seemed pretty normal between them. But he had to know what that was. He didn't want to go the whole summer having these questions weighing on him. He needed clarity or closure or whatever the fuck it was people needed after something like that.
Conner stepped through the door with his backpack slung over one shoulder.
"Hey." Kai caught his arm.
Conner looked him over, then yanked his arm free. "What?"
Kai bit his lip. *Am I really going to do this? Is it worth it?* His heart thumped in his chest. His mouth opened. "Uh, I wanted to talk to you, you know, about the party." *Too late to take it back now.* His mouth went dry.
Conner stared down the hallway, a frown creeping over his lips. "What about the party?" He narrowed his eyes at Kai.
He swallowed hard. "You know, what happened." He studied his face, the blue eyes, the scar on his cheek. "With us."
Conner freed a choked laugh, then smirked, shifting his weight. "You tell me. I was so fucking drunk, I don't remember a thing." He shook his head, the smirk fading. His brows

wrinkled and he licked his generous lips, his attention drawing to the hallway again. "Not a thing."

Kai blinked and furrowed his brows. *So that's how it's going to be.* "You sure?"

"Yeah, I'm sure. I gotta go." Conner turned and trotted down the hallway, opened the glass door and walked out onto the cement pathway.

Kai drew his brows together. *Conner remembers. I know he does.* He wasn't that drunk. What did it matter? Why the hell had he even asked? Now he looked like an idiot. An ache wrapped around his heart. Conner would never go for someone like him anyway. Even if he were a girl, it would never happen. He slumped his shoulders and released a rush of air. *This sucks.*

Chapter Two

Five Years Later

"Bryce, your order is sitting at pick-up. Get it before it melts." Kai shook his head at Bryce and smiled. He was a good waiter, but damn if he didn't let things sit too long at the bar. As he washed a glass at the hand sink, he scanned over the restaurant. A wall of windows looked out over a patio, and beyond, the green grass, sporadic olive and palm trees surrounding Fountain Lake took over the view in the fading evening light. The fountain centering the lake shot up a plume of water, going up over three hundred feet before cascading off to the side. He smirked. If the wind got up, the people walking in the park would enjoy a fine mist of smelly, green water today.

His attention drew down the long bar that ran the length of the restaurant, the gray, quartz bar top and high slatted-metal bar stools sitting at the front of it. He loved it here. Learning to tend bar had been the right choice, no matter what his mother thought about it. He dried the glass on a towel and stacked it with the others on a counter above the glass cooler.

"Hey, can you put the ASU game on here?" An older man pointed at a television hanging down from the ceiling over his head.

"Sure." Kai smiled and twisted around, his ponytail flinging across the back of his black t-shirt with the restaurant logo emblazoned on the front. He grabbed up a remote sitting on an island behind the bar that held the drink blenders, taps, stacks of glasses and the POS station, then switched the feed to the game and scanned across the other televisions lining the wall. Most already had this game on, but apparently this guy wanted it dead center. He set the remote down and looked across the room at the televisions lined up over the windows and glass doors to the patio. Looked like the game was on over there, too. *Hope no one complains.* He curled a corner of his mouth.

Kai stepped to the ticketing machine at one end of the island and ripped off a drink order. Lots of beer today, probably because everyone was here for college football. He smirked, grabbed two cold beer glasses from the glass cooler, then tilted one under a tap and flipped it forward. With all these beers, he didn't have the chance to try out the new bottle trick he'd learned last week. Doing flair bartending always got him better tips. As he filled the second glass, he let his gaze wander over the fake brick walls of the restaurant and out into the crowd sitting at high-top tables, eating, drinking, and chatting.

"Fuck me." Bryce stood next to him with dirty but empty white plates in his hand. "Guess who just walked in?"

"Huh?" Kai lifted his brows and pushed the tap back, then turned around.

Conner ambled to a high-top table, wearing a gray, polo shirt and jeans, his wide shoulders pulling the fabric of the shirt tightly over his chest, a brunette on one side and a blonde on the other.

Kai's breath caught. His heart skipped. *Holy shit.* He gulped hard. He hadn't seen Conner since that chem final. "What the fuck?"

Bryce came closer. "Right? Where the hell has he been? And where's Paige?"

"No idea. I haven't seen him around either. He couldn't

still be with Paige after all this time." He stared at Conner, dropping his mouth open. Damn, he still looked gorgeous and pretty much the same. He let loose a long exhale, brought the beers to the pickup station and dropped them off, then searched the people at the bar for empty plates and glasses. Everyone seemed okay for now. His gaze caught on Conner.

Conner chatted with the brunette, then looked across the bar at him. A faint smile tickled his lips. He hung his head and fingered his menu.

Kai's heart pinched. What was Conner doing here after all this time? He'd figured Conner would have moved away or something. *And why the fuck am I still feeling this way about him?*

A few more orders scratched out of the machine. Kai stepped to it and tore them off, one by one. Finally, something fun. He perused the order. Four lemon drop shots. He smirked and set up four lowball glasses on the drip rail, then grabbed four shakers from the underbar and lined them up. As he glanced out at people watching football, he picked up a bottle of vodka from the well, swung it around his head and flipped it over, pouring clear liquid into each shaker, raising the bottle high in the air before moving on to the next one. He repeated the performance with a lemon juice bottle and simple syrup, then scooped ice into each shaker, set one on top of the other, held them tightly together and brought all four to hover over the lowball glasses, straining the liquid into each one.

Clapping sounded around Kai, and someone whooped. He let a wide smile spread over his mouth, and as he poured the last shot from the shakers, he peeked up.

Conner smiled at him, watching the performance with his chin resting in his hand, elbow on the table.

Kai's heart skipped a beat. If nothing else, Conner would see that he was good at something besides chemistry. He let a sly grin spread over his lips. Though bartending was sort of like chemistry. He lifted the shakers up and set them in the sink, then finished off the drinks with the twist of a lemon peel.

"That was pretty cool, kid," said an older gentleman a few seats down drinking a white wine.

"Thanks. Been working on my skills." Kai laughed, tucked all four glasses into his hands and brought them to the pickup station, then went back to pouring the usual beers and wines.

The restaurant filled with people, and more waited at the door to get in. *Time to kick it into gear. Focus.* The machine spat out more orders and a few customers stood behind the chairs at the bar, waiting for drinks.

Janice, her red hair pulled high in a bun, came around the far end of the bar, slid a pen behind her ear and started making drinks. "Jesus, it's crazy in here tonight."

Kai glanced at Janice, his hands working quickly to fill drink orders. "Why didn't you put somebody else on?"

"Well, Beth called in sick, or she would have been here. When I tried to call in Nick, he said he was busy." She snorted. "I figured it'd be like old times, just me and you if we got slammed." She filled several beer glasses at once under the taps.

"Well, you got your wish." He trotted to the kitchen to check for a food order, perused the dishes waiting under heat lamps on a stainless counter, then picked up a plate of wings and a burger. As he turned around, Bryce came barreling at him.

Bryce shimmied out of the way. "Fuck, Kai. Watch where you're going." He laughed.

"Right." He shook his head and strode out to the bar, then placed the plates in front of an elderly couple. He smiled at them. "Enjoy your food."

"We need to talk when this is over." Bryce brushed up behind him and nodded his head at Conner.

Kai glanced at Conner, then pursed his lips. "Don't tell me he's in your station."

"Of course. I overheard some very interesting things." Bryce wiggled his brows at him.

Kai poured red wine into a wine glass. *Oh no . . .* "Get back to work. I'm in the weeds here."

Kai sighed and dried beer glasses with a white towel, then set them on the top of the glass cooler, stacking them. He looked out over the restaurant. Now only a few stragglers left to go, and it would be time to head home. He sure hoped his old blazer started tonight. Probably needed a new battery. Maybe that was all it was. At least it was cool enough now to walk home if he had to.

Bryce wiped down a high-top table, then searched around him and sided up to the bar. "Hey."

Kai clenched his jaw. Here we go. Bryce was going to fill him in on Conner. He really wished he wouldn't. He'd be so much better off not knowing anything at all. *And especially not seeing him.* He'd worked long and hard to forget the guy. He sighed. "What?" He picked up a new glass from the dishwasher and wiped.

"So, Conner broke up with Paige about a month ago." Bryce glanced at the table Conner had vacated during the rush, as if Conner could still hear him. "He didn't say why, but he moved into town from Scottsdale and he's living at Park Place, right across the street. He's also working from home as a pharmaceutical rep." He narrowed his eyes and looked Kai over.

His heart pounded. Damn his emotions. "Okay. So?" He lifted his brows.

"So . . ." Bryce straightened his spine. "So, he'll probably be hanging out around here."

Kai shrugged. "Why do I care?" Though he did care,

probably too much. He should have been over this stupid crush by now. But seeing Conner again confirmed it. He wasn't. He continued wiping the same glass, going round and round with the towel.

Bryce scoffed. "Jesus, man, I don't know. Maybe you can quit hating him now."

"I don't hate him. I don't even think about him anymore." *Okay, that's a big, fat lie.* But whatever, Bryce didn't need to know that. He set the glass down on top of the stack and grabbed another. He should change the subject. "So, mountain biking or trail running on Monday?" He glanced at Bryce.

Bryce offered him a wide grin. "Mountain biking. I can't keep up with you when we run the trails."

Kai grinned. "Fine. McDowell Mountain Park? Let's do the whole Pemberton Loop this time. No pussying out on me."

"Fine." Bryce huffed and walked off.

A flash of light lit the park up beyond the patio, followed by the loud boom of thunder.

Kai startled and dopped his mouth open, peering out the row of windows to the patio of the restaurant. "Shit." Thick rain fell beyond the patio. As the rain made its way underneath the awning, a couple sitting at a low-top table grabbed up their drinks and came to a table inside.

Janice walked out from the kitchen doors to stand next to him, placing her hands on her hips. "Looks like we got us a late monsoon." She chuckled.

"Looks like." He dried a wine glass.

Another flash of light came, followed by deep rumbling.

"At least we didn't lose power. I heard this storm is bringing a lot of flooding." She tapped his arm. "Good thing you have an SUV."

He smirked. "Yeah, as long as it starts." *Damn battery.*

Bryce trotted up to the front of the bar. "Hey, my customers are saying some of the roads are getting shut down. The washes are all overflowing. You should see the flooding in the park already."

Kai glanced at Janice. "I hope this settles down before we have to go home." Last thing he wanted to deal with was figuring out how to navigate closed roads. He set the dried glass on the counter.

"The trails might be crap tomorrow." Bryce gave him a sly smile.

"They'll be fine. Don't try to wuss out on me. We're still mountain biking tomorrow." He chuckled.

Kai, dressed in a grey t-shirt and black cycling shorts, parked his tan blazer in the carport of the beige adobe-style two-bedroom duplex he shared with Bryce. Turquoise handhewn wood vigas lined the roofline. He turned the key to shut the rumbling engine off. "Wasn't so bad, was it?" He snickered at Bryce, siting in the worn black cloth passenger seat in a multi-colored cycling shirt and shorts, wiping sweat from under his side-swept brown bangs with a red bandana.

"Not so bad if you like feeling like your lungs are burning up inside your body." He chuckled. "You killed me out there."

"You need to get out more." Kai opened the door on the SUV, stepped out and shut it, then looked up into a clear blue sky and pulled the hair tie off his ponytail, letting his hair fall past his wide shoulders. "Let's get the bikes off the rack and cool down. I need a shower."

Bryce got out of the vehicle. "Yeah, me, too."

Kai walked to the back of the blazer, taking in the splotches of sun damage in the paint on the roof and tops of the doors, then the dent in the back bumper. As he met Bryce at the back, he unfastened his bike and worked it off the bike rack stuffed into the hitch.

Bryce shook his head. "You spend all this money on your

bike and gear, but you can't afford a new car."

He grinned. He'd heard this before. "I don't need a new car. I can walk to work if I have to, and right now, this old thing gets me where I need to go."

"But it's so ugly." Bryce burst out in a hardy laugh. "And it doesn't have Bluetooth."

"Shut up." Kai set the bike on the cement driveway and rolled it into the carport, then rolled the bike inside the duplex, setting it against the wall in the kitchen.

Bryce followed and stacked his bike against Kai's. He hit his arm. "Hey, Kai, what the fuck? Did we get mice or something?" He pointed toward the sink.

Kai searched over the oak cabinets of the kitchen, the white laminate counter, to the stainless sink, then down to the beige, ceramic tile floor. Several glasses lay sideways but unbroken. As he wrinkled his brows, he stepped to them and picked them up. "How the hell did they fall off the counter and not break?"

"No idea. That's so weird." Bryce approached him and stood beside him. "Whatever, just put them back."

"Yeah." Kai set them on the counter and walked into the main room, taking a quick scan of the wooden front door. *Still locked.* He drew his brows together and perused the worn puffy brown leather couch and chair that sat under a large window looking at the neighbor's house and Ashbrook Wash beyond. In front of the couch rested a black coffee table and matching end tables with iron lamps topped off with cream shades. Nothing looked out of place in here. *Weird.*

As Kai walked into his bedroom, he flicked on the light from the wall and looked over his queen-sized bed with a red quilt and beige sheets, then at the dark, mission-styled headboard and nightstands. The bed rested beneath a window looking out over the trees and bushes of Ashbrook Wash, the scruffy palo verdes and mesquite trees hovering over brittlebush and desert marigolds. Again, nothing out of place. So maybe not mice, and maybe no one had broken in either. He brushed his hand over the back of his head, twisted his mouth, then made for the hallway.

As Kai stepped into the bathroom of oak cabinets, white laminate counters and a shower-bathtub combo sitting behind a plastic sliding door, his cell phone dinged. He unzipped a mesh pocket on the side of his shorts, slid it out, and held it up to his face.

Brandon
When can we get together?

"Fuck." Kai huffed. What did he have to do to get Brandon off his back? He never should have hooked up with that guy. *What a price to pay for a few drinks and a blowjob.* His image in the mirror caught his gaze and he twisted around. He'd filled out a lot in the last few years and it was all muscle. He smirked. Maybe that was why he couldn't make Brandon go away. Maybe he was too nice, though. At least that's what Bryce and May always said. He held up the phone and typed.

Kai
Not sure.

The phone chimed. "Damn it." He peeked at it.

Brandon
When do you work next?

"Shit." What should he say? It was a trick question. Brandon knew he always worked weeknights with Sunday and Monday off. This was the problem with hooking up with people he met at work. They always knew where to find him. Maybe it was time to stop doing that. He peeked at the phone.

He couldn't lie, could he? He scowled.

Kai
Tomorrow night.

He watched the screen, the little dots taunting him.

Brandon
See you then.

"Fuck." He shut the door, locked it, then turned on the chrome shower spigot.

Chapter Three

Kai gnawed on his lip and sliced into the lime on top of the prep area behind the bar. He glanced at the hostess stand and frowned. When would Brandon show up? He focused on the lime and cut into it.

"Hey, beautiful."

Kai cringed, then looked up.

Brandon took a bar stool in front of him, his curly, reddish-blond hair cut short around the sides of his head and long and bushy on top. He wore a tight, white athletic shirt over his wide chest. He took Kai in with his green eyes and licked his lips. "It's good to see you." He set his elbows on the bar and raised his hands, wrapping his fingers together.

"Yeah. Good to see you, too." *Not really.* Kai lowered his brows and stared at the lime. "What can I get you to drink?" He faced Brandon straight on.

"How about one of those fancy drinks, you know, where you twirl your bottles around." Brandon gave him a coy grin.

Kai released a long breath. "Come on, it's not even that busy in here right now. I only do that when we're busier."

"Won't you do it for *me*?" Brandon raked his teeth over his lower lip. "Come on." He stretched over the bar and touched Kai's forearm.

He drew his arm out of reach, pressing his lips together, then forced a smile. Brandon was a customer. He had to remember that. "Sure. What do you want?"

"How about a mojito?" Brandon beamed at him.

Kai wrinkled his brows, grabbed a highball glass, and set

it on the drip rail, then seized a shaker and looked out over the bar.

Conner stepped past the hostess stand, his hands in the front pockets of gray shorts and a white, V-neck shirt covered his strong shoulders.

Kai's breath caught and he blinked. *Shit.* He watched Conner stroll into the near-empty bar area and take a seat two chairs down from Brandon.

Conner folded his hands on the bar and offered Kai a quick grin.

He lifted his chin at Conner. His hands trembled. He had to focus, especially with Conner here. He picked up bottles, gauging how full they were. *You can't flip full bottles.* After finding the right ones, he twirled them in the air, one by one, landed them in his hand, then poured the liquid into the shaker, pursing his lips. Don't look at Conner. *Don't look.* He shoveled ice into the shaker, set the top on it, then held it up and shook it at the side of his head.

"Smile, beautiful. You're supposed to smile when you do that." Brandon placed his chin in his hands, giving him a wide grin. "You're so hot, Kai."

He flinched, then lifted the corners of his mouth and flashed his eyes at Brandon. He stopped shaking, cracked the top on the shaker, and strained the liquid into the highball glass, then grabbed mint, slapped it into his hand and stuffed it in the glass. After shoveling ice into the mojito, he shot the top with soda and set a sprig of mint over it and a lime wedge on the side of the glass, then dunked a straw into it. "Here you go." He twirled a bar napkin, watched it land in front of Brandon, and set the drink on it.

Brandon offered him a coy smile. "Kai, you're so great." He clapped his hands and scanned over Kai's body, circling his tongue over his lips.

"Sure." *Quit looking at me like that.* He drew a deep breath, then focused on Conner. *Fuck, he's watching me, too.*

Conner grinned at him, then shifted in his seat, dropping his gaze to the bar top, wrinkling his brow. "Kai . . ." He bit his lip, then focused on him. "You, uh, didn't we used to be chemistry partners?"

Brandon stared at Conner, sucking the mojito from the straw.

"Yeah, we were." Except there was also the little thing that happened at the graduation party. He should keep this professional. *Keep your cool.* He tensed his jaw.

Conner nodded. "Good to see you. It's been a long time." He let a faint smile creep over his generous lips. "You're pretty good at making drinks." He glanced at the bar top, then fixated on him with ice-blue eyes, lifting his straight dark brows. "Can I, uh, get a beer?"

"Sure. What kind?" A knot churned in Kai's gut. He placed his hands on his hips. He was a mess inside, but he sure wasn't going to show it.

"Do you have an IPA on tap?" Conner looked him over, chewing his bottom lip.

"Yeah." Kai blew a stray hair off his forehead, grabbed up a beer glass from the cooler and poured the beer from the taps. This was a really fucked up time to be here, when Bryce had the night off. There was no one to keep him sane through this. Why did they both have to come in when it was so dead? At least if it were busy, he'd have other people to deal with. He pushed the tap back and brought the beer to Conner, setting a napkin down underneath it.

"You're not going to twirl the napkin for me?" He wiggled his brows and sipped his beer.

Kai offered him a wide smile. "If you want, I can do that for the next one."

Conner set his beer down. "I'd like that."

The blonde woman from last weekend sided up to Conner.

"Hey." She flashed her brown eyes at him and kissed him on the cheek.

"Hey, Liz." Conner's smile faded and he focused on Kai. "Can we get some menus?"

"Sure." An ache pricked his heart. This was going to be a long, fucking night. He wrinkled his nose and pulled two menus off a stack, then gave them to Conner and Liz.

"What about my menu, Kai?" Brandon snickered at him.

Kai grabbed another menu from the stack and handed it to Brandon. He had to get away from this situation and gather himself. "I'll be back." He strode to the end of the bar, out across the dining floor, and ducked into a hallway. As he pushed on the restroom door, he sighed. He walked into an iron stall, shut the door, and exhaled, rubbing his forehead. So, now he had to watch Conner on a date and at the same time, try to keep Brandon from eye-fucking him all night. Jesus. Maybe he could tell Janice he didn't feel well, and she could tend the bar tonight. He shook his head. No, he needed the money. He had to get a damn battery for his blazer. With a huff, he opened the stall and made his way to the bar.

Kai approached Conner with a brand-new smile. "What do you want to eat?" He set his hands on the bar top.

"Well, get her the strawberry salad and I'll have the trout." Conner set the menus down.

He grabbed them up. "House salad or soup with the trout?"

"House salad."

"What kind of dressing?" He glanced at Brandon.

"Blue cheese." Conner gave Liz a coy grin. "It's really good here."

"Yeah?" She touched his arm.

Kai turned his attention to Brandon. "How about you?"

"I'll have the shrimp with corn." He raised a brow at Kai and sucked on his straw.

He walked to the POS system and entered their orders on a screen.

"Hey, beautiful, I need another drink."

Kai shut his eyes and clenched his teeth. This was like a living hell. He plastered a smile to his face and turned around. "Of course."

"Twirl the bottles again."

He widened his smile. *Of fucking course.*

Kai inspected the empty restaurant one last time before heading to the POS system and clocking out. A wave of exhaustion washed over him. What did Conner think of Brandon? Did he think anything of him at all? It seemed all Conner's attention was focused on Liz after she showed up. He frowned. It was going to take some getting used to if Conner was going to be bringing dates in all the time. He slumped his shoulders and walked through the kitchen and the dishwashing area, all stainless steel and red tile floor, then waved at Janice, sitting in a small office the size of a closet. "Goodnight."

She twisted at a gray desk chair, a bare light bulb hanging over her head. "See you tomorrow."

He nodded and slapped a gray metal door open, then stepped out into a breezeway built into the first floor of the brick building housing the restaurant. The door shut behind him. The cool night air shivered over his skin, making him shudder.

"Cold?"

Kai startled and twisted. "Brandon?"

Brandon walked toward him, lifting one brow. "Why don't we go grab a drink somewhere?" He stopped chest to chest with Kai.

Oh, no. He didn't ever want to grab a drink with Brandon again. The first time was all right. The blowjob was good, but

Brandon couldn't take a hint and go away. He shouldn't encourage him. He took a step back, bringing his hands up. "I'm really tired. I need to go home."

Brandon gave him a sly grin. "I don't mind going to your place." He came closer. Alcohol puffed out on his breath.

Kai flinched and his back hit the brick wall. Brandon was drunk. He shouldn't have served him that last mojito. He should have cut him off. He looked around, at the empty street in one direction and the parking lot in the other. "Uh, I d-don't think that's a good idea."

Brandon whacked his hand to the building over Kai's head. He pushed his chest against Kai's. "Come on, Kai. Give me a chance." He leaned forward, pressing his lips together.

Is Brandon going to kiss me? Kai shut his eyes and grimaced, turning his head. Brandon's lips brushed over his cheek.

"Get the fuck off him."

Kai popped his eyes open.

Conner seized Brandon's shoulders and tossed him.

Brandon stumbled and fell to the cement on his ass, his hands smacking behind him. "What the fuck?" He glared up at Conner.

"Don't fucking touch my friend." Conner sneered, his nostrils flaring.

Kai stared at Conner, dropping his mouth open. *His friend?* Did he hear that right?

Conner studied him, placing his hand on his wrist. "You okay?"

Kai nodded. "Y-yeah." Was this really happening?

Brandon stood up, rubbing his hands together. "Who is this guy, Kai?" He wrinkled his nose and looked Conner up and down.

Kai opened his mouth. What should he say?

Conner shifted to stand between Kai and Brandon, holding his arms out to separate them. "None of your fucking business." He glanced back at him. "Do you like this guy?"

"Uh, well . . ." Kai peeked over Conner's shoulder at Brandon. "Not really."

In a low rumble, Conner said, "Did you hear that? He doesn't like you."

"I suppose you think he likes you." Brandon snarled. "You're just a player. I could see it the moment you walked in." He crossed his arms over his chest and stomped down the walkway to the street.

Kai's heart skipped a beat. *Holy shit.* He lowered his brows. What just happened? Brandon had left the bar right before closing, so of course he was out here waiting for him. But Conner left an hour ago.

Conner twisted around. "Who is that guy?" The muscle in his jaw bulged.

"Uh . . ." He peeked at Conner, then focused on his black Vans shoes. "Just a regular." This was awkward.

"So, you've never dated him or anything." Conner's body relaxed.

Kai chewed his lip. "Dated? No. I mean, we went out for a drink once after work." No need to tell him they hooked up. His attention was drawn to Conner's face, the scar still visible under his left eye.

"Oh." Conner huffed. "You should be more careful." He raked a hand through his brown wavy bangs and they swept over his forehead as they released. "I'll see you later." He looked Kai over, then strode down the walkway to the street.

He let loose a long breath. "Fuck." What a crazy night. He strolled in the opposite direction from Conner, to the parking lot and his waiting blazer.

A few days later, Kai stood behind the island at the bar in his black restaurant t-shirt and jeans, watching the stragglers leave. His shift was almost over, all the prep and cleaning were done, and he only had two more nights until his days off. He cell phone dinged from his back pocket. He slid it out and held it to his face, taking a drink of water from a red, plastic, glass.

Bryce
The glasses are on the floor again in the kitchen.

Kai
WTF is doing that?

Bryce
Not sure. Mice? Maybe we should call an exterminator.

Kai huffed. How much was that going to cost?

Kai
Let's wait. I haven't seen any droppings, so I don't think it's that.

Bryce
Then what is it?

Kai
Maybe someone's coming in and fucking with us.

Bryce
Like who?

Kai
Fuck if I know.

Hearty laughing rolled in from the hostess stand. Kai looked up.
Conner waltzed into the bar with his arms slung around Ben and Lucas.

Looks like football jock central in here. Kai stepped out from behind the island as they all took a seat at the bar, Lucas to the left, Conner in the middle and Ben on the right.

Lucas peered up at him from under blond bangs, narrowing his blue eyes. "Kai? Kai fucking Nez?"

"Yes." He gave Lucas his best fake smile. *Lucas fucking asshat?* Surely, he wasn't going to bully him tonight. None of them were in high school anymore.

"Jesus, dude, you still work here?" Ben smirked, working Kai over with his brown eyed gaze under short gelled brown hair.

"I do." *I don't have a daddy to get money from like you do.* He cocked his head and placed his hands on the bar. "What can I get you?"

"Beer." Lucas slapped Conner's arm. "No gay pussy drinks." He chortled. "Right, Conner? Because none of us are *gay.*" He held his open palm up over Conner to Ben.

Ben slapped Lucas' palm.

Conner wrinkled his brows and focused on the gray bar top.

Kai pressed his lips together and ducked down to the glass cooler, grabbing up three beer glasses. Apparently, they hadn't changed a bit. When he came up, he smiled even wider. "What kind of beer?" He gestured to the taps. "We have all kinds."

"Coors." Ben laughed and slapped Conner on the back.

Conner lurched forward, placing his hands on the bar. "Settle down."

"Why? We're the only ones in here." Lucas spread his arms wide.

"We're about to close." *Thank, God.* Kai shifted his weight. "You all want Coors?"

Conner nodded, keeping his focus on his hands.

Kai stepped to the beer taps and filled all three glasses, then set them down in front of Ben, Conner, and Lucas.

"What you been up to, Kai?" Ben looked him over.

He shrugged. "Working, mountain biking, trail running, that sort of thing." What kind of stupid comment would they have for that? He peered at them.

"You're not as scrawny as when we were in high school." Ben smirked and sipped his beer. "You look good, man." He nodded at Kai.

That was an unusual comment, coming from Ben. He narrowed his eyes and grinned. "Thanks."

"Where's Bryce?" Lucas took a gulp of beer.

"He's out somewhere. I don't know. He's been working days this week." Probably a good thing they didn't work the same shifts all the time *and* live together. He wiped the bar with a white towel.

"He works here, too?" Lucas sniggered. "He always followed you around, didn't he?"

Conner finally looked at Kai, then sipped his beer.

"Guess so." The jocks always followed each other around, too, but you didn't hear him say anything about it. He drew a deep inhale. "Anyway, like I said, it's almost closing time. So, I'll have to get you to pay up for the drinks."

Conner pulled a black leather wallet out of the back pocket of his jeans, slid his debit card out and held it to Kai. "I got this."

Kai pinched the card between his fingers.

In one quick motion, Conner squeezed Kai's hand and released it, focusing on him, lips parting.

Kai freed a faint gasp. What the hell was that? He went to the POS system on the island and rang them up. Conner sure was quiet tonight, though. The machine spat out a bill.

Hushed voices sounded behind him. In a low voice, he heard, "That's so fucking gay, man. Why would he say that?" Laughter erupted. "No fucking clue."

That's quite enough. These guys hadn't grown up at all. How could they still be calling everything *gay* at this age? He clenched his teeth and turned around, then handed the bill to Conner along with a pen. "Here. Drink up. We're closing."

Conner wrinkled his forehead. "Kai."

His heart lurched. Hearing Conner say his name like that was no good. He was not going to stay late for these guys. "You heard me." He pursed his lips, looking them all over.

Conner stared at his beer, the smile fading from his mouth, then gulped it down. "Come on. You heard the man." He slapped Lucas on the arm and offered Kai a half-smile.

"Yeah, yeah." Ben finished his beer and plunked the empty glass on the bar top. He slapped Lucas. "Let's go."

Conner filled out the receipt and turned it over. He slid off the bar stool and waved. "See you around, Kai."

He waved at Conner. "See you." As they strolled out of the bar, he relaxed his shoulders and freed a heavy breath. "Damn." He cleaned up the glasses, then totaled up the bill. Conner had left him a twenty-dollar tip along with a note, reading, *Sorry.* He flicked his gaze at the door. "Damn, thank you, Conner." *Guess it was worth the hassle.* He closed out the sales, punched out, and made his way to the back of the restaurant, out the door, through the breezeway and to his blazer, parked behind a tan dumpster.

He pulled his keys out of the front pocket of his jeans, freed the tie from his long hair, and opened the door of the SUV. After putting the key in the ignition, he turned it. The engine whined a few times, then stopped. "Shit." He turned again. Nothing. "Fuck, the battery." He slapped his hand on the steering wheel. He'd have to walk home and deal with this tomorrow.

He climbed out of the SUV, locked it, and shivered, wiping his hands over his bare arms. It was cold out tonight, and he hadn't brought a sweatshirt. If he got too cold, he could always run. He trotted off down the parking lot and to the main road. Across the street, the lake gleaned in the moonlight and the trees were only shadows. This wasn't so bad.

The low rumble of an engine sounded behind him and slowed.

Who the fuck was that now? He looked to his right.

A metallic-green BMW M3 pulled up beside him and the tinted window lowered. "Hey, you need a ride?" Conner grinned at Kai from the driver's seat.

If he got in the car, what on Earth would he have to say to Conner? Too awkward. Especially after the scene with Brandon. "No, I'm okay." Another shiver rolled over him and his teeth chattered. He tensed his body and fisted his hands.

The car followed him. "You look cold to me. Just get in the car." Conner pulled up to the curb and stopped. "Kai."

His heart skipped. *Damn him for blurting his name out like that.* Should he? He halted and peered at Conner.

"I don't bite." He flinched and bit his lip. "Please." He lifted his brows.

What would it hurt? His house wasn't far, so how much talking would they do anyway? Besides, he was cold and damn tired. "Okay." Kai trotted to the passenger side of the car and slid into soft orange leather seats that hugged his body in an almost disturbing way. He looked over the sleek rectangular vents, buttons, and knobs in brushed chrome and patterned black. Rap music played softly in the background. This thing had Bluetooth. Hell, this thing could probably drive itself. He gazed at Conner. "Nice car."

"Thanks." He gunned the engine and it roared.

Kai's head struck the headrest, and he clutched the door handle. "Damn, it's fast."

Conner chuckled. "Over five-hundred horsepower."

Kai widened his eyes. "Jesus." It figured hot Conner would have an equally hot car.

"Want to go for a drive?" He glanced at Kai.

He narrowed his eyes at Conner. "Where to?" Though, did it matter?

"I don't know, we could take a quick drive down McDowell Mountain Road." He smirked. "Then I can show you how great this thing handles."

"Don't get a ticket." Kai snickered. This was weird. He was in Conner's ridiculously expensive BMW going for a drive, talking like this was normal. Hopefully, he wouldn't bring up the other night with Brandon.

"No tickets for me." He drove up Saguaro Boulevard, then took a right turn at Fountain Hills Boulevard and out onto McDowell Mountain Road.

Kai gazed out the window. As homes and businesses faded into desert hills, the scrubby bushes and cacti were lit up by moonlight.

"So, what have you been up to all this time?" Conner drove over rolling hills, the car hugging every one.

"Pretty much what I said at the bar. Trying to live simply, you know?" He studied Conner's profile, the straight, pointed nose, the upper lip vying for purchase over the lower one. God, he was still so attractive. Heat rushed his groin. He squirmed and licked his lips. "So, what's up with you? I heard you broke up with Paige."

Conner tensed his mouth. "Yeah. It was way overdue."

He nodded. Should he ask more about that? Maybe not.

Conner released a faint chuckle. "What about you? Who are you seeing? Besides that moron from the bar." He lifted a corner of his lips.

God, he had to bring that up. "Nobody, really. I'm trying to keep it simple, remember?" He freed a quick laugh. "Relationships are not simple." Though in truth, he'd never found the right guy and probably wouldn't in a small town like Fountain Hills. He frowned.

Conner huffed and smiled. "You got that right." He slowed the car and flipped it around, heading back to town. "You have dated, though, right?" He peeked at Kai.

"Yeah, I've been on dates." Not really. More like drunken hookups from the bar when he'd been desperate enough. If it weren't for those, he'd probably still be a virgin. He looked out the window and drew his brows together, then played with the hem of his black t-shirt.

"So, but nothing serious?"

Kai peered out at stucco houses of various shapes and sizes. They were back on Fountain Hills Boulevard. Time to change the subject. "Hey, take a left at Ashbrook."

"Sure." Conner clenched his jaw. "Where do you live?"

"On Ashbrook, two houses down."

Conner nodded and turned the car onto Ashbrook Drive. He scanned the area. "Where?"

Kai pointed at his adobe-style house with the turquoise rough-hewn vigas poking out from the corners of the flat roofline. "There."

Conner pulled the car up to the curb and stopped. "You live on Ashbrook Wash?" He widened his eyes, then peered out the car windows.

"Yeah, why?" Kai fingered the door handle.

"It's haunted." Conner chuckled and studied him.

"What?" He must be fucking with him. Kai narrowed his eyes at Conner and gave his head a slow shake.

"I'm serious. You've never heard that?" Conner rested one wrist over the steering wheel, the other hand between them on the center console. "How long have you lived here?"

Kai glanced at the dash, then focused on him. "About ten months."

Conner nodded. "Well, let me know if anything weird happens. I know some guys who do ghost hunting." He gave Kai a wide grin. "It could be a lot of fun."

Weird, like glasses falling off the counter and not breaking for no reason? Should he tell Conner about that? A shiver raced up his spine. Ghosts were not his thing. Grandma up in the Navajo Nation called them *chindi,* everything bad about a person that was left before they died. *And they make you sick.* No, it was nothing. "Sure." He opened the door.

Conner placed his hand on Kai's wrist. "Hey, see you soon."

He peered at Conner. "Yeah, see you soon." He got out of the car, shut the door, and walked over the driveway to the carport door.

Chapter Four

Kai, dressed in his black restaurant t-shirt and jeans, wiped a wine glass down with a towel and watched the diners from the dinner rush leave the restaurant, group by group. He surveyed the bar, stepping across its width. Did anyone need a refill or a check?

"Almost done." Beth walked to him and stopped, placing her hands on her hips, releasing a soft sigh. She brushed a lock of blonde bang off her brow and looked at him, her blue eyes curious. "Got any plans for your days off?"

He smiled at her. "Just the usual. Probably a trail run tomorrow, then I'm going to try and get Bryce back on the mountain bikes on Monday." Maybe this time Bryce wouldn't complain as much.

She chuckled, crossing her arms over her thin waist. "Good luck with that."

Bryce sauntered by the front of the bar with empty plates in his hand.

"Bryce." Kai lifted his chin to him.

He stopped and focused on Kai. "What do you want now?"

"Mountain biking Monday?" He smirked.

"Only if you promise to take it easy on me." Bryce strode off toward a swinging door leading into the kitchen.

"So, you do that a lot?"

Kai searched for the source of the voice. "Conner?" His heart skipped.

He sat on a bar stool to the right of Kai, wearing a blue button-down shirt, resting his forearms on the bar. "Can you make me a mojito?" He offered him a crooked smile. "And throw the bottles."

"Sure, I can do that for you." Conner looked good tonight. When would his date arrive? Kai pursed his lips and glanced at the floor, shaking his head once, then set the wine glass on the glass cooler.

Beth slapped his arm. "Evidently, you've got a new admirer." She went behind the island.

I wish. Kai let a shy smile spread over his mouth, set up the high-ball glass and shaker, then perused the bottles and twirled them in the air, one by one, pouring and mixing the drink, slapping the mint, stealing peeks at Conner.

Conner gave Kai a wide grin, wrinkling the corners of his eyes, then propped an elbow on the bar and rested his cheek on his hand. "You're so good at that."

Kai's heart warmed. At least there was something Conner liked about him. He twirled the napkin at Conner, watching it land in front of him, then placed the drink on top of it. "Thanks." He searched the clientele at the bar. Did anyone need anything, or could he chat with Conner while he was still alone?

Beth grinned at him, then took a few empties and debit cards from customers.

She had it covered. His attention returned to Conner. "Good?"

"Yeah, very good." He released the straw from his mouth, then raked his teeth over his bottom lip. "So, did you get your blazer fixed?"

How did Conner know he had a blazer? He knit his brows and narrowed his eyes. "Yeah. How did you know about that?"

"Bryce. I came in for lunch yesterday." Conner sipped his drink from the straw.

"Oh." Figured. Bryce and his big mouth. He grabbed a

bottle from the speed well and the towel, then wiped it off.

"You ever see that Brandon guy again?" Conner pressed his lips together.

"No, he hasn't bothered me since you threw him on the ground." Maybe he was rid of him for good. He snickered.

Conner furrowed his brows and leaned against the bar top. "How does it work, you know, when you're gay?"

He dropped the bottle in the speed well and placed his hands on the bar. "What do you mean by that?" Was this a sexual question? Surely he understood the dynamics of anal sex.

Conner stared at his mojito, stirring it with the straw. "Well, how do you know when a guy is interested? How do you know when he's gay?"

"Oh . . ." He freed a quick chuckle. But still, why was Conner asking him something like this? "Well, uh, it's pretty obvious when a guy hits on you. I suppose it's not all that different from when you hit on a girl or when a girl hits on you."

Conner looked up at him, squinting his eyes. "Do you always wait for the guy to hit on you? Or do you ever hit on anyone?"

He widened his eyes. Okay, this was interesting. How to handle it? He'd never even thought about it. He stepped back and rubbed his fingers on his chin. "I guess I just wait to be hit on." He snickered. It was a hell of a lot easier that way. Maybe he wasn't one to take chances with his heart.

Conner looked him over, licking his lips. Under his breath, he said, "Good to know." He shifted back in his seat, then sucked down the rest of the drink, lowering his brows. "Can you make me another one?"

"Sure." Conner wasn't making a whole lot of sense tonight. Kai set everything up and worked the bottles, making Conner's mojito, then placed it on the bar top. "There you go."

Conner sipped it. "I fucked up."

"What?" Conner wasn't talking about the graduation party thing, was he? He lifted his brows, holding his breath.

Conner fixated on him, his eyes dazed. "I fucked up." He grit his teeth. "My whole fucking life, I've only done what everybody else wanted. I never did what I wanted. I listened to assholes and signed up for shit I knew I couldn't follow through on. I never let myself be *me*."

Kai bent forward, placing his hands midway on the bar top, studying Conner. Maybe he shouldn't have another drink. "Were you out drinking before you came here?"

"Yeah." Conner huffed and frowned. "Nobody ever expected anything out of you, did they?"

He wasn't sure that was a nice thing to say, but he'd go with it for now. "No, I guess not."

"I mean, you never had a dad riding your ass to be a doctor, or a mother wanting you to be fucking perfect. Perfect grades, perfect athlete, perfect girlfriend . . ."

Kai twitched the corners of his mouth. How should he respond? This wasn't funny. In fact, it was downright sad. He had no idea Conner felt like that. "No. The only thing I was expected to be was pathetic, just like my dead father." Why did he have to blurt that out? *Shit.* He flinched and straightened, glaring at the floor.

Conner widened his eyes and looked at him. "Who told you that?"

He scowled. "My mother." He let loose a long exhale and scanned the bar for empties. This conversation wasn't going right. Maybe he could look busy somewhere else.

"Kai."

His breath stuck. His heart pinched. Did Conner have to say his name like that? "What?" He examined Conner.

"You're not pathetic. I don't think you're pathetic." He wrinkled his forehead, sipping his drink, swaying in his seat.

Kai chuckled and shook his head. This was really weird.

"Well, then that's one person." He wiped the sink.

Beth approached him. She glanced at Conner, then focused on Kai. Slowly, she said, "Everything all right here?"

He smiled at Conner. "Yeah, everything's fine." As good as having a secret crush drunk at the bar could be. At least Brandon wasn't here this time. *Or Liz.*

Conner gave him a faint grin. With a slight slur, he said, "Kai's the best."

She leaned to Kai and in his ear, whispered, "So, we've got an *I love you, man* drunk going on?" She chuckled.

He nodded. Under his breath, he said. "I'll get him a water."

She shook her head once and stepped to the other guests, picking up their empties and getting their checks.

At least she knew to pick up the slack for him so he could handle Conner. He grabbed a red plastic cup, scooped ice into it, then poured water in from the soda gun.

"Kai."

His heart skipped. *Damn.* "Yes, Conner." He set the water in front of him and forced a wide grin.

Conner drank the remainder of his mojito and slapped it on the gray bar top. "Can you make me another one?" A sloppy smile spread over his lips.

"How about you drink that water first?" Kai glanced at the POS system, 10:45 p.m. Almost closing time. "We're about to close anyway."

"Kai, talk to me." He flung his arm out across the bar and laid his cheek on it.

Bryce stepped to Kai from behind and tilted his head at Conner. "What the fuck?"

He could see in Bryce's eyes he was gearing up to have a good time with this. Conner didn't need any shit right now from him. "Ssh." He glared at Bryce. "Just leave him alone."

He lifted his brows and jutted his chin. "Fine." He stomped

off.

Kai placed his hands on the bar top in front of Conner. He knew how to play this game. "I'll talk to you, but only if you drink that water." He smirked.

Conner lifted his head and sipped the water, then rested his cheek on his arm. "Why are my friends such assholes?"

He choked out a laugh. This might get very interesting. "You think that, too, huh? Question is, why do you hang out with assholes?"

Conner furrowed his brows. "I don't mean to. They're not always assholes." He raised his head and rubbed the bar with his fingers. "They just, I don't know. We grew up together. We went through the same things." He squinted at Kai. "You're my friend though, right?"

Oh, boy. "Sure." What the hell was going on with Conner? This wasn't like him at all. "Conner."

He straightened in his seat. "Yeah?"

Kai cocked his head. Maybe he could get to the bottom of it. "What's up? Did something happen tonight?"

He scrunched his face and shook his head. "No." He sighed. "I'm just done with all of it." He came forward, setting an elbow on the bar top, pointing at Kai. "Do you know I used to go to all the best clubs in downtown Scottsdale? I'd get in for free. I'd get bottle service. They fucking treated me like I was a VIP. I *was* a VIP." He pouted. "But that's all done. I don't have to do it anymore. It was all Paige wanted. All she cared about was money and how everything looked to everybody else. Then, then she caught . . ." He slapped his hand to his mouth and rounded his eyes.

"Are you okay? You going to puke?" Kai raced to the end of the bar and sped around the front, then wound his arm around Conner's shoulders. Last thing he needed was to clean up puke. "Let's go into the bathroom."

"No, no, I'm okay." He laid his head on Kai's shoulder.

"I'm not going to puke. I almost said something I shouldn't."

What the hell had he been about to say? Something about being caught. Caught doing what? *Shit, Conner's head is on my shoulder.* His heart hammered in his chest. He propped him up in the bar stool and released him.

Janice walked out from the swinging kitchen doors, opened her mouth, and trotted to Kai. "Hey, Beth can handle closing. Why don't you take him home?"

"What?" What was wrong with her? He knit his brows together.

"Bryce said he lives across the street and he's a friend of yours. Just get him out of here and make sure he gets home okay. Get me his card, so he can pay his bill, then I'll clock you out."

"Conner, give me your debit card," Kai said.

Conner slid out his leather wallet from the back pocket of his jeans, pulled out the debit card, then handed it to Kai.

"Here." He gave it to Janice.

She trotted behind the bar, ran the card, then handed the bill and a pen over the bar top. "Get him to sign this."

Conner sniggered. "I'm giving you a twenty-dollar tip again. Because you're my friend." He signed the paper and dropped the pen on the bar top.

"That's very generous of you." Janice chuckled and waved her hand at Kai. "Go."

"Oh, for fuck's sake." *Thank you, Bryce.* Janice was really making him take Conner home. He drew a deep breath and looked him over. "Come on, we're leaving."

Conner let a coy grin quirk his lips. "I thought you didn't hit on guys?"

"I'm not hitting on you. I'm doing you a favor." Only because hitting on him would be a complete waste of time. He let the ghost of a smile play on his lips.

"Why aren't you hitting on me? Am I not your type?"

Conner spat out a snicker.

You're very much my type. "Stop it." He wrapped an arm around Conner, under the armpits. He was going to kill Bryce when they went mountain biking. "Stand up and let's go."

Conner slid off the barstool and draped an arm around Kai's shoulders. He sniffed his head. "You smell nice."

"Really." Kai twisted his head and bit his lip, holding in a laugh. This whole thing was ridiculous. "Come on." He walked Conner to the door of the restaurant. "How much did you have to drink before you came here?"

"I don't know. I quit counting after the fifth beer." He stumbled.

Kai grabbed him up and adjusted his hold. Damn, he was still a muscular guy and had to be four inches taller. "Okay, work with me here." Conner had seemed fine when he got there. *Guess everything just hit him.* He'd seen it happen before, someone looked normal one minute, then shitfaced the next. He walked him out the glass doors of the restaurant and down a concrete sidewalk, passing by shops in a mish mash of sizes and styles, some stucco, some brick, one story and two, and bushy palo verde trees sticking out of the pavement every twenty feet. "Which apartment is yours?" He took deep breaths, working to keep him steady.

"I got the best one." Conner pointed to the three-story apartment complex across from them, beyond a median with grass, pathways, fountains, sculptures, and tall trees. "It's on the third floor, corner. Looks out over the fountain."

Kai nodded. *Figures. Probably the most expensive one, too.* He scanned the apartments, the tall glass windows lining the bottom floor with shops, the modern tri-colored architecture in lime-green, dark-gray, and cream sections. This place wasn't like anything else in town. It looked like it belonged in Scottsdale, where Conner belonged apparently.

Kai walked him to the corner, then out over a crosswalk,

past the grassy median and to the sidewalk next to the apartments. He'd seen these places a million times but had never been inside. "How do we get up there?" He looked up and down the avenue, at the shops and palm trees standing tall every thirty feet.

"You go in there." Conner nodded at an open hallway between shops with a red handicapped railing and a ramp.

Kai walked him into the hallway and started up cement stairs with a red railing.

"I can't believe you're coming home with me." Conner stumbled on a step, then righted himself.

"Me, neither." All he had to do was get Conner into his apartment, then he could go home, and this weird mess would be over. Panting, he peered up at the flights of stairs. Only two more to go. He reached the top of the stairs and looked out over a white landing with dark, gray, metal doors. "Which one?"

"Here." Conner tightened his hold on him and led him to a door on the right. He pulled out a keychain from a front pocket, then unlocked and opened the door.

"Okay, so you've got it from here, right?" Kai unwound his arm from Conner's back and massaged a tense muscle in his own neck.

"Come in with me." Conner grabbed his hand and tugged him through the doorway.

Kai sighed and floundered into the main room of the apartment, taking in the sleek wooden cabinets with long brushed nickel handles in the attached kitchen. *God, can I please go home now?* He flicked on the lights from a switch at the wall and looked Conner up and down. "What do you want?"

Conner swayed on his feet, then plopped his hand on Kai's shoulder, peering at him with one eye shut. "The least you could do is help me get to my bed." He worked a lopsided grin over his face. "I mean, I did give you a nice tip and I did drive you home the other night."

He scowled. "Yeah." Damn, he had him on that. "Okay, where is it?" He wrapped his arm around Conner's back.

He flung his arm over Kai's shoulders. "In here."

He let Conner walk him over wood-plank flooring, past a tan, suede couch with a cream, oval, coffee table, sitting on top of a cream and gray shag rug, and into a bedroom with a gray and white striped duvet.

Conner tripped. "Shit." He toppled backward over the bed.

Kai fell onto him, his chest flush against Conner's, his cheek on his shoulder. "What the fuck, man?" He lifted up on his elbows and gazed down at Conner's stunning face, the ice-blue eyes staring back at him. This was just like the night of the graduation party, except Conner was on the bottom. He widened his eyes and swallowed hard.

"Uh, Kai."

"What?"

"Stay with me." Conner hooked his arms around Kai's waist. "I don't want to be alone tonight." He shut his eyes.

Holy shit. Holy shit. Holy shit. Heat rippled through his groin. His cock hardened. A wave of lust washed over him. "N-not sure this is a good idea." He shifted his hips off Conner. Did Conner feel his hard-on? Kai's mouth went dry, and he licked his lips. His groin tingled against the mattress. He had to get out of there.

"Can you just . . . stay? Please?" Conner loosened his hold on him. His breathing became rhythmic and deep.

Shit, was he asleep already? Kai searched Conner's face, the thick lashes, the scar under his eye, the plump lips, slightly parted. Damn, he'd love to kiss those lips again. He sighed. Should he? Conner was passed out. What would it hurt? Desire hummed up his spine. His heart thumped in his ears. *Maybe just once.* He lowered his head and pressed his lips, ever so lightly, to Conner's.

Conner pressed back and released a soft moan. In a breathy whisper, he said, "Kai . . ."

Maybe he wasn't asleep? Kai lifted his head and stared at Conner. It didn't matter—he had to go before it got out of hand. The last thing he needed was to relive the day after the graduation party all over again. He pushed up off the bed, Conner's arms falling off him, then rolled him to his side. Once he was sure Conner couldn't vomit on himself, he stood, straightened his t-shirt, and snuck out of the apartment.

Kai drove his blazer into the carport of his duplex, parking behind Bryce's white Toyota Corolla, turned the engine off, and let out a long exhale. What a crazy night. He peered down at his groin. His dick was still at half-mast after being in bed with Conner. *Damn it.* He was horny as fuck now. With a huff, he got out of the blazer and went for the carport door. Hopefully, Bryce wouldn't want to bother him.

As he came through the carport door, he shut it as quietly as he could. A movie droned on in the main room. Maybe Bryce would be asleep and he could tiptoe by him. He snuck through the kitchen and peeked into the main room.

Bryce lay on the couch, his head tilted up, his mouth hanging open. A beer can rested on the black coffee table.

He crept past Bryce and into his room, then shut the door, locked it, and hurried to undress, tossing his clothes in a heap on the floor. *Fuck, I need to get off. Now.* As he flipped the red quilt down, his cock hardened. He lay on his bed and shut his eyes, images of Conner flooding his mind. Who needed porn when he had memories of Conner? He twitched one side of his mouth and wrapped his palm and fingers around his shaft, placing slow strokes over it. Sweet friction tingled through his groin. His breath became quick and heavy. He rocked his hips, savoring the sensation. He lost himself in visions of Conner kissing him, thrusting against him, moaning, whispering his name. His cock hardened further and jerked in his hand. His peak teased him. He half whispered, half moaned, "Fuck."

He pumped faster, need thrumming inside him. He thrust his hips, and as his balls became heavy with release, he fondled his sac with his other hand. "Oh, God." He tensed his face. Delicious sensation built to an urgent crest. He shuddered over the edge and bucked his hips, his cock spurting seed over his fingers, over his stomach and chest with each surge of orgasm, gasping each time. As it slowed, he let loose a ragged breath and whispered. "Holy shit, Conner, what you do to me." He pursed his lips. He was never going to get over this fucking crush. *Never*. Not with Conner living right across the street from the bar.

He sat up, tossed his legs over the side of the bed, and grasped his shirt, then wiped his chest and fingers off. What the hell was he going to do? He tossed the shirt to the floor. Not even five years of not seeing the guy made a difference. He rested his elbows on his knees and placed his face in his hands, his long hair draping around his head. The whole thing was hopeless. He was destined to a life of longing for something he'd never have. His mother was right—he was pathetic, but not like his father. This was a whole different kind of pathetic. Tears stung his eyes. He rubbed them away. Crying about it wasn't going to help.

He lay down in his bed and drew the sheets and quilt up, staring at the ceiling. Conner was messed up tonight. What the hell had gotten into him? Why did Conner want to be his friend so badly? Did he think he was going to be treated like a fucking VIP at Fountain Bar and Grill if they were friends? He placed his hand over his mouth and chuckled. *What a douche.* That was so not going to happen.

He rolled to his side and tucked a hand under the pillow. He had the next two days off. He would stay away from the center of town. Then he wouldn't have to see Conner. Then Conner couldn't fuck with his heart. He closed his eyes.

Chapter Five

Banging broke out in the duplex. Kai fluttered his eyes open in the dark. "What the fuck?" More banging snaked through the door. Was someone in the house? With a swift inhale, he sat upright in his bed and listened. More banging. He stepped off the bed and fumbled through his clothes on the carpeted floor for his cell phone, then held it up to his face. The time read 3:05 a.m. Maybe Bryce just woke up? He smirked. Banging and a slam sounded out. "Shit."

He slid his jeans up his legs and fastened them, then snuck to the door and opened it, peeking out through the hallway and into the main room. It was empty. The banging came again from the direction of the kitchen.

"Kai." Bryce whispered from his bedroom doorway.

He opened the door further and peered down the short hallway to Bryce's room. If he was here, he wasn't in the kitchen.

Bryce stared at him, wide-eyed. "What the fuck is that?"

"I thought it was you."

A loud thud reverberated in the room.

Kai startled. "Holy shit. Someone must be in here." He stepped out from the doorway, gulped hard and motioned to Bryce. "Come on, I'm not doing this alone."

"Fine." He stepped out of his doorway, wearing his black boxer briefs.

"Bro, you going to put some clothes on?" Kai covered his mouth and released a muffled snicker.

Bryce looked down at himself. "Shit. I'll be right back."

He tried to focus on the direction of the kitchen through the dark, trying to see any shadows. A loud thud resounded in the room. He jumped and his hands trembled. What was in the kitchen? He widened his eyes. Maybe someone was after the bikes. "Fuck that." He puffed out his bare chest and strode into the main room, then stopped at the kitchen entrance, scanning the area, his hands fisting, adrenaline racing through his body.

Bryce stopped behind him. "What is it?"

He raised his brows and blinked a few times. "I-I don't know." He searched over an empty kitchen. All the cabinet doors were open and a few of the drawers. "What the fuck?" *Ashbrook Wash is haunted.* Fuck, no. A shiver raced down his spine.

Bryce placed his hands on Kai's upper arms, standing behind him. "Mice don't fuck with your cabinets, do they?"

His skin prickled. "No . . . Rats?"

Bryce squeezed Kai's arms. "Are there raccoons around here?"

He turned to Bryce, focusing on his rounded blue eyes. "Maybe. We are right on the wash." He relaxed his shoulders. "Shit, maybe that's what it is. The little fuckers have hands. Maybe they were putting our glasses on the floor." He released a tense chuckle.

Bryce stepped out from behind him and looked the room over. "So, where did they go?"

"I don't know. There's got to be a hole or a door or something." He flicked on the light, then swiped his long hair behind his shoulders and walked around the room, searching for gaps. "Look in the cabinets and under the sink. Maybe there's a hole somewhere." He opened cabinets, peeked inside, and went to the next one.

Bryce opened door after door, knelt down on hands and knees and searched the lower cabinets. "I got nothing, Kai."

"I don't see anything either." He furrowed his brows. "Maybe it's time to call an exterminator. Maybe there's something we're missing." He placed his hands on his hips and turned in a circle, surveying the kitchen one last time.

Bryce stood up and scratched his head. "Fucking weird."

"Yeah, I'm going to bed." Kai sighed and walked to his bedroom. "We can call an exterminator tomorrow."

Kai ran the trail in mid-morning sun, wearing black running shorts, bare-chested, his hair in a pony-tail flopping on his back. He took nimble steps over stones and dirt, breathing in a rhythm that matched his stride, his arms pumping. Alternative rock music played through the AirPods in his ears, his iPhone strapped to his right bicep. He surveyed the rocky trail, the spiky staghorn and chaotic cholla cacti lining the sides, the saguaros reaching high. Lizards and rabbits scattered every few feet under scrubby bushes. He ran up rolling hills, then came down and wound around a wide desert broom bush, its scruffy branches reaching out onto the trail.

Conner sat on a rock, rubbing his ankle, in black athletic shorts and a white t-shirt.

Kai's breath caught. He widened his eyes and halted, taking heavy breaths, then removed his AirPods and stuffed them into his pockets. "Shit, Conner. What are you doing out here?"

He squinted up at Kai. "Well, I was trying to hike off a hangover, but I stepped wrong on a rock." He smirked. "Maybe I was still too drunk to be out walking." He let out a sharp chuckle.

Kai stepped to Conner and knelt down. He probably didn't remember anything from last night. *Good.* "Let me take a look." He touched Conner's ankle and pressed a few spots around the bone. "Doesn't look swollen or bruised. Where does it hurt?" He focused on his face, looking deeply into ice-blue eyes. *He's so close.* He swallowed hard, then glanced at Conner's mouth. Last night's kiss flashed through his head. Desire quivered up his spine. He had to stop this.

Conner gazed at him, parting his lips, the edges of his mouth raised in a slight curl. "I tweaked it here." He grabbed Kai's hand and rubbed it around the outside bone of his ankle joint.

His heart thumped. His mouth went dry, and he licked his lips. His attention was drawn to Conner's ankle and he caressed it, dropping his whole hand over the joint. God, even this part of Conner felt good to touch. Heat rushed his groin. He cleared his throat and drew his hand away from Conner's ankle. He certainly didn't need a hard-on in these shorts. "Um, doesn't seem too bad. You should ice it, though. I have an instant ice pack in my blazer. Can you walk on it?"

Conner winced. "I think so." He stood up, balancing on the other leg, and grasped Kai's shoulder. "Maybe you could help me back?"

"Sure." He stood up and hooked his arm around Conner's back. Wasn't he doing this same thing last night? He released a quick chuckle.

Conner threw an arm over Kai's shoulders, standing on his good leg. "What's so funny?" He grinned at him.

"I've been helping you walk a lot lately." What a switch. The rich athlete needing help from the poor scrawny kid. He sniggered.

"Well, since I need so much help, it's a good thing you're around." Conner tightened his hold on Kai's shoulders. "How far is it?" He set the foot of his bad ankle on the trail.

"Not far. Maybe two hundred feet?" Kai took a few steps. Conner limped next to him.

"You okay?" Kai kept his attention on the ground. He didn't need to be looking at Conner's face when he was this close.

"Yeah, it's okay." Conner hobbled along next to him.

Kai led him to the parking lot and his waiting blazer.

Conner leaned his back against the side of the SUV. "What year is this?"

He pursed his lips. *Here we go with the wisecracks about his vehicle.* "Nineteen-ninety-eight." As he unwrapped the Velcro strap on his cell phone holder from his arm, he glanced at Conner.

Conner hung his head, snickering. "This thing is fucking ancient."

Of course. "So?" Kai didn't have a rich daddy and a college education. He couldn't afford a fancy car. He glared at Conner and removed his key from the phone holder, then unlocked and opened the back gate. He rummaged inside the back, through blankets, t-shirts, and tools for his first-aid kit. He grabbed a blue graphic t-shirt and slid it over his head, then pulled it down his chest. "A-ha." He found and opened a red, plastic box, prepared an instant cold pack and handed it to Conner. "Here." He held it out. "You can use my phone holder to tie it on."

He grinned at Kai. "Shouldn't I sit down somewhere for this?"

Kai scanned around them. Wasn't there a bench or something?

"How about we go to lunch? It's about that time." Conner limped toward the passenger door of his blazer. "I could put this on while we eat, and I can grab a beer. Hair of the dog."

Lunch with Conner. He was supposed to be avoiding him. *Oh well, it's too late now.* He lowered his brows and glanced at him. "Yeah, guess so. Where's your car?" He searched the parking lot.

"It's on the other side of the lot. Drive me to it and we can meet up somewhere in town." Conner opened the door and climbed inside the blazer.

"Sure." What on Earth would they talk about? He didn't have much in common with him. He stepped to the driver's side door and opened it. "Where do you want to go for lunch?"

"You like sushi? How about Katana?" Conner set the ice pack on his ankle.

"Yeah, that works." Katana Sushi was one of his favorites. They had the best sushi in the area. they must both like it, so that was one thing they had in common. His stomach grumbled—apparently, it liked that idea, too. He climbed into his SUV.

Holding the ice pack in one hand while Conner walked, Kai helped him into a black low-back metal patio chair, propped Conner's foot on an empty chair, and took a seat next to him at the four-top table. "Here's the ice pack back." He handed it to him, taking in his muscular legs. He must still work out pretty hard. He looked like he could still play football.

"Thanks." Conner set it over his ankle and wound Kai's cell phone holder around it.

What should they talk about? "Nice day." He looked out over the grassy median in the center of town, the trees and sculptures surrounding a winding brick walking path, then at the tall glass windows of the restaurant that sat on the first-floor corner of Conner's apartment complex.

"Sure is. Glad summer is over." Conner chuckled and picked up the menu. "You going to join me in a beer?"

"I sure am. It's my day off." Time for someone else to serve him, for a change. He perused his menu, looking over the offerings of sushi rolls, bento boxes and salads.

"So, what days do you typically work?" Conner studied him.

"I work weeknights, Tuesday to Saturday, then have

Sunday and Monday off. No use being there when it's not all that busy and my hourly pay is less." He smirked at Conner.

"Yeah, I hear you." He set his menu on the table. "Do you want to share a few rolls?"

"Sure." Kai watched a dark-haired waiter approach the table.

"What can I get you to drink?" The waiter looked them both over.

"I'll take an IPA. How about you, Kai?" Conner smiled at him.

"I'll have a wheat beer, whatever you have on tap." He glanced at Conner.

"Are you ready to order as well? The waiter shifted his weight.

Conner tapped Kai's arm. "You ready?"

"Sure. I like pretty much anything. Just pick your favorite rolls and I'm good." He watched an older woman walking her terrier on the median.

"Okay. So, how about the Sunkist roll, the baked lobster roll and the baked salmon roll?" Conner handed the menu to the waiter.

Kai nodded. "Those sound really good."

The waiter picked up Kai's menu. "Be right back with your beers."

"Thanks." He liked being a pleasant customer, since he'd had to deal with so many jerks in his own restaurant. He smiled at the waiter, then peered down at Conner's leg. "How's your ankle?"

He leaned back in his chair. "Good, now that it's elevated and iced."

The waiter dropped off their beers.

"That's what I need." Conner picked up his beer and sipped it. "I got really fucked up last night." His cheeks flushed.

"Yeah, you could say that." Kai took a gulp of beer. Damn, it was good to finally be drinking a beer instead of serving them. "You remember anything?" Though, based on past experience with him, he doubted Conner would say it if he did remember.

"A little." He gave Kai a shy smile. "I do remember you walking me home." He touched Kai's forearm. "Thanks for that."

"You should probably thank Bryce and Janice. It was their idea." He was sure Bryce thought he was being helpful somehow. He grinned and rested his elbows on the table.

"So, you like bartending?" Conner chewed his lower lip.

He released a soft exhale. "Yeah, I do."

"Why?" Conner cocked his head.

He glanced out at the median, then focused on him. "I don't know. I guess I get to be someone else when I'm behind the bar. I'm in a place where people are generally happy, and I get to be a part of that." He pursed his lips and stared at his beer, twisting it in a circle.

"So, normally you're not in a happy place?" Conner came forward in his seat, narrowing his eyes.

Kai rimmed his beer with his index finger. How should he answer that? It felt like he was talking to a therapist. "Let's say I've been in some very unhappy places in my life. Right now, everything's better." He peered at Conner.

Conner nodded and gulped his beer, then tensed his jaw. "I know you were bullied in high school, and I heard your situation at home wasn't the best." He gazed at Kai. "I probably didn't help the situation."

Holy shit, was Conner finally going to bring up the graduation party? He stared at him, his heart pounding. He opened his mouth, waiting.

Conner twitched a corner of his lips and focused on his beer. "It's such a nice day, we should talk about other things."

He offered Kai a forced grin. "Like, how are things going over there on Ashbrook Wash?" He snickered.

He gave his head a shake and gulped his beer. Should he tell him what happened? Sure. It wasn't anything anyway. "Fine. I think we have raccoons."

"Raccoons?" Conner lifted his brows and shifted in his seat.

He'd opened this conversation up, might as well finish it. "Bryce and I woke up to our cabinets slamming in the middle of the night, and when I got to the kitchen, the bastards were gone."

Conner blinked, then parted his lips. "So, anything else happen?" He set his forearms across the table.

Kai huffed. This was so stupid. "Glasses we left on the counter were knocked on the floor but weren't broken. We have a tile floor." He drew a deep inhale. "Raccoons could have done that, right? I mean, they can grab things." He held up his hand and opened and closed his fingers against his thumb.

Conner sat back in his chair and rubbed his chin. "I suppose it could be raccoons. I've never heard about raccoons being a problem around here, though. Have you?"

He scoffed and drank his beer. Conner had a point, but he was not going to entertain the alternative. "No, guess not. We're having an exterminator come out tomorrow to be sure."

"So, if it turns out to not be raccoons, we should set up a camera in your kitchen and see what's really going on." Conner chuckled. "I have a camera we can use."

We . . . Now suddenly he and Conner had become *we.* "Sure." He frowned. It wouldn't get to that. It had to be animals.

The waiter stopped off at their table and set down white rectangular plates of multi-colored sushi rolls, along with wrapped chopsticks and square soy sauce bowls. "Need anything else?"

"How about another round of beers?" Conner lifted his brows at Kai.

"Yeah." The beer was going down too well. He drank down the rest of his beer and handed the empty glass to the waiter, while Conner did the same.

Kai poured soy sauce in the bowl and mixed wasabi into it. Maybe he'd humor Conner on this ghost thing. "So, what exactly do you know about the haunted wash?"

Conner ripped open his chopstick wrapper and slid them out, then pulled them apart. "So, my friends told me there's an old story about a little girl that was murdered in Ashbrook Wash. It became a missing persons case because they never actually found the body." He glanced at Kai and wrinkled his forehead. "You okay?"

He never should have asked. This was too creepy. The chindi was nothing to mess around with. A shiver raced up his spine. He stared at his sushi, frowning. "Yeah, I'm okay. It's just . . . I'm not one for ghost stories. I don't even like horror movies. I can't watch them."

Conner swallowed a bite of sushi and fixated on him. "Why? They scare you too much?"

"I can't sleep if I watch them. I get nightmares." He tightened his jaw. Conner was going to think he was a pussy. He was though, wasn't he? Just another thing his mother was right about. He rocked once and gazed at him.

"Hey." He placed his hand on Kai's forearm. "Don't worry. I'll be right there with you if we find something scary."

He peered at Conner's face. Was he serious, or was he fucking with him? He seemed serious. Kai forced a grin. "Yeah, right. It's probably just raccoons." He ate a sushi roll.

"Kai."

He flinched. God damn if Conner saying his name didn't

get his blood going every damn time. "What?" He turned to him.

"I mean it. I won't let you down." He tightened his hold on Kai's arm.

He looked at Conner's hand on his arm and nodded. This was getting weird. "Okay. Let's talk about something else."

"Like what?" He gave Kai a warm smile and moved his hand to the table.

Good question. "So, Bryce says you're a pharmaceutical rep now?" He stuffed a sushi roll into his mouth.

"Yeah. My dad wanted me to be a doctor, but I didn't want to be in school forever. So after I got my bachelor's in biology, I got a job." Conner swallowed a sushi roll down.

The waiter dropped off a new round of beers.

Kai sipped his beer. He didn't even know there was such a thing as a pharmaceutical rep. "So, what's that like? What do you do exactly?"

"I basically go around and talk to doctors and sell the benefits of my company's drugs. I visit most the doctors here in Fountain Hills, then down by HonorHealth in Scottsdale, and I go up to Payson about once a week." He dunked a sushi roll in soy sauce and popped it in his mouth.

"Sounds like fun." And easy money. He smiled at Conner.

He thinned his lips. "Yeah, it's really flexible, and I have the freedom to do my own thing. It's not easy to get into, though. I got some help from my dad."

"Yeah?" Figured. Rich kids always seemed to have an in. "How so?" He gazed at Conner.

"My dad's an anesthesiologist, so he knows a lot of people in the drug industry." He slowly shook his head. "He was unhappy when I didn't want to go to med school."

The memory of Conner asking to cheat off his test for the chemistry final flashed in Kai's head. "I see. You were really going to be a doctor, even though you sucked at chemistry?"

He released a quick laugh.

Conner snorted. "Yeah, maybe you should have gone to med school."

Kai stared at a sushi roll sitting in his soy sauce mixture. College was never in the cards for someone like him. "I'd be in debt up to my fucking eyeballs if I'd gone to college."

"No shit? I thought natives got to go for free?" Conner narrowed his eyes and drank his beer.

The question was so typical. "No, we do not. We're just like everyone else and have to pay or get scholarships. We just happen to have scholarships available only to us." He popped the sushi roll in his mouth and chewed.

"Oh." Conner peered at him, holding a sushi roll up in his chopsticks. "How native are you? I mean, you look native."

Here we go. How to quantify his identity as a person into the separate pieces of it? He'd go with the official American government answer. "I'm one-quarter Navajo, on my father's side. He was half."

"So, your mom's white?" Conner cocked his head, looking him up and down, as if seeing him for the first time.

"Yeah. She's a full-on colonizer." He freed a belly laugh. Would Conner even know what he was talking about?

Conner frowned and gazed at his sushi plate. "So am I, I guess."

"It was a joke." He put his hand on Conner's knee. *Shit, what am I doing?* He yanked his hand away and cleared his throat, his mouth twitching. "Bryce and I talk pretty candidly about race."

"Well, whatever half, quarter, shit you are, it turned out well. I mean . . ." His face flushed. Under his breath, he said. "You ended up being pretty attractive." He gulped hard, inhaled deeply, and looked at Kai.

Kai's breath caught in his throat and his heart thumped in his ears. Had Conner just said he was attractive? "Uh, thanks." He knit his brows and focused on Conner's lips.

Conner's gaze focused on Kai's mouth. He took a heavy breath. "Yeah."

Stop it, Kai. This was stupid. *Conner is not attracted to you.* Kai blinked and slapped his hand to the table. "Anyway, looks like we've eaten all the sushi." He released a nervous laugh. "I should probably get home and shower. How's the ankle doing?"

Conner straightened in his seat and dropped his hurt leg off the chair. "It feels pretty good now." He unwound the phone holder from his ankle and handed it to him, then placed the ice pack on the table. "Thanks for helping me. Again." He gave Kai a wide smile.

"Of course." He did sort of owe him for getting rid of Brandon. He peered at Conner's ankle. "Can you make it to your apartment?"

"Let's see." Conner stood up, putting weight on the bad ankle. "It actually seems fine now."

"Good." Time to go back to the creepy house. He lifted his hand to the waiter.

The waiter came to the table.

"Can we get our check?" Kai asked.

"Sure." The waiter trotted off.

Conner sat in his chair. "Hey, listen. I got this." He set his hand on Kai's shoulder, then released it.

He might not have the money Conner had but he could pay for his own lunch. He shook his head once. "No, I can't let you do that."

"Yes, it's my treat. You helped me last night and today. I owe you one. Or two." Conner smirked at him.

He had him there. "All right." Kai drank the rest of his beer.

Chapter Six

Kai looked out over the restaurant and wiped a beer glass with a towel. It was already Wednesday, and Conner hadn't come in all week, or at least not on his shift. He glanced at the front door, behind the hostess stand. Maybe Conner was avoiding him? He had told Conner what his schedule was. *Don't be silly.* The guy was probably busy.

Bryce walked up behind him. "Hey, only another half hour and we can go home."

A shiver raced up his spine. "Yeah, to how many open cupboards this time?" At least they weren't finding glasses on the floor anymore.

"I know, right? This is getting really creepy." Bryce twisted his mouth. "What do you think it is? I mean, just because the exterminator didn't find any signs of raccoons doesn't mean it's not raccoons, right?"

There had to be a logical explanation. He shook his head. "I have no idea." He scanned the bar. Only one older gentleman sat at the end, nursing a red wine. "At least it stopped happening in the middle of the night."

Bryce chuckled. "That was fucking annoying, man."

Janice walked out from the kitchen doors, placed a pen behind her ear and stopped next to Bryce and Kai. "Hey, where's your new guy?" She placed her hands on her hips and winked at Kai.

The teasing about walking Conner home was never ending. He pinched his mouth. "Stop it. He's not my guy. He's just an old acquaintance from high school."

"Really." Bryce smirked at him.

"Could have fooled me. You know, every time he comes in here, no matter who he's with, he's always fixated on you." She gave him a wry grin.

What was wrong with them? "That's ridiculous. He's a-a friend. That's it." Heat rushed his face, and he hung his head. "In any case, he hasn't been in all week." Maybe Conner really was avoiding him. His mind went over Sunday's lunch. Had he said something to piss him off? He wrinkled his brow.

"Anyhow, let's get this place cleaned up and get out of here." Janice chuckled and sauntered into the kitchen.

Kai poured a beer from the tap, then brought it to a young couple seated at the bar. "Here you go." He looked out over the restaurant, watching groups at tables pay their bills and get up to leave. Another night almost done. He glanced at the front door. Friday night and still no Conner. He scowled. Conner must be avoiding him. *That's it.* For whatever reason, Conner probably didn't like hanging out with a poor native, gay guy. His heart pinched and he frowned. Maybe Lucas and Ben gave him shit about it. He fisted his hands.

Beth stepped to him with a white towel in her hand. She flung it over one shoulder. "So, I hear there's a good band playing tonight at The Alamo."

Could be fun. "Yeah?" He glanced at her and picked up a towel.

"Yeah. Mid-Life Vices. They play 80s and 90s rock. We're all going after work. You should join us." She smiled at him.

He turned to her. "So, who exactly is *all*?" He lifted his brows.

"Me, Janice, Bryce—"

"Bryce? Why didn't he tell me?" He was joking, but it was time to give Bryce some shit. He smirked.

"Tell you what?" Bryce strode across the restaurant floor and stopped at the front of the bar top.

"That you were going to The Alamo tonight?" He snickered.

"I was, but as you can see, I was busy." Bryce waved his arms around him.

Now he could get him. "Is that also why you let those margaritas sit at pick up so long I had to remake them?" He placed his hands on the back bar and forced a mock scowl.

"Shit, man. I had seven tables come in all at once." Bryce pursed his lips, then smiled. "You going or what?"

He released a short laugh. "Yeah, yeah, I'm going." He wiped the bar top. "You're driving."

Kai, wearing a tan V-neck shirt and jeans, walked through a small parking lot and looked over the single-story cream stucco plaza. A sign lit up in green on the roofline read *The Alamo Saloon*. He followed Bryce and Beth under an overhang with brown shingles and stepped over the cement walkway.

Bryce opened a heavy wooden door next to a window filled with neon beer signs. Loud rock music sounded from inside. "After you." He waved them through.

He followed Beth into the bar, taking in the room, the round high-top tables and two pool tables to his left, then the low-top tables and band playing on a stage to the right. A few Elk heads hung on the wall behind the four-piece band, on wood paneling. He tapped Bryce. "This place is packed." It looked like the whole town was out tonight.

Bryce smiled. "Yeah. Let's get drinks."

He strolled through the crowd of people up to a bar with a wooden bar top under an overhang that matched the one on the building. Strings of multi-colored lights lit up under the overhang, and behind the bar, mirrors hung on the wall with tiers of bottled liquor. He looked over the bottles, then at a blackboard with Jell-O shots written in neon colors. Those looked good. "Want a Jell-O shot?" He snickered at Bryce.

He sided up on Kai's left. "Sure. Strawberry banana?" He glanced at Beth. "How about you?"

She stood on the other side of Bryce. "Of course. Can't come here and not get a Jell-O shot." She laughed.

A female bartender with blonde hair pulled up into a ponytail stepped to them. "What can I get you?"

Bryce leaned forward. "Three strawberry banana Jell-O shots, a wheat beer, and two pale ales." He glanced from Beth to Kai.

The bartender went to work on their drinks and set them down on the bar. "Run a tab?"

Kai shook his head. "No." He slid his wallet out from the front pocket of his jeans. "I got this round." He slapped forty dollars on the bar.

The bartender took the money and brought back the change.

Kai left a few dollars on the bar and faced Beth and Bryce, his back against the bar top. "Jell-O shots?" These looked interesting. He handed out the red Jell-O in white plastic containers to each of them, then stuck his tongue into the edge of the container, licked all around and sucked the Jell-O out, swallowing it.

"That's hot."

Kai looked to his left. *Fuck.* He huffed. "Hi, Brandon." How was he going to get away from Brandon tonight? He set the empty Jell-O container on the bar top.

Brandon looked him up and down, holding a clear drink in his hand with a straw. "I didn't know you came out to places like this."

"I do." More like he didn't like going to places Brandon was at. He grabbed his beer and sipped it.

Bryce smirked at Kai. "Beth got a table with Janice. I'll be over there."

"No, don't leave." He swatted at Bryce's arm, missing it.

Fucking Bryce. The last thing he wanted was to be left alone with Brandon.

Brandon watched Bryce walk off. "I missed you, Kai." He placed his hand on the bar behind Kai and leaned his chest against his side.

He certainly didn't miss Brandon. He forced a grin at him. "You did, huh?"

"Where's your big player tonight?" Brandon lifted his chin at him.

Under his breath, Kai said, "Don't know. Don't care." But he did care. Probably too much. He scoffed.

Brandon wound his arm around Kai's waist. "Guess we get to have a drink together after all."

Kai gulped hard. How could he get out of this without being rude? Brandon was a still a customer of the restaurant. He searched around the room and his gaze caught on Beth. "Hey, my friends are waiting for me." He stepped from the bar.

Brandon tightened his hold. "Sure. I'll go with you."

God, this guy was clingy. Kai shut his eyes tight, then opened them.

Conner, Ben, and Lucas stood at the other end of the bar. Conner fixated on Kai, narrowing his eyes.

His heart skipped a beat. Pain pierced his chest. Conner was avoiding him, and it was probably because of Ben and Lucas. He wrinkled his brows and gulped his beer, then looked at Brandon. If he was going to have to deal with him all night, it would be easier if they weren't alone. "Fine. Let's both go sit at the table." He walked through people with Brandon behind him and sat at a stool with Bryce on one side, Beth, and Janice across from him and Brandon standing behind him.

Bryce looked Brandon over. "What have we got here?"

"Everyone, this is Brandon." He motioned to him. "Brandon, this is Bryce, Beth and Janice."

They nodded at each other, then Beth and Janice returned to the conversation they'd started.

Kai drank the rest of his beer and scowled. He didn't want to be here anymore. Maybe he could cut out and walk home. He had to think this through. He stood up, holding his empty beer glass. "Be right back. I'm going to take a piss."

Brandon set his drink down. "I'll go with you."

How could he keep Brandon away from him? He placed his palm on Brandon's chest. "No, go get me another beer, okay?" He gave him his most charming smile.

Brandon lit up. "Sure."

Kai meandered through the crowd, a mixture of old and young, and into a small restroom with short, wooden stalls. After using the urinal, he washed up, looking himself over in the mirror, his long brown hair hanging around his shoulders.

Conner walked into the bathroom and stepped up behind him. "Kai."

His breath caught and his heart quickened. Great, just what he didn't need tonight. He glanced at Conner and grabbed paper towels from the chrome dispenser, then wiped his hands, drawing a deep breath. "What do you want?" He was angrier than he wanted to be. He should tone it down. Conner didn't owe him anything. He certainly didn't owe him an explanation of why he didn't come into the restaurant this week. He frowned.

Conner clutched his arm and flung him around. "Are you here with Brandon?"

What the fuck? Kai furrowed his brows and looked him up and down, his white, button-down shirt stretching across strong shoulders, his jeans hugging narrow hips. "What's it to you?"

Conner wrinkled his nose, then clenched his jaw, the muscle bulging. "I thought you didn't like him." He thinned his generous lips.

"I don't." Kai yanked his arm free. "What do you care?" He threw the paper towel in the garbage. As he glared at Conner, anger built inside him. "Where the fuck were you all week?" He widened his eyes. Shit, he shouldn't have said that. He turned, placed his hands on the sink and hung his head, releasing a loud exhale.

Conner came flush behind him. "I was out of town at a conference. Sorry, guess I forgot to tell you on Sunday. I don't have your number. So it's not like I can text you."

Uh . . . what? This was weird. He took a deep breath, fighting to calm the thrumming of his heart. He straightened and faced Conner.

He took a step back, smirking. "Need help with Brandon?"

Kai glanced at the door. This was too much. He needed to get out of here. "I don't know." He couldn't look at him. If he did, more stupidity would probably come out of his mouth. He sidestepped Conner and made for the door.

Conner caught his arm. "Kai, don't leave."

With a scowl, Kai yanked his arm free and strode out of the bathroom, across the crowd and to his table, then sat down. What the fuck was that all about?

"Here's your beer." Brandon, sitting next to Kai, pushed a fresh beer toward him.

Kai surveyed the table. It was empty. *Not good.* "Where is everyone?"

Brandon poked at Kai's arm. "Out dancing. Want to dance?"

"No." He picked up his beer and slugged half of it down. Maybe he needed a shot, or maybe he needed to leave.

Conner walked up from behind him. "Brandon. What are you doing with my boyfriend?" He slid in between Kai and Brandon, his back to the table, resting an elbow on it.

Kai hung his mouth open and stared at Conner. *What the actual fuck is going on tonight? Has everyone gone insane?*

Brandon scoffed. "Since when is Kai your boyfriend?"

"Since last weekend." Conner puffed out his chest. "Right, Kai?" He glanced at him and lifted his brows.

Conner must be doing the fake boyfriend routine to try and help him get rid of Brandon. He'd go along with it for now. He snapped his mouth shut and wrinkled his forehead. "Y-yeah. Last weekend." He glanced at Brandon, then focused on his beer. He'd need more than this one to get through this night.

Brandon leaned over the table, glaring at him. "Why didn't you say something?"

"I-I don't know." He wasn't a good liar. He hugged his beer.

"It's still new. Isn't it, baby?" Conner wrapped an arm around him and squeezed, then kissed him on the head.

Baby? Is he nuts? Kai snarled and shook his head. "Yeah, it's new." *Conner kissed me. Holy fucking shit.* He bit his lip, then peeked at Brandon.

Brandon slid off his stool, glared at Conner, then stomped off.

He dropped his arm from Kai's shoulders, then sat at the barstool vacated by Brandon. He came close to Kai. "So, I guess I need your phone number if you're going to be my boyfriend."

"Stop it. I am not your boyfriend." What was Conner trying to pull? He straightened and faced him.

"I still want your number." Conner shimmied his cell phone out of the front pocket of his jeans, opened the interface and handed it to him. "Please? Then I can tell you when I'm going out of town, so you won't get mad at me." He snickered.

Heat flushed Kai's face. He must have been pretty obvious in the bathroom. "Yeah, okay." He relaxed his shoulders and entered his number, then handed the phone to Conner.

He called the number.

Kai's phone buzzed in his back pocket and he slid it out, then turned it off.

"There, now you have my number, too." Conner smiled at him. "Want to get a Jell-O shot with me?

"Where's Ben and Lucas?" They probably wouldn't approve. He scanned the bar.

"They left. They're getting up early to play golf at Firerock." Conner grabbed his hand. "Come on, let's get a shot."

That figured. All the rich boys had memberships there. Now he knew why Conner was hanging out with him. His friends had left. He wriggled his hand in his hold. "What are you doing?"

Conner tightened his hold and leaned in, whispering over his ear. "We're supposed be boyfriends, remember? You don't want Brandon thinking otherwise, right?"

Kai freed a choked laugh. He could play this game. "Jesus, okay." He climbed off the barstool and Conner did the same. "How about we get something stronger than a Jell-O shot?" He chuckled.

Conner led him through the crowd to the bar, tugging him along. "What sort of shot do you want?"

He perused the bottles of liquor behind the bar. "How about tequila?" Nothing else looked good.

"Okay." Conner lifted his hand and the bartender nodded at him.

"What can I get you?" She placed her hands on the back bar.

"Two shots of tequila." Conner slid his wallet out of his back pocket.

"With training wheels." He glanced at Conner.

He gave Kai a warm smile. "With training wheels."

The bartender left and came back with the shots, lime wedges and a saltshaker. "There you go. Ten dollars."

Conner pulled a twenty-dollar bill out of his wallet.

Kai set his hand on Conner's, over the wallet. "Hey, you don't have to buy for me."

Conner snickered. "I always pay for my dates."

If only it were real. "Fine." He twisted his mouth.

Conner handed the twenty to the bartender, then pushed a shot glass filled with tequila toward him. "Drink up, baby." He smirked.

"Don't call me baby." This whole thing was ridiculous. He chuckled and gave his head a shake, then lifted his hand to lick it for the salt.

"Let me." Conner seized his hand, gazed deeply into his eyes, then slowly ran his tongue over Kai's hand at the base of his thumb.

Lust flickered up his spine. Kai parted his lips and a soft moan escaped. His breath became heavy, and heat filled his cock. "Um . . ."

Conner poured salt on his wet hand. "Now you can do me." He held his hand up to Kai's mouth.

He licked his lips, gazing into Conner's intense blue eyes. His heart quickened. Was this really happening? He shut his eyes and licked Conner's hand. A vision played in his head of licking his cock instead. His shaft hardened in his jeans. He opened his eyes.

Conner's eyelids hooded and his lips parted, showing the tip of his tongue. His chest heaved with a deep breath. "Damn, Kai. I think you might turn me gay."

He blinked hard, then rolled his eyes. "Stop it." Now he really needed that shot. He licked the salt from his hand, threw the tequila back, grabbed up the lime and sucked on it. The tequila burned down this throat.

Conner poured salt on his hand, licked it, then drank the shot and pushed the lime into his mouth.

The band stopped playing and set their instruments down, letting the house music take over.

Kai searched the crowd. Brandon was nowhere in sight. "I think Brandon left, so we can stop playing the fake boyfriend game."

"Who says I was playing?" Conner hooked his arm around Kai's waist and drew him in close.

Kai's breath hitched. God, how he wanted this to be real. He studied Conner's stunning face, so near to his own. He focused on his lips. This was no good. He was going to lose it and kiss him and that would be the end of everything.

Conner leaned into his ear, his lips brushing his cheek. He whispered, "Brandon is right behind you."

Kai rounded his eyes. *So that's why he's still doing this.* A prick of pain pinched his heart. "Oh." He needed to leave. The charade might be funny to Conner, but it was starting to hurt.

Conner kissed Kai's cheek. "What are you staring at, Brandon?"

Kai turned at the bar top and glared at Brandon. If only he would go away. Then everything would go back to normal.

"I just can't believe you'd settle for one guy, when you're all over the hookup apps." Brandon smirked at Conner.

Kai dropped his mouth open and stared at Conner. "What?" Hookup apps were not his thing. He got all the action he wanted from tending bar.

Conner freed him and snarled. "You're obviously mistaken." He walked around Kai to stand chest to chest with Brandon. "Take that back."

Brandon curled one side of his mouth. "There's no mistaking that scar on your cheek. You didn't put your whole face on your profile, but the scar is there." He gave Conner a satisfied nod.

"Bullshit. I'm sure I'm not the only guy in the world with a scar on my cheek." In one swift move, Conner grabbed Kai's arm, hauled him through the crowd and out the front door of the bar, into the cool night air. He shoved him up against the cream stucco of the building.

What just happened? *Why is he pissed off at me? I didn't say anything about any hookup apps.* He winced and stared at Conner.

He scowled, then wrinkled his forehead. "You don't believe him, right?"

"Believe that you use gay hookup apps?" Kai erupted in a belly laugh. "Why would I believe that? You're not gay, right? Why the hell would you be using gay hookup apps?" He stifled another round of laughter. He couldn't help himself. Picturing Conner using something like that was funny. "Besides, those things are kind of creepy."

"You think they're creepy?" Conner placed his hand on the building above Kai's head and studied him.

"I guess so. I don't use them." He pursed his lips, gauging Conner's reaction. "Why do you care?"

"You're my boyfriend, remember?" Conner snickered. "I don't want you thinking I'm doing something creepy." He smirked at him and dropped his arm from the building. "Anyway, I'm about done here. How about you?" He looked Kai up and down. "You need a ride home?"

"Well, I drove with Bryce." Should he let Conner take him home, or go back with Bryce? Going home with Bryce was probably safer.

"Let me take you home. You don't want to go back in there with Brandon hanging around, right?" Conner tensed his jaw.

"No, I don't. Let me text Bryce." Conner had a very important point. He pulled his cell phone out of his back pocket and opened the text app.

Kai
Heading home with Conner.

The phone chimed.

Bryce
Don't make out on the couch. I don't need to see that.

Conner peered at his phone and snorted. "Really?" He lifted a brow at him.

Kai jerked the phone away and stuffed it in his pocket. Conner shouldn't have seen that. "Bryce is just fucking with me."

"Sure. My car is over here." Conner walked off across the parking lot.

He trotted behind Conner and caught up to him at his BMW, parked along the street.

Conner unlocked the car and got in the driver's seat.

Kai slid into the passenger seat and watched him.

Conner started the car and drove off down the street. He glanced at Kai. "So, whatever happened with the raccoon thing?"

"The exterminator couldn't find any evidence of them, or any rodents for that matter."

He looked out over the houses and plazas, the bushes, cacti, and occasional palm tree speeding by them.

"Is it still happening?" Conner turned the car onto Palisades Boulevard and drove past businesses in stucco buildings.

"Yes, it's still happening. In fact, I'll probably come home to a bunch of open cabinets." A shiver tingled up his spine. He'd be alone until Bryce got home. He was finding it harder and harder to be alone in that house, especially at night. He sighed.

"So, can I come in and see it?" Conner took a right turn at Fountain Hills Boulevard.

What could it hurt? At least he wouldn't have to face it alone this time. "Sure."

Conner pulled up on the street in front of Kai's duplex and shut the engine off. He peered out at the house. "Looks pretty normal to me. I don't see any raccoons scurrying off now that we're here."

"Yeah." No one ever saw the little bastards. He wrinkled his brow and got out of the car, meeting up with Conner in front of it.

"Let's go." He walked to the carport door and waited for Kai.

He pulled his keys out of his jeans and slid the key into the round, brass, doorknob. "Here we go." He opened the door.

Conner stepped inside the kitchen and placed his hands on his hips, surveying the room.

Kai came in behind Conner, locked the door, then looked around. The cabinet doors were all open and most of the drawers hung ajar. A few pieces of silverware rested on the tan, tile floor. He grit his teeth. "That's new." He pointed at the silverware.

Conner approached the silverware and crouched down, then picked up a fork, twisting it front of his face. "This is just bizarre."

Kai pursed his lips. "Yeah. It's really starting to creep me out." Goosebumps rose up on his skin. He wiped his hands up his arms.

Conner stood and stepped to the cabinets. "So, what happens if I close all these?" He shut the cabinets doors, one by one.

He shrugged and gulped hard. His heart raced. Somehow having an outside person witness this thing made it seem even more real. "Nothing. It usually happens once a day and then it's done."

Conner pushed the last drawer closed, then faced him. "You look terrified." He wrinkled his brows and placed a hand on Kai's arm. "I'll stay with you until Bryce comes home."

He didn't really need to be alone in the house with Conner.

It was way too tempting. He freed an exhale and raked a hand through his long hair. "No, you don't have to do that. It's no big deal." He released a tense laugh. "It's just animals, right?" At this point, he wasn't even sure *he* believed that anymore.

"I'm staying. This looks like poltergeist activity." Conner scanned over the room.

"P-poltergeist? You mean like in that movie with the kid who sat in front of a blank TV?" Trembling started in his body. He wrapped his arms around his waist.

"Yeah. Let's go sit on the couch." Conner took his hand. "But no making out. Bryce doesn't need to see that." He snickered.

Desire flickered through him. He didn't need to think about making out with Conner. "Shut up." He scowled and followed him to the main room, flicking on the lamps at the ends of the couch from a light switch on the wall, then sat on the couch next to Conner.

"So, I'll bring over my game camera tomorrow and we'll set it up while you're at work. It takes video, not just pictures. We'll get to the bottom of this. Is Bryce working tomorrow night, too?"

"Yes, he's working." Kai chewed his lower lip.

Conner brushed the back of a hand over his cheek. "Your face is so pale."

He tilted his head, removing his cheek from Conner's touch. His cock didn't need any more encouragement. It was bad enough the two of them were sitting so close on the couch. "I'm really not okay with this whole ghost thing." Should he tell him about the chindi? No, he'd think he was nuts.

"Yeah, I see that." Conner licked his lips, then focused on Kai's mouth, drawing his brows together. He placed his hand on Kai's cheek.

He widened his eyes. *Is Conner going to kiss me?* No fucking way. He stared as Conner's face came closer.

Bryce burst through the front door.

Conner dropped his hand and cleared his throat, then stood and rubbed his neck. "Hey, Bryce."

Bryce halted part way into the room, cocking his head. "The fuck?"

Conner stared at the floor. "I uh, better go." He glanced at Kai. "I'll bring that game camera over tomorrow." He flashed a grin at Kai, strode to the door and left.

Bryce stepped to Kai. "What's going on? Were you making out with Conner? I was joking when I sent you that text."

He scoffed and sank into the couch. "No, we were talking about the fucking ghost we have in our house." He shivered.

"Ghost?" Bryce narrowed his eyes. "Are you sure? You'd tell me if something was going on, right?"

"Yeah. Nothing is going on." Kai thought back over the night. It was all a show for Brandon, right? But Brandon wasn't around just now. He was probably seeing what he wanted to see. But Bryce saw something, too. Kai focused on Bryce. "Hey, what did you see exactly when you came in?"

Bryce plopped down on the couch. "Bro, it looked like Conner was going to kiss you, or that he already had."

His heart skipped a beat. "Huh." But really, he hadn't kissed him, and the whole thing at the bar was fake. "Well, he didn't." He rose from the couch. "I'm tired and I'm going to bed." He took a stride toward his bedroom. "By the way, Conner is bringing a game camera over here tomorrow to run while we're at work. He thinks we can catch whatever or whoever is messing with our stuff in the kitchen."

"Good, then we can prove to the exterminator that it's animals." Bryce huffed. "Ghosts..." He shook his head and chuckled.

"Yeah." Kai forced a smirk and walked to his bedroom, fighting off a round of goosebumps.

Chapter Seven

Buzzing sounded in Kai's bedroom. Who the hell was that? He opened his eyes and grabbed his cell phone off the nightstand, then held it to his face.

Conner
Lunch today?

He smirked. Suddenly Conner had become his best buddy. What was that all about?

Kai
Sure. Where and what time?

The phone dinged.

Conner
Pick you up at noon. Your choice on the restaurant.

Kai
OK

He looked at the time on his phone, 11:15 a.m. "Shit." He needed to get going so he could shower before Conner picked him up.

Kai stood in the front window of his duplex, wearing a slim white button-down shirt untucked over jeans, and tapped his hand on his thigh. Conner invited him to lunch. Conner was taking him to lunch. How weird was that? Something was definitely going on here, but he wasn't sure what.

Conner's BMW pulled into his driveway, angling slowly over the curb.

He rushed out to the car, then trotted to the passenger side and slid into the soft leather seats, giving Conner a wide smile. "Hey." Conner looked absolutely stunning, as usual. The guy really should have been a model.

"Hey." Conner, in a gray polo shirt and black jeans, grinned and backed the car out of the driveway, being careful of the front end over the curb. "So, where do you want to go for lunch?"

It would be good to get out of Fountain Hills for a change. "How about something over the hill in Scottsdale, like Ling and Louie's?" He hadn't been there in months and it was one of his favorites. He gazed at Conner.

"Yeah, sure." He drove the car out onto Fountain Hills Boulevard, then took a right at Palisades. As they passed their old high school, he shook his head and chuckled. "We had some fun times in that building."

Kai looked out over the clay-colored brick building with turquoise metal accents. "Some bad times, too." The memory of Conner denying what happened between them flashed through his head. When would they ever talk about that? Probably never. He thinned his mouth.

He glanced at Kai and lifted his brows. "How bad were things for you there?"

"Oh, it wasn't that bad. I guess it just never felt like I fit in anywhere." He stared at the dash. He was taking the fun out of this little outing. He should change the subject. "Anyhow, fill me in on what you've been doing since high school. I mean, I've only heard bits and pieces of it."

Conner smirked and turned onto Shea Boulevard, heading up a hill, then down the other side into a sea of Tuscan-style houses all painted in desert brown. A small mountain rose up on the left with the remnants of an ancient lava flow falling down its sides underneath cacti and brush. "After high school I moved down to Tucson and went to U of A for biology. I was going to do what my father wanted and get into med school." He frowned. "But you know that didn't happen."

Kai scanned over the houses and apartment complexes on either side of the road, hiding behind masonry walls, and the deep dirt wash running next to them. Maybe he could figure out what happened between Conner and Paige. "So, did Paige go down there, too?"

"Yeah. We lived together for a few years. We both stayed in the dorms the first year." He stopped the car at a light and studied Kai. "Why didn't you ever go to college?"

Kai lifted a corner of his mouth. "Me? Why?"

"You were good in school. You totally could have gotten in." He started the car back up.

Kai gave his head a shake and adjusted the rectangular, chrome vent. "It just wasn't for me. I wanted to work." He needed to work, more like. Maybe that was something Conner would never understand. He didn't have a lot of choices like Conner had.

"Live simply?" He smiled at Kai and drove the car into a parking lot.

"Yeah." That was one way to put it. Though he didn't have much of a choice but to live simply, either. He took in a brown building in Hacienda style. A tall square turret rose up at one corner with natural stone covering a few feet in from the edges and tiles at the roofline. A large covered patio stood in front of the building. Kai opened the car door and stepped out, then shut the door.

Conner got out of the car and strolled to him. "Patio?"

"Definitely." He looked up at a clear blue sky. "Too nice to sit inside." He followed Conner to a short iron gate and stepped inside the patio. "Let's sit at the bar." After all, that was where he felt most comfortable.

"Sure." Conner walked up to the bar, which was half facing the patio and half facing inside the restaurant. He took a seat and set his cell phone on the wooden bar top.

Kai sat next to him, scanning the racks of liquor bottles hanging over their heads and wine glasses dangling upside down. He'd always liked this setup. It was small, but efficient. Everything within quick reach. "I have to work tonight, so I'm not drinking."

"I don't, so I'm having a beer." Conner smirked at him.

A male bartender with short spiked, blond hair approached them. "What can I get you?" He dropped menus on the bar top.

"Iced tea for me." He picked up the menu.

"Pale ale on tap for me." Conner lifted a menu to his face.

"Be right back." The bartender walked off.

"What do you like here?" Conner perused the menu.

"The Evil Jungle Princess Chicken is good." Once he found something he liked, he usually stuck with it. He set his menu down and glanced at Conner. "In fact, that's what I'm getting."

Conner nodded and rubbed his chin. "I'm getting the Drunken Shrimp."

The bartender set their drinks down. "Did I hear an Evil Jungle Princess Chicken and a Drunken Shrimp?" He set his hands on the back bar.

"Yep." Kai handed his menu to the bartender and looked him over. This guy was good.

"Be right up." The bartender took both menus and sauntered off.

Kai stirred his iced tea with the straw. Maybe he could find out what Conner's deal was. "So, you said some things last week when you were drunk." He sipped his tea and peered at him.

Conner released a quick exhale. "Yeah, well, I was drunk. People do that." He shifted in his seat and drank his beer.

Kai examined him. He seemed a little uneasy. *Why?* "You said you fucked up," he said. "Were you talking about the break-up with Paige? Like are you sorry you broke up with her?"

"No, breaking up with her was definitely a good thing." Conner nodded, then tilted his head and twisted his lips. "But that's part of it." He focused on Kai, gazing into his eyes. "I was living a life that wasn't real."

Kai narrowed his eyes. "What do you mean by that?"

"I, uh . . ." Conner chewed on his lower lip and stared at his beer, then snapped his brows together for moment. "What was it like before you came out? How did you get the nerve to do that?"

Kai blinked. That was quite a change in subject. Conner obviously didn't want to talk about whatever had happened to make him move back to Fountain Hills. Kai lifted his chin, thinking back. "I didn't get the nerve. I was outed."

"By whom?" Conner's attention focused on him and he leaned toward him.

"Bryce." Kai released a quick laugh, the memory flooding his mind. He was so stupid back then, even more stupid than now. "I tried to kiss Bryce when we were freshmen. He told his mom, then his mom told my mom, and I was outed."

"Bryce?" Conner pinched his lips. "But you guys are such good friends."

"He was the boy next door. Literally." And as usual, he'd mistaken a close friendship for something more. He let a faint grin work its way over his lips. "Bryce was cute, but he's very straight."

Conner frowned. "Do you still think he's cute?"

He choked out a laugh. "God, no." He sipped his tea.

"We're best friends now. I got over him." He took Conner in from head to toe. "Found someone else to crush on." What would he say to that? He held his breath. He was playing a potentially dangerous game. Maybe he should have kept his mouth shut.

"Dare I ask who?" Conner offered a sly grin.

Of course, he went there. "No, you may not." Heat flushed his face and he gazed at his tea. Conner would never have pretended to be his boyfriend if he knew. They might not be sitting here right now if he knew. He tensed the edges of his mouth.

The bartender came up and set down plates of food. "Here you go. Enjoy." He walked off.

Now maybe he could change the subject. "This looks good." He tore open the wrapper on his chopsticks and shoveled rice and chicken into his mouth.

"Is it someone I know?" Conner picked up a shrimp with a chopstick and ate it.

"Who?" Apparently, Conner was going to keep this going. Why did he care so much? He gulped some tea from his straw.

"This guy you had a crush on. Do you still have a crush on him?" Conner sipped his beer, then set it down and fixated on him.

Kai looked him over, the side-swept, wavy brown hair, the ice-blue, narrowed eyes, the pointed nose, the generous lips, the gentle scar on his cheek. One day, he'd love to kiss that damn scar. Longing squeezed his heart. "Yeah. Yeah, I still do. I'm not telling you who, so quit asking." He furrowed his brows and slipped chicken and vegetables into his mouth.

Conner scowled. "I want to know, Kai." He glared at him.

"Why?" Jesus, the guy was persistent. He gazed at Conner.

"Does Bryce know?" Conner gulped hard.

Kai scratched his cheek. "Well, yeah."

"Fine. Then I'll ask Bryce." Conner chuckled.

He lifted his brows. "No, you won't." He slapped Conner's knee.

Conner seized his hand and tugged him close, focusing on his mouth. "I want to know, and I will know." He licked his lips, his breathing heavy.

Kai's heart thumped in his chest. Fuck if he didn't want to kiss Conner right this very second. He drew a deep inhale, gazing into Conner's intense eyes. "Maybe someday I'll tell you. When I'm ready. If I'm ready." Except that day would never come.

Conner freed his hand and cleared his throat. "Yeah, okay." He straightened in his chair, grabbed his napkin, and wiped it on the side of Kai's lips.

"What are you doing?" He swatted his hand away.

"You had some stuff on your mouth." Conner sniggered and sipped his beer.

Kai laughed. *So that's why he was looking at my mouth. Figures.* "Okay." Time to change the damn subject again. He thought back to last night. "So, do you have the game cameras?"

"Yeah, I can show you how to set them up when we get back." Conner ate a shrimp and some rice.

"This thing really terrifies me." A chill flickered up his spine and he brushed his palms over his arms.

Conner placed his hand on Kai's arm, wrinkling his forehead. "I told you not to worry about it. I'll help you get to the bottom of this. I know these guys who can figure out what's going on and probably settle things back down."

"But what if they can't?" His body shuddered. He really hated thinking there might be a chindi in his house.

"Then I guess you'll have to move in with me." Conner laughed and drank the rest of his beer.

He snorted. "Yeah, right."

Kai pulled his blazer into the carport of his duplex, shut the headlights and the engine off and climbed out into the dark, wearing his black restaurant t-shirt and jeans. He really didn't want to look at the camera footage. Maybe he was better off thinking it was raccoons, even if it wasn't.

Bryce stepped out of the passenger side of the blazer. "Here we go."

"Yeah." He turned to see Conner pull his BMW up to the curb and turn off the headlights. As goosebumps broke out over his skin, he wrapped his arms around his waist. Hopefully, he wouldn't lose his shit too badly and look like a pussy in front of Conner.

Conner got out of his car, wearing a gray polo and black jeans, then trotted up to Kai. "Ready?"

At least he wasn't alone. "No." He shuddered and took a deep breath, then followed Bryce to the carport door with Conner following.

Bryce pulled a key out of his front pocket, then opened the door. He glanced at Kai. "You, first."

"No, you go in first." *Fucking Bryce.* He clenched his jaw.

"I'll go." Conner straightened his shoulders and stepped inside.

"Well?" Kai walked in behind Conner and looked around. All the cabinet doors and the drawers were opened. Silverware rested on the tile floor. "Fuck this." His voice cracked. It was already too much to deal with. He trembled.

Conner grabbed the game camera from a round, glass and ratan dinette, then flipped the back open and turned on the screen. "Come here." He waved to Bryce and Kai.

He stepped to Conner with Bryce close behind.

Conner hit buttons on the camera, rewinding it, then stopped and hit play.

The small screen showed the cabinet above the sink opening, then slamming shut. A few doors down, a cabinet opened slowly and stopped. The silverware drawer groaned open. A fork flew out, clinking on the floor. No raccoons at all. Nothing.

Fear prickled up Kai's spine. He shuddered. His breath hitched. *This is too much. Too damn much.* "Fuck this shit. I'm out." He sped to the door, slammed it open and ran out into the street, panting. It wasn't real. It couldn't be real. He paced back and forth, glancing at the duplex, fisting his hands in his long hair at the temples. How could this be happening?

Conner ran to him and wrapped him up in a tight embrace. "Kai, it's okay."

A pack of coyotes howled and yipped from beyond the duplex in the tree-laden wash, piercing the quiet night.

Kai startled. "Holy shit. Not coyotes, too." Under his breath, he said, "Chindi . . ." He shook in Conner's hold, his arms drawn up between them. "It's not okay. It's fucked up." He peeked at the duplex. "What am I going to do? I can't go back in there. I can't. I-I could get sick."

"Hey, a lot of times the entity is someone we know who's passed on. Maybe it's a relative coming to visit and see how you are?"

He stared at Conner. "My fucking dead father? Are you shitting me?" Tears stung his eyes. "He's probably pissed off that I let him die." *Where did that come from?* He blinked and a tear tumbled down his cheek. He was losing it. The thing he didn't want to do. "Oh, shit." He bit his lip.

"What?" Conner kept his hold on him with one arm and brushed the tear from his cheek with his thumb. "Kai, what are you talking about?"

Kai's gaze darted over the street, the duplex, then landed on Conner. Years of pent-up emotion crashed through his heart. "I-I didn't remind my dad to take his insulin. H-he died in a diabetic coma. It was my fault. My mom said so all the time." *Was it possible the chindi had only found him now?*

"Jesus, Kai. How old were you?" Conner watched him, wrinkling his brows.

"I-I was five." Kai's breath hitched. His voice breaking, he said, "I was only five." The tears came, one after the other, falling down his cheeks. He couldn't stop it. He let out a soft sob.

"It wasn't your fault. You were just a kid." Conner hugged him tight to his chest. "Damn it, what kind of a mother would say something like that?"

Bryce trotted down the driveway and stopped at Conner and Kai. "I closed all the . . . What the fuck?" He stared at Kai and placed his hand on his back.

Conner twisted Kai around, out of Bryce's reach. "I've got him." He wound both arms around him. "Can you give us a minute?"

"Jesus, yeah. I'm going to go grab some bourbon. I think we all need it." Bryce strode to his white, Toyota Corolla, sitting against the curb on the other side of the street, got in and drove off.

Kai took a ragged breath against Conner's shoulder, his vision blurring with more tears. Why was this hitting him so hard? Why now? He nuzzled into Conner's neck and sniffled. It felt so good to be in his arms. Downright heavenly.

Conner released him enough to look into his face. "Kai, I'm here. I won't let whatever is in there hurt you."

He gazed into Conner's eyes, his mouth so close to his own. He swallowed and licked his lips. "C-Conner?"

Conner closed his eyes and placed a feathery kiss over Kai's cheek, brushing his hand down the back of his head. "I'm here." He kissed closer to his lips. "I'm not letting you go." He claimed his mouth with his own.

Kai widened his eyes, then shut them, taking all he could from the gentle but firm kisses teasing and tasting him, the exploring tongue dancing inside his mouth. He broke the kiss and whispered, "Oh, God."

Conner entwined his fingers in Kai's hair, jerked his head back, and placed more insistent kisses over his mouth, filled with need. He strengthened his hold around his chest.

Kai surrendered to the solid embrace, lust shivering up his spine, his cock hardening.

Conner moaned a deep growl, rubbing his stiff shaft against Kai's thigh.

He's not straight. He's not fucking straight! Kai fluttered his eyes open and broke the kisses, taking deep breaths. "W-we better get out of the street." He looked into his hooded blue eyes. Damn, he looked hot as hell. *God, I want him.*

Conner cleared his throat and freed Kai, except for his hands, squeezing them. "Kai, obviously I'm, I'm . . . I like you." He rounded his eyes and searched his face, his lips turned down in a pout. "I-I don't know who you have that crush on, but I want it to be me."

Kai dropped his jaw open. *Holy shit.* Should he admit his feelings? "Uh . . ." No, he wasn't ready. There was some serious explaining to do first. "Conner, we should probably talk." He had to be sure that Conner's feelings were real first.

Conner shut his eyes tight and released a quick exhale. "Okay." He opened his eyes.

"But not here." Kai glanced at his duplex. "I can't go back in there right now." He tilted his head at the house. "But I don't know what to do about Bryce. I can't just leave him here."

"How about we go back to my place for tonight and figure out what to do in the morning?" Conner drew a deep inhale.

"Yeah, that would probably work." Kai glanced at the house, then focused on Conner. There was nothing in there he needed badly enough to go in for. "Let's just go and I'll text Bryce on the way. I seriously can't go in there right now." A shiver prickled over him.

Chapter Eight

Kai watched Conner open the door to his apartment, then followed him inside. How should he start the conversation he'd waited five years to have? The drive over in his car had been quiet, too quiet.

Conner flicked on the lights and walked into the modern kitchen of sleek, dark wood cabinets, long nickel handles and white quartz countertops, and opened a stainless-steel refrigerator. He frowned. "Want a beer?"

"Yeah." Bryce would be here soon. He had to start talking.

Conner handed him an opened bottle of beer. "Here."

He took a sip. "Your graduation party." *Way to blurt it out.* He flinched.

Conner snapped his brows together and opened his beer bottle. "Yeah." He stepped past him. "Let's sit on the couch." He motioned to the main room.

Kai followed him past a round dinette in dark wood with green, upholstered chairs, to a tan, suede couch with a low, squarish back, sitting over a gray and cream shag rug. He sat down and set his beer on an oval coffee table made of white marble with iron legs. "So . . ." He lifted his brows.

Conner sat next to him. "I bet you think I'm a real asshole." He released a breathy sigh and raked his hand through his bangs, then let them fall across his forehead. "Guess I was." He drank a few gulps of beer and stared at his hand, resting in his lap.

Kai watched him closely. Was he going to get the truth out of him this time? "I didn't know what to think, actually. I never really thought you were an asshole. I guess I thought maybe you decided to experiment with me because I'm gay."

Conner's shoulders shook with an exhale of breath and the corners of his mouth twitched. "It wasn't an experiment, Kai. And it's not now."

"Then what was it? You do remember what happened, right?" His heart pounded in his ears. Finally, they were talking about this. He straightened his spine and lifted his brows.

Conner looked him over, wrinkling his forehead. "Of course, I remember. I remember it all the damn time. I can't ever get it out of my head. Even after five years."

Kai widened his eyes. "What?" His heart swelled with emotion. Could he have had feelings for him all this time? *No way.* That wasn't a possibility. There had to be another explanation. He opened his mouth to speak.

Conner scowled. "Look, do you even like me at all?" He fixated on him, bowing his lips down, his eyes glassy.

Kai nodded. He had to be careful. He shouldn't say too much. Not yet. "I-I do. Like you. I do." *So God damned much.* He gnawed his lower lip and glanced at the large television hanging on the opposite wall, then focused on him. "I just need to know what this is."

Conner crept closer and grasped Kai's hand. "This is me wanting to start something with you. Not an experiment, not . . . whatever that was at my graduation party." He wrinkled his brows and tensed his lips. "I liked you then, too."

"But you were with Paige." Kai's gut wrenched. None of this made any sense. How was he supposed to react? It was too good to be true. He studied him.

Conner tightened his hold on his hand and looked into his eyes. "I'm not with Paige now. That's over."

Kai rocked once and took a deep breath, glancing at his beer resting on the marble tabletop. He had to put this into some sort of perspective that made sense. "S-so, you're bisexual, or you're just gay for me?" He focused on him.

Conner pressed his lips together. "I like you. I want to be with you. That's what I know."

Under his breath, he said, "Gay for me . . ." Was that even a real thing? He stared at his hand, still tucked inside Conner's. Fear rippled through him. What was he supposed to do with that? He gulped hard. "Okay."

Conner growled, then stood up and paced to a sliding glass door with a set of vertical blinds half shuttered across it. He rubbed his eyes. "Look, Kai." He twisted around. "If you don't want to be with me, I get it. I-I guess I'll uh, back off." He wrinkled his brows and frowned, his eyes glistening.

Kai hung his mouth open. *What am I doing? Conner fucking Mitchell wants to start something with me and I'm saying no? The fuck is wrong with me?* He stood up, then walked to him. "No, Conner, I do want this. I want to try, you know, starting something with you."

Conner wound his arms around Kai for a tight embrace, nuzzling his face in his neck. In a choked whisper, he said. "Kai . . ." He sniffled and released him enough to peer into his face, then placed a long, passionate kiss on his lips.

Kai kissed back with equal intensity and wrapped his arms low on his back, drawing their hips together, his cock hardening. This was so good. Way better than anything his imagination had come up with over the years. A chime rang out from his back pocket. *Damn it.* He broke the kiss. "Shit, Bryce." He pulled his phone out of his back pocket.

Conner took in heavy breaths. "Too bad we couldn't get rid of him."

Kai flashed his eyes at him. "That's not nice." But he was right. He held the phone up to his face.

Bryce
I'm here.

Kai
Come up to the third floor. We'll meet you.

Conner peered into Kai's phone. "Guess we'll have to talk more later." He hugged him into his side and kissed his head, then walked to the door and opened it.

Kai's breath caught in his throat. This was going to take some getting used to. What would Bryce think about it? He followed him out the door and to the top of the stairs, then looked down.

Bryce's mop of dark hair came into view on the stairs, his footsteps clomping on each cement step, a brown bottle of bourbon swinging in his hand. As he came to the top, he stopped and looked Kai and Conner over. "Okay, what's up with you two?"

Kai stuffed his hands in the front pockets of his jeans and curled one side of his mouth. "Uh, nothing."

"We've decided to start dating." Conner gave Bryce a sly grin.

"The fuck?" Bryce focused on Kai. "Is he serious?" He pointed at Conner.

He wrapped an arm around Kai's shoulders. "I'm very serious."

Kai glanced at Conner, and heat rushed his face, then he dropped his gaze to the cement floor, his heart still pounding as if he were sprinting. Maybe he'd wake up tomorrow and find out this whole thing was a dream. "Yeah."

Bryce spread a wide smile over his face. "Guess we've got some celebrating to do." He slapped Kai's shoulder and waltzed into the apartment. "About fucking time, Kai."

Conner watched Bryce and smirked, then tightened his hold on his shoulders. "Sounds like maybe he knows something I don't."

"Shut up." *He knows a hell of lot that you don't.* He broke free from Conner's hold and followed Bryce into the apartment.

Bryce went through cabinets in the kitchen. "A-ha." He took a few low-ball glasses out and set them on the white quartz counter, then opened the bourbon and poured some into each glass.

Kai, with Conner following, stepped into the kitchen, and picked up a glass. A little bourbon would be just what he needed right about now. Bryce was a genius. *Sometimes.*

Bryce held a glass out to Conner. "Here you go."

He took the glass.

Bryce lifted his own glass high in the air. "To whatever the fuck is in our house. It finally got the two of you together."

Kai sputtered. "What?" He stared at Bryce.

"Come on, Kai. I think the cat's out of the bag, now, isn't it?" He sipped his bourbon.

"Uh . . ." *Bryce has a very big God damned mouth.* He flashed his eyes at Bryce. Conner didn't need to know the extent of his feelings quite yet. He focused on Conner and heat rushed his face. What was *he* thinking about all this?

"I'll drink to that." Conner let a playful grin work over his mouth, then took a gulp of bourbon.

Kai drew his brows together, shook his head, and sipped his drink. Maybe he wouldn't pick up on what Bryce was talking about.

Conner grabbed Kai's hand. "Let's go sit on the balcony with our drinks and talk." He led him through the main room and out the sliding glass doors to a balcony enclosed in a red metal railing, overlooking Fountain Lake and the surrounding park. The fountain sprayed up high, sparkling in the moonlight in front of the shadows of the far-off, jagged peaks of the Superstition mountains. He sat at a resin wicker outdoor couch with green cushions and tugged Kai down to sit beside him.

Bryce set the bottle of bourbon on a glass and resin wicker coffee table and took a seat in a matching chair, then scanned the view. "Damn, Conner, this is a nice place."

He smiled. "Yeah, I like it here. It's peaceful."

Peaceful and expensive. A chill worked up Kai's back and he shivered.

"You cold?" Conner brushed his hand up and down his back.

"Yeah, a bit." This was so, so, weird. Kai set his drink down on the coffee table, stealing a peek at Conner.

"Bryce, go grab some blankets from the bin over there." Conner pointed to a wicker bin sitting in the far corner of the balcony.

"Sure." Bryce stepped to the bin and pulled out a few brown blankets, then handed one to Kai. As he sat down on his chair, he threw a blanket over himself. "Brrr. Gets cold at night already."

Kai tossed the blanket over himself.

"What about me?" Conner sniggered and pulled some of the blanket over him. "You'll have to get closer." He draped an arm over his shoulders.

This is really going to take some getting used to. Kai chewed his lip and shimmed close into his side.

Conner tucked the blanket in around them, then picked up his glass and handed it to him. "Here."

"Thanks." Kai sipped his drink, letting it warm his insides. Conner was being so attentive.

"So, what do you really think is going on, Conner?" Bryce narrowed his eyes. "I mean, just because we didn't see animals doesn't mean there aren't any, right?"

He shook his head. "No, I think that's exactly what that means." He wrinkled his brows and glanced at Kai. "You going to be all right talking about this now?"

"I guess so." Goosebumps broke out over his skin. Could it really be his dead father coming to visit him? No, that didn't make any sense. "I mean, we have to talk about it." He frowned at Conner.

"Okay, I'll be straight then. I think you have a poltergeist in your house." Conner sipped his drink. "A poltergeist is just an active ghost that has the ability to move objects."

"Jesus. That's kind of scary." Bryce pinched his lips. "Is there a way to get rid of it?" He took a gulp of bourbon.

"I think so. First, I think we need to make contact. Some of the guys I work with are into paranormal investigating, and they have the equipment. We can set up an investigation and see if we can figure what or who this thing is." Conner watched Kai.

Kai widened his eyes and his mouth went dry, fear spiraling up his back. He knew what this thing was. His Shinálí would never lie to him about something like that. "Chindi." He gulped his bourbon.

"Why do you keep saying that word?" Conner brought his head closer to Kai's.

He gazed deeply into Conner's blue eyes. "It's what my grandmother called them when I lived on the Navajo Nation. She said it is everything bad about a person that's left behind after they die, and it becomes a spirit."

Conner lowered his brows. "You actually lived on the Navajo Nation? You mean up at Four Corners?"

"Yeah." He studied Conner. What would he think about that? It wasn't something he told everyone about.

Bryce chuckled. "You got yourself a real native, there, Conner."

"Shut up, Bryce." His jokes about his ancestry were not funny right now. He flashed his eyes at him and focused on Conner.

Conner toyed with the shoulder of Kai's t-shirt. "So, when you said you were blamed for your father's death, were you also told that his chindi was going to get you?"

Kai burst out a nervous chuckle. "No, no. I put that one

together myself." He shook his head. Stupid. He was going to look like a superstitious idiot.

"No wonder you freaked out." Bryce sniggered.

Kai released a long exhale and glared at Bryce. He didn't need to be reminded of what a pussy he'd been. "Let's focus on how to get rid of this thing." As a chill worked its way up his spine, he snuggled into Conner's side. It was nice, having him this close. Maybe he'd get used to it quicker than he thought.

Conner tightened his hold on his shoulders, a faint grin creeping over his lips. "So, you've lived in this place for a long time already, and nothing happened until recently, right?"

"Yeah." Bryce stared off in the distance and sipped his bourbon. "The timing is a bit odd. I mean, why would it show up now?"

"Who knows. We did have that nasty last monsoon right before we noticed it the first time." Kai widened his eyes at Bryce. A chindi might come after the resting place was disturbed. "Do you think the storm could have upset something in the wash? I mean, they were all flooded." He gulped down the rest of his drink.

Conner grabbed his empty glass, then picked up the bourbon bottle and refilled it. "I think you need this more than any of us."

Kai let a dim smile quirk his lips. "Thanks." He drank some down. "So according to what I was told, if you disturb the resting site or bones or things of the dead, then their chindi can want to seek revenge." He glanced at Bryce, then focused on Conner. What the hell was he thinking about all of this?

Conner narrowed his eyes and nodded his head. "So, and water is said to be a conduit for spirits, which is probably why the wash is haunted in the first place."

"How do you know all this stuff?" Bryce turned to Conner.

He shrugged. "I hear a lot of stories from the guys I work

with. It's interesting."

Kai drank a gulp of bourbon, the liquor now creating a pleasant buzzing in his head. He gazed at Conner and grinned. *We are together. He likes me.* If this was all just a dream, he didn't want to wake up.

Conner squeezed his shoulders with a smirk playing on his lips. "What are you thinking about? It doesn't look like ghosts."

Kai blinked at the glass coffee table. "Never you mind." No way could he tell him, and especially with Bryce here. He widened the grin and kicked at the table with his sneaker.

Bryce stood up from the chair and yawned, stretching his arms over his head. "Okay. I'm tired. What are the sleeping arrangements tonight?" He dropped his arms.

"There's a queen-sized bed in the guest room right in there." Conner pointed to a French door at the far end of the balcony.

"Great." Bryce went to the sliding glass door, opened it, then winked at Kai and disappeared into the apartment.

What was that about? He gulped down more bourbon. "I suppose we should finish up and go to bed. I can sleep with Bryce."

"The hell you will." Conner puffed a breath. "You'll sleep with me."

"Do you really think that's appropriate? I mean, we just started dating." He giggled and hiccupped. Damn, the bourbon was getting to him. He swirled the liquid in the glass and drank the rest down, then set the glass on the table. *Shit, I could have sex with Conner tonight.* He widened his eyes and stared at Conner.

He furrowed his brows. "You're not sleeping with Bryce. You kissed him. I'm not letting you sleep with him."

Kai erupted in a sharp laugh. Why would he say something like that? "Jesus, it was a million years ago, and we live together. If I were going to do something with Bryce, I would have already."

Conner frowned and twisted the blanket between his fingers. "You're sleeping with me. If you don't want me to touch you, I won't."

But he *did* want him to touch him, and damn, did he want to touch Conner. Every tiny speck of him. Was he ready for all his fantasies to come to life? He let his smile fade and brushed the hair from Conner's forehead. "I-I don't know what to do. I've honestly never been in this situation."

"I thought you'd dated guys." Conner lifted his brows and shifted to face him.

"Uh, well, I really just sort of hook up with guys at the bar." This was really awkward. As heat flushed his face, he bit his lip.

Conner spread a coy grin over his mouth. "Let's just go to bed and talk."

He chuckled. *Yeah right.* "Okay."

Conner stood from the couch, grasped his hand and pulled him up, then led him through the main room, past the dinette and into his bedroom, flicking off the lights along the way. As he stepped to the other side of the bed, he shimmied his gray polo over his head and tossed it to the floor. With a smirk, he unfastened his jeans and shoved them down his legs, then toed out of his shoes and stepped out of the jeans.

Kai took Conner in from head to toe, the muscled chest and shoulders, the toned abs, the hard cock jutting out of his boxer briefs, his thick thigh muscles. *Damn, he's already hard.* Lust flickered up his spine. Heat filled his groin and his cock jerked. He licked his lips, and his breath grew heavy.

Conner threw the duvet down and climbed over crisp, white sheets to lie on his back. He lifted his arms and tucked his hands behind his head with a coy smile. "Coming?"

Under his breath, Kai said, "Not yet." He released a soft

snicker.

"What?"

"Nothing." Kai undressed down to his boxer briefs and slid into the bed beside Conner on his side, facing him. He slipped his hand under a pillow and in a teasing tone, he asked, "So, what did you want to talk about?"

Conner rolled to his side. "Tell me who you have that crush on." He brushed his fingers down Kai's rib cage and hip with a light touch.

His cock twitched and he bit back a moan. *God, that was good.* He took a deep breath. "Come on, what else do you want to talk about?"

"That's all I want to talk about. I don't want you having a crush on anyone but me." Conner caressed down Kai's hips, then skimmed his fingers over Kai's solid shaft.

His breath caught and he swallowed. "Um . . ." He could barely think. Should he just come out with it? No, he couldn't admit something like that yet.

Conner's eyes hooded and he parted his lips. Heavy breaths escaped his chest. He stroked Kai's side, over his hips, up his rib cage and circled his shoulder. He bit his lower lip, then released it. "Kai, just tell me. Please." He placed his hand between his thighs and rocked his hips forward, releasing a soft moan.

This is too much. How was he supposed to watch this and not give in? His cock ached with need. "It's you. I have a crush on you." He dropped his mouth open. *Shit.*

A grin flashed over Conner's lips, then he licked them. "God, I'm so fucking hot for you right now." He pressed on his own swollen cock, pre-seed seeping through his boxer briefs at the tip. He rocked his shaft into the palm of his hand.

"I'm, I'm, yeah, me too." A pulse of desire shivered up his spine and twitched his cock. What should he do? This was Conner he was in bed with. Not some guy from the bar. He had to be careful. He gulped hard. "C-Conner?"

"Can I kiss you, Kai?" Conner raked his teeth over his lower lip and stroked his solid cock through his briefs.

"Um, yeah."

Conner inched closer to him, set a hand on his cheek, and placed long, slow kisses over his mouth, each one more and more intense, tangling Kai's tongue with his own. He slid his other hand up and down his own stiff cock, moaning into Kai's mouth. Inside of a breath, he said, "I want to touch you, Kai." He pressed hard between his legs, then groaned. "Can I?"

"Yeah." Kai's cock ached for attention. How he wanted to feel his touch. His skin burned with anticipation. He kissed Conner's hot, wet mouth, devouring him with hungry kisses.

Conner brushed his hand up Kai's shoulder, then down to his chest to tease his nipple.

His breath hitched. "Fuck." His cock jolted, spilling a dab of pre-seed into his briefs. As his tongue laid claim to the inside of Conner's mouth, he reached a tentative hand out to stroke his muscled chest. He yearned to touch all of it, to taste all of him. He kneaded at the firm flesh, then rubbed and pinched Conner's nipple.

Conner's body shuddered. He halted the motions of his hand over his own cock. He whimpered, then broke the kisses, panting. "Shit, you almost made me come."

He swallowed, then licked his swollen lips. "R-really?" God, this was a thousand times better than his fantasies and a million times better than anything he'd ever had before.

Conner bit his lip and gazed at Kai with an intense craving in his eyes. "D-do you want to touch me more?"

Do I. "Yeah." He slipped his hand down Conner's side, then slid his briefs down his hip, exposing his weeping cock. He wrapped his fingers around it. It was thick, and the skin was soft. He rubbed his thumb over the slit, swiping pre-seed over the top.

Conner shut his eyes, gasped, and tensed his mouth. "I'm so fucking close right now."

He studied Conner. What should he do? "D-do you want me to make you come now?"

Conner opened his eyes. "No." He moved Kai's hand around to his back and brought their hips close, then placed heated kisses over Kai's mouth, moaning and rocking his hard cock against Kai's hip.

Kai thrust against his thigh, wrapping his leg around Conner's. Sensitivity built in his aching shaft. He clutched at Conner's back, yearning to touch every inch of his skin. He groaned into his mouth, kissing with intensity, years of fantasy on display in every second.

Conner broke the kisses to lick and nibble a trail down Kai's neck, then to his nipple. He sucked and swirled it with his tongue, teasing it into a hard nub.

"Oh, fuck." As a pulse shivered through Kai's body, he flung his head back. He bucked his swollen cock into Conner's hip, desperate for contact.

Conner licked and kissed down Kai's stomach, then stopped and looked up. "Can I suck you off, Kai?"

"Hell yes." As a shiver worked its way over his skin, he bit his lip. Conner was going to suck him off. *Conner!* A shudder of need rolled over him. He fought to steady himself. He wanted this to last.

Conner pulled Kai's briefs down and devoured his cockhead, sucking and swirling it with his tongue. He dove in, taking Kai's cock all the way to his throat, licking up and sucking down, releasing greedy moans.

Kai clenched his teeth, holding in release. He didn't want to come yet, but damn, Conner was making it hard. Wet heat enveloped his cock, bringing a surge of delicious pleasure quivering over him. His balls grew heavy and tightened. He slapped his hand to Conner's head. "C-Conner, I'm, I'm going to come." His toes curled. As he shut his eyes, he freed a muffled cry. He spilled over the edge, letting waves of intense sensation jolt through his body, spurting his seed into Conner's lapping mouth.

Conner sucked until Kai was spent, then slid his mouth off with a pop. His voice trembling, he said, "C-can you do it to me?"

Could he? *Hell yes.* Kai drew deep breaths, steadying himself, and lifted a corner of his mouth. This was definitely like a dream come true. A wet dream. He nodded, focusing on Conner, his face full of need.

Conner slipped his briefs off and rose up on his knees, bringing his weeping cock to Kai's head.

Kai backed up onto the pillows, resting against the headboard of the bed, and took the hot cock between his lips. The bitter-sweet taste of Conner's pre-seed slicked his tongue. *God, he tastes good.* He wrapped a hand around the base and pumped his stiff cock with his mouth.

Conner rocked his hips into Kai's sucking mouth, releasing throaty groans. "Fuck, Kai, that's good." He tangled his hands in Kai's hair, driving him harder, faster over his cock.

Kai took it in, licking and sucking, groaning over the swollen head, while fondling his sac.

Conner's shaft hardened further and twitched. "I'm coming," he rasped.

Kai sucked hard, and seed spurted over his tongue and down his throat. He looked up.

Conner's face tensed. His head arced back and he erupted in sharp gasps.

As it slowed, Kai swallowed it all down, freed his spent cock, then licked the shaft one last time, not wanting to let it go. "Mhmm."

"Fuck . . ." Conner shuddered, bit his lip, and slipped his

fingers out of Kai's hair, then sat with his legs tucked underneath him, gazing at him, grinning. "I've dreamt of that forever."

Kai shook his head. "What are you talking about?" His hand brushed over his own cock. *Damn, I'm getting hard again.*

Conner leaned close to place a lingering kiss on his lips. "I don't know. Something about you has always turned me on, I guess."

"Come on." He pursed his lips and focused on the wall of the bedroom. How was he supposed to believe that?

Conner placed his hand on his shoulder. "Kai, look at me."

"No." He drew his brows together and turned his head the other way. He must be one of those sweet talker guys. "Why are you saying things like that?" He frowned.

Conner grabbed his chin and brought them face to face. "I've always liked you. Even in high school. How many ways do I have to say it?"

He gazed deeply into Conner's eyes. Was he fucking with him now? "Then why didn't you say something? Why did you disappear for five years and why the fuck were you with Paige?"

"I was confused and stupid." He slid his boxer briefs up and moved next to Kai, then draped an arm around his shoulders. "Just know that I'm not confused and hopefully not as stupid anymore." He kissed his cheek. "Come on, lay down with me."

Kai shimmied down into the bed and brought his boxer briefs up over his hips. What was going on here? He gnawed on his lower lip. *Conner just gave me a damn good blowjob.* He widened his eyes and glanced at him.

"Come here." Conner laid on his back and patted his chest, his arm stretched out.

Kai rolled to his side, one arm resting over Conner's chest, his head on his shoulder. *Wait. Has he given a blowjob before?* It didn't seem like he had any hesitation. He just did it. He furrowed his brows. Something wasn't adding up.

Conner wrapped his arm around Kai and kissed his head, then flung the covers over them. "Am I really the one you have a crush on, or did you just tell me that?"

He hid his face in Conner's neck. "Jesus, you figure it out." He huffed, then smiled against Conner's skin. Whatever was going on, it felt good to be here in his bed, in his arms. That much he knew. Maybe he could find out more in the morning when his head was clear. "Goodnight."

"Goodnight, baby." Conner snickered, kissed his head, then sighed.

He closed his eyes.

Chapter Nine

Kai, wearing his restaurant t-shirt and jeans from yesterday, looked out over his duplex in the late afternoon sun and frowned. He couldn't believe was actually doing this. He glanced at Conner, who sat in the driver's side of his BMW in a black long sleeve t-shirt and jeans, then at Bryce, crammed into the back seat, wearing his restaurant attire, and typing on his phone.

Bryce set the phone down. "Time for some fun." He tapped Kai's seatback and got out of the car, closed the door, then stretched.

Conner gnawed at his lip. "Kai?" He faced him.

"Yeah?" He looked Conner over. Something was up. "What?"

"So, these guys from work don't know about us. I mean, it's sort of new..." He wrinkled his forehead, then grabbed Kai's hand. "You understand, right?"

He widened his eyes. Conner wasn't out. Which begged a bigger question. What the hell *is* he anyway? "Yeah, I get it. You're not out at work."

Conner flinched and dropped his gaze to their hands, resting on the center console. "Yeah."

He tightened the hold on Conner's hand. "Don't worry about it."

Conner focused on him. "Thanks." He rubbed Kai's shoulder. "You ready? The guys will be here any minute."

"Yeah, guess so." There would be enough people here, so how bad could it be? He took a deep breath and climbed out of the car, then waited for Conner to get out.

Conner stepped up to him and touched his arm. "We have to grab your things anyway. You need clothes." He grinned at Kai.

"I know." Depending on how this investigation went, he might be staying with Conner for a short time. He furrowed his brows. Suddenly things were happening really fast. He didn't have time to think it through.

Bryce walked up to them. "Hey, I think they're here." He pointed at a newer black Chevy Tahoe SUV.

The vehicle pulled up behind Conner's car and stopped. Two men in their thirties stepped out, in t-shirts and jeans, one with dark blond hair, the other with brown hair. They waved. "Hey, Conner."

A wide smile spread over Conner's face and he left Kai's side to great them. "Hey."

Kai followed Bryce to the SUV. Hopefully, these guys could help them and everything would go back to normal. Or at least normal in his house. He smirked.

Conner held his hand out to him. "Kai, this is Brent and Eric."

He held out his hand. "Hi, I'm Kai." Hopefully, these guys were as good as Conner said they were. He shook Brent's hand and then Eric's.

Bryce stepped up. "I'm Bryce." He shook their hands.

Brent nodded. "Nice to meet you both. We'll get our stuff set up and then let you know when we're ready."

Conner lifted his chin to them. "Sounds good." He focused on Kai. "Come on, let's go and get your things."

He nodded.

Bryce followed Brent to the back of the SUV. "Here, let me help you."

Conner walked with Kai to the carport door of the house. "Hand me your keys."

He pulled his house keys out of the front pocket of his jeans and handed them to Conner. What would they find after not being home all night? "Do you really think they'll find anything?"

Conner turned the key in the knob and opened the door. "Yes. They always do." He wrinkled his brows. "You okay? You sure you want to be here?"

Kai pursed his lips. "Yeah, I'm sure. I want to see this for myself." As he stepped inside the house, goosebumps shivered over his skin. He rubbed his arms. A strange feeling overcame him, as if something was watching him. It seemed worse, somehow. "C-Conner?" He looked out over the kitchen. The cabinets were open in a haphazard pattern, along with the drawers. Silverware littered the floor. "This is fucking creepy."

"Yeah." Conner shut the door, then wrapped an arm around Kai's shoulders and kissed his head. "Don't worry, I'm here. We'll get to the bottom of this."

He twisted in Conner's hold and draped an arm around his waist, then swallowed hard. What would he have done if Conner hadn't come back into his life right now? He gazed into Conner's stunning face, the intense, ice-blue eyes, the generous lips, the scar hovering on his high cheekbone. A flood of emotions filled his chest. *What are these feelings? They're so intense. Am I falling in love? Shit.*

Conner gazed into his eyes. He licked his lips. "Kai, I promise you, I won't let anything hurt you."

Kai nodded. Statements like that weren't helping the feelings in his heart. "Yeah." He cleared his throat and freed Conner. "How about we pick this place up first, then we can go get my stuff."

"Sure." Conner crouched down, picked up the silverware and set it in the drawer.

Kai closed all the cabinet doors, then slid the drawers shut. He didn't want to pussy out of it this time. He should face this thing. He stood up and walked out of the kitchen and into the main room with Conner following.

A shadow in the outline of a person walked from Kai's room toward Bryce's room and disappeared.

Kai startled. "Holy fuck." The hair stood up on the back of his neck. "C-Conner, d-did you see that?" Instinctively, he hooked his arms around Conner's chest and buried his face in his neck.

"What?" Conner held him tight.

"There was a black something walking in the hallway." Maybe he didn't want to face this after all. He trembled.

"You saw a shadow figure?" Conner peered toward the hallway.

"If that's what you call it. Yeah." His heart pounded in his ears. He fought to calm himself. *Get a grip*. Nobody else was behaving this way, not even Bryce.

"I'm not surprised. That's pretty common with poltergeist activity." Conner kissed his head and held him tighter. "You want to leave?"

"N-no. I have to get my stuff." He freed Conner and glanced at the opening to the kitchen. He'd have to control himself around Conner's friends, too. The last thing he wanted was to out him if he wasn't ready. With a sigh, he focused on Conner. "But I'm not staying here until we're certain this thing is gone."

A faint grin played over Conner's mouth. "You've got no complaints from me."

Brent and Eric entered the room with Bryce following. Cases of equipment swung in their hands.

"Hey, Kai just saw a shadow figure in the hallway." Conner turned to face them.

Brent smiled. "Awesome. Let's see if we can get some EVPs." He pulled a small recorder from his back pocket and strode to the hallway, holding it out in front of him.

The Haunting Crush

Eric set a case down, opened it up and pulled out a black, round canister with lights and an antenna poking out of the top. "Here, we can try this REM pod, too." He followed Brent to the hallway.

Bryce stood next to Kai and Conner, placing his hands on his hips. "Was everything fucked up when you got in?"

Kai glanced at Bryce. "Yeah, more silverware on the floor." A shiver raced up his spine. He drew a deep breath and shut his eyes for a moment.

"We know you're here. Can you talk to us? Maybe tell us who you are?" Brent stepped through the hallway, holding out the recorder.

Eric crouched down, set the REM pod on the floor and turned it on. A few lights flickered. "Looks like we've got something."

Brent licked his lips and gulped. "This is your chance to talk to us. You can talk into this device in my hand, and we'll hear it."

A faint whisper laced through the room. The REM pod lit up and set off a tone.

Brent motioned to Eric. "Turn it off."

Eric shut off the REM pod and stood up.

Brent walked to Conner, Kai, and Bryce, still holding the recorder out. "Okay, let's listen."

Kai stared at the recorder, his mouth going dry. Maybe they didn't pick up anything. Maybe he was seeing things. *But the REM pod . . .* He peeked at Conner.

Conner's attention focused on the recorder.

Brent punched buttons with his thumb. The recorder came on.

We know you're here. Can you talk to us? Maybe tell us who you are?

A girl's whisper replied. *Mommy.*

Kai widened his eyes and focused on Bryce. "What the fuck?" A tingling sensation swept over him, making the hair on his arms stand up.

"Damn, that's a class A EVP." Brent's eyes lit up.

Bryce bit his lip. "I-I don't know, man. Are you sure that's not someone outside?"

Eric shook his head. "No, that's an EVP."

Brent hit the buttons again. "Okay, everyone be quiet." The recorder started up again.

This is your chance to talk to us. You can talk into this device in my hand, and we'll hear it.

The girl's voice came through. *Go home.* A few seconds later, a voice said, *bones.*

Kai's trembling grew. His knees knocked. "Th-that's it. I-I need to get out of here." Fuck it. This was the creepiest thing he'd ever seen, and he couldn't even have Conner close to get through it.

"Let's get your stuff and go, then. They can continue this and tell us what they find." Conner placed a hand on Kai's arm, then released it.

"I'm not going back there. Are you fucking kidding me?" Why wasn't anyone else as scared as he was? He glared at Conner.

Brent touched Kai's back. "Hey, take it easy. They can feed off negative energy."

He twitched the corners of his mouth. "Great." He had plenty of negative energy to feed off.

"Hey, at least it doesn't sound like it's the chindi of your father, right?" Conner examined him, furrowing his brows.

Kai nodded. He had a point. This thing, whatever it was, might have nothing to do with him. The fear filling his chest dissipated. "Yeah, maybe it *is* that girl that went missing in the wash. Maybe she's just lost?"

"Maybe she's asking to go home to her mother. Maybe it's her bones that are lost?" Conner pursed his lips, then came in close to Kai's ear. "You're really pale." He drew back and looked him up and down. "Want to leave the house for a while and then see if you want to come back in?"

Kai thought for a moment. If he left now, he wasn't really facing anything. He glanced at Bryce, Brent, and Eric, all watching him. He couldn't look like a pussy. "No, I'll stay." He nodded at Brent. "Go ahead and keep going."

"Okay. Eric, grab the MEL meter and I'll get the spirit box and we'll try the kitchen, since there's been so much activity there." Brent walked to a case and crouched down, then picked up a device resembling a walkie talkie.

"So, what do these do?" Bryce narrowed his eyes.

Brent stood up. "This spirit box scans frequencies and allows the spirits to talk to us directly. The MEL meter detects changes in temperature and electromagnetic field. If a spirit is around, the temperature will drop, and we'll get a reading on this."

Bryce lifted his brows. "Wow, you guys really know your stuff."

As a shiver rolled over his body, Kai wrapped his arms around his waist.

Conner placed his hand on Kai's lower back. "You don't have to do this."

Kai furrowed his brows. "Yes, I do. If you all can handle this, then so can I." *I'm not going to be a wuss.* He pinched his lips and looked at Conner.

Conner released a long exhale. "Okay."

Eric walked into the kitchen, holding the MEL meter out in front of him. "Got a reading in here."

Brent trotted up behind Eric, holding the spirit box. "Awesome. This place is super active." A wide smile spread over his mouth.

How can these guys be so damn happy about this? Kai walked with Conner and Bryce to the doorway of the kitchen and watched.

Eric held out his free hand. "The temperature dropped ten degrees. Feel how cold it is here."

Brent stepped to Eric, holding out his hand. "Damn, it's super cold right here." He glanced at Kai. "The AC isn't on, right?"

Kai shook his head. "No. Nothing's on." They kept if off as much as possible to save money.

"Come here and feel this." Brent chuckled.

Conner grabbed the back of Kai's arm, above the elbow. "You want to feel it?"

Kai huffed. "I suppose." He'd show them he wasn't afraid of a little cold air.

Conner, Bryce, and Kai walked into the kitchen and huddled around Brent and Eric, everyone holding out a hand.

Kai's body shivered. This was like stepping into the walk-in freezer at the restaurant. "Jesus, it *is* cold." He glanced at Conner.

He pursed his lips. "You okay?"

Kai nodded. Somehow, he was getting used to it, and it didn't seem as scary. Just a bit of cold air and a little lost girl. That was all this was.

"Okay, everyone, I'm going to turn on the spirit box now." Brent hit a button the spirit box and white noise filled the room. "Okay, you can use this box to talk to us. Focus your energy on this."

Kai went to the corner of the room, opposite the cabinets and the dinette, wrapping his arms around himself.

Conner followed. In a whisper, he said, "These guys are good, huh?"

Kai nodded, his attention drawn to the spirit box. What would this spirit have to say?

Brent focused on the spirit box in his hand. "Why are you here?"

Through the white noise, a man's voice rang out. "Kai."

A jolt of adrenaline shot up Kai's spine. His breath caught. "Fuck." His gaze darted around the room. Everyone looked at him with wide eyes. "N-No . . ." He shook his head. "C-can't be." His knees knocked and his teeth chattered. As tears stung his eyes, his breath came in quick pants. He focused on Conner. "I-I have to leave." He raced for the door, opened it, and ran down the driveway to the street. He fisted his hands in his hair and paced. He wasn't going to break down over this. He wasn't. A sob burst from his throat. He squeezed his eyes shut and clenched his teeth. There was no way his father's chindi was here. There must be something wrong with that device. That's all it was.

Conner caught Kai and held him in a tight embrace. He kissed his head. "Kai, I'm here."

As Kai glanced at the house, he pushed at Conner's chest. "Stop, what if your coworkers see us?"

"Shit." Conner freed him, seized his hand, and hauled him behind the SUV, then wrapped his arms around him. "I'm sorry."

Kai buried his face in his neck, draping his arms around Conner's waist. His voice shook. "What was that?"

Conner kissed his head. "I don't know. I hate to say it, but what if your father's spirit *is* here?"

Kai shut his eyes tight and clenched his jaw. His father's chindi was here to seek revenge on him. He should have remembered the insulin. *It's my fault he died so young.* A lump formed in his throat. Tears broke through and pooled in the corners of his eyes. His breath hitched. "It's him. He hates me." He let a ragged breath slip. "No . . ."

"Kai, he doesn't hate you."

He shoved Conner away and glared at him. *How would he*

know? "Then why the fuck is he here throwing shit around in my kitchen?" He blinked and a tear tumbled down his cheek. He swiped it away and sniffled.

Conner lowered his brows and pressed his lips together. "I don't know, maybe to get your attention?" He snatched Kai's hands. "Maybe he has a message for you. Maybe he doesn't want you to think that way?"

He thought on Conner's words and stared at the tan wall of the duplex. None of this made any sense. "I-I don't know."

"Maybe you should go back in there and find out." Conner rubbed his thumbs over the top of Kai's hands.

He dropped his mouth open. "Are you fucking serious right now?"

Conner grabbed him up in a tight embrace. "It sounds like maybe you have a chance here most people never get."

In a thick voice, Kai said, "But what if he hates me?" He nuzzled his face into Conner's neck, wound his arms around his waist and drew a jagged breath. Tears found their way down his cheek. He bit them back. "I don't know if I can do this."

"I'll be right by your side." Conner kissed his cheek.

"But your coworkers are there." Kai's breath hitched. Was he really going to try this? He didn't want to break down in front of everyone and he didn't want to out Conner by mistake.

"How about if I ask them to let us use their spirit box alone? Then it would be just you and me."

"Okay." That might work. It was time to face this thing. He took a deep inhale, releasing Conner, then wiped his face. "Let's go before I change my mind."

Kai paced in the kitchen while Conner sat at the dinette with the spirit box and a REM pod resting on the glass tabletop. The only light filling the room came from the cooking light over the stove.

"Come here." Conner held his arm out and beckoned him with his fingers.

Kai walked to him. "I-I can't sit down for this."

Conner grasped his hand. "Just stand next to me then."

Kai glanced out the kitchen window next to the table, looking out into the dark, over the shadows of the scrubby cactus in the rock yard to the street. "The SUV is gone. We probably have a half hour or so until they come back with dinner." How did Conner talk him into this? "So let's get this over with." He bit at the nail on his index finger.

Conner turned the REM pod on. The lights lit up and a tone sounded. "Something's already here." He shut it off and turned on the spirit box. White noise filled the room. "Kai is here. Who's with us?"

Kai stared at the device and drew a deep breath. Was his father really here with them? A chill worked its way up his spine. His skin tingled with goosebumps. "It's getting cold in here. You feel it?" He glanced at Conner.

"Yeah, the temperature definitely dropped." He moved his hand around the table, then pushed the spirit box closer to Kai. "If you have a message for Kai, then say it now."

The white noise broke. "Shizhé'é."

It's him. Kai whimpered and his knees weakened. What should he say? He placed both hands on the table, holding himself up.

"What?" Conner narrowed his eyes and looked at him. "Did you get that?"

"It said *father* in Diné." His voice trembled and his body shook. He fought to keep his composure.

Conner hooked his arm around Kai's hips. "Is that the Navajo language?"

Kai nodded, tears blurring his vision. He had to hold it together. If his father were here to get revenge, then so be it. He bit harder on his nail and moved to the next finger.

Conner focused on the spirit box. "Do you have a message—"

"Kai," the spirit box said.

Kai furrowed his brows and stared at the box. He wasn't sure if he wanted to leave or stay. Both options seemed like a bad choice. But if this was real, then this was his chance to make amends.

"Say something, Kai." Conner pulled him close and kissed his stomach. "Don't be afraid. This is your father."

"I'm sorry." Kai's voice broke. His lower lip trembled. He blinked and tears plunged down his cheeks. Maybe his father could forgive him somehow.

Conner stood and draped his arms around Kai's shoulders. "It's not your fault."

The white noise broke. "Two spirit."

Kai widened his eyes. "Oh, my God." He pushed away from Conner and stared at the device. Was his father trying to tell him he knows about him being gay? Was he saying he has two spirits?

"What? Is he saying there are two spirits in this house?" Conner peered at Kai.

"Two spirit is a native term for people who have two spirits, male and female. It's sort of a term for gay people. There's more to it than that, but I guess that's the best explanation I have right now." He took deep breaths. How was Conner going to react to this?

Conner dropped his mouth open. "Seriously? Is he acknowledging your sexuality?"

"I-I don't know." He focused on the spirit box. What should he say? Ask a question? Tell him something? What?

"Love you," the voice said.

His breath caught and pain shook through his chest. In a strangled voice, he said, "I love you, too, Shizhé'é." *My father loves me, even though I'm gay. Even though I forgot the insulin.* A sob erupted from his throat and he fell to the tile floor, lying over tucked legs, his forehead on his wrapped forearms. A well of grief rose up inside him. He wept, his shoulders shaking, sobs breaking free.

Conner shut the spirit box off, skidded the dinette chair across the floor and knelt beside him, holding him as best he could, shushing him. "It's okay, Kai. I'm here."

He took deep, ragged breaths, struggling to calm himself. God, he was a baby. "I'm sorry, Conner."

"For what?" Conner kissed his head.

"For being such a pussy." Kai clenched his jaw, willing the emotions to subside. He had to settle down.

"Jesus, you're not a pussy." Conner lifted him up to sitting and embraced him, kissing his cheek. "Shit, I'd break down, too, if this happened to me. In fact, I lose my shit for a lot less."

Kai sniffled and looked at him with wet eyes. "Really?"

Conner shrugged and placed his hands on Kai's cheeks. "Yeah." He wiped the tears from his cheeks with his thumbs. "I almost lost it last night when I thought you didn't like me." He let a faint grin creep over his lips.

"Really." Kai looked him over. Maybe Conner was a pussy. He smirked and released a soft chuckle.

"What's so funny?" Conner's gaze darted over his face.

"Nothing."

Bryce burst through the carport door. "Kai, are you all right?"

He flung himself backward, landing on his hands. "Fuck, Bryce. Way to scare the shit out of me." He sniffed.

As Conner rose to his feet, he searched behind Bryce. "Where are Brent and Eric?"

Bryce pointed behind him. "They're getting stuff out of the Tahoe." He took Kai in. "Were you crying?"

"Shut up." Kai stood up and wiped himself off. Bryce

certainly didn't need to know what happened. "Why did you come in like that? Ever think of knocking?"

"It's my house. Plus, I was worried about you. Did you talk to your father?" Bryce glanced at the equipment sitting on the dinette.

"I think I did." Kai sighed and raked a hand through his long bangs.

"So, what happened?" Bryce glanced at Conner, then focused on Kai.

"We think Kai's father came through the spirit box and gave him some closure." Conner placed his hand on Kai's shoulder.

Bryce swallowed and grabbed Kai's hand. "I'm sorry, man. I know how hard that must have been for you."

Conner scowled and pulled Kai's hand out of Bryce's. "He's okay now. We dealt with it."

Kai gazed at Conner. *Damn, he does not like Bryce touching me.* He smirked. He sort of liked it.

Brent and Eric strolled through the carport door with bags of takeout. Brent held up a bag. "Dinner is served."

Conner rubbed his hands together. "Good, I'm starved."

Eric set a bag of food down on the dinette. "So, fill us in while we eat and then you guys can take off while we finish up."

"Sure. You're going to sage the place, right?" Conner opened a bag and pulled out a wrapped hamburger.

"Yes, we'll start there and see how things go." Eric focused on Bryce. "Will you be staying here tonight?"

Bryce looked at Conner. "I think I'll stay at Conner's another night. I'd like to see what the cameras pick up after all this."

Conner nodded. "Sure."

Chapter Ten

Kai closed the door on Conner's apartment and rolled his suitcase into his bedroom, then strolled into the kitchen. It had been a mentally exhausting night, and he was already tired. He sighed.

"Drink a bourbon with me on the balcony?" Conner offered him a wide grin.

"Sure. That sounds perfect." Kai watched him take out two low-ball glasses, then pick up the bourbon bottle from the back of the quartz kitchen counter and unscrew it. "It's nice having someone else serve me drinks."

Conner poured the bourbon in the glasses. "Yeah? Maybe you'll have to teach me some of those tricks you do." He handed a glass to Kai.

"Sure." An image flashed though his mind of Conner throwing bottles. He smirked, then sipped the bourbon and puckered his lips. It burned down his throat. "Damn, I need this after today."

"Yeah? Come on." Conner cocked his head and walked toward the sliding glass doors.

Kai followed him out the doors and sat next to him on the couch. If he could believe what had happened tonight, then his father forgave him for everything. A feeling of contentment washed over him. He took in the view of the small lake and surrounding park down the street, the far-off jagged outline of the Superstition mountains in the moonlight. The fountain wasn't running for the moment.

Conner tugged a blanket from the armrest and threw it

over them both, then rested his arm over Kai's shoulders. "Come close."

As Kai curled a corner of his mouth, he shimmied into his side. It felt so nice being here with Conner. Without his help, he wouldn't have been able to deal with this chindi-ghost thing and find some sort of closure with his father's death. He glanced at him. A swell of intense emotion rose up inside him. His heart skipped a beat. *Damn, if this is love, I'm falling hard.*

A jingle rang out.

"Shit, my phone." Conner shifted and tugged his phone out of the front pocket of his jeans. It read, *Brent,* across the top. "Hello?"

Kai watched him and sipped his bourbon. Hopefully, this chindi thing would end tonight.

"So, all you're getting now is the girl's voice?" Conner glanced at him. "Yeah. Sounds good. We'll check that out this week." He touched the button and hung up the phone.

"So?" Kai lifted his brows.

"So, no more male voices on either the spirit box or the recorders. All they get now is the girl's voice talking about bones." Conner drank his bourbon and looked out over the view, furrowing his brows.

"What does that mean, do you think?" Kai studied him. Maybe it wouldn't end as easily as he'd hoped.

"Well, first we need to see if the activity in the kitchen stops. If it does, then I think maybe that was your father trying to get your attention. If not, then it's the girl and maybe your father just came through because of the equipment or something." Conner tightened his hold on him. "Maybe your father is always with you. You just never knew it before."

Shizhé'é is always with me . . . It wasn't a scary thought anymore. Instead, it was calming. Kai rubbed his chin. "Okay. But they're doing the sage tonight, right? Wouldn't that stop it?" If they couldn't end it with the sage, then what?

"Yeah, they're doing that now. But it doesn't always work. I was thinking if the cameras pick up activity in the kitchen even after they sage the place, then we should start looking to see if there are some bones somewhere. Maybe in the wash. I mean, you said this all started after that storm that flooded everything, right?"

A shiver ran up Kai's spine. "Yeah." Come to think of it, it was also the first night he saw Conner again since high school. He narrowed his eyes at him. Coincidence? *Maybe . . .* "So, if there's activity, we'll start searching the wash for bones."

"Yeah." Conner sipped his bourbon, then drew a deep breath. "Kai?"

"Yeah." He focused on him.

"Maybe you could start working some day-shifts." Conner chewed his lower lip.

He scoffed. What was this all of a sudden? "I make better money working nights."

Conner shifted to face him. "Yeah, but . . . I work days." He wrinkled his brows. "And, um, then we could see more of each other during the week." His gaze flicked to the blanket and a blush grew across his cheeks.

"Conner Mitchell, are you trying to say you're not seeing enough of me?" Kai sniggered. He could have some fun with this. "We just started dating and I'm already staying at your house." He let a wide grin spread over his mouth.

Conner thinned his lips and huffed. "Well, we need to have time to go look for bones, if there are any, and if you're working nights and I'm working days, how are we going to do that?"

"We can go when I get off work. I only work until nine-thirty during the week." He liked seeing the ever-confident Conner ruffled. "Or I can always go look with Bryce during the day." He smirked.

"I don't want you doing that with Bryce. What if you get

scared?" Conner wrinkled his nose and peeked at him. "And it's dark after you get off work."

"Ever heard of flashlights?" Kai snickered. *Oh, this is fun.* "Damn, Conner, I had no idea you were so clingy."

He gave Kai a sly grin and slapped his arm. "I'm not clingy. It just makes sense to try and get out in the wash when it's daylight, and you'd get off at four if you worked days, right?"

"Well, I can't do anything about this week's schedule. It's already set. Maybe next week I can work a day or two." When was the last time he'd opened the restaurant? He couldn't even remember when that was. Conner did have a point, and it would probably be better to go look before the sun set. If he found something creepy, he would much rather Conner was there than Bryce anyway. Goosebumps broke out over his skin. He wouldn't touch anything they found.

Conner sipped the last of his bourbon down, then wiggled his brows at him. "Almost ready for bed?"

Kai's breath caught and heat rushed his groin. Damn, just thinking about getting in bed with him had him going. "Almost." He sipped his bourbon. How much had Conner done with other guys? Maybe he could put this question to rest. "Hey."

"What?" Conner set his glass down on the table, then glanced at him.

"I want to ask you something." What was the best way to ask something like this? Kai twisted his mouth. "I uh, was just wondering, you know, how much, I mean, have you ever, uh . . ."

Conner lifted his brows. "Just ask me."

Kai gulped hard. "What have you done with guys, you know, sexually?" His heart pounded. Why was he so nervous asking this question?

Conner frowned and stared at the table. "I'm not sure I want to talk about that."

Kai shifted to see him better. Conner's arm fell off his shoulders. "Why not?"

"I-I don't know. It's just not something I talk about." Conner tensed his mouth.

"But, so, you have done things with other guys. Not just me." Kai's heart pinched. The thought of him doing anything with anyone else hurt. *Guess now I'm jealous. Damn.* He grit his teeth.

Conner slumped his shoulders with a sigh. "Can we just not talk about it?" He hung his head. "Why do you need to know that?" He fingered the blanket.

Kai straightened in his seat, then sank into the couch, biting the nail on his index finger. Why didn't Conner want to talk about it? Did something happen to him that he doesn't want to bring up? Wait, wasn't he with Paige all this time? How could he have any experiences with guys if he was with Paige? *Oh shit.* The memory of the graduation party flashed through his mind. He widened his eyes. Maybe he wasn't the only one Conner did that to. He was probably embarrassed about it. He looked him over. "I guess I don't have to know details. I just wanted to know, so I know how much, um, experience you have." *That sounded stupid.* He flinched.

"I have enough." Conner scoffed. "How much experience do you have?" He dropped his mouth open and held up his palm to Kai. "Stop. I don't want to hear it."

"Sure." Kai smirked and shook his head, gazing at him. "I think I got my answer anyway."

"Really. Then let's stop talking about it." Conner stood from the couch, the blanket falling off them both to the cement floor. "Let's go to bed."

Knocking sounded on the door.

"Oh, must be Bryce." Kai trotted to the door and opened it.

Bryce stepped inside and shut the door. "Hey."

"Hey. Sorry, but we're headed to bed." He pointed to the

kitchen. "There's more bourbon if you want some."

Bryce sighed. "No, I'm exhausted. I just want to go to bed, too. See you in the morning."

"Yep."

Kai shimmied out of his boxer briefs, climbed into the crisp white sheets of Conner's queen-sized bed, and waited for Conner to join him, lying on his back. Anticipation swelled his cock. What would tonight be like? Last night might have been the best night his sex life had ever seen. He brushed his hand over his erection, then pressed. A pulse of sensation shivered through him. He released a sharp gasp. Damn, Conner had him so fucking hot just waiting for him.

The lights shut off in the other room and Conner appeared in the doorway, bathed in the ambient light from the avenue streetlights coming in through the window blinds. He shut the door and came to the bed, then bit his lip, shimmied out of his long-sleeve t-shirt, dropped his jeans and boxer briefs to the floor, and stepped out of them. His cock stood firm over his stomach, the tip almost reaching his navel.

Kai's shaft jerked at the sight. *Looks like Conner is just as hot for this as I am.* He watched him climb into bed and lie next to his side.

Conner placed hungry kisses on his shoulder, then lifted up on an elbow to gaze down on him. "Kai, I don't want to rush this." He licked his lips and ran a hand down Kai's chest, to his stomach and hips, then skimmed over his solid cock. "I'm so close already I don't think you should touch me for a little while."

"What?" Kai widened his eyes. Did Conner have the stamina of a pre-teen? *Fuck that.* "No, way. How about if I just make you come twice?"

Conner shuddered and moaned. "That works." He rolled to his back and rocked his hips, his cock lifting off his stomach. He released another, softer moan and pre-seed dribbled out the tip to pool on his abdomen.

Damn. Kai's gaze locked on Conner's erection and he licked his lips. Lust surged over him. "Can you come like that?"

Conner gazed at him with hooded lids, then skimmed his teeth over his lower lip, nodding. "Yeah. All I have to do is think about it enough and I can make it happen." He thrust his hips again and his cock surged up, dripped, then fell back onto his stomach. He writhed on the bed and groaned. "It's only when I think about you though." He rubbed his hand over Kai's stomach and down to his cock, then placed lazy strokes over his shaft.

Shit, is he for real? He shut his eyes and gasped. Intense pleasure rippled up from his groin. "Fuck, I think you've got me going now, too." His breath grew heavy. He came down over Conner and placed hot, wet kisses on his lips, dancing his tongue inside his mouth, writhing over him with the soft strokes of Conner's hand over his cock.

Conner whimpered and thrust his hips in an urgent rhythm.

Kai grabbed Conner's cock and pumped. He couldn't help himself.

Conner cried out, his head arcing back, his body shuddering, seed spurting up over his stomach and chest.

A surge of sensation swept over Kai's body. His peak teased him. *Damn Conner's soft touch.* He wanted more, now. "G-go harder."

Conner pumped his cock faster, then stopped. "I want to suck you off."

"Really." Good idea. Kai lifted a corner of his lips, then licked down Conner's chest and stomach, lapping up the droplets of seed. When he reached his groin, he licked his semi-firm cock. "I think I'm going to get you hard again first."

Conner freed a sharp gasp. "Yeah."

He worked Conner's shaft with his mouth, licking up and down, sucking the head and swirling with his tongue. It swelled and hardened. He fondled Conner's sac, letting saliva drip down to his fingers, then toyed with his entrance.

"Fuck, Kai." Conner bit his lip and bucked his hips. "D-don't go there yet."

"Why?" He smirked. This might be the hottest thing he'd ever seen. "You going to come again already?"

Conner forced a quick glare at him. "Don't make fun of me."

Kai stopped and glanced up at Conner. He was right. That wasn't nice. "I'm sorry." He crept up to his face and gazed into his eyes. "Hey, I'm sorry."

Conner's eyes shimmered in the ambient light. He parted his plentiful lips.

Kai placed gentle kisses on Conner's mouth, then cheek, and finally, he kissed the scar under his eye. "I love this scar." *And apparently the man it belongs to.* He drew a deep breath, then brushed his index finger over it. He'd wanted to do this for as long as he could remember.

Conner took his hand. "It's only for you. I'm not like this with anyone else. I don't know what it is about you. I tried to tell you last night."

Kai widened his eyes. So that was what he meant. Damn, this dream was getting better by the second. "Okay, so . . ."

"Maybe in time it'll settle down. Maybe it's just because these are my first times with you." Conner flushed.

Kai smirked and kissed him on the lips. "Maybe I don't want it to settle down. Maybe I think it's hot." He placed more intense kisses over his lips and skimmed his hand down his muscled chest to play with his nipple, kneading it, teasing it.

Conner arched his back and groaned. In a strained voice, he said, "Fuck, Kai."

He licked down Conner's cheek, then sucked on the nipple,

while sneaking a hand down to stroke Conner's shaft.

Conner bucked his hips, his lips parting with faint gasps.

Kai's cock ached for something solid. He ground it against his hips, the friction pulsing pleasure through his groin. His breath quickened and sensitivity grew in his cock. Inside a breath, he said, "Oh, fuck . . ."

Conner rolled him to his side, then crawled in a circle, putting his cock at Kai's head and his own head at Kai's groin. "Suck me off, Kai." He engulfed Kai's cock with his wet mouth and pumped with a hand at the base.

Intense pleasure raced up Kai's spine from his cock. "Oh, shit." He licked up Conner's shaft, then slid his mouth over it, diving down and sucking back up. He wrapped one hand around the base and fondled his sac with the other, then with slickened fingers, he teased his entrance.

Conner whimpered and thrust hard into his sucking mouth. He stopped his motions on Kai's cock. "I'm going to come if you keep that up."

Kai smiled over his shaft and slid a finger inside his entrance, then curled and pulled it back out while sucking on his weeping cock.

Conner cried out, spurting seed into Kai's lapping mouth, panting against his thigh. Breathless, he said, "You are a fucker, you know that?"

"I know I want to fuck *you*, that's for sure." *God, do I want to fuck him.* In fact, he couldn't think of anyone he'd wanted to fuck more in his whole—Wet heat engulfed his cock, sliding up and down, sucking the head. As his peak surged, he released a long moan. "Oh, shit!" He thrust into it. Delicious pulses of sensation ravaged his senses. He shut his eyes tight and gasped, curling his toes, clutching at Conner's thigh.

Conner pumped Kai's cock, swallowing it all down as if famished. As it ended, he wiped his mouth, then licked his shaft a few times more.

"Easy." Kai chuckled and drew his hips away, then rolled to his back. "Damn, it tickles now."

Conner grinned and swung himself around to lie beside him, over his arm, then set his hand on Kai's cheek and placed passionate kisses on his lips, opening his mouth and penetrating him with his tongue. He rocked his hips against his thigh.

"Holy shit, are you getting hard again?" Kai released a soft breath, wrapping his arm around his muscular shoulders. How was he going to keep up with this guy?

Conner grinned and shook his head once. "I'm just playing." He laid his head on Kai's shoulder and nuzzled into his neck, pressing his semi-hard cock against Kai's thigh. In a soft voice, he said, "But I probably could." He brushed his hand over Kai's shoulder and down his stomach. "I can't get enough of you, I guess."

This is too good to be true. Somebody should wake him up from this dream . . . or maybe not. "I can't get enough of you either." Were those words really coming out of his mouth? Heat rushed his face and he snuggled against Conner. He was so done for. *God, I love him.* Could Conner love him back? Or was this more of a sexual thing for him?

"I have to work tomorrow." Conner pulled the covers over them both and placed lazy strokes up and down Kai's arm.

"Yeah. I don't." Kai smiled and kissed his head.

Conner tilted his head up. "I have to be out of here early. My first appointment is at eight o'clock down by the hospital."

"Okay. Guess I'll go to the house with Bryce and start looking in the wash." Kai looked up at the ceiling, a faint pattern of light filtering in from the sides of the blinds in the window.

"I wish you wouldn't. I'd rather you waited for me." Conner stopped his motions on his arm.

"Why?" Kai moved his head to peek at his face.

"If you find something that scares you, I want to be there

with you. Not Bryce." Conner pressed his lips together.

Kai snickered. "Jesus, okay. Guess I'll just go for a run or something." Was he really jealous of Bryce? Somehow, he liked the idea. It was cute. As long as he didn't get too possessive.

"I better go to sleep. Goodnight, baby." Conner kissed his cheek, then shut his eyes.

"Goodnight." With a deep sigh, Kai went to sleep.

Kai opened his eyes to sunlight shining in through the sides of the blinds on Conner's bedroom window. Damn, he didn't remember Conner leaving. Must have been so tired he'd slept right through it. He threw off the sheet and comforter, then stepped into his jeans from yesterday. Did Bryce get up yet?

He strolled out of the bedroom and into the main room. No Bryce. Maybe he was as tired as Kai was after all the ghost hunting. As he scanned over the contents of the room, his gaze caught on a folded tented paper and a key resting on the white quartz bar counter that separated the kitchen from the main room. He walked to it and picked it up.

I made breakfast. There are plates for you and Bryce in the refrigerator. Just heat them up in the microwave.
Conner

His heart warmed and a faint grin crept over his lips. Conner was surprising, and not just in bed. He strode to the guest bedroom door, on the other side of the kitchen, and knocked. "Hey, you awake yet?"

A groan snaked through the door. In a raspy voice, Bryce said, "Yeah."

"You want me to heat you up some breakfast?" He chuckled.

"Sure."

Kai made his way to the refrigerator, took out two white plates covered in tinfoil, then removed the tinfoil and heated them up in the microwave. He smirked. Conner had made them fried eggs, bacon, and hash browns. He brought the warmed food along with silverware to the dark-wood, round dinette table.

Bryce ambled from the guest bedroom to the table and took a seat in a green, upholstered chair. "Wow. Who made breakfast?" He raked a hand through his bangs and let them fall across his forehead.

"Conner," he said. "What some juice?" He smiled.

"Yes." Bryce picked up his silverware and cut into an egg. "Can you make coffee, too?"

Kai shook his head and smirked. "Yes." As he made his way into the kitchen, he noticed a silver coffee carafe sitting on the counter. "Perfect." Conner had thought of everything. He found the coffee cups, poured the coffees, then brought out cream and orange juice from the refrigerator. After putting cream and sugar into the coffee cups, he poured the orange juice into glasses and brought everything to the table.

"Damn, Kai, I don't know how you balance all those glasses in your hand." Bryce snickered.

"Practice." He'd never do well at the bar if all he could carry was two glasses at a time. He sat down and picked up his fork. "How is it?" He shoveled hash browns into his mouth.

"Damn good. Conner can cook. Breakfast, at least." Bryce sipped his coffee. "So, how are things going with you two?" He studied Kai.

Kai nodded. "Good." *Maybe more than good.* He ate a bite of bacon.

"So, is he gay or bisexual or what?" Bryce lifted a forkful of hash browns to his mouth.

Kai furrowed his brows. That was a good question and not

one he'd gotten a straight answer to. "I don't know." He drank some juice.

Bryce spat across his coffee. "What? How can you not know? Aren't you guys fucking?"

He released a soft chuckle. "Jesus, that's a bit personal, don't you think?" He offered Bryce a mock glare.

"Come on, Kai. You've had a thing for Conner since . . . well, since you found out I wasn't gay. How can you two be sleeping together and not be fucking?" He lifted his brows, and the hint of a grin quirked his lips.

Kai sipped his coffee. Should he talk to him? Bryce had a big mouth. He narrowed his eyes. But he was his best friend, and Conner was a little confusing. He focused on him. "Look, if I tell you what's going on, you've got keep your mouth shut. You hear me?"

A wide smile grew over Bryce's face and he leaned forward in his chair. "Sure. You can trust me, you know that."

"I know I can trust you. It's your little remarks you can't keep in check." Kai sighed. He glanced out the sliding glass doors at the mid-morning sun making long shadows from olive and palm trees on far-off grass in the park down the street. *How much should I tell him?* He looked back at to Bryce. "Just be careful. I think Conner isn't all that open about his sexuality or something." He thought back to last night's questions. Why didn't Conner want to answer him about his experiences with men?

Bryce widened his eyes. "This sounds good. Tell me."

He pressed his lips together, then sipped his coffee, staring at the table. "I don't know what he is. He doesn't want to say." He glanced at Bryce.

"Okay." Bryce lifted his brows. "And?"

"And he's obviously had sexual experiences with guys but doesn't want to tell me anything about it."

Bryce came back in his seat, rubbing his chin. "But he was

with Paige until recently, right?"

"Remember his graduation party?" Kai raised his brows.

"Yeah . . ." Bryce dropped his mouth open. "Oh, shit. You think he's into open relationships?"

"Open relationships?" Kai wrinkled his brows. *God, I hope not.* "What do you mean, exactly?"

"Maybe he and Paige had an open relationship back then and he was trying you out first, to see if he wanted to get you into bed with him and Paige?" Bryce waggled his brows, sipping coffee, then ate some eggs.

Kai's heart pinched. How could Bryce say something like that to him and then go on eating breakfast? *He knows how I feel about Conner.* "Bryce."

"What?" He looked up at him with a forkful of egg at his mouth.

"You don't really think that do you? I mean, he seems pretty monogamous to me." Kai stared at his plate of food, his forearms resting on the table, a bad feeling forming in the pit of his stomach.

Bryce shrugged and chewed the eggs, then looked him over. He stretched across the table and touched Kai's forearm. "Maybe he wasn't as into Paige as he is you. He seems to really like you."

Kai drew his brows together. An open relationship was not something he would ever consider. "Yeah, I hope so."

"Kai, it was just a suggestion. It doesn't mean I'm right. I'm sure there's some other reason why he did that and why he doesn't want to tell you about certain things. Maybe it's too soon for him."

"Yeah." Maybe it *was* too soon for Conner to talk about those things. He frowned. "What are you doing today?"

"I'm going to go and check out the wash and see if I can find anything weird in it." Bryce drank some orange juice.

"Okay. I'm going for a run. Can you drop me off at my

Blazer?" He ate some eggs.

"Sure." Bryce chuckled, then slapped his arm. "Come on, I'm sure you two will work things out."

"Yeah."

Chapter Eleven

Kai, dressed in a red t-shirt and jeans, checked the clock on the stove top. Almost six. Conner should be home soon. He opened the oven and checked the pork chops in a broiler pan. They looked like they needed a few more minutes.

Bryce opened the door on the apartment, wearing a white t-shirt and jeans. "Hey."

Kai glanced at him. "Hey, did you see anything?"

Bryce shook his head. "No, not a thing. I took a good look all around, too." He walked into the kitchen and stood next to Kai. "What are you doing?"

Kai checked the broccoli, set up in a steamer on the stove top. "Cooking dinner." He'd decided it was the proper thing to do, since they were staying in Conner's place and he'd made them breakfast.

Bryce chuckled. "Damn, look at you, all domestic and shit."

"Shut up." He huffed.

"You made some for me, too, right?" Bryce walked to the refrigerator and pulled out a bottled water, screwed off the cap, then gulped it down.

"I did, but comments like that are going to make you go hungry." Kai grinned and with a fork, checked the potatoes boiling in a pot on the stovetop.

Conner came in through the front door in a white, button-down shirt and black slacks, a computer bag slung over his shoulder, and stopped at the kitchen. A wide smile spread over his face. "Hi, honey, I'm home." He stepped to Kai and kissed him on the cheek.

Bryce erupted in laughter.

"Very funny." *Bastards.* Kai shook his head, then removed the pork chops from the oven and set them on an open area of the stovetop. "Go get your plates from the table."

Conner set his computer bag against the wall of the entryway. "You set the table and everything?"

Kai drained the potatoes, then seasoned them and added butter, leaving them in the pot, and took the top off the steamer. "Yes, I did."

Conner came into the kitchen with two plates and handed one to Kai. "You go first, since you cooked."

Kai smiled at Conner. "Thanks." He grabbed a pork chop with a pair of tongs, then spooned out potatoes and broccoli onto his plate. He stole a peek at Conner filling his plate with food, then grabbed a bottle of beer from the refrigerator and went to take a seat at the dinette.

Conner sat next to Kai with his plate of food and a beer, then Bryce sat across from him.

"So, what did you two do today?" Conner cut into his pork chop.

Bryce sipped his beer. "I went to the wash. Didn't find anything weird."

"And you?" Conner focused on Kai.

"I went for a run in the park." It was a great way to clear his head. Especially after the conversation he'd had with Bryce at breakfast. He ate a bite of broccoli.

Conner focused on Bryce. "So, did you take a look at the game camera while you were at the house?" He gulped some beer.

"Hell no, I wasn't going in there alone." Bryce shook his head once and stuffed a bite of potato in his mouth.

Conner swallowed down some food. "So, let's head over there after dinner and take a look at the game camera. If nothing's on it, I think we should let it go again tonight ,and if it's still clear, then I think we're done."

Kai peered at Conner. "And if not?"

Conner pressed his lips together. "If not, then we keep looking in the wash."

"What if we never find anything and it keeps going on?" Bryce lifted his brows.

"Then I guess we call in a medium." Conner cut more pork chop.

"A medium?" A shiver raced up Kai's spine. Was he serious? This was getting weirder all the time. "Where are we going to find a medium?" He freed a puff of air. "Wait, don't tell me. You work with one." He snickered.

Conner shook his head and smirked. "No, Brent and Eric have a few they work with."

"Great." He couldn't believe he was talking about things like this. But here he was. He gulped down some beer.

Kai followed Conner and Bryce into the carport door of the duplex, flicked on the kitchen lights, and stopped. Goosebumps shivered over his skin. He rubbed his arms. "Guess it's not over." *This is so fucked.* He pointed at the kitchen cabinets, all open to some degree.

"Were they all closed when you left last night?" Conner paced in front of the open cabinets.

"Yeah. At least there's no open drawers this time or silverware on the floor." Bryce narrowed his eyes. "Plus, it must have happened during the day or after we left last night. It was happening while we were at work before the investigation."

Conner rubbed his chin. "So, it's changed up a little, I guess." He walked to the glass and rattan dinette and picked up the game camera, flipped the back open the pressed buttons by the screen. "Let's see what we've got."

Kai leaned in close behind Conner, peering at the small

screen.

Conner hit the play button.

The video started. The cabinet door over the sink opened and shut, then the one next to it, then next to that, as if something invisible were walking down the counter and opening and closing them one by one. Finally, they all opened and slammed shut, then opened again.

"Fuck this." Fear trembled through Kai. He gulped hard.

Conner wrapped an arm around Kai's waist and kissed the side of his head. "I'm here."

"S-so what do we do now?" Kai edged into Conner's side. He was getting really used to having Conner close like this.

"I'll ask Brent and Eric to schedule a medium to come out. In the meantime, let's keep looking in the wash, and we'll keep the game camera rolling." Conner backed up the video and set the camera down on the glass table.

"Listen, I can't stay at your place forever, Conner. I'm going to go stay at my mom's place instead, until this thing is over." Bryce glanced at Kai.

"Sure," Conner said.

"Why would you do that?" Kai lifted his brows.

Bryce poked Kai in the side and jutted his chin at Conner. He whispered, "You'll thank me later." He winked.

Kai widened his eyes and heat rushed his face. As usual, Bryce was trying to be *helpful*. "Oh . . ." He stole a peek a Conner.

As Conner set up the game camera, a coy smile spread over his lips. "There."

Bryce slapped Kai's arm, then slid a small black flashlight out of his front pocket. "Come on, let's go check out the wash."

Kai pulled a small, red flashlight from the front pocket of his jeans and followed Bryce. "Come on, Conner. You're the one who insisted we had to do this together." Though he if they found something, he'd be damn happy to have Conner with him.

"I'm coming." Conner left the game camera to follow Kai and Bryce out the carport door, around the front of the duplex, then down the side and into the back yard.

Kai, standing twenty feet from the back of the duplex in the natural desert landscape of rocks, brush, and cacti, shined his flashlight at the wash. The sun was almost set, leaving everything in shadow. Scrubby palo verde mixed with mesquite and ironwood trees, all unkempt with boughs bending all the way to the ground. Underneath the trees lay large milkweeds interspersed with brittlebush. "How are we even supposed to get in there?"

"There's a path over there." Bryce pointed his flashlight to an opening in the bushes and weeds between two palo verde trees. He walked toward it.

Kai and Conner followed, pushing aside spiked branches, and kicking away errant tendrils. After a few feet, the wash opened up, exposing dry beds of dirt and rocks laid out in trails between shorter weeds and bushes.

Kai darted his flashlight over the area, hitting the trees on either side, then down around the dirt and weeds. There was so much underbrush, how would they ever find anything in the dark? "Where did you look today, Bryce?"

"More over there." Bryce shined his flashlight at the trees behind their duplex.

"So, Kai, you come with me and we can walk down the wash to the road." Conner grabbed his hand.

He smiled. "Sure."

"I'll go to the other side." Bryce hopped over a patch of weeds and walked up the trail bed on the other side of the wash.

Kai strolled beside Conner for a few feet, shining his light from side to side. Maybe this was pointless. It was hard to see anything at all.

Crackling sounded under the trees.

Kai's heart skipped. "Shit." What the hell could that be? The hair on the back of his neck stood up.

The crackling sounded again.

Conner hooked an arm around Kai's waist and set his light in the direction of the noise. "Shh. It's probably just an animal."

Just outside the periphery of Conner's light, a pair of yellowish-green eyes came into view, bounced, then stopped.

"What is that?" Kai deepened into Conner's side. *Thank God Conner's here.*

Conner moved his light.

A coyote stared at them, one back leg raised, sniffing at the air, fluffy tail straight out behind it.

"Fuck." *We should know better than to be in the wash at night.* "Conner, this isn't a good idea."

The coyote sprinted off toward the road.

Conner drew a deep breath. "Maybe."

"Maybe? If there are coyotes out here, then there are javelina. I don't feel like getting attacked out here."

"Yeah, you're right. This might be too dangerous at night." Conner moved his light to Bryce. "Hey, we just saw a coyote. Maybe we should head back."

Bryce stopped in his tracks. "Yeah? Shit. Good idea."

Yipping and howling rang out through the wash.

Kai startled and flung his arms around Conner, hiding his face in his shoulder. "Damn it." He was looking like a pussy again. He frowned.

Conner clicked off his flashlight and held Kai close, nuzzling his neck. "Sometimes I kind of like it when you're scared." He found Kai's mouth and placed a lingering kiss over his lips, then parted them with his tongue, pressing his swelling cock against Kai's hip.

He lost himself in the insistent kiss, kneading the muscles

of Conner's back with his hands. Coyotes be damned. This was too good.

The howl of a lone coyote called out through the chill night air.

A shiver raced up his spine. *Or maybe not.* He broke the kiss, gazing into Conner's intense eyes. "Let's get out of here." Tapping prodded his shoulder. He yelped and jumped.

"Jesus, Kai, settle down." Bryce laughed.

A grin played over Conner's generous lips.

He scoffed and turned in Conner's hold. "You scared the shit out of me."

"Everything scares the shit out of you." Bryce grinned. "The trail is over here. Let's go." He walked off down the bed of dirt.

Kai glanced at Conner.

Conner watched him, his grin widening.

Kai pointed a finger at him. "Don't say a word. I told you I hate this shit." Could everything go back to normal now, so they didn't have to do this anymore?

"I didn't say anything." Conner sniggered. "Let's go home."

Kai followed Conner into the kitchen. "Bourbon?" He grabbed two low-ball glasses from the cabinet, unscrewed the cap from the bourbon bottle and poured. What sort of surprises would tonight bring?

Conner stepped up behind Kai and wrapped his arms around his waist, resting his chin on his shoulder. "Looks like you already know the answer to that."

"Think we'll have to get a new bottle tomorrow." He emptied the bottle into the glasses and looked them over. It was probably two full ounces, but who was counting? He handed a glass to Conner.

"Balcony?"

"Of course. It's our thing now, isn't it?" He snickered and followed Conner through the main room, out the sliding glass doors and to the waiting outdoor couch, then sat down.

Conner took a seat and flung the blanket over them.

He sighed and looked out over the park and the fountain, spraying high against the far-off stars. No moonlight tonight. No wonder the wash was had gotten so dark as soon as the sun set.

Conner rested his arm over Kai's shoulders. "Come here."

He snuggled into Conner's side, then drew the blanket up and sipped his bourbon. The day's events replayed in his mind, stopping at the conversation he'd had with Bryce over breakfast. He had to find out if Conner had been in an open relationship with Paige. "It was really nice to make breakfast for us before you went to work."

Conner tugged him closer. "Glad you liked it."

Kai studied the bourbon as he tilted his glass. "So, um, I was wondering."

"What?" Conner kissed the side of his head.

Kai shut his eyes a moment, savoring the affection. "What are your views on open relationships?" Hopefully, he'd asked it the right way. He focused on him.

Conner widened his eyes. "Why are you asking me that?"

"I don't know . . ." What should he say that wouldn't put him off? He had to be careful. "Just curious, I guess."

Conner's gaze darted over his face and he frowned. "Kai, I don't want you being with anybody else." He huffed. "Why, are you seeing someone else besides me?"

"No, of course not." *Conner wants to be exclusive.* Kai twisted his head away, hiding a grin. "Have you ever tried something like that?"

Conner's mouth opened, then shut. He stared at the drink in his hand, resting in his lap. "I don't know why you're asking me this."

Kai shifted on the couch and placed a hand on Conner's cheek, then kissed his lips. Maybe that would ease his concerns. "I'm just trying to figure you out."

Conner glared at him, knocking his hand away. "Do you want an open relationship?" He flared his nostrils. "I don't want you being with anyone else."

Kai blinked. "I don't either." *He looks pissed.*

"Okay, then it's settled. We're not having an open relationship." Conner pursed his lips and drank some bourbon, then looked him over. "Right?"

That went nothing like I planned. "Yes, okay." Kai furrowed his brows, glancing at the view. "By the way, I wasn't asking to *have* an open relationship."

"Good. Then we can stop talking about it." Conner tugged him in close to his side and nuzzled his neck. "Hurry up with your drink, so we can go to bed."

Kai lay nude on his back in Conner's bed, the sheets and covers drawn down, watching Conner's muscles as he climbed in next to him.

Conner lay on his side, propping his head up with an elbow, his breath coming in deep draws. The tip of his firm cock glistened with a bead of pre-seed in the ambient light from outside the window.

Kai licked his lips. *He's already so aroused. But then, so am I.*

Conner touched the side of Kai's hip.

His breath caught. Lust shivered over his spine. His hard cock jerked. He bit his lip and gulped.

Conner skimmed his hand up Kai's side, circled it over his shoulder and came back down to settle over his cock, focusing on his face.

Kai shut his eyes. Every inch of skin tingled. All Conner had to do was touch him and he was on fire. He opened his eyes and drew a deep breath.

Conner slid his hand over Kai's shaft, lazily caressing, then stroking with more pressure. "You want to touch me, Kai?"

He nodded and raked his teeth over his lower lip. *Do I.* He'd start there and then—

Conner pumped Kai's cock, over and over.

Pleasure pulsed through him. He freed sharp moans and rocked his hips. His cock dribbled pre-seed onto his stomach. In a breath, he said, "Oh, shit." How many times was he going to make Conner come tonight? Three? He licked his lips and lifted the edge of his mouth.

Conner stopped his hand. "What are you thinking about?"

Kai rolled to his side and grasped Conner's erection, then pumped it, hard and fast. "How many times I'm going to make you come tonight."

Conner whimpered, then shuddered, his mouth falling open. "Fuck, Kai." His cock jerked, then seed spurted up between them, landing on Kai's chest and dripping over his fingers.

"God damn, Conner." Kai devoured him in deep kisses, rolling over him, rocking his hard cock against his thigh. *I need to fuck him, right now.* Their tongues tangled in the wet heat of their mouths. He kneaded his hands up and down Conner's side, his muscled chest and rubbed over a nipple, then pinched.

Conner groaned and thrust against him, wrapping his legs around Kai's, increasing the pressure and friction.

Breathless, he said, "Can I fuck you, Conner? Please." He kissed down Conner's stubbled chin to his neck and nibbled at his earlobe, then gave it soft bites.

Conner arced his head back. "Yes." He writhed under him, slapping his hands to his ass, bringing their thrusting hips closer still. "Fuck, yes."

His cock twitched and a pulse of pleasure jolted through him. Did he hear that right? He was going to let him fuck him?

He lifted his head, panting, and gazed deeply into his intense eyes. "You'll let me do that? Tonight?"

Conner nodded.

A wave of desire shivered over Kai. His cock surged with intense sensation. "S-stop moving."

Conner stopped all motion. "What's the matter?" He lifted his brows.

"I almost came." Kai offered him a wicked grin. "You have no idea how long I've wanted to do this." He flinched. *Damn, Kai, way to spill the beans.*

Conner slowly rocked his hips. "Really." He brushed his hand down Kai's cheek. "How long?"

Kai placed a deep, sensual kiss over his lips. *What the hell. The secret is out anyway.* "A very, very long time." He rocked against his thigh, kissing him with more intensity, then shifted to the side, bringing his hand down, the fingers still slicked with Conner's seed. He snuck between Conner's thighs to tease his entrance, circling, then slid a finger inside.

Conner gasped and his semi-firm cock hardened. He rocked into his fingers. "More."

Kai slid a second finger inside and curled, then pumped.

Conner's face tensed, his thighs quivered, and he moaned. "Fuck me now, Kai." His head twisted to the side.

Holy fuck if this isn't the hottest thing I've ever seen. He brushed his free hand over Conner's forehead and claimed his mouth in deep, heated kisses, thrusting against his thigh, delicious pleasure humming through him, his fingers sliding in and out of his tight entrance.

Conner's moans quickened and his body shuddered. In a choked voice, he said, "Kai, I swear to God if you don't fuck me now, I'm going to come again, and you'll miss your chance."

Kai rounded his eyes and halted all motions. "Shit. We can't have that." He gave him a quick smirk and lifted onto his knees. "Uh, where's the lube and stuff?"

Conner pointed to the dark-gray nightstand with long, silver handles. "Top drawer."

Kai slapped it open and fumbled through it for a condom and lube, then opened the condom and rolled it over his solid cock. After slicking his fingers with lube, he threw it in the drawer and laid next to Conner.

"I have a confession." Conner gave him a sly grin.

"What, now?" Kai slicked his entrance with lube and slid two fingers inside, curled and pulled out.

Conner tensed his face, bit his lip, and groaned. "Damn it, Kai." He lifted his knees up, then placed a hand on Kai's cheek. "I've wanted to do this with you for a very, very long time, too."

Kai gazed into his eyes. Was he serious? He looked serious. Now was not the time to think on that. *Damn if I don't love the shit out of him right now.* He kissed him with all the emotion swelling his heart. He should slow down and make this first time last. With a deep breath, he lay over him and dropped his hips between Conner's legs, then positioned his hard cock at his entrance. He pressed his mouth to Conner's, parting his lips and kissing him fully, taking him all in, then slowly rocked his hips.

Conner wrinkled his brows and freed a sharp gasp, then found Kai's ass with his hands and pressed, wrapping his legs around his hips, driving him deeper.

"Oh, God." Tight heat enveloped Kai's cock, the friction sweet and intense. He stayed on Conner's mouth, penetrating him with his tongue, then wiped his hand in the sheets and brushed it over his cheek, breaking the kisses. He gazed into his hooded, intense eyes, then down to his parted, swollen lips, all the time pulling out and thrusting deeper into Conner. God, he was stunning. He dropped his head down to his neck and nibbled and sucked soft skin, his peak taunting him with each rock of his hips. *Conner feels so good, so damn, good.* It wasn't sex. It wasn't fucking. He was making love for the first time in his life. As his sac grew heavy with the need to release, he slipped a hand between them and pumped Conner's firm cock.

Conner dug his fingers into Kai's side and cried out, his body shuddering, seed spurting up between them.

Delicious release surged through Kai's body, curling his toes, sending waves of sensation pulsing through his cock, gasping with each one. As it slowed, he laid his head on his shoulder, panting. He'd done it. He had finally had sex with Conner fucking Mitchell.

Conner embraced him and kissed his head. "That was fucking awesome."

He nodded, holding Conner's shoulders. There was no going back now. He was all the way in. *I am completely, hopelessly, desperately in love.* A prick of fear fluttered his heart. He was so fucked.

"Kai." Conner attempted to move him.

He held still, biting his lip. "What?"

"You okay?"

"Yeah, I'm fine." If he got up, would Conner see his true feelings? They had to be written all over his face.

Conner chuckled. "Come on, we need to clean up."

Kai tightened his hold on Conner's shoulders and took a deep breath, then lifted his head. He couldn't look at Conner. *If I do, he'll see.* He climbed off the bed and walked into the bathroom, discarded the condom, then grabbed a washcloth off a chrome towel rack and washed up. He rinsed the washcloth then brought it to Conner. "Here."

Conner sat up in the bed and wiped off. "You sure you're okay? You seem weird."

He pursed his lips. He couldn't talk. If he did, it might spill out of him. He nodded.

"Damn it." Conner threw the washcloth to the floor and

seized his hand, then tugged him down to the bed. "Come here." He pushed him to his back and lay over him.

Kai stared at the wall, keeping his lips pinched together. *Don't say it. Don't fucking say it.*

Conner kissed his cheek and brushed his hand over Kai's forehead. "Are you okay with what we did?"

Kai turned to him and he widened his eyes. "Yeah, I'm very okay with it. I loved it." He flinched. *Fuck, I need to keep my mouth shut.*

Conner smiled. "I loved it, too." He laid on the bed and flung the covers over them both. "I have to get up early." He wrapped an arm and a leg around Kai from the side, then kissed his cheek. "Goodnight, baby."

"Goodnight." *My love.* He snuggled closer into Conner's side and closed his eyes.

Chapter Twelve

Kai looked out over the restaurant, the tables and bar almost full of people, but manageable. He grabbed a wine glass out of the dishwasher and dried it with a white towel, then scanned over the bar top for empty drinks. Everyone seemed fine for the moment. His gaze caught on Conner, in a blue button-down shirt and black slacks, walking past the hostess stand, then the windows with a view of the park. He must have come straight from work. He glanced at the clock on the POS station—6:05 p.m. He grinned.

Conner took a seat on a barstool and gave him a wide smile, his intense ice-blue eyes focused on him. "Hey, baby."

He wasn't sure he'd ever get used to Conner calling him that. As heat flushed Kai's face, he set the wine glass down, then grabbed a menu from the island and stepped to him, his ponytail swaying across his back. "Hey." He handed the menu to him and rested his hands on the back bar. "Beer?"

Conner licked his plentiful lips and smiled. "Yep." He perused the menu.

Kai grabbed a beer glass from the cooler and poured him a beer from the tap. He knew exactly what beer he liked. The last few days flashed through his mind, the easy way their lives meshed and the hot nights in bed. His cock jerked in his jeans. He should stop thinking about that. He cleared his throat, then brought the beer to Conner and set it in front of him. "So, what do you want to eat?"

"Just get me a burger." Conner handed the menu to him. "Too bad I can't have your home cooking tonight." He

The Haunting Crush

smirked.

Kai rolled his eyes. "Don't worry, it's already Thursday. I'll cook you dinner soon enough." He walked to the POS station and entered his order. He didn't have to ask him what type of burger, what sides or how he liked it cooked. He already knew. Seemed he was getting to know Conner pretty well. His gaze caught on movement behind him.

A young man with blond hair held up an empty wine glass, waving it in the air. "Hey, bartender."

Kai turned around. "Want another one?" How'd he miss that? Conner was too distracting.

The young man gave him a coy grin. "Yes."

Kai went to work, pouring a new white wine, then brought it to the young man.

"Hey, what's your name, anyway?" The young man leaned into the bar front on his elbows and bit his lip.

"Kai." He narrowed his eyes. Was this guy about to hit on him?

"Kai . . ." He smiled. "I'm Samuel. You native or Mexican?" He sipped his wine.

Kai pursed his lips. *Here we go.* "I'm part native."

"Looks like you got the best part." Samuel flashed his blue eyes at him, then looked him up and down.

"Excuse me?" Kai cocked his head.

Samuel licked his lips. "You're very attractive."

Heat flushed Kai's face. He stared down at the sink. What was he supposed to say to that? Conner was sitting right here. He turned to Samuel. "Uh, thanks."

Conner stood up and stepped a few bar seats down to Samuel, resting his hand on his seatback. "Hey, he's taken."

Samuel gave Conner the once over. "By whom, you?" He laughed, then placed his fingers at his mouth. "Hey, haven't I seen you somewhere before?"

Conner grimaced, then glared at Samuel. "No, I'm sure you

haven't." He tensed his mouth and pointed at Kai. "Anyway, he's taken. Kai's my boyfriend. So, lay off."

His boyfriend? Kai widened his eyes. When was that decided? Not that he minded. Not at all. It was finally real. He held his hand out to Samuel. "Nice to meet you Samuel, and yes, this is my boyfriend."

Samuel shook Kai's hand. "Nice to meet you, Kai." He focused on Conner. "And you are?"

"None of your business." Conner scoffed and went back to his chair.

Kai offered Samuel a quick grin, then trotted to Conner, leaning over the back bar. "Hey. Don't be a dick to the people who come in here, okay?"

Conner scowled. "He's the one being a dick." He thinned his generous lips, then fixated on Samuel. "Who does he think he is, coming in here and hitting on you? Did he really think you'd be hot for him?"

Kai lifted his brows. *Hot for him?* "What?"

"Do you get that a lot? People hitting on you while you're working?" Conner wrinkled his nose, then gulped his beer.

Kai took a quick look around. Hopefully, no one was listening to their conversation. "It happens. I work in a place where people are drinking and hooking up."

Under his breath, Conner said, "Maybe you shouldn't work here anymore." He frowned.

"You can't be serious." *I won't even entertain such a comment.* Kai shook his head, then picked up a rag and wiped down the area next to Conner, now vacated by a couple.

Janice walked through the black swinging door from the kitchen with a plate of food in her hand, then set it down in front of Conner. "Burger?"

Conner smiled at her. "Yes, thanks."

"How's it going, Kai?" She stood next to him, crossing her arms.

"Good. Everyone seems happy." He glanced at Conner. *Except maybe him.* He chuckled.

Conner took a bite of his burger.

"So, I scheduled you for two day shifts next week, Wednesday and Thursday. You okay with that?" She scanned the restaurant.

He slapped the towel on the bar top in front of Conner. "Well?"

Conner swallowed his burger down. "Yes, I'm happy with that."

Her brows lifted. "Oh, so you're changing your schedule for him? You two finally ended up together?" She smiled at Conner.

"Yes." As Kai smirked, he held his hand out to her. "Conner, this is Janice, my manager."

Conner wiped his hands on a paper napkin. "Nice to meet you." He held out his hand.

She shook it. "Likewise." She touched Kai's arm. "Damn, Kai, he *is* good looking."

Kai grinned. "I know." *And he's mine.*

Conner widened his smile and shook his head.

"Well, got to get back to work." She tapped the bar in front of Conner. "See you later."

"Yep." Conner sipped his beer.

She trotted off.

A customer at the far end of the bar pointed to an empty beer glass and Kai refilled it, then came back to Conner and dried wine glasses from the dishwasher.

"Kai."

His heart skipped. Damn, Conner still had that effect on him. "Yeah." He watched him.

A shy grin played over Conner's mouth. "So . . . I took Monday and Tuesday off next week." He peeked at him.

Kai set the wine glass down and picked up a new one. "Oh,

and why is that?"

"I want to take you somewhere special."

"Where?" He looked at Conner.

"It's a secret, but I'm taking you out of town for two nights." Conner looked him over. "I wanted to get you out of here and maybe forget about this ghost thing for a while."

Kai's heart warmed. It sounded perfect. No one had ever done anything like that for him before. He sided to the back bar, grinning at Conner. "So, you're taking me on a romantic getaway?" He snickered.

Conner flushed. "Yeah, is that okay?"

"Oh, it's more than okay." Damn, Conner didn't even get that it was a joke. Kai picked up a new wine glass. If they were going to be gone this weekend, then when would they have time to deal with the ghost problem? "Did you ever find out when Brent can schedule that medium?"

"Yeah, he's not available until next weekend." Conner dipped a French fry in ketchup and ate it.

Kai let loose a long exhale. "Okay. Bryce isn't finding anything in the wash. I think the medium is our only hope of stopping the weird shit in my house."

Conner nodded and gulped some beer. "I think you may be right." He took a bite of burger, then swallowed it down. "Though I'm getting used to having you at my place." He gave him a shy grin.

Kai chewed the nail on his index finger. Come to think of it, he was getting pretty used to being at his place, too. Where was this thing going between them? He still didn't really know what his deal was. Conner wasn't all the way out. He knew that much.

"Hey, someone wants another drink." Conner pointed down the bar.

"Shit." He had to pay attention. Kai strolled down the bar to an elderly couple. "I'm sorry. What can I get you?"

Kai, dressed in a black long-sleeve shirt and jeans, sat in the passenger seat of Conner's BMW M3, squeezing his eyes shut. "When can I open them?"

"Not yet. Almost."

He clutched the handle on the door. Where the hell was Conner taking him?

"Okay, you can look."

Kai opened his eyes, brushed his bangs off his forehead, and peered out the windows of the car. Small shops of differing shapes and sizes, most colored in a clay-orange stucco, surrounded him with sidewalks and parking lots. He looked up behind the shops. Colorful water and wind worn sandstone mountains rose up with striations of red and orange, the noonday sun bringing out patterns in the cliffsides. Toward the bottom of the mountains, scrubby oaks and pinyon pine dotted the reddish clay dirt. "Sedona?"

Conner, wearing a gray button down shirt and jeans, grinned. "Yes, and we're staying here." He pointed at a small sign nestled in a bed of red rock, surrounded by flowers. "L'auberge." His grin widened into a full-on smile.

Kai's mouth fell open. "Are you serious? I've never been here." Jesus, how much had he spent on this get away? This was one of the most exclusive resorts in Sedona. He stared at him.

Conner drove the car down the side street. "Well, now you have. We have reservations for lunch here, too, so I hope you're hungry."

Kai gulped and placed his hand on his stomach. They'd had breakfast before they left, but nothing since. "Yeah, definitely hungry." He looked out the windows as the car descended. Scrubby brush gave way to greenery and tall cottonwood trees, their fall colors on full display. Small log-sided cabins with shingle roofs came into view, nestled among the trees in front of Oak Creek. "Shit, this place looks so peaceful."

Conner drove the car around a circular drive and parked under a high awning held up by columns of river rock, connected to a building of dark brown wood siding. "Stay here. I'll go check us in." He leaned over the seat, gave Kai a quick kiss, then got out and strutted through the double glass doors of the building.

Kai wrangled his fingers together in his lap, scanning the grounds of flower beds, vines on trellises and tall pine trees. He'd never in his life be able to afford to come to a place like this. Hell, he'd only stayed in the cheapest of motels whenever he'd been anywhere, and usually if he did go anywhere, he camped. No wonder Conner had asked him to bring shirts with collars. This place probably had a dress code. He bit his lip.

Conner trotted to the car, opened the door, and climbed in. He smiled at Kai, then patted his thigh. "This is going to be awesome." He drove the car along a smaller drive and parked in a spot in front of the last of a row of log cabins. "We're here. Let's get our stuff."

Kai got out and waited for Conner at the trunk of the BMW, surveying the area. The bubbling of the creek sounded off in the distance and the cool air chilled his skin. "Good thing you told me to bring a jacket."

Conner stepped to the trunk and opened it with his key fob. "I wouldn't let you come unprepared." He hauled out Kai's suitcase, then his own and shut the trunk. "Let's get these inside and head over to the restaurant."

"Sure." He rolled his suitcase through a set of tall pines, down a cement pathway with flower beds on either side and up the front steps of the cabin to stop on the covered portion of the porch. He looked out over the creek, flowing over boulders, and fallen trees, stretching across at least fifty feet to the other bank. "Wow, the creek is pretty big in this area."

Conner opened the door on the cabin. "I'm sure that's why they put the resort here." He stepped inside.

Kai followed Conner into the cabin, taking it all in, the king-sized four poster bed in dark wood with fine white linens and a navy-blue blanket laid out across the bottom, the brown leather settee bench at the foot of the bed, the square wooden table with two wicker chairs sitting next to a window looking over the creek and finally the sitting area of large beige upholstered chairs resting in front of a fireplace with a television hung over it. The walls and ceiling were all wood paneled but painted white. "This is a really nice fucking place, Conner." He grinned. "Holy shit."

Conner stepped to him and wound his arms around Kai's shoulders, then kissed his lips. "I wanted to take you someplace really special, because I want you to know how special you are to me."

Kai gazed into his intense blue eyes, warmth filling his chest. *God, I love him.* He swallowed and wrapped his arms around Conner's waist. "Thank you, so much. No one has ever done anything like this for me."

"Well, get used to it, because I'm only getting started." Conner smirked and placed a longer, more sensual kiss on his mouth, then rested his forehead on Kai's and swayed them both. "We're going to have such a great time here."

"We better." Kai snickered.

Conner released him. "Let's go to lunch."

Kai, now wearing a light black jacket over his shirt, followed Conner to a wooden deck looking out over the creek under a canopy of colorful cottonwood trees. Square tables were set up with white linen tablecloths and iron patio chairs. White ceramic vases held small bouquets of orange flowers.

Conner met with a maître d'hôtel. "Reservation for Mitchell."

"Right this way, sir." The maître d' wore a black vest over his white shirt and black slacks. He led them to a table on the creek. "Here you are. Will you be ordering wine?"

Conner sat down and picked up a wine list from the table. "Yes, this one." He pointed to the menu.

"Certainly, sir." The maître d' left.

"What did you order?" Kai unfolded the linen napkin and placed it in his lap.

"A nice chardonnay." Conner grinned. "I thought it would go well with the atmosphere."

Kai nodded and moved his long hair behind his shoulders. In a teasing tone, he said, "Perfect for such a lovely day." He snickered.

A female wine steward with her blonde hair in a bun stopped at the table, a napkin draped over one arm, and showed the wine bottle to Conner. "Here you are, sir."

He nodded.

She opened the bottle, set the cork on the table, and poured a small amount into Conner's wine glass.

He picked it up, swirled the wine, then sipped. He grinned. "Very good." He set the wine glass down and beamed at Kai.

She nodded and poured wine into Kai's glass, then more wine into Conner's glass, set the bottle into a marble bottle insulator on the table, and left.

Kai sipped the wine. A mixture of oak and honey filed his mouth. "Damn, this is really good."

"Yeah, one of my favorites, Cakebread Cellars." Conner drank his wine. "So, figure out what you want to eat. I'm starved." He picked up his lunch menu.

Kai perused the menu. "The chicken salad wrap looks good."

A male waiter came to the table. Conner ordered Kai's

wrap and some Italian sausage sliders for himself.

"So, what are the plans for today?" Kai lifted his wine glass and tilted it, watching the legs of the wine dribble down the sides in the mid-afternoon sun. Good thing he was in the food industry, so he'd know how to handle being in this high-end restaurant. Otherwise, he wouldn't have a clue.

Conner shifted forward in his seat, tenting his fingers on the table. "For starters, I have in-room massages scheduled for this afternoon, then maybe we can walk around Tlaquepaque's shops, and after dinner, of course, we can have our bourbon on the porch. Tomorrow, I was thinking we could hike to some of the old ruins. How does that sound?"

Kai lifted his brows. "It sounds, uh, great." He'd never had a massage before. He twisted his mouth. Should he ask Conner about it? He glanced at him. He didn't want to sound stupid. "So, um, will the massage be with a man or a woman?"

Conner smirked. "I asked for women. I don't want a guy touching you like that."

Kai pressed his lips together. But Conner would have a *woman* touching *him*. How did he feel about that? Maybe it wasn't a sexual thing anyway. But Conner was a pretty sexually wound-up guy to begin with. He narrowed his eyes at him.

"What?"

Kai fingered his fork. "So, what if I don't want a woman touching *you*?"

Conner chuckled. "Would you rather a guy did my massage?"

Kai pictured Conner on a massage table, his hard cock jutting up from under a sheet, coming as soon as a male masseuse touched his shoulders. He shook his head. "Shit, no." He squirmed in his seat. He'd rather be the one giving Conner a massage. "Maybe we should do each other?" He lifted a brow.

Conner laughed. "Are you serious? It'll be fine. These massage therapists know what they're doing. They're all trained in Swedish massage." He grabbed Kai's hand and rested them on the table. "There's no happy ending," he said. "Unless we want to give each other one after they leave." He wiggled his brows.

Kai's cock jerked. Damn, all this talk was already making him horny. Maybe they'd have to skip the shopping. He drank some wine and lifted a corner of his mouth. "I do like the idea of a happy ending after they leave."

"So do I." Conner squeezed his hand.

The waiter dropped off their food.

Kai picked up his wrap and took a bite, chewed, then swallowed it down. "Damn, that's good."

"So is mine." Conner took a bite of slider and sucked juice off a finger. "So, Kai, I want to know more about you. I mean, I know you, but I feel like there's a lot I don't know."

Kai sipped his wine and looked out over the creek, the sun shimmering off the water as it hit boulders and rocks and moved swiftly downstream. "So, what do you want to know?"

"Well, like how long did you live on the Navajo Nation? What was that like? Do you still go up there and visit relatives?" Conner ate a truffle fry.

Kai set down his wrap and studied him. That was a lot of questions. Where should he start? "So, my dad was half Navajo on his mother's side. He always lived there. He met my mom in Flagstaff, so I'm told. I don't know all the details." He frowned. There was so much about his parent's relationship he didn't know. It wasn't something his mother liked to talk about. "Anyway, I was born up there and we lived there until I was about five."

"Five . . ." Conner drank some wine. "Wasn't that about when your dad—"

"Yeah. He had diabetes and didn't manage it very well." Kai frowned. "My mom didn't handle it well when he died. My sister, May, and I ended up in foster care for about a year, somewhere around Flagstaff." He sighed. "My mom got into drugs."

Conner widened his eyes. "Oh, shit." He laid a hand on Kai's thigh. "I'm sorry. It sounds like it was pretty rough."

"Yeah, it was." Kai gazed at him, thinking back. How different would his life had been if his father hadn't died?

Conner focused on him, wrinkling his forehead. "Is it hard to talk about?"

Kai drew a deep breath. "Sometimes. It's not something I tell everyone." He fought against memories trying to surface of his mother passed out on a tattered couch while he'd tried to make something to eat for May and him, then finding no food in the house. During that time, they were always hungry. He stared out at the glimmering water of the creek, letting it sooth the pain hovering under the surface of his emotions.

"So, how did you end up in Fountain Hills?" Conner bit his sandwich.

Kai's attention returned to him "Oh, well, after my mom got out of rehab, she was able to get us from foster care and she decided to move far away to make a new start. I guess addicts need to get away from the people they used with."

Conner nodded. "So, you moved there when you were seven?"

"Yeah, but I didn't start school on time. So I was in the class behind you, even though I'm the same age as you."

"Seriously? We should have graduated together?" Conner gave him a warm smile.

"Yeah." Kai let a faint grin curl his mouth. "My family lived in The Village." He freed his hand and picked up his wrap, taking a bite.

Conner furrowed his brows. "Oh . . . I didn't know you

lived there. I guess Bryce lived there, too?"

Kai nodded, chewing, then swallowed. "My mom and Bryce's mom still live there." *And it pretty much looks exactly the same.*

"Shit, so Bryce is staying in The Village until this ghost thing is settled?" Conner took a bite of a new slider.

"Yeah." Kai finished off the first half of his wrap. Conner had no idea exactly how poor he really was. Maybe he hid it well. "Tell me about your family."

Conner freed a quick chuckle. "Oh, I don't know how much there is to tell. I mean, you saw the house I grew up in. It's not like I wanted for anything."

Kai poured more wine into their glasses. "You're an only child, right?" At least there weren't any siblings that he knew about when they were in school together.

"Yeah. And with that brought a lot of fucking expectations." Conner sighed. "But I think I told you about that." He laughed sharply. "Probably when I came into the restaurant drunk that night."

Kai poked at a side salad with his fork. "Yeah, you did." He snickered. "You also asked me how gay people hit on each other." He shook his head, chuckling. "Guess you figured that one out." Now that the pieces were fitting together, he was realizing *why* he'd asked those questions.

Conner flushed and sipped his wine. "Yeah, good thing, huh? You weren't going to do anything." He gazed at him.

Kai's gaze caught on his ice-blue eyes. His heart skipped. *Damn, he's so stunning. How did I ever get to be with him?* "Yeah, I'm glad you did."

"I want to ask you something, Kai." Conner came forward in his seat, resting his elbows on the table. "Did you have a crush on me in high school?"

"Uh . . ." His mouth dropped. *Shit.* What was he supposed to say?

"There was a rumor going around that you did." Conner grabbed his hand.

Fucking Bryce and his big mouth. He released a choked laugh. "Yeah, um, I guess I did."

"S-so, you had a crush on me all this time?" Conner kissed Kai's hand.

Kai slumped his shoulders. Might as well come out with all of it. "Yes, I've had a crush on you for so long, I can barely remember a time when I didn't."

Conner bent over the table and placed a long, tender kiss on his lips. "You have no idea how happy I am to hear that." He smiled.

Warmth flowed through Kai's heart. *It's not just a crush, now it's love.* He scanned his face, taking in his narrowed blue eyes, the full lips, the gentle scar under his eye. He'd kissed that scar. Now it was his. He inhaled deeply. It was time for Conner to spill it. "So, you told me you liked me in high school, too. Can you elaborate on that?" He smirked.

Conner went back in his chair and freed a puff of air. "Oh, wow. Well, I did like you, but I was really confused. I was dating Paige. My parents loved her." He glanced toward the creek, then focused on Kai. "Those minutes we spent in my bedroom confused the fuck out of me." He raked his hand through his side-swept bangs. "I had heard about you crushing on me, and I couldn't get it out of my head. So when I saw you standing there all alone in the hallway, I don't know, I couldn't stop myself." He sipped his wine. "I wanted to know what it was like to kiss you. I kept thinking about it when we were in chemistry class together." He snickered. "That's probably why my grade was so bad. I couldn't concentrate with you there." He looked Kai up and down. "I guess it was a sexual thing at first. After I got you in my bedroom, well . . ." He raked his teeth over his lower lip. "I couldn't stop thinking about what happened. I couldn't stop thinking about you."

His face went slack. "I daydreamed about you all the time." He pulled him close by the shoulder, brushing his lips over his cheek, then whispered in his ear, "I've been jerking off, thinking about that night all these years."

Kai widened his eyes. "Damn." His cock twitched in his jeans. They needed to find their bed fast. Oh, but they had massages scheduled. *Damn it, I'm going to be horny as hell through the whole thing.*

Conner freed him and licked his lips. In a soft voice, he said, "I'm fucking hard as shit right now."

Kai looked around them. Only a few guests were dining a couple of tables down. "Should we cancel the massage?"

A wicked grin played over Conner's mouth. "No, let's wait for it."

Kai shut his eyes, took a deep breath, then opened them. He'd wait. It would be almost impossible, but he'd wait. "Okay."

Chapter Thirteen

Kai lay on the massage table on his back with his eyes closed, a thin white sheet and blanket draped over his nude body. The knots in every muscle had been worked out. A relaxing hum permeated through him. Soothing music played in the background.

A female voice said, "Okay, we're going to leave now, and someone will come to get the equipment in an hour or so."

"Sure," Conner said in a gravelly voice.

The music shut off and the soft click of the door sounded in the room.

Kai opened his eyes and drew a deep breath, bringing his arms up over his head, stretching. "Damn, Conner, that was awesome."

Conner rolled to his side on his own massage table, the sheet and blanket falling around him. "I told you they'd be good."

Kai sat up and dropped his legs over the side, then ran his hand down his thigh, slicked by massage oil. "I'm all greasy."

Conner lifted up and climbed off the table, his back to him. "Guess we'll have to shower."

"Guess so." He'd always wanted to do it in the shower, but with the quick bar hookups he'd had, he'd never gotten the chance. He looked Conner over, the wide back, the tight ass, the muscled legs.

Conner turned around, his hard cock reaching up almost to his navel. "We have an hour." He bit his lip and placed lazy strokes over his shaft.

Heat rushed Kai's groin, hardening his cock in an instant. He didn't have to suppress it any longer. He lifted the edge of his mouth. "Let me do that." He jumped off the table and stepped to him, pressing his lips to Conner's, exploring with his tongue. He skimmed his hand down his slick toned stomach and stroked his cock, sliding easily over the skin with the massage oil on his palm.

Conner whimpered and moaned inside Kai's mouth. His breath grew heavy. He rocked his hips in time with his stroking hand.

Kai broke the kiss and stopped his hand. He wasn't going to miss this chance. "Let's take this into the shower."

Conner nodded, then grabbed his hand and led him into a bathroom of large white tiles and wood plank flooring with a separate free-standing tub and glass shower. He turned a chrome fixture in the shower and held out his hand. "It's warm already." He stepped into the shower and under a cascade of water streaming from a large, square head.

Kai walked in and swung the glass door closed.

Conner pushed him against the tile shower wall and claimed his mouth in hungry kisses, grinding his hard cock against his hip.

Kai tangled his tongue with Conner's, rubbing his firm shaft over his thigh. Intense sensation tingled over him. His sac tightened. "Shit, I'm close." All that waiting after the talk at lunch had him way too amped up. He pulled his hips away, willing the feeling to subside.

Conner raked his teeth over his lower lip and smiled. "Guess it's your turn to come fast." He wrapped his hand around Kai's shaft and pumped, devouring his mouth in a frenzy of deep kisses.

A surge of pleasure swept over Kai, sweet pulses shuddering through his body. He moaned as each one hit, his seed spurting up over Conner's hand. His knees grew weak, and he shut his eyes.

Conner held him up under the armpits. In a ragged voice, he said, "Fuck, Kai, that was hot." He thrust against his hip, rubbing his solid cock over him, taking quick breaths.

Kai opened his eyes and wrapped an arm around Conner's waist, then kissed him hard.

Conner broke the kiss, arching his head back, cried out, and slicked Kai's hip with seed, thrusting and grinding, his face tensing with orgasm. As it slowed, he rested his forehead on Kai's, panting. "We barely got into the shower. I wanted to soap you up."

"You can still soap me up." Kai offered him a crooked grin. This wasn't ending anytime soon, as far as he was concerned.

Conner kissed his lips, then released him and stepped under the flow of water, skimming his hands up his face and over his hair.

Kai picked up a bar of soap from a tile shelf, unwrapped it, and slid it over Conner's chest, caressing the muscle and skin with his other hand.

Conner brought his head out of the water and wiped his eyes. "That feels good."

Kai soaped up his arms and turned him around, then washed his back. He reached down and rubbed the soap over his groin.

Conner's breath caught.

Kai kissed the back of his neck and brushed over his chest with one hand while stroking his hardening cock with the other. "Can I make you come again?" His shaft filled with heat and he pressed it against his buttocks. A pulse shivered up his spine. Damn, he was starting to have orgasms like Conner.

"Probably." Conner drew deep breaths. He rocked his hips. "I want to feel you touch me all over, though."

Kai left his groin and crouched down, washing his

muscular legs, running his hand up to fondle his sac, the crease of his ass, then down inside his thighs and to his feet. His own cock ached and twitched, and pre-seed beaded at the tip. He placed quick strokes over his own shaft, sensation quivering through him, releasing a long moan.

Conner looked down. "What are you doing?"

Kai gazed up, lust humming through his body. "I-I don't know. Just can't stop."

Conner lifted him up and placed intense kisses over his mouth, holding him under the water, then wrapped both their cocks in his hand and pumped.

"Oh, God." Kai dropped the soap, shuddering with need, kissing him with urgency. He ran his hands up and down Conner's back, then around to his chest. *It's not enough. I can't get enough of him.*

Conner thrust his erect cock against Kai's, his hand pumping, his own tongue teasing his, gasping. He rubbed over his chest, then stopped at a nipple and pinched.

A shock of pleasure seared from Kai's nipple to his cock. His sac grew heavy and intense sensation pulsated through his shaft. Harsh waves of orgasm came on in a flood of pleasure. He cried out, clutching Conner's back, spurting seed over their stomachs.

The pumps of Conner's hand became erratic. He thrust hard, then spilled his seed between them, gasping against his shoulder. As it slowed, he embraced him and nuzzled his neck. "Fuck, what you do to me."

Kai freed a lazy chuckle. "No, what you do to me. You're turning me into a sex addict." He'd never wanted anyone more in his life.

Conner lifted his head and smiled. "Good." He crouched down, picked up the soap and lathered Kai up from head to toe, toying with his spent cock.

Kai jerked his hips and slapped his hand away, laughing. "Stop it. It tickles now, damn it."

Conner gave him a wide grin. "Yeah, but maybe . . ."

"Maybe nothing." He placed a quick kiss on Conner's lips. How would he ever keep up with him? "Maybe later. How about that?"

"Definitely later." Conner moved him under the water and rinsed the soap from his body. "Let's get cleaned up and head out to dinner at Tlaquepaque."

"Okay."

Kai, wearing a white and blue striped button down shirt under his black jacket and a pair of jeans, strolled next to Conner down a walkway over flat stone pavers of various sizes. Tall trees rose up out of holes in the walkway. He looked around him at the Mexican hacienda-style building, the textured, clay-colored stucco walls surrounding them, the columns holding up archways, and thick wood beams running under red tile roofing. He'd driven by the place so many times, but had never come inside. "So, this place is a replica of an old Mexican village?"

"Yeah, I think it was modelled after a place in Guadalajara." Conner, in a tan V-neck sweater and jeans, grabbed up his hand and kissed the back of it, then grinned.

Warmth flooded Kai's heart. He gave him a shy grin. *How I love this man.* The feeling was only getting stronger. He glanced out at clay flowerpots lining the bottom of a stairway, leading up to a second story of shops and restaurants.

As they passed a cement fountain with multiple tiers of flowing water, Conner stopped. "What do you want to eat?"

Kai touched his free hand to his lips. "How about Mexican? This place is making me hungry for it."

"Okay, there's a damn good Mexican restaurant in here." Conner led him to an arched, glass doorway and stepped inside. "We can sit on the patio."

A hostess greeted them at a stand, then took them to a table on the patio.

Kai sat at a low-backed rounded Equipale chair and rested his hands on a round, tile-topped table. Colorful umbrellas covered each of the tables in orange, yellow, red, and blue. The place was nice, not too fancy.

Conner sat next to him and took the offered menus from the hostess, then handed one to him. "The margaritas here are killer."

"Yeah? Guess I'll have to get one." Kai perused the menu and set it down. "I already know what I want."

Conner lowered the menu from his face. "What's that?"

"A chicken chimichanga with green chili sauce." Kai scanned the semi-crowded patio, taking in the view of the plaza and the tall fountain beyond, surrounded by a bed of flowers and small, deep-green bushes. "This place is so nice. I've never come in here before."

"Why not?" Conner set his menu on the table.

"I always thought it was too expensive. I figured I'd never be able to afford anything in here." When it came to the shops, he was pretty much right. His attention shifted to Conner.

Conner placed his hand over Kai's, resting on the table. "You'll never have to worry about that again."

Kai lifted his brows. What exactly was he saying? He smirked. "Yeah, right."

"From now on, I'm going to take care of you." Conner kissed his hand and set it on the table.

Kai gazed at him. It sounded too good to be true and probably too soon to be thinking that way. Conner was definitely a sweet talker sometimes. Kai needed to be careful of that and not get his hopes up too much.

A waitress with dark wavy hair came to the table in a colorful Mexican dress. Conner ordered a plate of chicken tacos for himself, Kai's chimichanga, and margaritas.

Kai thought over the conversation they'd had at lunch. He

was finally getting some answers for his behavior. Maybe he could get more. "So, what exactly went wrong between you and Paige?"

"Why do you want to know that?" Conner narrowed his eyes.

Kai shrugged. "I don't know, guess I've only heard bits and pieces, and I'd like to hear the whole thing."

The waitress set their margaritas on the table. "Here you are."

"Jesus, Conner, are you trying to get me drunk?" He looked over a large greenish, hand-blown margarita glass with a blue rim and a green saguaro cactus stem.

Conner let out a hardy chuckle. "Why get two small ones when you can get one large one?"

Kai huffed. "You *are* trying to get me drunk." Who said he needed two margaritas? They were always super strong in places like this.

"I've never seen you drunk, but you've seen me shitfaced out of my mind. It's only fair." Conner spun a thick black straw through the drink.

Kai sucked the drink through the straw, sweet and sour with the after taste of tequila filling his mouth. "Okay, we're off topic now. Paige. Spill it."

"Oh, shit, Kai. Okay." Conner drank his margarita. "Paige and I got along, still get along really well. We just . . . wanted different things, as it turns out."

"So, what were those different things?" Kai focused on Conner's stunning face, the way the evening light lit the back of his brown wavy hair and made his eyes a darker shade of blue.

"Like I said, we got into the party scene in downtown Scottsdale, and she loved appearances. She liked to look like we had even more money than we had. It got old." Conner frowned.

"So, you split up over money?" Kai tapped the straw through his drink. He had a hard time believing that, with the small fortune Conner was spending on this get away.

"Well, not really." Conner stared at the tile tabletop. "Bottom line was, I didn't love her." He fixated on Kai and chewed his lower lip.

Kai opened his mouth. "Like ever? You never loved her? Or you just fell out of love with her?" This was still so confusing. He shifted in his seat.

"I don't think . . . I ever loved her, not as a romantic partner." Conner looked him over, lowering his brows.

Kai blinked a few times. *What the actual fuck?* "How the hell do you stay with someone that long if you don't love them?"

Conner placed his hand on Kai's. "I thought I did, but now I don't think so. I think I loved her as a friend. And still do, actually."

Kai's heart pinched. "Still do?" He yanked his hand away. "What is that supposed to mean?"

Conner sank into his seat, straightening his legs out, a coy grin spreading over his mouth. "I love her the same way you love Bryce." He crossed his arms over his chest.

"Oh, you fucker." Kai shook his head once and chuckled. "Touché." He took a long draw of his margarita. Maybe they should stop talking about Paige.

The waitress set their food down. "Enjoy." She trotted off.

Kai cut into his chimichanga and ate a bite, thinking over the rest of their evening. "We need to get some bourbon. I'm really looking forward to sitting on that porch tonight."

"There's a craft liquor store in here that sells high-end blends of just about everything. They have the best bourbon I've ever had. Plus, we can taste it before we buy." Conner took a bite of his taco.

"So, we should head over there when we're done, grab a bottle, and go back to the cabin."

Conner tapped his nose. "Great minds think alike."

Kai stepped out of Conner's car, his head buzzing with tequila and multiple tastings at the craft liquor store. He stepped to the walkway of their cabin and stumbled, then righted himself. "Shit."

Conner grabbed him up, hooking an arm around his waist. "Jesus, Kai, for a bartender you sure don't hold your liquor well." He sniggered.

"I'm supposed to serve it, not drink it." Kai scoffed.

Conner walked him through the pines, down the path to their cabin and up the porch steps. "Do you still want to have a bourbon on the porch?"

Kai peered at him. "Yeah. We have to. It's our thing." He pouted. "I was looking forward to it." He steadied himself and straightened his shirt and jacket.

Conner opened the door to their cabin. "Okay, but drink some water first." He stepped inside, went to the bathroom, and filled a glass with water, then brought it out to Kai. "Here, drink this."

Kai gulped down the water and handed the empty glass to him, then wiped his mouth. "I'm fine. Get the bourbon and meet me on the porch." He placed a quick kiss on Conner's mouth, then grinned. As he walked out to the porch, he surveyed the two round-backed wicker chairs with puffy blue cushions. No couch. He wanted to cuddle up with Conner. He twisted his mouth.

Conner came to the porch with two low-ball glasses and the bourbon in a clear bottle, rounded at the bottom, with a cork top. "What's the matter?"

"There's no couch. How are we supposed to cuddle?" Kai stomped his foot.

Conner freed a sharp laugh. "Damn, you are funny when you're drunk." He kissed his cheek and sat in a chair. "Let me pour the drinks, then you can sit on my lap, okay?"

Kai pursed his lips and glanced at him. "There's not enough room."

Conner lifted his brows. "Okay, here." He set the bottle and glasses on a wicker table in front of his chair, then stretched over, grabbed the other chair, and brought it next to his. "Sit down."

"Fine." With a scowl, he plopped in the chair and crossed his arms. "Where's my bourbon?"

Conner chuckled and poured the bourbon, then handed a glass to him. "Here. You cold at all? There are blankets in the cabin."

"No, I'm okay." Kai took the bourbon and sipped, letting it calm him. He looked out over the gurgling creek, the moonlight shimmering off the ripples and waves of water clashing with boulders. "It's so peaceful here." He held the glass in his lap.

"Hey, hold my hand." Conner held his hand out.

Kai took his hand. "Conner?"

"Yeah."

"I had fun today. This is really nice." Kai bit his lip. He'd never get to experience something like this if Conner weren't in his life. He glanced at him.

"I had fun today, too. I'm really happy we could do this." Conner smiled at him.

"This is not something I'm used to, you know, being in fancy places." It was probably just another day for Conner. Kai drank some bourbon.

"Yeah, I know." Conner squeezed his hand.

"I mean, I grew up so poor. I only camp or stay in really shitty hotels if I go anywhere." This cabin was a hundred times better than the crappy townhouse he'd grown up in. He looked out across the creek bed at the shadows of tall cottonwood trees on the other side.

"How poor were you? Like were you on welfare or anything?" Conner shifted closer to him.

"I think so. At least part of the time. My mom only worked at grocery stores as a cashier, so she never made very much money. I know we went to the food bank in town every week." Kai focused on him. What would he think about all this?

Conner sipped his bourbon. "At least your mom was okay with you being gay."

Kai let loose a sharp belly laugh. "No, she wasn't. She hated it. She said all sorts of fucked up things about it." The smile faded from his mouth as stinging memories flooded his mind. "She always said that queers cried too much." He clenched his jaw.

"Shit, Kai, that's terrible." Conner tugged on his hand. "Come here and sit on my lap."

"No, that'll look stupid." Kai sniffed and rubbed his eyes. Damn the liquor. Now he was proving his mother right.

Conner set his glass on the table, then knelt down in front of him, placing his hands on his cheeks. "Kai, look at me."

As Kai pressed his lips together, he gazed into his eyes.

"It's sounds like you were dealt some really shitty cards when it came to your parents. I think you're a really strong person." Conner placed a lingering kiss on his lips.

Kai closed his eyes, savoring the taste of him. *God, I love him, so much.* "Conner, I . . ." He popped his eyes open. *Holy shit, shut the fuck up.*

"You what?" Conner's gaze darted between his eyes. "Tell me."

Kai's heart thumped in his ears. He twitched the corners of his mouth and shook his head free of his hold. "No, it's nothing." He sank into his seat.

Conner released a long exhale, then sat in his chair. "Okay." He picked up his bourbon and drank it. "I'm going to ask them to bring us a couch for our porch tomorrow.

You're right. The chairs suck." He snickered.

"See?" *That was close.* He had to be more careful. He drew a deep breath.

"I want to meet your mother. Would that be okay?" Conner peered at him.

How would that go down? Not very well. "I'm not so sure that's a good idea."

"Have you ever brought anyone home?" Conner shifted in his chair.

Kai released a short laugh, then bit at a nail. "No. No need to." There'd never been anyone that important in his life. *Until now.* He widened his eyes and stole a peek at him.

"But does Bryce know her?" Conner wrinkled his nose.

"Yes, he lived right next door." Kai twisted in his chair to face him. "Why are you so worried about Bryce?"

Conner furrowed his brows, focusing on his drink. "He knows more about you than I do."

How could he ease his Conner's mind about that? Kai lifted one brow. "He doesn't know what I look like when I come." He chortled.

Conner slapped his forearm and laughed. "Jesus, Kai. Guess you got me there." He drew a deep breath. "Where did May end up?"

"She went down to U of A. She's studying nursing. Got a full ride." She was smart and got out. Kai thinned his lips.

"Wow, that's tough to get into." Conner drank some bourbon, then moved his head to look at him. "You okay?"

"Yeah, it's just that May sort of got all the breaks, you know? She's straight and doesn't look native, so no one harassed her. Even my mother thinks she's way better than me." He forced a quick grin, then drank his bourbon.

"Sounds like there's a bit of tension between you and your sister."

Kai sighed. "Not really. May has always been there for me.

She sticks up for me around my mom." How did they get stuck on this topic? He needed to change it before his mood went sour. "So, what ruins are we hiking to tomorrow?"

Conner chuckled. "Well, we have to go to Palatki. But I know that's a pretty short hike for someone like you, so I thought we could hit that one first and then maybe hike in Boynton Canyon."

"Sounds perfect." Kai grinned. It would be fun seeing those places with Conner.

"Have you hiked there before?" Conner downed the rest of his bourbon.

"Yeah, but it was a long time ago." Kai twisted to face him, peeking at the empty glass. "So, you ready for bed?"

A coy grin swept over Conner's mouth. "Yes, I am." He rose from his seat and walked to the door, then opened it. "You coming?"

Kai smirked. "Not yet." Conner hadn't heard him the first time he'd used that line. This time was different.

Conner shook his head. "You're bad."

Kai drank the rest of his bourbon and followed him into the cabin, then shut the door.

Conner took his empty glass and set it on the wood table, then walked to the bed, shimmying out of his sweater along the way. "Get undressed." He shoved his jeans and boxer briefs down his legs, then stepped out of them.

"Anything you say." Kai undressed, his cock hardening, then walked to the bed and climbed under crisp, cool, white sheets to lie on his back. He was so looking forward to this. He couldn't seem to get enough of Conner Mitchell.

He lay next to Kai on his side, his head propped up on an elbow. He licked his lips, looking him over. "You're so beautiful, you know that?"

Heat flushed Kai's face. "No . . ." He was trying to sweet talk him again.

"No, really, Kai. You are. Haven't you ever wondered why you get hit on all the time?" Conner brushed his hand over Kai's chest and down his stomach, skimming over his hard shaft.

Kai's breath caught. His cock ached. God, his touch felt good. He bit his lip and released it. "I don't get hit on that much."

"More than me." Conner shifted to lie over his chest, pressing his solid cock into his hip. He glided his fingers over Kai's forehead, moving his hair to the side.

"I don't believe that. I'm sure you get hit on all the time." He gazed into Conner's intense eyes. "I mean, you're like a fucking model."

Conner pressed his lips to Kai's, parting them with his tongue, teasing the entrance. He lifted his head, rocking his hips against him, rubbing his hard cock against his skin. His eyes shut and his face tensed. In a raspy whisper, he said, "Fuck, what you do to me." He drew his hips away and took deep breaths. "I'm going to get you off first." He threw the covers down and wrapped his hands around the base of Kai's shaft, then crawled down and pumped it with his mouth.

"Oh, shit." As a surge of pleasure tingled up Kai's spine, he bucked his hips. *Damn, he was good at this.*

Conner licked his shaft, circling the head, then plunged down again, sucking hard, over, and over. He fondled his sac and as it slickened with saliva, he snuck his hand down to his entrance. "Can I do this to you?"

Kai peeked down. "Fuck, yeah." *What would it feel like to have him inside me?* He lifted his legs, exposing himself to him.

Conner groaned over Kai's cock. He teased his entrance, circling and toying with it, then plunged a finger inside, curled it just so, and pulled out.

A shock of sensation pulsated through Kai's groin, jerking his cock. He whimpered. *Damn, he's good at this, too.* "Do that more."

Conner added another finger and stroked inside his entrance while devouring his cock. He writhed over him, moaning, rocking his hips, pre-seed dribbling from the tip of his own firm shaft.

The sensation in Kai's cock built to a thrumming peak. He slapped his hands to Conner's head. "Fuck, I'm coming."

Conner sucked and licked, taking him all the way down his throat.

As waves of pleasure shivered over Kai, he cried out and arced his head back, thrusting into his mouth.

When it slowed, Conner released him and clambered up on top of him, grinding against his thigh, placing hungry kisses over his mouth, all the while moaning into him.

Kai fought to keep up with his relentless kisses, wrapping his arms around his shoulders. Hot wetness slicked his thigh.

Conner slid his cock in circles over the wetness, his body shuddering, his breath hitching. As he calmed, he lifted his head and peeked down. "Fuck, I made a mess." He dropped over him, nuzzling his face in his neck, panting.

What just happened? Kai wrinkled his brows and held him close, kissing the side of his head. "D-did you just come on my leg?"

Conner nodded against his shoulder. "Sorry."

Kai brushed his hand down the back of his head. "No, don't be. I just wasn't sure." He'd never had anyone do that before. *Oh wait, except at his graduation party.* But they were both clothed. "That was hot, actually." He raised a corner of his mouth.

Conner lifted his head and looked into his eyes. "You think?" He wrinkled his nose. "I mean, I almost didn't make it to your leg." He bit his lip inside a grin.

"You're so fucking cute, too" Kai tugged his head down for a quick kiss. God, if he could eat him up, he would right now.

"Sometimes I can't get enough of you."

Conner smiled. "I never get enough of you." The smile faded. "Kai, I uh . . ." He chewed his lower lip. "Um . . ." He widened his eyes, as they grew glossy.

"What?" He let a faint grin play over his lips. Why was Conner looking at him like that?

He fell down over Kai's chest, freeing a long exhale. "Nothing."

He stared at the ceiling, embracing Conner tightly, then kissed his cheek. Was Conner feeling the same way he was? Was it possible? *Holy shit. This could be real.* Should he say something? If so, what? He pressed his cheek to the side of Conner's head. "Hey, you okay?"

Conner sniffed and nodded. "I'm fine."

Maybe I should confess first? No, what if he was wrong? Then he'd look like an idiot. He tightened his hold around Conner. His heart raced in his chest. Someone had to go first. "Um, Conner, I uh . . ."

Conner lifted his head to gaze at him. "Yeah?" He rubbed his thumb across Kai's cheek. "Say it."

Oh, Jesus, he's looking right at me. His heart pounded in his ears. "Um . . ." He glanced at the wall, then focused on him, drawing a deep breath. "Fuck, uh . . ."

Conner closed his lips, holding his breath.

"We should get cleaned up." He grimaced. *Fucking idiot, what is wrong with you?"*

"Yeah, you're right." Conner rolled to the side of the bed and stood up, his back to Kai. "I'll get you a washcloth." He walked off to the bathroom.

With a growl, he clenched his teeth and pounded a fist into the mattress. He should have said it. It felt right, perfect even. He was being a pussy. Again.

Conner returned with a warm washcloth and wiped Kai's thigh, then handed it to him. "Here."

"Thanks." He cleaned the rest of himself off and gave the

washcloth back to Conner.

Conner made to get up.

I don't want him to leave. He seized Conner's arm and yanked him into the bed, snatching the washcloth and throwing it to the floor. "Get in here, now."

Conner fell over him, chuckling. "What the fuck are you doing, you lunatic?"

"I want to cuddle, and we couldn't do that on the porch." He just wanted him close. He worked his way up behind Conner's back, both of them on their sides. He kissed his neck, draping an arm around his chest. "That's better."

Conner grabbed Kai's hand and kissed the back of it. "You happy now?"

"Very."

"Good. We have a whole other day of this."

"That's fucking awesome." Kai closed his eyes.

Chapter Fourteen

Wearing a white workout shirt, black shorts, and his black jacket, Kai stepped out of Conner's BMW and waltzed up the curb of a brick convenience store with Conner following. His long ponytail swung across his back. "Palatki was pretty cool. It's such a beautiful spot, no wonder the Sinagua settled there."

Conner, in a thin gray hooded sweatshirt and blue shorts, opened the glass doors for Kai. "Wonder if any of them are related to you." He snickered.

Kai rolled his eyes. *Here we go with the ancestry jokes.* "We're all related at some point." He stepped inside and walked through an isle of snacks to the back cooler, opened the door, and grabbed two large water bottles. "Damn, I'm thirsty." He handed one to him.

Conner twisted off the cap on his bottle and gulped down some water. "Me, too. We should have gotten water before we went out there, but it wasn't that long of a hike."

Kai opened his water and drank it down. "Let's get a few more, just in case." He grabbed another bottle out, handed it to him, then took another one for himself.

"You going to pay for that?"

Kai startled, then twisted around.

A man in a red plaid shirt and dirty jeans with a long beard and graying hair glared at him, one hand on his hip, the other holding a large can of beer. "Well?"

"Of course." What the hell was this guy going on about? Kai attempted a grin.

"Fucking Mexicans. Always trying to get everything for free." The man stomped through the isle to the cashier and paid for his drink.

"What the fuck was that?" Kai stared at Conner.

"I think he just called you a fucking Mexican." Conner snarled, handed all the water bottles to him, then strode to the front of the store.

What is Conner going to do? Kai trotted up behind him, bumping his arm. "Hey, stop."

Conner's face reddened. "No one talks to you like that." He tapped the man on the shoulder.

The man, a few inches shorter than Conner, sneered at him. "What do you want?"

"You need to apologize to him." Conner pointed at Kai.

Kai widened his eyes. *Holy shit.* This guy would never apologize. He'd seen a million others just like him. Complete and utter assholes. It wasn't worth the hassle. He released a tense chuckle, holding his hand out. "Hey, it's okay. Just leave it alone."

"Why should I apologize to him? He should go back to Mexico if he doesn't like it." The man scowled and went through the front door.

Behind the counter, a young female cashier said, "Hey, don't start anything in the store. I'll have to call the police!"

"Fine, then we'll take this outside." Conner glared after the man and stomped through the door.

Kai's heart pounded. "D-don't call the police, please. I'll calm him down." He set the water bottles on the counter, then raced outside.

Conner stood chest to chest with the man on the sidewalk, towering over him. In a growl, he said, "He's not even Mexican, you fucking moron. If anyone belongs here, he does. You go the fuck back to whatever rock you crawled out from." He flared his nostrils, fisting his hands at his sides.

God damn it, this guy isn't worth it. "Conner. Stop. She's going to call the police." He pointed to the store and grabbed Conner's arm.

Conner yanked his arm free. "Well? Apologize."

"Fuck you." The man spat at Kai.

Kai shifted, the spittle landing beside him. *Oh . . . game on.* "No, fuck you." He sneered and lifted his fist.

Conner belted the man, square in the jaw. "Fucking asshole."

The man yowled and grabbed his chin, stepping back. He stared at Conner with wide eyes, then glowered, pointing at Kai. "Why would you defend him? You're white."

"I'm not a God damned racist." Conner lifted his fist and stepped close to the man. "Get the fuck out of here before I beat the shit out of you."

The man stumbled back, his gaze darting between Kai and Conner.

"You heard him, go. Or you'll have to take us both on." Kai stepped forward, puffing his chest, his fist still raised, his heart pumping hard.

The man grumbled, then walked off to a gray truck and got in.

Conner grabbed Kai's hands. "You okay?" He wrinkled his brows.

Kai drew deep breaths. "Yeah, guess so. It's not like that was the first time." He certainly wasn't expecting it here.

"Are you kidding me?" Conner looked him up and down. "I had no idea shit like that happened anymore."

"Well, it does." Kai twisted his mouth. "I'm sorry you had to see that." He peeked at his face.

"Don't be sorry. That asshole should be sorry." Conner growled and stomped his foot. "Fuck, what an asshole." He scanned around him, then wrapped Kai up in a tight embrace, kissing the side of his head. "Next time someone says something like that to you, I'll just beat them senseless. I won't even wait."

Kai smiled against his shoulder. It felt good to know he would defend him like that. "Thanks."

Conner released him. "Let's go pay for our water and get out of here."

"Yeah."

Kai followed Conner up a path of reddish-colored dirt, surrounded by cliffs with reddish, orange, and cream striations rising up out of the green pinyon pines and scrubby bushes and oaks. The noonday sun made shadowed patterns in the crags on the mountains. He plodded along, taking in the immense beauty around him. Every once in a while, a group of other hikers walked by them. "Damn, this place is something else. No wonder it's such a spiritual center."

Conner sipped some water from a bottle. "Yeah. Are you Christian?" He glanced at him.

"Not really. My mother is, you know, after the rehab stint." Kai chuckled. "She used to take us to church, but it never really stuck."

Conner nodded. "We used to go to Christ's Church in town. I don't go anymore."

Figures, that's where all the wealthy, popular kids went when they were in high school. "So, I guess Paige was also in your church?" Kai looked at the trail, as they headed up a small hill, toward some cliffs.

"Yeah, we met in youth group there." Conner freed a sharp laugh. "Along with Ben and Lucas, believe it or not."

"What's not to believe?" They were a pretty tight-knit group. He sipped some water.

Conner stopped. "The ruins are up there." He pointed to a huge overhang in the cliffside, almost a full-on cave. The remnants of ancient walls littered the underside of the overhang, made of flat, clay-colored, stone masonry, piled high, with doorways between.

"That's cool. Can we go up there?" Kai held his hand over his eyes, shielding them from the sun.

"Yeah, we go through Subway Cave." Conner grabbed his hand. "It's a little treacherous." He grinned at him.

He doesn't want me to fall. Kai hung his head and smirked, hiding it from him. It was a sweet gesture, but Conner was more likely to fall than he was with all the trail running he'd done. "Let's go."

They hiked up a path with a cliff ledge on one side falling down to the trees and bushes, and a sandstone wall on the other, rising higher with each step. Finally they came to a steep section where the clay-colored sandstone walls rose up on either side of them. As they reached the top, Conner stopped and turned them around. "Look."

"Holy shit." Kai looked out between two reddish cliffs with the sides rounded inward and the valley of green below them. Out in the distance were more sandstone mountainsides, rising sharply up out of the canyon. He squeezed Conner's hand. "Beautiful."

Conner turned to him. "Like you." He leaned in to place a tender kiss on his lips. "Kai, I uh . . ." He furrowed his brows and peered at their hands, entwined between them.

"What?" Kai searched his face. His heart hammered in his chest. There was that look again. Was he about to confess? *God, I hope so.* "Go on."

Conner licked his lips and swallowed. "Um . . ." He bit his lip and focused on him. "Kai, I—"

"Excuse us. Can we get by?" An older woman in hiking gear with a pole stood next to them.

Conner exhaled. "Yeah, sure." He moved to the side, letting her and a few others pass.

Shit, shit, shit. Kai looked up at the clear blue sky. Where the hell did they come from? His attention drew back to

Conner. *Romantic moment gone. Damn.*

Conner cleared his throat. "So, the ruins are over here." He pointed inside the cave.

"Yeah." He followed Conner into the cave, then walked along the edges of the ruins, peeking inside the one-room dwellings. "Hard to believe people actually lived in here."

Conner nodded, then drank some water.

They walked down the ruins, from dwelling to dwelling, each one in various states of decay.

"Kai?" Conner stopped and surveyed their surroundings.

"Yeah?" He faced him.

"Anyone ever give you shit for being gay? Like that guy today, I mean. You ever come across homophobic people?" Conner studied him.

Kai shrugged. "Sure, I mean people are assholes about a lot of things." *Like your friend Lucas in high school . . .* Wait, was he having second thoughts about what they were doing all of a sudden? He narrowed his eyes. "Why are you asking me about that?" Maybe he had it all wrong. Maybe Conner wasn't on the verge of confessing. Maybe he was questioning.

Conner took slow steps along the trail.

Kai followed, watching him. "Conner?"

He stopped and turned, smirking at Kai. He ruffled the hair on top of his head. "Just want to know how many times I'm going to have to fight for you." He went to count on his fingers. "Let's see, for being native, for being gay and for guys hitting on you."

Kai sniggered. "What about if a woman hits on me?" *Like that would ever happen.*

Conner wrinkled his nose. "You don't like women." He cocked his head, lifting his brows. "Okay, when women hit on you, too."

Kai snatched Conner's hand. "Guess I'm lucky. *I* only have to worry about people hitting on you."

Conner laughed and shook his head. "Yeah, but they don't."

"We'll see." That was utter bullshit. Kai placed a quick kiss on Conner's cheek. Maybe he shouldn't worry so much about Conner questioning what they had.

Kai, wearing a black fleece and jeans, sat on a wooden bar stool next to Conner at a square wrap-around wood bar top, the underside lit up in blue, the back wall filled with rows of high-end liquor bottles on dark, wood shelving and centered by a big screen television playing a football game. "Dinner was really nice." He perused the bottles of liquor behind a male bartender, dressed all in black.

"Yeah, I love this place. The food is good, and the views are awesome from that patio." Conner, dressed in a thin gray V-neck sweater and black jeans, picked up a drink menu.

"Watching the sunset over the red rocks during dinner was awesome." This place was magical, and being here with Conner was even better. Kai placed a hand on Conner's thigh.

"What do you want to drink? Since we walked here from the cabin, we can both drink, for once." Conner offered a sly grin.

"I'm going for a dirty martini on the rocks." Kai looked over at the bartender.

The bartender looked up from washing glasses. "What kind of vodka?"

"Tito's." It was the best, as far as he was concerned. Kai smiled.

Conner set his menu down. "I'll have the same."

Kai surveyed the establishment, checking the groups of people sitting at high-top tables, the bar itself half-full of patrons. Not too busy, just right. No one in need of refills at the moment. Funny how he even checked on people's drinks when he wasn't working. He let a grin quirk his lips.

Conner leaned in. "What are you thinking about?"

He freed a quick chuckle and shook his head. "Just checking on everyone, even though I don't work here."

"You're right. You don't work here. You're on a date with me." A wide smile swept over Conner's mouth.

The bartender set down their martinis. "Enjoy."

Kai picked it up and took a sip. "Wow, just right." He held it up to the bartender. "Thanks, man."

He gave Kai a nod and a smile.

"I'm not looking forward to going home tomorrow. Maybe we can call in sick and stay another day." Conner frowned at his glass, then drank his martini.

"I can't call in sick. I don't get paid if I don't work." Kai glanced at a young blonde woman, sitting behind Conner.

The blonde licked her upper lip, gazing at Conner. Her long hair was curled at the ends, and she wore dramatic make-up and a small black cocktail dress.

"But you're going to start working more days, right? Maybe more than two a week." Conner lifted his brows.

"No, two days a week. That's what I agreed to." How was he going to make someone like Conner understand something like this? He needed to work when he could get maximum pay, and Janice would give him any hours he wanted. He furrowed his brows, glancing at the blonde woman. Something was up.

The woman pointed at Conner, while smiling and chatting with another blonde woman, her hair cut blunt at her chin.

"Have you thought about going back to school, maybe getting a real job?" Conner set his glass on the bar top.

"What the fuck does that mean? I have a real job." Kai flashed a glare at him and removed the hand from his thigh, taking another peek at the blonde woman behind him. *He never gets hit on, huh?*

Conner set his elbow on the bar and rested his cheek in his hand, facing Kai. "Hey, I'm sorry. That's not what I meant.

You were so good in high school, I just think you'd do well in college, too. Maybe you could get one of those scholarships you told me about."

Kai released a long breath. He didn't need to hear this from him. He was happy where he was at. "Now you sound like my mother."

Conner lifted his head. "What?"

Kai fingered the rim of his glass. "She was never happy with anything I did, and she hates me tending bar." He frowned. "She always said I was pathetic." *Just like my father.*

"Jesus, Kai. I'm sorry." Conner touched his arm. "I want to meet her. I want to make her see you're not any of those things she thinks you are."

Kai gazed into his blue eyes. "Thanks, but I don't think anyone or anything can change how she thinks about me. I remind her too much of my father, who she apparently hates for leaving her with two young kids."

"So, do you look a lot like your father, then?" Conner looked him up and down.

Kai nodded, remembering the few pictures his mother had kept of him. "Guess so."

"No wonder your mom left Flagstaff to live on the rez with him." Conner sipped his drink, wagging his brows at him.

"Stop." Kai slapped his arm and chuckled, eying the blonde woman behind him. What would happen if he left? How would he react to being hit on? "Hey, I need to use the restroom."

"Sure." Conner straightened in his chair.

Kai slid off the bar chair and walked past a gold wall with booths lining it toward a hallway with a sign reading *Restrooms* next to it. As he entered the hallway, he stopped and turned to watch Conner.

The blonde woman sidled up to him, giving him a seductive smile.

Conner twisted in his chair to face her.

She laughed, tossing her head back.

Thought so. He gets hit on. Probably all the time. The question is, how does Conner react to it? He stepped farther into the hallway and rested his back against the wall, gnawing his lower lip. *So, what is he going to do about it?* He peeked around the corner. *I should let this ride for a bit and see how he responds when I go back out.* He curled the corner of his mouth, used the restroom, washed up, then walked out to his seat.

The blonde woman giggled, her hand resting on Conner's forearm on the bar.

"Hey." Kai took his seat and sipped his drink, resting his elbows on the bar top.

"Oh, Kai, you're here." Conner leaned back in his seat and gestured to the blonde woman. "Uh, Kai, this is Monica. Monica, Kai."

"Nice to meet you, Kai." She held out her hand to him, her palm facing down.

What, did she want him to kiss her hand? Kai gave it a brief squeeze, putting on his bartending smile. "Nice to meet you, too."

"She's a pharmaceutical rep for my competition. She calls on the same docs in Fountain Hills that I call on. She also went to bible camp with me, but I haven't seen her since then, so I didn't recognize her." Conner gave him a knowing look, then grinned at her.

"Oh, really. So, you two know each other?" This meant she was probably in Conner's little clique and they even sort of worked together. Conner wasn't out at work. They needed to be careful. Kai drank a gulp of martini, then pinched his lips as it burned down his throat.

"Yes, it's been a long time. I've seen him around at work, but didn't say anything. All the women in the doctors' offices talk about Conner, though." She licked her lips, then sipped her white wine.

"Really." This was getting more interesting by the minute. Maybe now he knew why Conner wasn't out at the office. He flinched. He shouldn't be thinking this way. He should trust him more. Didn't his father get him that job? Maybe that was why he wasn't out at the office. They all probably knew his father. He gazed at him.

"They all think he's very attractive," she said.

Conner flushed and hung his head, smirking. "I don't know about that."

"So, what are you two doing up here? Boys' weekend without the girlfriends?" She pouted.

"There are no girlfriends." Kai flashed his eyes at her.

"Oh, so you and Paige broke up? Well, my friend and I are single right now, too." She pointed at the other blonde woman, wearing a short red dress, smiling at them.

Kai thinned his lips. *Enough of this.* "Maybe we should—"

"Kai." Conner glared at him, then slowly shook his head. With his back turned to Monica, he said, "Just give me a minute."

Kai blinked. Conner wanted to hang out with them. His chest tightened. Through his teeth, he said, "Fine."

Conner wrinkled his brows. "Kai . . ." He cocked his head.

Monica grabbed Conner's arm, turning him to face her. "So, where are you staying? Maybe we could all go back to your place and catch up on the gang, you know, Ben and Lucas" She glanced at her friend. "Right, Steph? That would be fun."

Kai pressed his lips together, staring at his drink. Now this was getting out of hand. He didn't want to hang out with these women.

"Sure, uh, maybe." Conner tapped him on the shoulder. "That would be okay, right?"

Kai glared at him. Under his breath, he said, "Are you serious right now?"

Conner came close to him and whispered, "We practically work together. She's friends with my friends. What am I supposed to do?"

Kai whispered, "You can fucking say *no*. That's what you can do." That was apparently not something Conner was good at.

Conner offered her a wide smile. "Uh, we're pretty tired. Maybe another time?"

"That's too bad." Monica frowned. "Were you out golfing today?" She fluttered her eyelashes at Conner.

"No, we were hiking." Kai scoffed and drank some martini. She probably had a rich doctor daddy, just like Conner, and here they were, in another high-end place. So why wouldn't she assume they were golfing?

Monica drank the rest of her wine down. "Damn, I'm empty." A coy smile crept over her lips.

"Oh, I'll get you another." Conner flagged down the bartender and pointed at her glass.

The bartender lifted his chin at Conner. "On your check?"

"Yeah." Conner turned to Steph. "You want a drink?"

Steph smiled, the red lipstick stretching over her teeth. "Sure." She got up and took a bar chair next to Kai. "What's your name?"

He widened his eyes. *What the fuck?* He had not signed up for this. "Kai."

"Oh, that's unusual. Are you Hispanic?"

The bartender set new white wines on the bar top.

He bit his upper lip, stifling a laugh and shook his head once. This was so classic. "No, I'm not. I'm part Navajo."

She lifted her brows. "Oh. Do you have a spirit animal?"

"A what?" He stared at her, straightening in his seat.

Conner burst out in a belly laugh, slapping him on the shoulder. "What is that supposed to mean?"

Steph pressed her fingers to her lips. "Oh, I thought

Indians had spirit animals."

"Indians are from India. I'm not from India." How stupid was this woman? He turned to Conner. "Drink up. Let's go."

"Ah, come on, Kai. I wanted to have a few drinks with you here. I like this place." Conner downed the rest of his martini and grabbed Kai's thigh.

Kai looked down at Conner's hand on his thigh. He was going to out himself to his almost coworker and old friend. He moved Conner's hand away. Better keep him in check and get him out of here.

Conner lifted his hand to the bartender. "Hey, bartender, can I get another martini? And one for my boyfri—shit." As he rounded his eyes, his face went blank, then he glanced at Monica.

"Coming right up." The bartender went to work on their drinks.

Kai quirked a side of his mouth. The more Conner drank, the more he was going to slip up. He could feel it in his bones. Conner was a talker when he was drunk. He placed his chin in his hands, propped up on the bar top by his elbows. "Conner."

Conner focused on him. "What?"

Kai grinned. In a soft voice, he said, "You sure you don't want to head back to our porch, with our bourbon and the couch you ordered?"

Conner gulped and his face flushed.

"You know, and then we could . . ." He raked his teeth over his lower lip, glancing at Conner's groin, then released it.

Conner licked his lips, focusing on Kai's mouth, squirming in his seat, then adjusted his jeans. Under his breath, he said, "Fuck . . ."

The bartender set their dirty martinis on the bar and took the empties.

Monica tapped Conner on the shoulder. "What are you two

whispering about over there?"

"Just guy stuff." Conner tore his gaze from Kai, then drank his martini.

Kai lifted his glass to his mouth. They seriously needed to go.

Steph placed her hand on Kai's thigh and came in close to his ear. "You are very attractive."

He sputtered across his drink, widening his eyes. "Um . . . you think so?" He stared at her. He certainly didn't feel the same about her.

Conner jumped up from the chair, seized Kai's arm and hauled him toward the restroom hallway. As they turned the corner, he shoved him against the wall, then slapped a hand on it over his head, hovering over him.

Kai stared up at him. "What?"

"That woman is fucking hitting on you." Conner looked him over.

Kai dropped his mouth open. "You were being hit on, too. You might even have *enjoyed* it."

"That woman knows me." Conner flared his nostrils.

"So? That makes it okay?" Kai glared behind him at a gold wall. Conner got hit on, too and probably at work. No matter if he admitted it or not. *And he has a problem with me tending bar.* He focused on him, narrowing his eyes, curling his lip. "How do you behave when you go on those work conferences? Do you buy drinks for the women there, too?"

Conner blinked and dropped his arm. "I uh . . ."

"Uh-huh." Kai stepped forward and jabbed his index finger into Conner's chest. "Don't give me shit about tending bar if you think it's fine to buy women drinks at your fancy conferences. And don't give me shit about being hit on by women. I don't like women. *You,* on the other hand, *do.*" He scowled.

Conner claimed his mouth in deep kisses, wrapping his

arms around him, moaning softly.

Kai surrendered to the intense kisses, parting his lips, letting his tongue penetrate him. He broke the kiss, breathing hard. "Fuck, Conner, what are we fighting about?"

"I don't know." Conner dove in for another round of passionate kisses, roaming his hands up and down Kai's back, digging his fingers into his flesh.

Kai stole a breath, eyes closed, and brushed his lips against Conner's ear, lost in the moment, emotion swelling in his chest. "If I didn't love you so much . . ." *Oh shit.* He popped his eyes open. His heart thumped as if it would break free.

Conner held Kai out in front of him, staring into his eyes. "D-did you just say . . ." He took a hard swallow. "You love me?"

He scratched his head, staring at the floor. No words would come. *What have I done?*

"Kai." Conner moved his hands to Kai's shoulders and shook him. "For fuck's sake, look at me." His voice choked. "Please."

He forced a peek at Conner.

Conner's eyes glistened with tears. "Look . . . at me."

He bit his lip and gazed deeply into Conner's eyes. His heart ached. *God, now I love him even more.* "I love you, Conner."

"Fuck." Conner's breath hitched. "I love you, too, so much." He yanked him into a tight embrace and sniffled, kissing the side of his head. "Damn, I just want to take you home and cuddle on that damn porch."

"Yeah, but we have drinks to finish with those women." Kai sighed.

"I have an idea. Let's go out there and down the drinks, pay up and leave as quick as we can." Conner freed him, then wiped his eyes.

Kai released a sharp laugh. "You want to drink a dirty

martini like a shot?"

Conner nodded. "Let's see who can drink it faster." He gave him a full-on smile.

"You're on. Winner gets the first blowjob." Kai snickered and strode out from behind the wall with Conner following.

Chapter Fifteen

Kai strolled with Conner down the path to their cabin, hand in hand, smiling and laughing all the way. "Didn't know I could drink when I wanted to, did you?" Kai squeezed Conner's hand.

"I did not." Conner shook his head. "Guess you won the bet." A shy smile swept over his lips. "I don't mind though. I love giving you blowjobs."

"I love you giving me blowjobs." That was something he'd never tire of. Kai chuckled.

Conner led him up the steps to the porch and stopped. "But first, the cuddling? Or do you want to do that after."

"I'm afraid I'll fall asleep if we don't cuddle first and I've been looking forward to using this couch all day." Kai took him in, the wide shoulders and narrow hips, the chiseled features of his face. How did he get so damn lucky?

"I'll get the bourbon. You make yourself comfortable." Conner opened the door to the cabin and stopped. "Do you need a blanket?"

Kai sat on the couch and put his feet on the glass and wicker table. "Nope."

"Okay." Conner went inside.

Kai watched the ripples and bubbles of the creek glistening in the moonlight, the gurgling sound calming him. *Conner loves me.* Who'd have thought that could happen? Certainly not him. Even if he could go back in time and tell his eighteen-year-old self that this day would come, he'd never have believed it. He let a wide grin work its way over his mouth. This was the best trip he'd ever had.

Conner came out with two low-ball glasses and the bottle of bourbon. He set everything on the table, sat down next to Kai, and poured their drinks, then handed one to him. "Here."

"Thanks." Kai sipped the bourbon, puckering his mouth as the liquid burned down his throat. "This is so good." Conner had really good taste in bourbon. He sank deep into the couch.

Conner laid an arm over Kai's shoulders and drew him into his chest. "This is like heaven, isn't it?"

Kai laid his head against his shoulder. "More like a dream come true." He shut his eyes a moment, savoring the sound of the creek and the warmth of having Conner next to him. "I really don't want to go home."

"Me neither." Conner kissed his head. "Maybe next time we come up, I can book the cabin for a week."

"That works." He didn't care if it meant taking a week off work, he'd do it. Kai opened his eyes and glanced at him. How would things be when they got home? Would the haunting in his house still be happening? How much longer should he stay at Conner's place? Everything was happening so quickly. "Conner?"

"Yeah."

"So, we're officially uh . . . in a relationship, you know, boyfriends. Right?" It didn't come out quite the way he intended. He drew his brows together.

"Yeah, why are you even asking that?" Conner turned his body to peer into his face.

"I don't know. I guess we should talk about who can know and who can't. I mean, you're not out at work, so you couldn't tell those women about us, right?" How would that be? There were still things about him that were a mystery. "And that's because you're not out to your family?"

Conner pursed his lips. "Yeah, that's why I didn't tell them or anyone at work. I'm . . . I don't know." He hung his head. "Can you wait for me to figure this out?"

Kai faced him. "Sure. But it's probably okay if Bryce knows. I mean, he does already."

Conner nodded slowly and sipped his bourbon.

"Just so you know, it's hard for Bryce to keep secrets. He tries to, but he always ends up making some sort of joke and spills it without even realizing it. So, if they don't already, everyone at the Fountain Bar and Grill will know." Kai sighed. Plus, Fountain Hills was pretty small. It probably wouldn't take long for their relationship to get around no matter what. But Conner should already know that.

Conner traced the rim of his glass with an index finger. "Let's try to keep it under wraps as much as possible though, for now, okay?"

"Yeah." He could understand that, seeing as how Conner was probably just figuring himself out. He snuggled into his side. How would Connor's parents handle it? "What are your parents like?"

Conner released a short chuckle. "Why are you asking me about them?"

"I don't know. Just curious, I guess. We already talked about mine." Kai sipped his drink.

Conner drew a deep inhale. "Well, my mom is pretty nice. She's your typical nineteen-fifties housewife, you know, likes to cook and keeps the house really clean, even though we've always had a maid. They never cleaned well enough for her, so she cleans even more after they leave." He snickered.

"Wasn't she on the PTO at school? I seem to remember her being around the school sometimes." Kai thought back to seeing a well-dressed woman at the school resembling Conner, the same hair and eyes, and being told it was Conner's mother. He'd been too much of a pussy to say anything to her.

All he'd done was stare.

"Yes, she was always in the PTO, but was the vice president for the high school when we were there. Then she was on the board for little league." Conner thinned his lips. "She was very involved." He drank his bourbon.

"What about your dad?"

"My dad worked a lot, like any doctor in his field. There was a time when he was always on call in case there was an emergency surgery at the hospital. He missed a lot of ball games. Of course, my mom was always there." Conner tightened his hold on him.

"So you said there were a lot of expectations. What do you mean, exactly?" Kai gazed at him. Maybe he'd get some clarification.

"My father is pretty demanding. I think you have to be, to get as far as he has. He expected me to have the same drive that he has. Turns out I don't. I mean, I have some drive, but not like him." Conner furrowed his brows.

"So, how do you think they'll react to us being together?" *How did I blurt that out?* He wasn't going to go there yet, but he did. He held his breath. How would Conner respond?

Conner tilted his head back, as if looking up into the trees, for a long moment. His chest expanded with a deep breath. "I don't know. Let's stop talking about this." He drank the rest of his bourbon.

"Sure." Kai's gut clenched. He shouldn't have asked that question. It was too soon, and he should have known better. He finished off his bourbon. How could he lighten the mood? He shifted on the couch, placing his arms around Conner's neck. "Someone owes me a blowjob." He placed hungry kisses on his mouth, parting his lips with his tongue.

"That's better." As Conner returned the kisses, he snuck his hand under Kai's fleece, massaging his chest, then teasing his nipple.

Kai freed soft gasps, a jolt rocketing through him, his cock aching as it hardened against his jeans. He'd never get enough of this. He kissed his way to his neck and bit at soft flesh.

Conner groaned and tilted his head back.

Kai brushed his hand over Conner's erection under his jeans, rubbing it, then fondling it.

Conner gasped, rocking his hips into Kai's hand. In thick voice, he said, "Fuck, Kai."

Kai sucked on his neck, then bit his earlobe. "I want that blowjob." God, did he want it.

Conner clenched his teeth and his eyes shut. "S-stop, uh, touching." His breath came in fast draws. His face was strained.

Kai moved his hand up and under his gray sweater, kneading the muscles of his chest. "Are you close?"

"Yeah. Damn it. Why do you make me so fucking hot so fast?" Conner released him and gazed deeply into his eyes. "What the hell is it about you that does this to me?"

Kai kissed him, then smirked. "I don't know. You really aren't like this normally?"

"No. Not even with other . . ." Conner widened his eyes. "No."

He'd really like to hear the rest of that sentence, but they had better things to do. "So, let's take this inside."

Conner nodded, then rose up from the couch, taking his hand. "Get the bottle."

Kai grabbed the bourbon bottle and followed Conner into the cabin, then set it on the square wooden table. "So, get naked, Mitchell." He sniggered and undressed, throwing his clothes to the floor. He couldn't wait to feel his mouth on him.

"You're so demanding, Nez." Conner smirked, removed his sweater and jeans, then climbed under the sheets.

Kai got in the bed, lying on his side. He had an idea. He would try doing to Conner what Conner always did to him.

"Let's try something, shall we?" He flung the covers down, exposing them both. He took Conner in, the hunger on his face, the strong chest, the rock-hard cock, pre-seed beading at the tip, then the muscled legs. "You are so much fun to look at."

Conner licked his lips. "I don't want you to just look at me."

"I know." Kai skimmed his hand up Conner's side, over his shoulder and down his taut stomach, then brushed over his cock.

Conner's breath hitched and his cock jerked. "Fuck, even that's too much."

"I'm not even kissing you." Kai came down and kissed him, placing his hand on his cheek, dancing his tongue inside his mouth, moaning.

Conner rocked his hips, his cock jutting up each time, his body shuddered. "Fuck." He creased his brows.

Kai lifted his head and brushed a hand down his cheek. "Look at me, Conner." Maybe he could distract him enough to calm him down.

Conner's gaze met his.

"I love you." Kai placed a tender kiss on his lips.

Conner gulped hard. "I love you." His face relaxed, then he took a deep breath and lifted off the bed on an elbow.

It looks like it worked. "Turn around. We'll suck each other off at the same time. I'm going to suck you so hard you'll probably come twice." Kai grinned.

Conner pressed his lips together and shut his eyes tight, pre-seed dribbling from his cockhead. "Damn it, Kai, saying things like that doesn't help." He crawled down to Kai's groin and fisted his shaft, then pumped it with his mouth, taking him in deep.

Hot, wet friction swept over his cock. Kai shuddered and groaned, thrusting into Conner's mouth, watching another bead of pre-seed seep out of Conner's tip. He licked it off, the taste all bitter and all Conner.

Conner whimpered, sucking down on his shaft, then swirling the head.

Sensation built inside Kai, tingling over his groin. He licked Conner's shaft a few times, teasing it.

Conner moaned over Kai's cock, keeping a relentless rhythm, then fondled his sac.

"Oh, shit." Pleasure pulsed up his spine. His peak teased, a delicious humming inside him. He toyed with Conner's sac while licking only the tip of his swollen cock. It twitched with each flick of his tongue.

Conner sucked harder, faster, over and over, his hand pumping at the base.

The hot edge of release shuddered over him. "I'm coming." Kai devoured Conner's cock, sucking as hard as he could, his tongue pressing against the underside. As his own orgasm surged, Conner's shaft hardened and spurted against his throat. Waves of sensation quivered through him.

Conner freed muffled cries, thrusting into him while pumping his cock. As it calmed, he released him and panted, wiping his mouth. "Holy fuck, Kai, what a great idea." He lay flat on the bed, his chest heaving, a wide grin on his lips.

"Get up here." Kai released his spent cock and slapped at his thigh, taking deep breaths.

Conner shifted to lie next to him on his back. "I thought you were going to make me come twice?" He let out a lazy chuckle.

"There's still time." Kai rolled to the side and wound a leg around Conner's. Being in bed with him was simply the best.

"Yeah, we have all night." Conner kissed his head.

Kai played with Conner's nipple. He didn't want to go home. "Wonder if Bryce found anything in the wash."

"Wouldn't he have called you if he did?"

"Probably not. He knows how important going on this trip with you is to me. So I'm sure he didn't want to bother me while I'm up here." Kai kissed his chest.

"How important, huh?" Conner snickered. "How much more does Bryce know that I don't?"

"Everything." Kai quirked his lips, then peeked up at him.

"That has to change." Conner frowned.

"It will, in time." Kai nestled into his chest. "Love you."

"Love you."

Kai, in a white t-shirt and jeans, sat in the passenger seat of Conner's BMW, gazing out the window at the far-off, jagged mountains and the scrubby bushes and cacti speeding by on the sides of the freeway. "I don't want to work tonight."

Conner, wearing a gray, polo shirt and jeans, glanced at him. "I wouldn't want to either."

"I really could have used another day. I can't remember the last time I had more than two days off in a row." It was certainly more than a year ago that he and Bryce had gone camping for a few days. The time away had been so nice. He rested his elbow on the top of the door and placed his forehead in his hand.

"Maybe you should call in sick?" Conner lifted a brow.

Kai sighed. "I need the money." That was not an option. Though now it seemed he was paying rent on a place he wasn't living in. His phone chimed. He shifted in his seat and pulled the phone out of a front pocket, then opened the interface.

May
I'll be home this week for fall break. I want to see you.

Kai smiled. This was perfect. He had so much to tell her. "Who's that?" Conner leaned over, focusing on his phone.

"My sister. She's coming up for fall break." Kai hit buttons on his phone.

Kai
Cool. When and where?

"So, can I meet her?" Conner lifted his brows.
"Sure." Maybe they could grab a drink somewhere. Kai watched the three dots blinking on the text interface of his phone.

May
Mom's house. She wants to do a family dinner. Can you get a night off this week?

Kai scoffed. That was the last thing he wanted to do. "Shit, no." He dropped the phone in his lap and pursed his lips, glaring out the window.

"What's wrong?" Conner placed his hand on Kai's thigh.

"My mom wants to do a family dinner with May this week." Kai's chest tightened. Last time they'd tried that, it had ended in a screaming match. He bit the nail on his index finger.

"So, let's go. You can introduce me to both of them." Conner tapped his leg.

Kai focused on him. "You don't understand. There's about a fifty-fifty chance my mom will be in a pissy mood and she'll take it out on me." And it would be really uncomfortable for everyone.

"Let her. All the better reason for me to be with you." Conner wrinkled his brow, glancing at him. "I want to be there for you." He drove the car onto an overpass, entering a new freeway.

"Yeah." Kai freed a long breath. He wanted to see May, and he hadn't seen his mother in months. He should probably do this. But should he really bring Conner? If it went badly, it could be embarrassing. "I don't know."

"Kai, I want to meet them." Conner took his hand and squeezed it. "I want to know more about you than Bryce." He smirked.

"Oh, for fuck's sake." Kai huffed and picked up his phone. He'd have to call his mother and let her know about them. That wouldn't be a fun conversation either. "Fine. Let me talk to my mother about us first."

"Good. You know, even if she's hard to deal with, it's okay." Conner focused on the road. "It's one of the things that made you as strong as you are." He flashed his eyes at him.

I don't feel all that strong. Why does Conner see that in me? He picked his phone up and opened the text interface. "Let me see what May thinks."

Kai
I have Wednesday and Thursday night open this week.

His phone chimed.

May
Let's do Thursday.

Kai
Okay. I'm bringing my boyfriend.

May
What???

Kai sniggered and touched his fingers to his mouth. "I just told her I'm bringing my boyfriend."

Conner let a wide smile spread over his lips. "So, what did she say?"

Kai's phone lit up and rang. "She's calling now." Just what he expected. He smiled and brought the phone to his ear.

"Hello?"

"What the fuck, Kai? A boyfriend? Really?" May chuckled.

He glanced at Conner. "Yeah, you'll never guess who."

"Is it someone I know?"

"Yeah. Conner Mitchell." He grinned.

"No fucking way. He's not straight?" she said, excitement lacing through her voice.

"Apparently not. We . . ." What should he tell her? He stole a peak a Conner.

Conner lifted his brows at him, grinning from ear to ear.

"We started dating a few weeks ago. We're heading home from Sedona now." It was still hard to believe, even for him. He glanced out the window.

"Isn't that the guy you had a crush on in high school?"

"Yeah." He toyed with the hem of his t-shirt.

"You're going to have to tell me all about it when I get up there," she said. Her voice lowered. "Are you sure you want to bring him to Mom's?"

Not really. "He wants to come. He wants to meet both of you, and well . . ." He peered at Conner. "He knows how she is."

"Okay. I'll do what I can to make this easier on you. But you need to remember to not take every little thing she says the wrong way."

"I don't." It wasn't *his* fault Mom said the things she said. He pursed his lips. Maybe May could help. Mom would listen to her and probably not be so nasty. "Maybe you could talk to her for me and see how she reacts."

"Sure. I'll let her know and then I'll tell you what she says." She exhaled. "If it looks like it's going to be bad, I'll let you know."

"Thanks." He stared at the dash, frowning. Why couldn't he have normal parents like Conner's?

"I've got to go. I'll talk to you later this week."

"Sure, bye."

"Bye."

Kai hung up the phone and slid it into his front pocket. How would this go down? Either really badly or just fine. There was no in-between.

"So, what did she say?" Conner gnawed his lower lip.

"She's going to talk to my mom for me first and we'll see how she handles it. It's better this way." He drew a deep breath.

"So, you think she might not want me to come?" Conner creased his forehead.

"No, it's not that. It's just I never know how she's going to react to something. She might be fine with it, or she might get bent out of shape over it. It has nothing to do with you." How could he explain it to Conner? Unease built in his chest. He watched him.

Conner furrowed his brows. "But she knows you're gay. Has—"

"We don't talk about it. She knows, but we don't talk about it." Kai shifted in his seat. What was it really like? He'd never had to explain it before. "It's not like she asks me who I'm seeing or if I'm seeing anyone." He peered at Conner.

"Okay, so this would be the first time you're bringing someone home to meet her then, right?" A wide grin swept over Conner's face.

Kai scoffed. "It's not going to be what you think it is, and to tell you the truth, I have no idea what to expect at this point. We'll see what May says after she talks with her." A knot formed in his gut. This could be bad.

Chapter Sixteen

Kai, dressed in his work clothes, looked out over the few people drinking at the bar top, then focused on Conner. Everyone was set, for the moment.

Conner nursed a beer in a gray polo shirt and jeans and watched a baseball game on the television hanging on the wall.

Kai stepped in front of him and wiped the bar top down. Conner had come in shortly after his shift started. "Good game?"

Conner smiled at him. "So-so."

"You're taking your sweet time with that beer." Kai placed his hands on his hips. "You plan on staying here all night?"

Conner gave him a sly smile. "Yeah, got to make sure no one hits on you."

Kai shook his head and grinned. "Come on, it's a Tuesday night." Not that he minded him being here. He was nice to look at.

"So?" Conner sipped his beer. "I have to defend my property." He snickered.

"Really. Now I'm your property?" He laughed.

Conner's cell phone lit up and rang. He raised his brows and picked it up. "Hello?"

Kai walked to the other end of the bar and brought a check to a couple, then rang them up at the POS station. He glanced at Conner.

Conner set his phone on the bar top. "Hey." He motioned with his fingers.

The Haunting Crush

Kai set the receipt and debit card in front of the couple, then strolled down to Conner. "What's up?"

"That was Brent. Turns out the medium had a cancellation and can come to your house tomorrow night. Does that work?" Conner gazed at him.

A shiver raced up his spine. "Yeah, that works." Maybe they could finally get this chindi thing taken care of and he could move back into his own place. Kai glanced at him. How would he take that? "So . . ." His phone chimed. He slid it out of a back pocket and opened the text interface.

May
Mom says she'd like to meet him.

Kai blinked a few times. Holy shit, was this for real? His mother was going to acknowledge his relationship?

Kai
So, she's okay with it?

He watched the dots on the screen.

May
Yes, she even seemed happy about it.

Kai
Are you sure?

May
Maybe you should call her.

Fuck, no. He chewed his lip. He'd just face her when they went to her house on Thursday. That was enough.

Kai

Just let me know if something changes before Thursday.

May
Sure.

Kai slid his phone into his back pocket.

"Hey, what was that all about?" Conner lifted his chin to him.

Kai twitched a corner of his mouth. "My uh, mom wants to meet you." He still couldn't believe it.

Conner spread a wide smile over his face. "That's great." He drank his beer.

"Yeah." Kai massaged his neck, staring at the back bar. How would this really go down? Maybe it would be fine. May would be there. She'd help him if things went downhill.

"You okay?" Conner wrinkled his brows. "You look worried."

"I'm okay." Kai forced a grin. "It'll be fine." He drew a deep breath. He should change the subject. "Anyhow, so we'll get to the bottom of this ghost thing tomorrow night, right?"

"Probably. Brent says this medium is really good." Conner sat back in his chair.

"Good." Kai grabbed a wine glass from the dishwasher and dried it with a towel.

Bryce strolled up with a serving tray in his hand. "Did I overhear something about the medium?"

Conner turned to Bryce. "Yeah, he's able to come out tomorrow night. Are you working?"

"No, I'm on days tomorrow and Thursday." Bryce scanned over the tables in the restaurant.

"Oh, same shifts as Kai, huh?" Conner narrowed his eyes.

"Yeah, why?" Bryce lifted his brows.

Kai slapped the towel on the bar top. "Stop it, Conner." He smirked. He could have some fun with this. "Conner's jealous of you."

"Kai . . ." Conner growled, glaring at him.

Bryce shifted his stance, looking Conner up and down. "Bro, I don't swing that way. Besides, Kai's had a crush on you forever. You don't have to worry about him."

"I know." Conner fingered his beer glass and grinned. "We love each other." He gazed at Kai.

Heat flushed Kai's face. "I thought you didn't want to tell everyone." Maybe Conner didn't mind if it got out after all? Maybe he'd decided to use Bryce's big mouth to come out in a round-about way.

"I want to make sure Bryce knows." Conner flashed his eyes at Bryce.

"That's great, man. About time." Bryce slapped Conner's arm and smiled. "Anyway, I wanted to tell you both that there is nothing in that God damned wash. I was all over it this weekend and I didn't find anything but a few old liquor bottles."

Kai pursed his lips. "So, what was all that talk of bones?" They had to get this ghost thing figured out.

"Who knows?" Conner sipped his beer. "Tomorrow should be interesting.

Kai, still wearing his restaurant attire, parked his blazer in the carport of his duplex, shut off the engine and glanced at Bryce. "This is so fucked up."

"I know. I really want to get out of my mom's place." Bryce opened the door and climbed out.

Kai got out of the blazer and searched for Conner's BMW in the long shadows of early evening sunlight. He should have been here by now. "Wonder where Conner is?"

Bryce met him on the driver's side of the SUV. "I'm sure he'll be here soon." He studied him "We haven't had a chance to talk alone. How are things going with you two? Did you figure out what his deal was?" He placed a hand on his hip.

Kai twisted his mouth. "There are still some things that I'm not so sure about, but he does seem to really want to be with me."

"Really." Bryce peered at him. "What are you not sure about?"

Kai focused on him. He should be careful about what he told him, but it would be nice to get his opinion. "Something happened when he was living in Scottsdale, and I think he just up and left Paige and moved back here. I know that he has experience with men, but I don't understand how he would if he was with Paige all this time. Unless he cheated on her."

"Did you ask him about the open relationship thing?" Bryce thinned his lips.

"Yeah." Kai snickered. "He thought I was asking him to have an open relationship, and he got sort of pissed." He shook his head. "I don't think he's into that."

"Well, then he either cheated on Paige, like, a lot, or in the short time between him leaving her and hooking up with you, he did a lot of guys." Bryce laughed.

Kai's heart clenched. Was Conner a cheater? If he did that to Paige, would he do that to him? Wait . . . Brandon said something about a hookup app. "Shit."

"What?" Bryce touched his arm.

"That night we were at The Alamo, Brandon accused Conner of having a profile on some gay hookup app." Kai focused on him. "Do you think maybe he did go a little crazy after he broke up with Paige?"

Bryce shrugged. "It's possible. Anything is, I guess."

Kai widened his eyes. Conner wouldn't still be using hookup apps now, right?

"What are you thinking?" Bryce furrowed his brows.

Kai shook his head. "Nothing." That was stupid. When would Conner have time to use a hookup app? They were always together. Living in the same place, even.

Conner's BMW pulled up to the curb and the engine shut off. Conner got out of the car, wearing a blue button-down shirt and gray slacks. He strolled to Kai and smiled. "Hey, baby." He kissed him on the lips.

All the previous suspicions melted away. "Hey." Kai let a wide grin sweep over his mouth. He shouldn't be stupid about this. Conner loved him and it was obvious. "So, where is Brent with the medium?"

"He's on his way. Want to go in and check the place out while we still have some light?" Conner placed his hand on the small of Kai's back.

"Sure." Kai pulled his keys out of his front pocket and opened the door. "Feels like we haven't been here in so long." What would it be like to be to living with Bryce again?

Conner grabbed his hand and stepped into the kitchen with Bryce following. "Looks about the same."

Kai peered into the room. All the upper cabinet doors hung open. A shiver raced up his spine. "Damn. I was really hoping when we came in, we wouldn't find anything."

Conner strode to the game camera and picked it up off the glass and rattan dinette. "Is it even worth looking at the footage?"

Bryce walked the length of the cabinets, closing each one. "No. What are we going to see? These things opening up by themselves again? We already know that."

Conner glanced out the kitchen window. "Looks like Brent is here."

"Good." As goosebumps broke out over Kai's skin, he rubbed his hands up his arms.

Conner hooked an arm around him and kissed his cheek. "Scared?"

"Yeah." Kai chewed his bottom lip. He'd have to remember to keep himself in check. Brent wasn't supposed to know they were together.

A knock sounded on the carport door.

Bryce opened the door and stepped aside. "Hey, Brent, come on in."

Brent entered the room, wearing a black shirt and jeans.

A tall, bald man with kind eyes wearing a thin, gray sweatshirt and black jeans followed Brent.

Brent pointed to each of them. "This is Kai, Conner and Bryce." He gestured to the bald man. "This is John."

John bowed his head. "Nice to meet you all." He clasped his hands in front of him. "Shall we get started? I'm already feeling vibrations in here, and I don't want to lose them." He held his hands out and walked to the cabinets. "Yes, it's here." He placed his hand on the cabinet over to the right of the sink. "There was something in here that was special to someone."

Kai dropped his mouth open and looked at Bryce. "Holy shit."

Bryce's gaze caught on Kai's. "The locket."

John turned to them. "What did you say?"

"When we first moved in, there was a locket in that cabinet. We didn't know what to do with it, so we brought it to Goodwill." Kai glanced at Conner. "It's got to be gone now." Did that mean they were doomed to having this ghost here forever? "Do we have to try and find it?"

John shook his head. "No, there is something else." He shut his eyes. "I feel something terrible has happened here." He opened his eyes. "There's more than one."

"More than one ghost?" Kai shuddered and wrapped his arms around his waist.

Conner placed his hand on Kai's shoulder. "You okay?"

Kai gave a shaky nod. It was going to be nearly impossible to remember to stay off Conner. He wanted nothing more than to feel his arms around him.

"When we did the investigation, we think Kai's father

came through." Brent gestured to Kai. "But after Kai did a session with him on the spirit box, we didn't get anything more from him."

John nodded. "I'm getting the same word over and over again. Bones." He tented his fingers over his chest.

"That's what we got, too." Brent rounded his eyes.

John glanced at the door, then strode toward it and went outside.

Everyone followed.

John walked through the yard of rock, bushes and cacti and came to the side of the tan stucco house, then crouched down. "Get me something to dig with. Now."

Kai watched John, trembling. "Uh, isn't there a trowel in the kitchen, Bryce?"

"Yeah, I'll get it." Bryce trotted off.

Conner whispered in Kai's ear. "It's okay. I'm here." He placed a hand on his lower back.

Kai forced an unsteady grin at him.

Bryce returned with the trowel and handed it to John. "Here."

John dug in the dirt, looked up, then dug a bit more. "Can you give me a light?"

Brent slid a cell phone out of his back pocket and turned on the flashlight. "Here."

They all peered down. A white, rounded shape showed through the dirt.

"Holy fuck." Fear quivered up Kai's spine. He turned into Conner, winding his arms around his waist. "What is that?"

Conner embraced Kai, then unwrapped their arms. He whispered, "Sorry."

"Oh." *Shit, did Brent see that?* He twisted to the others. Everyone's attention was on the thing John was digging around.

John stopped digging. "We need to call the police. This is the skull of a baby, maybe premature. The bones aren't fused."

"What the fuck?" Bryce stared at it. "Who the hell would bury a baby on the side of a house?"

John peered up. "Point the light up there."

Brent moved the light to the roofline. A rain spout jutted out from the wall.

"I'm assuming that with the rain pouring off the roof right here, the bones were disturbed." John glanced at each of them, one by one.

"The late monsoon." Bryce sighed and turned to Kai. "Remember, Kai? All the rain must have dislodged the remains during that storm. It wasn't in the wash like we thought."

Kai nodded, holding his arms crossed over his chest. Why would someone abandon their child like that? What a terrible thing. Tears stung his eyes. He rubbed them away.

Conner watched Kai, wrinkling his forehead, then slipped his cell phone out. "I'll call the police. We probably shouldn't touch anything more, so they can investigate."

"Wait." John held out his hand and stood up, then handed the trowel to Bryce. "I feel that this is what the spirit wanted us to find. I believe the spirit is connected to this skull." He looked at Brent. "But there is more to it than that." He stepped toward the house. "Follow me. We need to have a séance."

Brent and Bryce followed John.

"A what?" Goosebumps shivered over Kai's skin.

"Come on. This should be interesting." Conner placed his hand at the bottom of Kai's back and walked with him through the yard, the carport door and into the house.

John moved the black coffee table from the couch to the center of the main room. "All gather around and place your hands on this table. We can use it to contact the spirit."

"Cool." Bryce walked to the table.

Brent slid an EVP recorder out of his back pocket and placed it on the couch. "I'll record, in case we can pick anything up while we do this."

Under his breath, Kai said, "No fucking way." Using spirit equipment was one thing, but participating in a séance? He shook his head, trembling.

Conner grabbed his arms, under the shoulder. "Relax, Kai. He knows what he's doing."

John, Brent, and Bryce sat with their legs tucked under them at the table, all on the same side, and set their hands on it.

"We need all of us, Kai. And with the one spirit calling out to you specifically, we need you more than anyone here." John held his hand out to Kai. "Come and take a seat across from me. Nothing can harm you."

"B-but can't I get possessed or something?" Kai frowned, glancing at Conner.

Conner whispered in his ear, "I'm here. I won't let that happen to you."

Kai's gaze darted between them all, then he slumped his shoulders. "Shit, fine." They'd better be right about this.

Conner and Kai knelt down at the table, placing their hands on it.

"Okay, now what?" As Kai watched John, he fought to keep his hands steady.

"Now we wait." John closed his eyes a moment. "They're here. I feel them."

The table jiggled.

"Who did that?" Kai narrowed his eyes, looking at each of them. "Bryce, are you trying to fuck with me?"

"No." Bryce sniggered.

"It was the spirits. They're letting us know they're here." John let his face go slack.

The table slid across the carpeted floor at Kai.

Kai screamed and jumped up. "Fuck this." No way was he going to do any more of this. His knees knocked together.

Conner stood and grabbed his arm. "Settle down."

"The fucking table just came at me all by itself, and you're telling me to settle down?" Kai glared at Conner.

"Kai, you need to be strong through this." John pursed his lips. "Come and sit with us again."

"Jesus, Kai, don't be such a pussy." Bryce chuckled. "Come on." He cocked his head.

Kai drew a deep breath. "Fine, Bryce. Let's see how you handle it if it comes after you." This was so fucked. He knelt down again, next to Conner, placing his hands on the table.

The table jiggled.

Kai whimpered.

As Conner wrinkled his forehead, he watched Kai.

"I feel the mother of the baby is here. Is that correct? Move the table if that is correct." John stared at the table.

The table rocked onto two legs lengthwise, then slammed down.

Kai froze in place, staring at the table, hanging his mouth open.

"Are you the Ashbrook Wash ghost?" Conner glanced at John.

The table rocked again.

John peered at Conner. "How did you know that?"

"Wild guess." Conner offered a faint grin.

John closed his eyes and his face contorted. His lips snarled.

Kai whispered, "Holy shit." He watched John's face change.

John opened his eyes. In a voice higher than his own, he said, "I miscarried. I didn't know what to do. I'm sorry." His head flipped back, then fell forward.

As John slumped, Brent grabbed him from the side. "Guess we have our answer."

John came to and scanned the room, straightening. "Sorry.

That was unexpected." He placed a hand to his forehead.

"You okay?" Brent released him.

"Yes. What happened?" John asked.

"I think you were possessed for a few minutes. But it sounds like the girl that went missing, the Ashbrook Wash ghost, was pregnant and had a miscarriage and buried the baby on the side of this house. I'm guessing if we could look up the records, she probably lived here." Conner examined Kai.

John nodded. "Yes, and her spirit is probably stuck here until the remains are properly disposed of."

"What do we do now?" Kai glanced at Conner, then focused on John.

"Now I think we have enough information to call the police, and once the police are done and the remains are gone, I think it would be a good idea to sage and bless this house. There shouldn't be any more disruptions after that." John rubbed his temple.

Kai released a long exhale and relaxed his shoulders. "Good."

Kai sat on the cushions of Conner's balcony couch, draped in a blanket, watching the tall fountain shooting up and shimmering in the moonlight in the center of the park.

Conner came onto the balcony and handed him a low-ball glass with bourbon and took a seat beside him.

Kai grinned and flung a section of blanket over Conner. "Weird to have to call the police tonight." He thought back. He'd never had to do that before. He sipped his bourbon.

"Who would have thought that the miscarried remains of a baby would be buried in your side yard and that it would belong to the infamous Ashbrook Wash ghost?" Conner set his arm around Kai's shoulders. "Come here."

Kai snuggled into his side. "How long do you think it'll

take to investigate the scene?"

"No idea, but I would think at least a day or so." Conner kissed the side of his head.

"Well, when should we do the sage thing again and blessing?" It better work this time. He wrinkled his brows. "I mean, maybe we could do it tomorrow and see if it works. Then I could move back in this weekend."

"Kai." Conner faced him, dropping his arm from his shoulders.

"What?" Kai gazed into his blue eyes.

"Do you really want to go back?" Conner swallowed hard.

"I uh, I still have a lease on that place. I'm paying rent." He searched Conner's face. What was he driving at?

Conner stared at his glass of bourbon, resting in his lap. The corners of his lips twitched with a faint grin. "I like having you here." He searched Kai's face. "When is your lease up?"

"About two more months." Kai pressed his lips together. "What are you saying? I should break my lease?" He narrowed his eyes. Was he asking him to move in already? "What about Bryce?"

Conner winced and sighed. "No, you're right. You should move back into your own place." He frowned. "Guess we won't get to do this every night." He swirled the bourbon in the glass, then drank it.

"We can still do this every night. I work right across the street. I can just walk over when I'm done." Kai placed his hand on Conner's cheek. He didn't look happy. "Don't get me wrong, I've loved staying here with you while this thing was going on. But it's a little soon to be moving in together, isn't it?"

"Is it?" Conner flashed his eyes at him. "So, you'll go back to living with Bryce." He creased his nose.

Kai released a puff of air. "Come on, you know there's

nothing between me and Bryce." Why in the hell was Conner still going on about that?

Conner fingered the blanket. "I know, but you two work together already and you'll be living together again. He'll always know you better than I ever will."

"Come on, Conner. That's not true. There are things I tell you that I don't tell Bryce." Kai kissed his cheek. What could he say to make him feel better about the situation?

"Like what?" Conner searched his face.

"I don't know." Kai sipped his bourbon and thought on it. He had to make it good, so Conner would stop worrying about this. He gazed deeply into his intense eyes. "I haven't told Bryce everything about my parents. He doesn't know that my mom blamed me for my dad skipping his insulin the day he died." It was the truth. He'd never admitting that to anyone before.

"Seriously? I'm the only who knows that?" A faint grin curled Conner's lips.

"Yes, well, you and May. But May was there, so I'm not sure that counts." Kai grabbed Conner's hand.

"May would have been three. She wouldn't have remembered that." Conner widened his grin. "But I don't care if May knows more. She *is* your sister."

Kai sipped his bourbon and looked out over the lake. "Does Paige know more about you than I do?" *Where did that come from?* Maybe all that talk with Bryce had him questioning things again. He glanced at Conner.

Conner turned his head.

"Conner?" He set his fingers on Conner's chin, bringing them face to face. He wanted some damn answers. "Well?"

Conner chewed the inside of his mouth. "She knows a lot about me." He snapped his brows together. "We were together a long time."

Kai's heart pinched. That was not what he wanted to hear.

"Do you still talk?" He thought back. He didn't remember her ever calling or seeing text messages from her on his phone, but it's not like he was looking for it.

"Yeah, we talk." Conner drank his bourbon. "I told you we're still friends."

I'm not sure how I feel about all this. "Did you . . . does she know about us?" This would be the test. If she knew he had someone else, then they were definitely done, at least in *his* mind.

Conner shook his head. "Let's stop talking about this."

That wasn't good either. "Why don't you want to tell me what happened to make you move back here? Something did happen, right?" He couldn't just go on wondering anymore. He rubbed his eyebrow. This conversation was getting out of hand.

Conner gulped hard. "Why do you think something happened? Can't I just decide that I need to change the direction of my life, and do it?"

"So, are you telling me that's what happened? You just woke up one day and decided to dump your girlfriend of six years and move back here and start dating men?" Saying it out loud really made it sound ridiculous. He lifted his brows.

"Not men. *A* man." Conner expelled a long breath. "Shit, Kai. This isn't something to fight about, is it? We should be happy tonight. We found the source of your ghost problems and however we ended up here, we're together." He kissed Kai's cheek. "I love you."

He was right. He cocked his head and smirked. "I love you, too."

Chapter Seventeen

Kai lay nude on his back in Conner's bed, the covers pulled up to his chin. The conversation they'd had on the balcony kept playing through his head. It didn't sound plausible that Conner would up and change his life like that. Those were some really big changes all at once.

Conner opened the door to the bathroom, shut off the light, and stepped to the side of the bed. He dropped his boxer briefs down and stepped out of them, his cock already hard. He climbed in next to Kai and lay on his side. "Why are you all covered up? Let me see you." He dragged the covers down, licking his lips. "You aren't still mad at me, are you?"

Kai rolled to his side, taking in Conner's stunning face. "No, I can't stay mad at you for long, anyway." He brushed his hand down Conner's side, over his hip and to his hard cock, giving it slow, soft strokes.

Conner bit his lip and shut his eyes, letting out a soft moan. In a breathy voice, he said, "There's no reason for you to be mad at me." He rocked his hips, pre-seed beading at tip.

Kai swiped his thumb over the end of Conner's erection, slickening it.

Conner whimpered, his body shuddering.

"Yeah, okay." He'd let it go this time. Secrets had a way of coming out on their own. "Are you close? Should I get you off now and then again?" He watched Conner's reaction, his own cock aching with need. He loved being in bed with this man. Every time was the best he'd ever had.

Conner opened his eyes, the lids hooded. "What do you

want to do?"

Kai claimed his mouth in ravenous kisses and placed quick jerks over his shaft.

Conner tensed his face. He broke the kisses and took heavy breaths against Kai's neck, wrapping an arm around him. "Fuck." He dug his nails into Kai's back and cried out, his seed bursting up between them. As it slowed, he rolled to his back and lifted his forearm over his eyes, panting.

"I decided you were coming twice. As usual. I mean, why change a good thing?" Kai licked the seed from his hand, then moved over Conner, hovering over him, and licked the droplets of come off his muscled chest and taut stomach. His cock twitched as a pulse of lust raced up his spine. "You are so fucking hot." He dropped down over him and placed chaste kisses over his lips, rocking his hips slowly over Conner's thigh, taking sweet friction from him a little at a time. He wanted to savor every second of their time together like this.

Conner moaned against his mouth, roaming his hands up and down Kai's back, then squeezed his buttocks, bringing their hips tighter still. "What do you want, Kai?"

Kai licked down his neck, then bit at the sensitive flesh with a groan. He could eat him up right now. "Damn, I don't know. You, I just want you." As he worked his shaft over Conner's thigh, pleasure knotted in his gut and shivered over him.

Conner's cock stiffened again. He arced his head back and released a soft gasp, writhing under him. "Do you want to fuck me, Kai?"

He sucked on Conner's earlobe, then whispered, "I want you to fuck *me* this time." He hadn't felt what it was like to have him inside him yet. It was time they did this.

Conner stopped moving. "Kai, I've never done that before."

Kai lifted his head. "Seriously?" He swiped his thumb over his cheek. "B-but that time I fucked you wasn't your first. Was it?" He searched his face.

Conner shook his head, gazing at him with wide eyes.

"S-so you've let guys do you, but you haven't done *it* to a guy?" Kai lifted his brows. Somehow, this was hard to believe. Conner was full of surprises.

"No." Conner blinked fast and turned his head.

Why does he seem embarrassed? "Do you want to?" Kai skimmed his hand over his forehead, swiping his bangs back.

"I-I don't want to hurt you." Conner focused on him.

Kai lifted the edge of his mouth. "You're not going to hurt me. I've done it more than a few times before." That might be an understatement, actually. He usually ended up being the bottom. Of course, Conner was different. Everything about Conner was different.

"I don't need to hear that." Conner clenched his jaw.

"Sorry." Kai watched him, caressing his cheek, then his forehead. What was going on in his head? "If you don't want to, you don't have to. I just thought—"

"I want to." Conner rolled him onto his back and crushed his mouth in deep, penetrating kisses. He thrust his hard cock against Kai's hip, gasping against his mouth. "Fuck, I want to."

Kai fought to keep up with his demanding kisses and thrusting hips. His peak taunted him, just under the surface. He took heavy breaths.

Conner broke free and rose up on straight arms, then opened the nightstand and snatched a condom and lube.

Kai's cock jerked and a pulse shot through his body. "Hurry." Damn, he was going to spill it before he even got it in if he wasn't careful.

Conner squirted lube over his fingers and lay next to Kai on his side, then gazed into his eyes and brought his slickened fingers to his entrance.

Kai lifted his knees, keeping his gaze affixed to Conner's.

Conner circled his entrance and slipped a finger inside, hitting his internal bundle of nerves.

A shock of pleasure jolted up his spine. "Oh, fuck." He bit his lip. "Keep going, right there."

As Conner slid a second finger in and stroked his insides, he pressed his lips over Kai's, his tongue tangling with Kai's.

Kai rocked his hips into the air, pre-seed seeping down to pool on his stomach, his cock and thighs twitching with each thrust of Conner's fingers.

Conner ground his hard cock against him, rubbing himself on the side of his hip. In a gravelly voice, he said, "You ready? 'Cause seeing you like this is making me so fucking hot."

"Yeah. I'm ready." God was he ready.

Conner pulled his fingers out, rolled the condom over his engorged cock, slickened it with lube, and moved between his legs, sitting up. He lifted Kai's bent legs back and pushed his cock at his entrance, coming down over him on straight arms. He looked at him and bit his lip. "Tell me if I hurt you."

"I will. You won't." Kai wrapped his legs around his waist, driving Conner's cock harder against his entrance.

Conner released a sharp gasp, then rocked his hips, sliding the tip inside him.

The familiar burning sensation rolled through him. He wanted more. Now. "Deeper."

Conner dropped to his elbows and slowly drove his cock inside him. He hung his head. In a choked voice, he said, "You're so fucking tight." He pulled out and pushed back in, taking deep, ragged breaths, his body shaking. "This is so damn good."

A shudder of sensation twisted inside Kai's gut. "I'm close, go harder." Damn if Conner wasn't going to make him come like this.

Conner thrust into him, over and over, his hips slapping against him, placing hungry kisses over his lips. He snatched

Kai's hair and jerked his head back, then licked and sucked at Kai's neck.

As tingling prickled Kai's neck, pleasure built in his groin and his sac tightened. "Holy shit, Conner, I'm coming." He clenched his teeth as sensation coiled deep inside and pulsated over his body, curling his toes, spurting seed onto his chest.

Conner shuddered over him, arcing his head back and crying out, his hips thrusting in an erratic rhythm. As it slowed, he pulled out and lay on Kai's chest, his head on his shoulder. "Fuck, that was good." He took deep draws of breath.

Kai wrapped his arms around him and kissed his head. "No one has ever made me come like that, you know, without jerking me, too."

"Really?"

"Really. Guess we both had a first."

Conner nuzzled into his neck. "I was so afraid I was going to lose control and hurt you."

"Well, you didn't." Kai tightened his hold. "You were perfect."

"No, you're perfect." Conner lifted his head and looked into his eyes. "I love you, so much."

Kai let a contented grin work its way over his mouth. "Love you, too."

Conner tapped his nose. "Let's get cleaned up. I have to work in the morning."

"Yeah, yeah."

Kai, wearing a white, button-down shirt and jeans typed in the text interface on his phone as he paced from Conner's kitchen to the main room, then bit at his thumbnail. His heart pounded as if would break free from his chest.

Kai
How's mom? Should I really do this?

Kai watched the three dots as they blinked at him, then glanced at Conner, sitting on the couch in a blue shirt and black jeans.

"Kai, it'll be fine. Relax." Conner held out his arm. "Come here."

Kai stepped into Conner's arm as it wound around his waist.

Conner pulled Kai down into his lap and embraced him. "It'll be fine. Let's just go."

"No, I have to be sure." He fixated on the phone. Why wasn't she answering? Was Mom already starting something with her? The phone chimed.

May
It's fine. Come over.

Conner peered into the phone. "See? She says it's fine. Lets' go."

Kai stood up and rubbed the sweat off his hands on his jeans, still fixated on his phone.

Conner stood and seized Kai's hand. "We're going. Stop looking at your damn phone."

Conner pulled his BMW up to the curb at The Village in front of the familiar plain cream-colored building in wood siding, the bottom floor a two-car carport and the top floor holding the living quarters. The sun was setting behind the walls of the complex. He turned to Kai, placing a hand on his shoulder. "Stop worrying. What's the worst that can happen? She says something nasty to you and we leave?"

Kai peeked at him, his nerves fraying. "It's not what she might say to me that I'm worried about. It's what she might say to you." He rubbed his eyebrow, frowning.

Conner grabbed his hand. "Stop it. There is nothing she can

say to me that's going to change how I feel about you."

Kai's turned to him. "Are you sure?" He certainly wasn't so sure about that. He attempted to swallow, but his throat was dry.

"I'm sure." Conner leaned over the center console and kissed him on the mouth. "Come on."

Kai opened the car door and stepped out.

May came trotting up to the car, her long dark hair bouncing across her shoulders, wearing a red blouse and jeans. "Kai." She clapped her hands together.

Kai walked around the car and threw his arms around her shoulders. "May." She was already making this easier for him.

She wrapped him up in a strong embrace. "Settle down, you're shaking." She brushed a hand down the back of his head.

He released her. "I'm sorry. I'm just so fucking nervous." This might be the best or the worst day of his life. He'd find out soon enough.

She glanced at Conner and held out her hand. "Hi, Conner, I'm May."

Conner took her hand and kissed the back of it. "I'm really happy to formally meet you. I know we saw each other at school." He released her hand.

"Oh . . ." She giggled and gave him a shy grin, tapping her fingers to her mouth. "Well, everyone knew who you were in school."

With a wide grin, Conner grabbed Kai's hand. "Well, shall we?"

Kai freed a long exhale. Under his breath, he said, "Fuck." How did he let Conner talk him into this?

As they strolled into the carport, Conner yanked Kai close and kissed his head. "Relax. We got this."

Kai looked at him and his heart swelled with emotion. God,

how he loved him.

They trotted up the steps, behind May, and into to the main room of the townhome.

Kai looked around him, the memories piling up in his mind, some good, but mostly bad. The old green couch was as worn as ever and the same old oval oak coffee and end tables surrounded it with the white ceramic lamps and maroon shades.

Kai's mother approached them, wearing a gray frilly blouse, and jeans, drying her hands on a green kitchen towel. Her cropped dark hair was streaked with gray, and her blue-eyed gaze caught on Kai. "Kai, it's about time you came home." Her eyes wrinkled as she smiled at him.

"Mom . . ." He tightened his hold on Conner's hand.

His mother stepped closer, then looked at their entwined hands. Her smile faded. She gestured to Conner. "So, this is the boy May's been gushing about?"

"Mom." May touched her mother's arm and whispered in her ear.

His mother pursed her lips, then held out her hand to Conner. "Pleased to meet you. Conner, is it?"

"Yes, ma'am." Conner shook her hand and nodded his head at her. "It's a pleasure meeting you."

"Aren't you going say he's told you so much about me?" She turned around and walked toward the kitchen of white cabinets with round, gold handles and white appliances. "I'm sure he has."

May followed her, talking too low for them to hear.

Kai's heart sank. It was going to be the worst day of his life. His lower lip trembled. A lump formed in his throat. This can't be. Under his breath, he said, "Fuck. Let's go." He went for the stairs, tugging Conner's arm.

"Stop." Conner said, between his teeth. Conner yanked him back and looked him in the eyes. "Don't run away. Face her."

In a soft, but stern voice, Kai said, "You don't know what you're saying. She's not someone you *face*, unless you want your face ripped *off*." They had to get out of there before things got worse.

His mother brought a large platter with spaghetti in marinara sauce to an ova, oak dining table with farm chairs, all just off the kitchen. The table was already set with plates, silverware, and glasses of water. "Come and eat."

"Come on, Kai. Let's just go and eat. Okay?" He took both of Kai's hands in his. "Come on."

"Kai, get your ass over here and eat. I didn't make all this food for nothing." She placed a hand on her hip and scowled.

Conner's eyes widened. "Jesus."

"See?" Kai wrinkled his forehead. "Now we stayed too long, and we have to go eat." *Yep, this is nothing like the nice family dinner Conner had imagined.*

"Come on, Kai and Conner. You two can sit here." May smiled and placed her hands on two chairs sitting opposite to where his mother stood.

Kai scoffed and took a seat, being careful not to look at his mother. Maybe she'd get better somehow. Maybe May would say something to keep her from berating him.

Conner sat next to him, grinning. "Looks great, ma'am."

"Thank you, Conner. And by the way, you can call me Margaret." She sat in a chair next to May and spooned pasta and sauce onto brown plates. "The parmesan is over there." She tilted her head.

Conner nodded, picked up the green container of parmesan and shook it over his noodles.

Kai stole a peek at his mother.

She twisted her fork in the pasta and glanced at him. "Son, you want me to get you a beer or something?"

And just like that, she changes. "Uh, no, I'll get it." Kai stood up and trotted over white linoleum to the refrigerator. "You want one, Conner?"

"Yes, please," Conner said.

"Me, too, Kai," May said.

He grabbed up three cans of beer, popped the tops on them and brought one to May, set one each in front of Conner and himself, then sat down and took a few gulps. Too bad they didn't bring the bourbon. He grinned.

"Guess you're pretty comfortable getting beers for people, being as you're a bartender and all." His mother shoved pasta into her mouth.

"He's a very good bartender, Margaret." Conner chuckled. "You should see the way he flips the bottles around at the bar." He drank his beer.

"I know. I've seen him. He's great." May grinned at Conner.

"What, like a circus act?" Margaret sniggered.

Kai set his fork down and stared at his plate. She was going to berate him all night. He knew it. His gut clenched.

Margaret pointed her fork at her daughter. "May here is going to be a nurse. She's a great catch, Conner, if you know what I mean."

"Mom!" May slapped her hand to the table.

Kai flinched and bit back tears. This was going to end with him running from the house. He knew it.

Conner took a deep breath, then grabbed Kai's hand and set them on the table. "Margaret, I love Kai. He's really special to me, and for me, he's perfect." His voice became thick. "In fact, there are a lot of people I could probably be with, but I only want him. He's everything I'm not. Everything I wish I could be."

Kai gulped over the thickness in his throat. *God, I love him. He's trying so hard.*

Margaret watched Conner, then ate more pasta and swallowed. "So, Kai is all that to you?"

"Yes. You raised a decent, strong man." Conner met her gaze straight on.

May clasped her hands at her chest. "Isn't that sweet, Mom? Kai found a really good guy who loves him."

"Conner, you passed the test." Margaret gave him a wide smile.

Kai blinked a few times. "What?"

"Conner doesn't look like a queer to me. I wanted to be sure he liked you. Guess he does." She sipped at her water.

"Jesus, Mom. What's a queer supposed to look like?" Kai lifted his brows. What sort of a thing was that to say?

"Like *you*." His mother snickered. "And don't use the Lord's name in vain. Did I raise you in a barn?" She shook her head.

Conner laughed. "That's sort of funny."

"No, it's not." Kai grinned and slapped at his arm. He thought over his mother's previous comment. *She wants to be sure Conner likes me.* His heart skipped and he watched her eat. That must be her way of looking out for him. It wasn't warm and fuzzy, but he'd take it.

"So, Kai, what's this stuff I hear from Bryce about a ghost in your house?" May sipped her beer.

Fucking Bryce. He didn't want to talk about this in front of Mom. Bringing up the little ghost chat he had with his father, if that was really what it was, would not be good. "Uh, nothing. We had some weird stuff happen in the house, but it's resolved now." He ate his pasta.

"Ghosts? What the hell, Kai?" His mother's eyes narrowed.

Shit. "It's nothing. It's done." He stared at his pasta, twirling his fork in it.

Conner swallowed his food and glanced at May. "Kai was getting some poltergeist activity in his house, swinging cabinet doors, silverware on the floor, that sort of thing. I had some friends that are paranormal investigators come and do an investigation. Turns out—"

"It's handled." Kai glared at him, squeezing his arm. "Right, Conner? It's handled."

Conner cocked his head. "It's uh, handled." He studied him.

"Not a big deal." Kai moved pasta around his plate and shook his head. They should hurry and get out of there before something else came up.

"Oh, but paranormal investigators, you mean like *Ghost Adventures*? I love those guys." May beamed at Conner.

"Uh, yeah," Conner glanced at Kai.

Kai slid his cell phone out of the back pocket of his jeans and opened the text interface.

Kai
I'll tell you about it later. We can't talk about this in front of Mom. It involves Dad.

May's phone, resting next to her plate, chimed. She picked it up and looked at the display, widening her eyes, then nodded at Kai.

Margaret scowled. "Okay, you two. What's going on? You think I'm stupid?"

May chuckled and touched her mother's arm. "No, of course not, Mom. You don't believe in ghosts anyway, right?"

Margaret gazed at May, then at Kai. "No, I don't. That's all bullshit. I can't believe you'd do something like that, Kai. I couldn't even get you to walk by the neighbor's house when they decorated it for Halloween. You were such a scaredy-cat."

Conner grinned at Kai, then cleared his throat and wiped his face with a napkin.

"I'm not a scaredy-cat. Anymore." Kai flashed his eyes at Conner. *Better keep your mouth shut.*

Conner placed his hand over his mouth, attempting to

stifle a laugh.

"What's so funny?" Kai lifted his brows at him.

"It's just... I can't..." Conner giggled and rose from the table, grabbing Kai's hand. In a soft voice, he said, "Come with me a minute."

"What?" Kai glanced at May, then his mother. What was wrong with him?

"Maybe he realized being queer wasn't for him after all." His mother snickered.

Conner freed a choked chuckle. "Funny, but no, that's not it."

Margaret poked her fork at Conner. "Then maybe you've lost your mind." She focused on Kai, smirking. "What have you done to him, Kai?"

Conner tugged on his hand. "Excuse us a moment." He lifted his chin at Kai.

"Oh, for fuck's sake." *What now?* Kai stood up and followed Conner down the hallway.

"Language, young man!" His mother called out.

Kai followed Conner down the hallway and stopped. "What's going on?"

Conner giggled. "I'm sorry, Kai. Your mother is actually pretty funny. You know that?"

Kai shifted his stance, his chest tightening. "Are you shitting me right now?"

Conner nodded. "I've never met anyone like her." He smiled at Kai. "I mean, she loves to tease you, and you take everything she says so seriously. I don't even think you realize it."

Kai pinched his lips. This wasn't fair. He wasn't seeing it right. "Conner, she may be funny right now, but it could change in an instant, and then she says things that aren't so funny. Cutting things."

Conner's face slackened. "I'm sorry. It's just, with how you were acting about coming here, I didn't know what to think. At least she's trying to be nice right now, right? In her own way, I mean." He took Kai's hands in his.

"Yeah." He'd never looked at his mother this way. May had told him the same thing before. Maybe they were right. Maybe he should stop being so suspicious of everything she said. "So, but don't say anything more about the ghost stuff. I don't want to have to bring up my father."

Conner lifted his brows. "Oh, yeah. Guess I didn't think of that. Sorry." He kissed his cheek. "So, let's go back out. Try to lighten up, okay? Just laugh at her little jokes."

He drew a deep inhale. "Okay."

Chapter Eighteen

Kai strolled hand in hand with Conner to his BMW, waiting at the curb, with May following. He looked up between a mixture of pines and palm trees at the starry night sky, then at Conner's car, lit by low, landscape lighting. Having a family dinner hadn't been so bad after all. It wasn't normal, but it wasn't terrible, either. He stopped at the car.

"So, I'm dying for you to tell me what happened in your ghost investigation." May widened her already large brown eyes.

"I think we talked to dad." How would she take it? Kai watched her reaction.

She dropped her mouth open. "Are you serious? Why do you say that?" She grabbed his arm.

"A man's voice came through on the spirit box. He said my name, and then Shizhé'é." Kai bit his lip. It was still hard to believe.

Her eyes shimmered as she brought her hands to her mouth. "Oh, my God."

Kai wrapped her up in a tight embrace and glanced at Conner.

Conner wrinkled his brow, placing his hand on Kai's back.

"At one point he said *love you* on the box." Kai shut his eyes, biting back tears. He wouldn't mention the whole two spirit thing. He was sure that last message was for both of them.

Her shoulders shook with a sob. "Kai, I wish I could remember him."

"Yeah, I barely do." The memory of his father's death flashed through Kai's mind. He shut it away. He should be strong for her. "Anyway." He patted her back and released her.

She swiped at her eyes and choked out a sharp laugh. "That's really fucking awesome. I wish I could have been there to hear it."

Conner hooked an arm around Kai's waist.

"Guess we should have recorded it." Kai nestled into his side. "It would have been really cool if you were there."

She glanced from Kai to Conner. "But you had Conner with you." She grinned.

Kai gave her a shy smile. "Yeah." He never would have been able to handle it without Conner.

"We also figured out the mystery of the Ashbrook Wash ghost." Conner offered her a wide grin.

"You did? What was it?" She lifted her brows.

Kai peered at her. "You know about that?"

"Sure, some guys in my grade at school used to go looking for it." She touched Conner's arm. "So?"

"So, it's a very tragic story. Turns out she was a teenage mother who buried a still born premature baby on the side of Kai's house. She couldn't leave the wash until the baby was properly buried. Or at least that's what we found with the medium in the séance we performed." Conner gazed at Kai.

"The police are still investigating." Kai took a deep breath and caught his gaze. Once that was over, he could move back into his own house.

"Wow, that's terrible." She furrowed her brows, covering her mouth. "The poor girl. Does that mean the Ashbrook Wash ghost is gone?"

"According to the medium, yes." Conner thinned his lips. "It's really sad . . ."

"Very sad." She shook her head. "I can't believe you guys

even brought in a medium." She smirked at Kai. "And you got my scaredy-cat brother to sit in on a séance."

"Hey." Kai slapped her arm. "I'm getting better with that."

Conner kissed his cheek. "I was with him."

"Well, I'm glad he has you, Conner." She cocked her head, grinning. "You know my brother had a crush on you in high school, right?"

Conner glanced at him. "Yeah. I think we both had crushes on each other. Too bad I was too chicken to do anything about it."

Her mouth dropped open. "You did? But weren't you with—"

"Yes, he was with Paige." Kai rolled his eyes. He was done bringing Paige up. "Anyhow, we need to get going."

"Sure." She touched Kai's arm. "Hey, I'll be around until Sunday. I know you work, but maybe we can figure something out."

"Yeah." Kai smiled at her. "Tonight . . . wasn't as bad as I thought it would be."

"Maybe mom's getting soft in her old age." She chuckled.

"I can hope." He bumped Conner's side. Dinner was over and it was time for their bourbon on the balcony. "Let's go." He released Conner and hugged May, then stepped to the car.

Conner gave her a quick embrace. "Bye, May. It was nice meeting you." He freed her.

"Nice to meet you, too." She waved. "Take care of my scaredy-cat brother."

Conner sniggered. "I will."

"Shut up," Kai said.

Kai waited on the outdoor couch under a brown blanket, watching the fountain spray high into the night air in the center of the park. A sliver of moon hung over the far-off shadows of mountains. He'd done it, he'd taken a guy home to meet his mother, and it didn't end in an argument or tears.

A cell phone rang from inside the apartment. Kai turned around. The sliding glass door was still open. He'd forgotten to shut it.

Conner placed his cell phone to his ear. "Hello?" He stopped at the dinette and set their glasses of bourbon down.

"Can't tomorrow. I'm out of town." Conner looked out toward the balcony.

Kai twisted around, facing the park. Was Conner going out of town this weekend and didn't tell him?

"Maybe. Yeah, I'm at a conference right now. I should be back this weekend." Conner chuckled.

What the fuck? Why was Conner lying about where he was? He pinched his lips.

"I don't know. I might have to uh, see my parents this weekend," Conner said. "Yeah, I'll let you know." He released a sharp laugh. "Talk to you later. Bye."

Kai gnawed his lower lip. What was that all about? Should he ask? He fingered the blanket. They were boyfriends now, he had a right to know what was going on, didn't he?

Conner stepped onto the balcony and slid the glass door closed. "You left this open?"

"Guess so." Kai took a deep inhale. He had to say something.

Conner took a seat beside Kai and handed him a glass of bourbon. "So, how are you feeling after—"

"Who was that on the phone?" *Way to blurt it out.* He thinned his lips.

Conner peered out over the park, then sipped his bourbon. "Lucas."

Kai's gut clenched. He wasn't sure what to think about that. Lucas had never liked him. Lucas was the asshole who'd bullied him the most. "So . . ."

"So, I'm going out with him and Ben on Saturday night."

Conner clenched his jaw. "I mean, you work, right?"

An ache grew in Kai's chest. Why did it hurt to hear this? "Where are you going?" He watched Conner closely.

"A club in Scottsdale." Conner glanced at him, then stared out at the park. "That's all right, isn't it? I mean, it's okay for me to see my friends on the nights you work, right?"

"S-sure." Was he going to get his bottle service and VIP treatment when he was out with Ben and Lucas? Would it be just like old times? He knew what those clubs were like. Women got into the VIP lounges for free to keep the guys happy and everyone was dressed to kill. Would Conner decide the life he'd left behind was better than this one and go back? The ache in his chest grew. "Why are you doing this?"

Conner gulped hard. "Doing what?" He drank a gulp of bourbon and hissed. "I'm not doing anything, Kai. I'm just going to hang out with my friends. I haven't seen them since . . ." He glanced at Kai. "Since we hooked up."

Now we're a hookup? He didn't like this. Not one bit. He knew exactly what was going on. It was the same thing that was going on in Sedona with the girls, the same thing that went on with Brent and Eric during the investigation. When was he going to come out? He could at least start with his friends. "You don't want to admit to them that we're together, do you." He glared at Conner.

Conner's breath caught. He stared at his bourbon, sitting in his lap, pouting. "I'm sorry, Kai. It's too soon for me. You know how they are. I can't tell them yet." He sniffled and rubbed his eyes.

Damn, he is closeted as fuck sometimes. Conner had been understanding about his mother — maybe it was time for him to be understanding about this. "Okay, but at some point, it's going to come out whether you want it to or not." He wrapped an arm around Conner's shoulders and kissed his cheek. "It's okay. I'll wait."

"Thanks. Maybe I'll break it to them on Saturday. Okay?" Conner gazed at him and kissed him on the lips. "I love you, Kai. You know that, right?"

"Yeah, I know." He sipped his bourbon. "I love you, too."

Kai rolled onto his side on the bed, dozing lightly. Warmth pressed up behind him. Something hard poked at his backside. He woke, but kept his eyes closed. Light caresses skimmed up his chest, then plunged to his groin, placing soft strokes over his cock. Feathery kisses shivered over his neck and shoulders. A soft, hungry moan sounded behind him.

"Kai . . ." Conner's breath quickened. He whispered, "I need you."

"Mmm . . ." Kai rocked his hips back, his buttocks meeting with Conner's solid cock. In a mumbled voice, he said, "You want it again?"

Conner freed a ragged breath, kissing his neck with more intensity, stroking faster. "I dreamt about you."

As Kai's cock hardened with Conner's touch, he curled the corners of his mouth. "Let me guess, a wet dream?" A jolt of pleasure shook through him. He gasped.

"Yeah." Conner thrust against the crease of his buttocks. "I woke up before I came, though." His body shuddered and he released a deep groan.

"Good." He twisted to face Conner, biting his lip. "I'd rather you save that for me." He slicked his hand with saliva, then rubbed Conner's seeping cock, swirling pre-seed over the tip, devouring his mouth in intense kisses.

Conner whimpered, thrusting into his palm, pumping Kai's shaft with erratic jerks of his hand.

As sensation buzzed inside him, he licked down Conner's neck and bit at an earlobe.

Conner groaned. "Fuck, Kai. I'm close." His body quivered. "Go fast and hard."

Kai opened his eyes, taking in the pure lust in Conner's gaze, the swollen, parted lips. He quickened the pace of his hand and watched. He'd never tire of seeing him come.

As Conner closed his eyes, his brows wrinkled, and he raked his teeth over his lower lip. His cock hardened further, and his body shook, seed spurting up between them, harsh gasps erupting from his throat.

Fuck that's hot. "Oh, shit." As Conner continued pumping his shaft through it all, a surge of sensation pulsed Kai's cock and waves of delicious orgasm coursed through his body, shooting his seed to mix with Conner's. As it calmed, he took heavy breaths. He thought back over the evening. He'd jerked Conner once and gave him a blowjob before bed already. *Damn.* "Shit, Conner. How many times can you come in a day?"

A lazy grin quirked Conner's mouth and he rolled to his back. "With you, or normally?"

Kai freed a short chuckle. "Okay, with me."

"I'm not sure. I don't think we've hit that limit yet." Conner shifted to his side, looking him over, then kissed his lips. "No one has ever turned me on like this."

"So you keep saying." Kai smiled, wiped his hand on the sheets, then placed it on Conner's cheek. "Someday, we should spend the whole day in bed and see what that limit is."

Conner grinned. "Maybe this weekend."

"Yeah, maybe this weekend." Kai kissed Conner's cheek.

Kai, wearing his work attire, strolled to the POS terminal and clocked in. He was one more shift away from having two days off and boy, did he need them after this week.

Bryce came up behind Kai. "That was cool of Conner to get his pastor to bless our house." He clocked in at the POS.

"Yeah, now that we've done the sage again, blessed the

house and the police are gone, we can finally go home." Kai looked out over the restaurant, thinking through what needed to be done before the dinner rush came.

"I'm going home tonight. I'm not waiting for the game camera footage. I mean, John said the ghost should be gone now." Bryce sighed. "I need to get out of my mom's house."

"Yeah, that has to be hard." Kai touched his arm. "Thanks for doing that, though. You know, letting me stay at Conner's alone."

Bryce gave him a sly grin. "You deserve it. I've never seen you so happy."

That was an unusual comment from Bryce. Kai narrowed his eyes at him. "You're not going to give me shit about it?"

"No. I got sick of watching you pine over Conner." Bryce laughed.

"I wasn't pining." Kai scoffed. There was the typical Bryce.

Bryce took a step toward the kitchen, then stopped. "Oh." He tapped Kai's shoulder. "I forgot to tell you. The police sergeant called me. He said he can't give me specifics, but the girl that was abducted used to live in the house next door. Not our house. Back then, our house wasn't even built. So they think the baby was buried there when the land was empty."

"So, the Ashbrook Wash ghost girl never lived in our house?" Kai cocked his head.

"Yeah, it's funny no one found the remains when they were building the place." Bryce scratched his head.

Kai shrugged. "Well, maybe it moved when that big storm came through. Who knows?" A shiver tickled up his spine. "All I know is I'm glad it's over."

"Yeah, me, too." Bryce drew a deep inhale. "Get to work." He slapped Kai's arm.

Kai chuckled.

Kai dried a wine glass with a white towel, scanning over

the mostly full bar.

Beth poured beers at the taps, then lifted her chin at him, her focus beyond him.

He turned around.

Brandon stepped through the high-top tables, wearing a black shirt and jeans, then took a seat at the bar. "Hi, beautiful."

Shit, not tonight. "Hey, Brandon. What can I get you?" He set the wine glass on the cooler.

"How about one of your delicious mojitos?" Brandon let a coy grin work over his mouth. "And do it the right way." He winked at him.

"Sure." Kai perused the bottles in the speed well, finding the ones he could flip, then set about making the drink, twirling the bottles in the air, pouring liquid into the shaker on the drip rail, then shaking it and slapping the mint before giving the drink a shot with the soda gun. As he gave Brandon his best smile, he twirled the napkin at him, then set the drink on it.

A few claps rang out in the restaurant.

Kai widened his smile. "Menu?"

"Yes, please." Brandon sipped his drink. "This is great, as usual."

Kai grabbed a menu off the stack on the island and set it down in front of Brandon.

Brandon grabbed his wrist. "Where's your big player tonight?"

With a huff, Kai yanked his hand back. "He's not a player. He's my boyfriend."

"Really." Brandon slid his phone out of the front pocket of his jeans and opened the interface.

Kai furrowed his brows. "What are you doing?" Whatever it was, it couldn't be good.

"I have something to show you." Brandon swiped across

the display, then tapped it. "Here, take a look at this and tell me that's not him."

"Shit." Kai snatched the phone from him and peered at it. The lower half of a man's face displayed on the screen, a pointed nose, generous lips, and an inch-long scar under the left eye. His gut wrenched. His breath caught. *My scar. The one I love so much. There's no mistaking it.* "What the fuck is this? You taking pictures of Conner now?"

"It's his profile picture, Kai. Swipe to the right." Brandon gave him a smug grin.

He gulped over a lump in his throat. *Can't be. This must be a mistake.* He swiped. Text displayed on the screen.

Only interested in quick hookups. Bottom. Willing to do —

Kai tossed the phone on the counter. He refused to read any more. It didn't mean anything. "So, he used gay hook up apps. Lots of guys do, right?" He glared at Brandon. "If you can see his profile, you must be on there, too, right?"

"Yeah, but I don't have a boyfriend. Why wouldn't he shut it down if you two are together?" Brandon lifted his brows.

"Maybe he hasn't had time to." Kai's chest tightened. It had been weeks. Why was Connor still on there? Was Conner with his friends right now, or having a hookup tonight? He picked up the towel, staring at the back bar. He hated feeling like this. It hurt.

"Kai, it's not the only one. He's on several."

Tears stung his eyes. "So? What are you trying to say?" He clenched his jaw. Nausea balled up in his gut. He forced himself to face Brandon. Between his teeth, he said. "What are you trying to say?"

Brandon widened his eyes and held up his palms to Kai. "Hey, if I'm in a relationship with someone, that shit stops. Know what I mean?"

Beth walked down the bar and placed her hand on Kai's

shoulder. "Hey, what's up?" She glanced at Brandon, then focused on Kai. "You okay?"

His breath hitched. "I'm not okay." He sniffled. He couldn't break down at the bar if that was where this was going. "I need to go outside for a moment."

"Sure." She patted his back. "You go, I got this."

He swiped at his eyes, then plodded through the kitchen and out the heavy, gray metal door, into the breezeway. "Fuck." Pain wrenched his chest. He paced up and down the cement walkway, fisting and opening his hands. There had to be an explanation. This had to be how Conner had gotten experience with guys while still dating Paige. But that meant he was cheating on her. Or did they have an open relationship? Or had this all happened in the brief time after they broke up?

He growled and continued pacing. Why was Conner so secretive about everything? The memory of the allegation at The Alamo flashed into his mind. *I told him I thought hookup apps were creepy.* That was why. It had to be. But why the fuck did he still have active profiles? If he texted Conner right now, would he even text back? If he was hooking up with some guy, probably not. He slid the phone out of his back pocket and opened the text interface.

Kai
Hey, where did you end up?

He watched the interface, gulping hard. *Delivered* showed under the text, then, *Read 6:57 PM.* Dots flickered at him. He rubbed his nose and sniffled.

Conner
Having dinner at a Thai restaurant. I have to bring you here next time. It's really good.

God, I'm so stupid. Nothing sounded out of the ordinary.

Why didn't he trust him? Maybe Conner hadn't thought to turn the profiles off. Maybe it just slipped his mind. Conner couldn't have met up with anyone since they started dating—they were together all the time. They'd have to talk about this later. He drew a deep breath, wiped his eyes, and walked into the kitchen of the restaurant. He'd let Beth take Brandon's order and deal with him the rest of the night.

Kai sat on the outdoor couch, wrapped up in a brown blanket, glass of bourbon in his hand. He looked out over the park, watching the glow from a full moon shimmer off the lake. The fountain wasn't running. It was too late. He thought back. This was his third glass of bourbon. He held it up and tilted the glass, watching the liquid ripple. Conner was still out. He picked up his phone, resting in the folds of the blanket and held it to his face. It read *1:17 A.M.* He opened the text interface and read the messages.

Kai
When will you be home? I'm off work.

Kai
Where are you?

Kai
It's late. Are you okay?

The messages were all delivered, but none of them read. Could something have happened to him? Pain pierced his heart. This wasn't like Conner. Something must have happened. Should he start calling hospitals or something? What if he was hurt?

A white Mercedes coupe drove up the avenue and stopped below the building.

He set his bourbon on the glass tabletop and stepped to the

red railing, then looked down, bending over it.

A woman wearing a tiny red dress and heels got out, her dirty-blonde hair falling in loose waves around her shoulders. She trotted to the passenger side of the car and opened it. "Conner, we're home. Time to get out."

Kai's heart lurched. "Fuck." He grabbed his chest. "No . . ." This wasn't happening. It wasn't what it looked like. Conner was still friends with Paige, right?

She reached in the car and yanked on an arm. "Conner, you have to get out."

"Fuck this." Kai dropped the blanket, flung the sliding glass door open, raced through the front door and took the stairs two at a time, his heart pounding against his breastbone, his breath coming in quick pants. As he reached the bottom of the stairs, he sprinted to the street.

Conner's arm was wrapped around Paige's shoulders, his head hanging forward. Slurring, Conner said, "Take me to bed."

Kai halted, staring at them.

Paige's gaze caught on Kai. She dropped her mouth open. "Kai? Kai Nez? What are you doing here?"

"Kai?" Conner lifted his head. "Fuck, Kai." He wrenched his arm free from her shoulders and stumbled toward Kai. "Baby, take me to bed."

"Baby?" Paige furrowed her brows. "What's going on here?"

Conner threw his arms around Kai's shoulders. "I missed you so much." He nuzzled Kai's neck.

What the hell am I supposed to do? He's fucking outing himself. He hooked an arm around Conner's waist. "Boy, he's uh, drunk, huh? He even called me baby." He freed a strangled laugh.

Conner laid his head on Kai's shoulder.

She blinked a few times. "What are you doing here?"

He had to think quick. "I had some problems at my place, and I work across the street." He pointed at the restaurant. "Conner was nice enough to let me stay here for a few, uh, nights." He gave her his best forced smile. "I uh, was just on the balcony upstairs and saw you pull up. I figured you could use some help."

She placed her hands on her hips, then looked them up and down. "Okay, well—"

"I'll take care of him. Don't worry." They needed to leave. Now. He turned them both around and walked Conner to the stairwell. "Bye." He waved behind him.

As they trudged up the stairs, a hot knot tightened in his chest. Fucking Conner had been out with Paige all night. Was that why he didn't text back? Was he too busy looking at her to look at his fucking phone? He reached the top of the stairs and opened the door, led Conner into the bedroom and tossed him on the bed. *This feels fucking familiar.*

Conner held his arms up. "Kai, come lie down with me."

"No." He'd get him undressed and then go to sleep. It could wait until morning. He scowled and slid Conner's shoes and socks off, then knelt on the bed, his knees on either side of Conner's hips. He unfastened his jeans.

Conner propped up on his elbows, a lopsided grin spreading over his mouth. "Are you going to suck me off?"

"Fuck, no." He shook his head, clenching his jaw. This was just perfect. Conner was so drunk he had no clue what was going on. As he tugged Conner's jeans down his legs, he glanced up.

Conner's hard cock jutted up from his boxer briefs. "Come on, Kai. I'm so fucking hot for you right now."

He released a harsh exhale. "No, Conner. Not tonight." He wouldn't be swayed. He tugged Conner's jeans off his legs.

Conner dropped to his back. "Fine." He rubbed his hand over his swollen cock through his briefs and moaned, rocking his hips.

Kai jumped on the bed, seizing Conner's hand, hovering over him on straight arms, peering into his face. Conner really had no fucking clue. "Stop it. Look at me, damn it."

As Conner's gaze caught on Kai's, his face went slack. "A-are you mad at me?"

"Yes, I'm fucking angry as hell." Which was worse—Paige taking him home, the app profiles, or all the fucking worry he'd been through tonight? He glared at him, then sat on the bed and drew up his knees, his arms wrapping around them.

Conner rounded his eyes. "Why?" He came up to sitting and raked a hand through his bangs. "What's wrong?"

"For starters, you didn't text me back and I was worried as fuck about you." Kai rested his head on his arms. This was so messed up. He shouldn't be talking to a drunk. It wasn't worth it. He knew better.

"Kai, I'm sorry. I-I didn't see—"

"Why, because you were with fucking Paige all night?" He punched the bed. "Fuck."

Conner flinched.

I have to stop before I bring up the app profiles. That was better left to the morning. Kai breathed deeply. He needed to calm down, and Conner was in no shape to listen to anything. He probably wouldn't even remember tonight. He stared at the wall. "Let's not talk about this right now. Let's just go to sleep. We can talk in the morning when you're sober."

"I'm pretty sober right now." Conner swallowed and looked around the room. "I-I need some water." He climbed off the bed and left.

Kai squeezed his eyes shut. What should he do? This discussion should wait. But he'd already said so much.

Conner entered the room with two open bottles of water, wearing only his black button-down shirt and boxer briefs. He handed a water bottle to Kai. "I told you I was still friends with Paige." He gulped the water down. "I'm sorry I didn't see your texts."

"Okay, well, you told me you were going out with Ben and Lucas. You didn't say anything about Paige." Kai sipped the water, keeping his gaze on the gray and white striped duvet.

Conner sat on the bed. "You're jealous." He placed a hand on Kai's knee.

He grimaced. "Why wouldn't I be? You two were together forever. You only just broke up. You got shitfaced with—"

"Nothing happened." Conner crept next to him and draped an arm over his shoulders. "I love you, not her." He kissed his head. "I swear it. We're just close friends now, that's it."

Kai scoffed, rubbing his forehead. "But she doesn't know about us." Nobody in Conner's world knew about them.

Conner let loose a long exhale and removed his arm from Kai's shoulders. "You need to give me time."

The scent of alcohol floated in on Conner's breath. Kai focused on him. Was he really as sober as he said he was? Probably not. This was pointless. "Let's just go to bed. Okay?"

Conner frowned. "We shouldn't go to bed mad at each other. My parents always said that."

And at the rate we're going, will I ever meet them? "I'm not really all that mad anymore. I mean, there are some things we need to talk about, but not now." He climbed off the bed and went through the apartment, shutting off lights, clearing his head, then walked back into the bedroom.

Conner lay on his back, under the covers of the bed, watching Kai.

Kai undressed, shut the light off, then made his way under the covers, lying on his back next to Conner. Hopefully, he could go to sleep now and wouldn't lie awake thinking about this all night.

Conner rolled onto his side, nuzzling into Kai's neck,

wrapping a leg and arm around him. "All I wanted all night was to be with you like this. I didn't want anyone else."

"Yeah, okay." Kai kissed his head. Then why didn't he come home sooner or check his text messages? He shook the thought from his mind. He needed sleep first. Then he'd see how everything felt in the morning.

"I love you, Kai."

"Love you, too."

Chapter Nineteen

Kai, wearing a white shirt and jeans, sat on the patio at the restaurant, overlooking the park and fountain in the mid-morning sunshine. It was weird eating there on his day off, but with football season they had good a breakfast menu on Sundays, and he could take advantage of his employee discount. He peered at Conner. "What are you thinking?"

Conner, dressed in a tan, long-sleeve t-shirt, and jeans, scanned a small menu. "Probably the all-meat omelet. I need some grease." He rubbed his belly.

Kai nodded. Conner hadn't said a word about last night. Did he even remember what happened?

Bryce walked up to them with an electronic tablet in his hand. "If it isn't the lovebirds."

Kai released a quick laugh. "Right." Maybe before last night. He frowned.

"Hey, I slept at the house last night." Bryce scanned around him. "No ghost."

"Seriously? So it's really gone?" Kai lifted his brows. He could finally go home.

Conner thinned his lips. "How can you be so sure?"

"There's been no activity, nada, for at least twenty-four hours. That would have been a record before." Bryce tapped his finger to the tablet. "I don't feel anything there, either. Before, you could feel something watching you, you know?"

"Yeah . . ." A shiver raced up Kai's spine. "So, it doesn't feel creepy in there anymore?"

"Not one bit." Bryce lifted his chin at Kai. "Anyway, I got

to get to work. Do you guys know what you want?"

"Get us both the all-meat omelet and an IPA." Kai grabbed Conner's menu, then handed both of them to Bryce.

"Sure." Bryce trotted off.

"You ordered me a beer?" Conner smirked and glanced toward the park.

"I figured you needed it. Hair of the dog." Kai shifted in his seat, studying him. When would they talk about last night? "Do you uh, remember much from last night?"

Conner winced and stared at the table. "I remember you being so mad at me about Paige you didn't want to have sex."

"Jesus." Kai shook his head. Did everything have to revolve around sex? "Conner, it wasn't just that. I uh, found out something last night." He narrowed his eyes, watching him. He had to be very careful.

"What do you mean?" Conner tapped his finger on the table.

"You have um . . . you use ah . . ." Shit, he couldn't say it. He released a breath of air, then bit his lip.

"What?" Conner straightened, focusing on him. "Just say it already. What did you find out?"

"I know you have profiles on some gay hookup apps." *Way to blurt it out, as usual.* Kai furrowed his brows.

"No, I don't." Conner glared at him. "Who the fuck told you that?"

Kai bit his lip, then released it. Why would he lie about this? "I saw it. I saw the picture." He shook his head, grimacing. "It was definitely you. No mistaking that scar under your eye." The scar he loved. His heart ached. This wasn't going well.

"So, what, do you think I'm a creep now? Is that why you didn't want to do anything last night?" Conner's voice broke. He rubbed his eyes, clenching his jaw.

Bryce dropped off their beers, stared at them both for a

moment, then scurried off.

"No." Shit, Conner was losing it. Kai placed his hand on Conner's knee, caressing it. "I know a lot of guys use those. It's just not something I do."

"Then why are you bringing it up?" Conner looked at him with glossy eyes.

"Why are your profiles still active?" He bit at his thumbnail. All he wanted at this point was to know that they'd be shut down. Why he had them didn't matter anymore. "I mean, shouldn't you shut those down now?"

"Yeah, sorry." Conner sighed and sipped his beer, staring at the tabletop. "How did you know?"

Shit, how am I supposed to tell him about Brandon? But he had to. He couldn't lie. "Brandon showed me last night." He braced himself.

Conner growled. Through his teeth, he said, "Fucking Brandon? Was he in here last night while you were working?" He curled his lip.

"Y-yeah, but I let Beth take care of him. I only served him one drink." He parted his lips, taking deep breaths. He didn't do anything wrong. He was not the one with profiles on multiple hookup apps.

Bryce dropped off their food and looked from Conner to Kai, squeezing Kai's shoulder. "Everything all right here?"

Conner hung his head. "Yeah, it's just fucking fine." He wrung his hands in his lap.

Maybe they should have had this conversation before they left the apartment. He sipped his beer, keeping his gaze on Conner. He looked way more upset than he should be. Maybe there was more to it.

Bryce focused on Kai, furrowing his brows. "*You* okay?"

Conner glared at Bryce, snarling. "He's fine. Leave us alone."

"Jesus, man. Settle down." Bryce widened his eyes, holding

The Haunting Crush

his hands out. "Maybe you two should just eat your food and quit talking. Cool off a bit."

Kai peered at his food. He wasn't all that hungry now. "Yeah. You're right." He placed a hand on Conner's forearm. "Let's just eat, and we can continue this another time."

Bryce walked off.

Conner nodded his head. "Let's talk about something else."

What else was there? "Uh, I should probably go back to my place today, since the ghost seems to be gone." He cut into his omelet and took a bite.

"So now you're moving out." Conner set his silverware on his plate.

Kai dropped his mouth open. What was he supposed to say to that? It wasn't like they were formally living together. He looked out at the park, the sunlight shimmering off the water of the lake. He guessed the timing was bad. Maybe Conner thought he was leaving because of the hookup apps. "Look, I'll uh, leave a toothbrush at your place, okay?" He forced a chuckle. He had to lighten the mood somehow.

Conner picked up his fork and cut into his omelet. "No, don't."

What the fuck does that mean? He should leave it alone. They shouldn't argue here. He worked here. He shoveled food into his mouth.

Kai followed Conner out of the glass front doors of the restaurant. Breakfast had been tense. Something was definitely not right with Conner. He strolled beside him up the palm and palo verde tree-lined avenue toward Conner's apartment.

"I don't want you to leave." Conner grabbed Kai's hand.

Kai drew a deep inhale. What could he say to that? "Conner, I—"

"I don't want to fight anymore." Conner glanced at him,

pinching his lips. "Can we just go home and be together today? Let's not talk anymore." He quickened his stride, tugging him along.

Kai trotted to keep up with him. What was the hurry? "I have to go—"

"Stop it, Kai. Just stop." Conner ran across the street, hauling Kai behind him.

Kai's long hair bounced along his back as he ran. What the fuck was going on?

Conner hauled him into the bottom of the stairwell of the apartment and shoved him up against the wall.

Kai's back hit with a thud. "What are you doing?" He gazed at him.

Conner crushed his lips in an intense kiss, his chest flush with Kai's. He broke the kiss, his face strained. "I'm sorry you had to see those. The profiles. It's not—"

"What the fuck, Mitchell? You a faggot now?"

Fuck no. Kai twisted his face toward the street. "Lucas."

Conner jumped off Kai, widening his eyes, his body trembling. "L-Lucas? B-Ben?"

Lucas and Ben strolled into the bottom of the stairwell, smirks on both of their faces, then stopped.

Lucas looked Kai up and down. "I mean, we all knew about Kai. But you?" He pointed at Conner. "What the fuck? Did he turn you gay?" He burst out into a harsh laugh.

"N-no." Conner hung his head.

"Paige said she saw you two together here last night. We didn't believe her. But I guess she was right." Ben shook his head, snickering.

Lucas stepped toward Conner and lifted his head by the chin, sneering. "All those years we played ball and showered together. I bet you were checking us all out, weren't you, Mitchell? Did you like what you saw?"

Conner looked away.

A hot ball of rage built in Kai's chest. He smacked Lucas' hand away, putting himself between him and Conner. "Fuck off, asshole." He clenched his teeth.

"Oh, look, the little gay boy speaks." Lucas leered and puffed out his chest. "Or what?"

Kai fisted his hand and brought it to head level. "Just fuck off. You've always been a nasty motherfucker. Looks like you never grew up. Still bullying people after all these years?"

"You going to hit me, Kai?" A wicked smile spread over Lucas' mouth.

"Hey, that's enough." Ben grabbed Kai's hand and pushed Lucas back. "You don't have to be such a dick, Lucas. We were just going to give him shit. You're taking this too far."

"Yeah, whatever. But we didn't think we'd find him fucking around with Kai . . . literally." Lucas stepped back and raked a hand through his short, blond hair, growling. "Conner, we need to talk. Now." He turned and stepped toward the street.

Kai grabbed Conner's hand.

Conner yanked free. "Not now, Kai." He flashed his ice-blue eyes at Kai. "I'll be back." He walked off, following Ben and Lucas.

"No fucking way." He furrowed his brows, staring after Conner. Why the hell would he go with them after that? It made no fucking sense. He glanced up the stairwell. What was he supposed to do now? *Just sit here and wait?* He shook his head. What other choice did he have? He trudged up the stairs to the apartment.

Kai sat on the couch and brought his phone to his face to read the time. Two hours had passed since Conner walked off with his asshole friends. He glanced at his suitcase, packed and ready to go to his own place. At this point, he was very ready.

He stood up and walked out the sliding glass door to the balcony, then leaned over the red railing and looked up and down the street. No sign of Conner. Where did they take him? What the hell did they have to talk about? He pursed his lips. Conner did say he'd be back. But when?

With a sigh, he turned and stepped inside, then shut the door. He should try texting. He held up his phone and opened the text interface.

Kai
When will you be back?

He watched phone for an answer. *Delivered* showed up under his text, then *read*. The three dots blinked underneath.

Conner
Not sure.

"That's fucking great." What was he supposed to do now? He was tired of waiting. He released a long exhale. He should just go home. He opened the text interface again.

Kai
I'm heading home. Let me know when you want to get together.

Conner
OK

"That's it, then." He grabbed the handle on his suitcase and trudged out of the apartment, locking the door on his way.

Kai pulled his blazer into the carport of his duplex and parked. He studied the stucco wall in front of him. What would he do if he went in and all the cabinet doors were open? Go back to Conner's? Somehow, that didn't feel like an option anymore. Conner hadn't protested his leaving at all, this time. Something felt . . . off.

He got out of the SUV and tugged his suitcase out of the back tailgate, then rolled it up to the door and unlocked it. As he swung the door open, his heart quickened. He gulped hard. What would he find? Was the ghost really gone? He scanned over the kitchen. The cabinet doors were all closed, glasses sat on the counter by the sink, no drawers open or silverware on the floor. He curled his lips in a faint smile. "Goodbye, Ashbrook Wash ghost girl."

He walked inside, rolling his suitcase behind him, and stopped in the main room, searching for anything out of place. Everything was right where it should be. No weird feelings anymore. Bryce was right. It was gone. Everything could go back to normal now. He rolled his suitcase into his bedroom to unpack.

Kai lay on the couch on his side, dozing while the television droned on with a random action movie.

"Hello, hello?" Bryce's voice snaked in from the kitchen.

Kai opened his eyes and rose to sit on the couch. "Shit." What time was it? If Bryce was home, it had to be after four. Why hadn't Conner contacted him by now?

Bryce walked into the main room in his restaurant t-shirt and black jeans. "Hey. So, any activity?" He stopped in front of Kai and placed his hands on his hips, looking around him.

"Nope." Kai rubbed his eyes. "So peaceful I apparently fell asleep." Plus, he was still tired after the late night he'd had. *Fuck Conner.* Where was he?

Bryce sat next to him. He tapped Kai's thigh. "So, what's up with you and Conner? You two didn't look so happy at breakfast and I see he's not here."

"Yeah, some shit went down." He rested his elbows on his thighs, thinking through the last day. So many bad things had happened all at once. Where to start? "I found out he's on a bunch of gay hookup apps."

"No shit?" Bryce widened his eyes and sank into the couch. "Like he's still using them even with you two being together?"

Kai wrinkled his brows. "No, I don't think he was using them. But his profile was still active." He hung his head. Memories flashed through his mind. "Fuck, he was out on Saturday night with Lucas, Ben and Paige and got shitfaced. She drove him home and saw us together. So Lucas and Ben came to . . ." He thought back over the exchange. "Actually, I don't know what the fuck they were trying to do. They saw us kissing by Conner's apartment and called us faggots."

"Seriously? What a couple of morons. Those guys were always assholes." Bryce shook his head. "So, did you tell them off?"

"Yeah." He stared at the black coffee table. Why didn't Conner tell them off? He had never backed down in the past. Why now? Because it was his *friends*? "Fucking Lucas was being a real dick. Ben calmed him down. I was about to punch the fucker." He sighed. "Anyway, they said they had to talk to Conner, and he went off with them. I guess he's still with them." But that was hours ago. Had Conner texted while he was sleeping? He picked up his phone from the coffee table.

"So, is Conner coming over?" Bryce wiggled his brows.

"I don't know, actually." Kai opened the text interface. No new messages. "I haven't heard from him for a few hours." He should text him.

Kai
Do you want to come over here?

Delivered showed under the message, then *read*. Kai watched for the three dots, but nothing came up. "Something's not right." He chewed his lower lip. His heart pinched.

How could Conner still be out with them? He said he'd be back.

Bryce laid a hand on Kai's shoulder. "What do you mean?"

Kai set the phone down. Maybe Conner was busy and couldn't text back. Maybe he was driving or something. "I don't know. It just feels like something is off." He glanced at Bryce, his chest tightening. What if Lucas and Ben were making Conner have second thoughts about them? "You don't think . . ."

"What?"

Kai drew a deep breath. "You don't think Lucas and Ben could talk Conner into breaking up with me, do you?"

"Dude, it's so fucking obvious that Conner is totally in love with you. I doubt it. I mean, how could they do that? *Why* would they do that?" Bryce shifted on the couch and laid an arm over Kai's shoulders. "If anything, they should be happy for him. If they aren't, then they're even worse jerks than I thought they were."

Kai released a ragged breath. "I don't know. Conner isn't out. He's been really secretive about some things, and maybe he's rethinking it. He said he would be right back, but it's been hours." He picked up his phone and peered at the display. "He isn't texting back now."

"Maybe he needs some time and space to think things through." Bryce pursed his lips. "You two have been together nonstop for weeks now."

Kai's heart lurched. "What do you mean by that?" He studied Bryce. He was pretty sure this wasn't something he wanted to hear.

Bryce cocked his head. "Well, if you're saying that he's not out and Paige basically outed him, then maybe he needs some time to regroup and figure out how to actually *come* out." He tightened his hold on Kai's shoulders. "Relax, remember when I outed you? You were pretty upset. I didn't think you'd ever talk to me again."

Kai freed a choked chuckle. "Yeah, that's true. It takes some time to figure out." But why wouldn't Conner want to figure it out together? Conner knew he'd been through it before.

"If I were you, I'd just give him the space he needs. He'll come around. You'll see." Bryce dropped his arm from Kai's shoulders. "Anyway, I need to shower."

"Yeah." Kai nodded his head. His chest ached. He didn't want Conner to have to face this alone. He should be with him. But Bryce was right. He should let Conner come to him when he was ready. He shouldn't force anything.

Kai ran down the trail in the mid-morning sun, fighting off the ache in heart. He focused on the cacti, scrubby bushes and short trees surrounding him, the birds fluttering as he sprinted by them. Sweat beaded and rolled down his face and back. His AirPods played a hard rock song. Conner hadn't texted. Conner hadn't come to see him. Conner had vanished. Just like the ghost. They were both gone. He was alone.

It was Tuesday—he had to start his work week tonight. He had a whole day to feel shitty about it. He'd decided to give Conner space, but this was getting ridiculous. Now it was time to make peace with it. His running pace matched the beat, panting, his lungs burning. He came to a brittlebush, its scruffy branches almost blocking the path. He sped around it. *There's the rock I found Conner sitting on that day.*

His breath hitched. He slowed, taking deliberate steps, and stopped, bent over, his hands on his knees. In a strangled voice, he said. "Fuck." He clenched his teeth. Tears stung his eyes. He wasn't going to cry, not yet. Conner needed time. Or was he gone, just like before? His chest shook with a sob. He shouldn't think like that. Conner wouldn't do that.

He glanced at the rock Conner had sat on when he'd twisted his ankle. A hot tear journeyed down his cheek.

"Fuck, Conner. Where the hell are you?" He sat on the rock and placed his face in his hands, his elbows resting on his knees. He drew deep breaths. Conner had disappeared before. He was probably doing it again. *He's not strong like I am.* That's what Conner had told him. Maybe he couldn't handle it. "But you said you loved me . . ."

The tears came in a torrent of pain, overwhelming him. His chest heaved with sobs. He surrendered, weeping into the palms of his hands, the tears falling one after another. The ache in his chest was unbearable. How was he going to get through this? He'd never hurt like this before. He'd never been in love before. It had only been a crush. That's all it was ever supposed to be. Why had he let Conner in? He knew better. Between sobs, he said, "I'm so fucking stupid." He wrapped his arms around his waist, rocking, hanging his head. He was more than stupid. "I'm so fucking pathetic." He wept.

Kai looked out over the restaurant, the groups of people coming in for their evening meal and a few drinks. He scanned the bar for empties. An elderly man had an empty wine glass in front of him. He stepped to him. "You need another?"

The man smiled at him. "Sure, kid."

He grabbed a wine glass and the bottle from the island, poured the wine and set it down. "There you go."

"Thanks." The man sipped his wine.

Kai sighed. He needed to keep busy. It was the only thing keeping him from falling apart. Everything in the restaurant held memories of Conner now. He had to stop thinking about him and get over him. It was Thursday already, and he still hadn't heard anything since Sunday. *Not one text. Nothing.* Obviously, Conner wasn't strong enough to be out and had decided this whole gay relationship thing was not for him. He pinched his lips. The fucker could have at least told him to his face it was over. This was a pussy way out.

He picked up a white towel and opened the dishwasher, then pulled out a beer glass and wiped it down. His gaze captured a familiar blonde woman stepping through the high-top tables, following a hostess. Under his breath, he said, "Fuck, Liz."

Liz sat at a high-top table for two and hung her black purse over the back of the chair.

His chest tightened and a lump formed in his throat. *Fucking Conner better not start bringing his God damned dates in here now.* Didn't he have any clue how much that would hurt him? He turned around and swallowed hard, biting back tears threatening to surface. If Conner came in to sit with her, he was leaving. He glanced at Beth, pouring drinks at the other end of the bar. Beth could handle it. It wasn't very busy tonight. Janice would understand.

Bryce strolled out from the swinging kitchen door with an electronic tablet in his hand, scanning the tables, then glanced at him. He frowned and switched his stride to stand next to Kai. "Hey, you okay? You don't look so good."

The pain in Kai's chest heightened. He drew a deep breath, grabbing the edge of the island counter. "No, I'm not okay." How could he possibly be okay with any of this?

Bryce twisted his mouth and peered out into the dining area. "That woman Conner used to hang out with is here."

"I know." *Master of the obvious, Bryce.* Kai blinked a few times. He had to hold it together.

"You think Conner is coming to meet her?"

Kai clenched his jaw, clutching the counter, taking ragged breaths.

"He wouldn't do that, Kai. That's just fucking sadistic. I mean, come on, would he really do that to you?" Bryce wrapped his hand around Kai's forearm. "Take it easy."

Through his teeth, Kai said, "I'm trying to fucking take it

easy." He slumped his shoulders and hung his head. "I'm not going to look out there. Keep an eye out, and if you see Conner coming in, get your ass over here and warn me, so I can leave. Tell Janice what happened for me." If he was meeting Liz here for a date, then for sure it was over. Even if Conner wanted to get back together, it wouldn't matter. It would finally be over for *him*.

"Yeah, sure." Bryce freed his arm. "Don't worry. I'll make sure to take care of it."

"Thanks." Kai stepped to the dishwasher and focused on drying the glasses. He had to keep his mind off it and his gaze away from that table. He wiped a few down, then poured a beer from the taps.

Bryce sided up to the pickup area and motioned with his hands. "Hey, Kai."

He walked to Bryce. "What?"

"She's meeting a girlfriend. It's safe." Bryce grinned at him. "See? Conner wouldn't do that to you. In fact, he's out of town."

Kai's heart pitched. "I don't want to know." He held his hand up. Bryce thought he was being helpful. He wasn't.

"Kai, I'm just telling you, so you don't have to worry about him coming in all night. He's in San Diego at some work thing." Bryce shook his head. "Fuck, you have no faith at all."

Kai glared at him. "Why should I have any faith, huh? The son of a bitch disappeared on me and doesn't even have the balls to tell me he's out of town or—or—that he's fucking dumping me. Apparently, he told *her* he was going out of town. He's an asshole. Just like his friends."

Bryce widened his eyes and dropped his mouth open. "Damn, dude. You were supposed to be giving him space, not giving up on him."

Kai flared his nostrils. "There's a limit to how much space I'm willing to give." He didn't understand. He didn't know

Conner the way he thought he did.

"Okay, okay. Jesus . . ." Bryce walked off toward the tables.

Chapter Twenty

Kai pulled his blazer into the driveway behind Bryce's Toyota Corolla and shut it off. Only one more day of work left, and he'd have his two days off. He looked at Bryce's car. He must have had Beth drive them to The Alamo tonight. The band was playing again, but he was in no mood to go with them this time. Dealing with Brandon there would have been excruciating.

With a sigh, he hauled himself out of the car and stepped toward the carport door. A form came into view next to it, not quite as tall as the doorknob, the neighbor's carport light catching on the outline. He squinted in the darkness.

"Kai, I'm sorry." Conner's voice broke.

Kai's heart jolted. A hot lump filled his throat. He took a step forward, straining to see in the dark. "C-Conner?" Was he seeing things? How did he get here? He hadn't seen his car.

Conner sat against the carport wall, his knees drawn up, his arm lying across them. He held a bottle to his mouth and tipped it back, then hung his head. "I'm sorry. C-can we talk? Or do you hate me already?"

Kai crouched down in front of him, taking him in.

Conner lifted his head. The trails of tears shimmered on his cheeks. His hair was disheveled. His blue button-down shirt was buttoned in the wrong holes. Patches of dirt littered his jeans.

Even in this state, Conner was stunning. Kai's heart ached. "What happened to you?" He reached a hand out to him, stopped, then drew it back. Conner had ditched him. He needed to be careful and remember that.

"I-I need to talk to you. Everything is all fucked up." Conner choked out a sob. "Shit, Kai, please talk to me."

"Okay. Come in, then." Kai stood up and unlocked the door. *I better be doing the right thing. If Conner is here to finally end it, at least I'll have some closure.*

Conner stumbled up, then righted himself, the bottle swinging from his hand.

Kai opened the door and studied him. "Are you drunk?"

"No . . . maybe." Conner creased his forehead, tears shimmering in his eyes.

As Kai nodded, he knit his brows, and stepped inside the house. Hopefully, Conner wasn't too drunk to say what needed to be said. As he inhaled a deep breath, he flicked on the lights to the main room and plopped down on the leather couch. "Fuck me." What was he going to do now? He should keep his mouth shut and listen.

Conner plodded to the couch and sat next to Kai, then set the bottle of bourbon on the black coffee table.

"So, talk." Kai's heart pounded in his ears. This was it. He stared at the television. He didn't want to look at him right now. If he did, he might not be strong enough for whatever Conner was about to say.

Conner released a held breath. "Kai, I'm gay."

"The fuck?" Kai glared at him. "What sort of bullshit are you trying to pull?" He absolutely was not going to put up with any lies.

Conner's lower lip trembled, and his eyes filled with fresh tears. "See? No one believes me when I tell them. I've done such a fantastic fucking job of making everyone think I'm someone I'm not that no one believes me when I tell them the truth." He blinked and tears tumbled down both cheeks. "I've been gay my whole life. I've hidden it my whole life. I don't like women *at all*." He pouted. "So there was no reason to be jealous of Paige."

He hung his mouth open. *No God damned way.* He was going to listen. He needed to keep quiet.

Conner gulped hard, grabbed the bourbon bottle, and took a sip, then set it on the table, hanging his head, his hands wrangling in his lap. "I was using the hookup apps to meet up with men. God, I just wanted to be with men. I hated being in bed with Paige. I had to force myself to do it, and a lot of the time, well, I couldn't, you know . . ." He shook with a sharp laugh. "Unless I thought about you. That time in my bedroom when we . . ." He sniffled. "I used that a lot." He lifted his chin. "You should know, you were my first."

Kai raised his brows. *Holy shit. He's finally telling me everything.* It was falling into place. He set a hand on Conner's thigh. "Go on."

"I got a little crazy with the apps, though. It was kind of fucked up. I sort of looked for guys who would degrade me. I guess it made me feel better about what I was doing, you know, cheating on Paige. I was getting what I needed but punishing myself in the process." Conner glanced at him, creasing his brows. "I'm so sorry you read my profiles. That must have looked really fucked up."

"I didn't, uh, read them." Kai stole a peek at him.

"Thank God." Conner freed a long sigh. "I deleted everything. They're all gone."

Kai pressed his lips together. "Why didn't you delete them when we started dating?"

As Conner shook his head, a tear tumbled down his cheek. "I don't know. Guess I was so caught up in you I didn't even think about it. Looking back, I should have." As his voice cracked, he said. "I fell so hard and so fast in love with you. You have no idea. I've never felt like this before." Tears rolled down his cheeks. He wiped them away. "When Ben and Lucas showed up, I got scared. I didn't know how to tell them. I didn't know how to let everyone know who I really was. But

I knew I had to." He drew a deep breath. "You see, we had this . . . pact. Lucas started it at bible camp. We were all the perfect kids. The ones that had everything. We laughed at kids like you. Well, they did. I just followed along. I didn't want anyone to know I was different, and deep inside I was like the kids they laughed at and bullied."

"Holy shit." Kai squeezed his thigh and took a deep breath. He needed to know it all. "So, what happened to make you finally break up with Paige and move back here?"

"Paige caught me with a guy in a club. I realized I couldn't do that to her anymore and I needed out of that whole scene." Conner bit his lip. "I talked my way out of it. I told her it was just a messed-up thing from drinking too much and she bought it." He shut his eyes tight. "But I knew it was going to happen again." He shook his head. "It was like my whole sense of self was unwinding and I couldn't stop it."

Kai rubbed his forehead. "Jesus, Conner." He examined him. What kind of pressure was he under to do this to himself? "So, what about your parents? Are they like, homophobic or something, too?"

Conner thinned his lips and let out a sharp laugh. "Fuck if I know. They had nothing to do with it. I brainwashed myself into thinking that being the perfect son meant not being gay. So I made sure they'd never suspected a thing. It was all me, being led by my friends, nothing in particular they said or did."

Kai's heart hurt for him. What if Bryce hadn't outed him? Would he have resorted to something like this to keep it from *his* mother? *Maybe* . . . But there was a bigger question at stake here. "S-so what do you want to do now?" He held his breath.

"I want to be with you, Kai. I want to be myself, finally. I want to get out of this fucking closet." Conner breathed heavily. "D-do you still have any feelings left for me?" He wrinkled his brows, his blue eyes glistening with tears.

"Are you serious? Do you really think I could get over you that fast?" Kai's heart swelled with emotion. As his vision clouded, he threw his arms around Conner's shoulders and yanked him to his chest. "God damn it, Conner, I still love the shit out of you." A hot tear fell down his cheek. He kissed his head. It all made sense now and Conner was his, even after all this.

As Conner buried his face in Kai's neck, his shoulders shook with gentle weeping.

Kai held him tightly, shushing him. "It's all right now. We'll figure this out together, okay?" He'd help Conner through this. He'd be strong enough for both of them.

Conner nodded against his shoulder, calming. "I'm not friends with Lucas anymore." He lifted his head, peering into his face. "He's such a fucking homophobe. I knew he was bad, but I didn't know how bad until last Sunday."

"So, you're still friends with Ben?" Kai gazed into his stunning face, taking in the scar under his left eye, the generous lips, the stubble on his chin.

"Yeah. He's all right. He follows Lucas around. I guess you could say that Lucas was the leader of our little trio." Conner snickered, then sniffled. "I punched Lucas."

"Really?" Kai let the corners of his mouth curl. The fucker deserved it.

"Yeah." Conner glanced at the television, then focused on him. "He was talking shit about you, so I decked him and knocked him on his ass. I can't have someone talk shit about my baby." Conner offered a lopsided grin.

It felt so good to finally have everything out on the open and nothing weird between them. Kai released a quick chuckle. "So, what about Paige?"

"I had a chat with Paige. She was pissed off that I led her on all those years, but I think it finally answered a lot of questions for her and probably gave her some closure. She was my best friend all those years. It was really hard doing that to her. The last thing I wanted was to hurt her. Turns out, she still had romantic feelings for me." Conner laid his head on Kai's shoulder. "I guess, when she drove me home, she was expecting to spend the night with me."

A hot jab stabbed Kai's heart. He wrinkled his nose. "I figured as much. She was not happy to see me there." He wouldn't ask any more about that night. Images of her flirting with Conner in the VIP lounge floated through his mind. *No, not going to think about that.* Conner came home to *him* that night. "Next time you go to one of those clubs, we go together."

A smirk spread over Conner's lips. He fingered Kai's restaurant t-shirt. "I'd love to take you there." He raised his head. "There are so many places I want to go with you."

Kai thought back over the week. Now was the time to get answers to all his questions. "Hey, who is that Liz woman I've seen you with?"

"Oh, she works in the clinic in town. She's the office manager. Sort of a work friend." Conner lifted his brows. "Why?"

Kai tensed his mouth. "She came into the restaurant last night and knew you were out of town this week. I guess I thought maybe—"

"Well, now you know there's no way there'd be anything between us." Conner closed in and placed a long kiss on his lips. "There's only you."

"Yeah." Kai took a deep breath. God, he missed those kisses. "So, you went out of town this week?"

"Just for one night. I was in San Diego yesterday for a business meeting. I came home today." Conner's gaze focused on his mouth. "What else do you want to know?" He licked his lips. "'Cause I think we have better things to do."

Heat rushed Kai's groin. He was right. But he had to know everything first. "Why are you such a mess and where were you all week?" He flipped his finger through the openings between the buttons on Conner's shirt.

Conner looked himself over and frowned. "I spent the week talking to my friends about us and getting my head together. I wanted to be sure that I was ready to come out before I saw you again. When I came home from the airport, I decided I was ready, and I went for a walk to figure out what to say. I was afraid I'd blown it. That you wouldn't want to talk to me. Anyway, I sort of fell down."

Kai smirked. "Where? Were you walking in a wash or something?"

Conner freed a soft chuckle. "No, took a wrong step in the field out by the grocery store and fell into a ravine. I got my bottle there first and I sort of drank a lot early on in my walk, then slowed down when I got here, so I could sober up before talking to you."

"Jesus, Conner, walking in the desert when you're not sober is not something you should be doing." Kai laughed. "You didn't hurt your ankle or anything, right?" He wasn't even going to ask about the buttons on his shirt.

"No, I didn't hurt my ankle this time." Conner stuck his tongue out at him.

"I got a better use for that tongue of yours." Kai draped his arms around Conner and tugged him down on top of him on the couch, kissing him with all the pent-up emotion from the week.

Conner broke the kiss. "God, I missed you." He nuzzled his neck. "I don't ever want to be apart for that long again."

"Me neither." As Kai's cock hardened, he rocked his hips against Conner's thigh, taking sweet friction. He ran his hands down Conner's back and squeezed his buttocks.

Conner moaned, his solid cock pressing against Kai's hip, rocking at an insistent pace. In a breathless voice, he said, "Do we want to do this here, or will we freak out Bryce if he walks in?"

"Yeah, you're right. Better move to my bedroom." Kai placed deep kisses over his lips, rocking his hips again. Sensation flickered up his spine. "But I don't want to stop."

"Me neither." Conner ground his hips, rubbing his erection over Kai through his jeans, gasping against his mouth. "Damn, it's been too long." He devoured him in penetrating kisses, his body shuddering against Kai. He broke the kisses, panting. "I could get off right now."

"R-really?" Kai's cock pulsed with pleasure. There was no way he could stop now. He watched Conner, pushing against him, lust tingling through his body.

Conner thrust hard against Kai's hip, groaning. His face tensed and his eyes shut. "Fuck. I'm coming." He thrust in an urgent rhythm against him, gasping as his body shook. He opened his eyes and gazed at him, his eyes hooding. "Now I'm ready to move."

"Damn, Conner. How the hell do you do that?" Need coiled in his gut, twitching his cock in his jeans.

"It's you. I can't help it." Conner kissed him on the lips, brushing his hand over Kai's cheek.

"Now you've got me so fucking hot, I'm not going to last when we get in my room."

"So? We have all night, right?" Conner climbed off the couch and held out his hand. "Come on."

Kai grabbed his hand and rose from the couch, then followed him into his bedroom and flicked on the nightstand lights.

"I need to clean up. I'll be right back." Conner walked off down the hallway.

Kai undressed and pulled down the sheets and quilt on his bed, then slipped inside, lying on his back. This was the first time Conner would be in his bed. It sounded like the only thing left was to break the news of their relationship to

Conner's parents. What would it be like meeting them?

Conner stepped into the room and closed the door, his bottom half bare, his shirt now buttoned correctly, his hair combed. He held his jeans and boxer briefs in his hand and flung them to the floor.

Kai took him in, the muscled thighs under the tails of the shirt. The tip of his cock peeking out from underneath. His own erection twitched. "Damn, Conner, that's a good look for you."

Conner smirked. "You like that?"

"Yes, now get in here." He flipped the covers down. He wasn't waiting any longer.

As Conner stepped to the bed, he unbuttoned the top of his shirt.

"No, don't take that off. Leave it for me." Desire quivered over Kai's body. God, did he want him.

Conner flicked off the lights, then climbed into bed, next to Kai, on his back. "What are you going to do to me tonight?"

Kai rolled to his side, biting his lower lip. "This." He kissed his chest through the opening in the top of the shirt, then unbuttoned one button and kissed lower.

Conner groaned and writhed on the bed, his cock hardening. "Fuck, Kai."

As Kai rubbed his solid cock against his thigh, he skimmed his hand over Conner's shaft, giving it lazy, soft strokes. Sensation built in his groin. He wanted all of Conner tonight. He was his and he wanted to take him. "Can I fuck you tonight?" He bit at his nipple.

"Yeah." Conner's shaft jerked and pre-seed dribbled onto his stomach.

Kai swiped his thumb over the tip, then pumped.

Conner gasped, thrusting his hips.

Kai rose up and opened the drawer of his nightstand, then pulled out a condom and lube. He slickened his fingers with lube, then dove his hand down to Conner's entrance, circled it, then slipped one finger inside.

Conner shut his eyes and moaned, lifting his knees.

Kai placed hungry kisses over his mouth, plunging his tongue inside to tangle with Conner's. A pulse of pleasure rocketed through his cock as it rubbed over Conner's skin. It was too good. He wouldn't last if he kept this up. He drew his hips away and slid a second finger inside Conner.

Conner groaned, his breath quickening, his hips thrusting, his solid cock twitching off his stomach. "Come on, Kai, do it."

Kai pulled his fingers out, moved between his legs and positioned the tip of his shaft at his entrance. He lifted Conner's legs.

Conner dragged Kai down to him, driving his cock slowly inside. He released a strangled whimper.

Kai brushed his hand over Conner's forehead, rocking slowly, in and out, going further in a little at a time, the tight heat of Conner's slick entrance knotting sensation in his cock. "I love you, Conner."

Conner opened his eyes, the lids hooded with lust. "I love you." He wound an arm around Kai's shoulders and drew him down for passionate, open mouthed kisses. He hooked his legs around Kai's waist and quickened the pace.

Kai's peak wound in his groin. His sac tightened. "Oh, fuck." He wrapped his hand around Conner's engorged cock and pumped it.

Conner let out sharp gasps, his face tensing. His head arched back and he cried out, his seed spurting up between them.

Kai's orgasm came on in a torrent of pleasure, wave after wave jolting through his body. His toes curled and his hips bucked. He dropped down over Conner, clenching his teeth, moaning deeply. As it quieted, he lay panting against

Conner's neck. How did he ever get here? It was all too good to be true, but it *was* true. Conner was all his. There was nothing between them now. His heart ached in a good way. He wiped his hand on Conner's hip and pulled out, then rolled to the side. "Fuck, Conner. We are definitely doing that again tonight." He rested his forearm over his eyes.

"Yeah, I agree. We have to make up for everything we missed this week." Conner snickered.

Kai lifted on an elbow and gazed down at him. "This week? I think we have five years to make up for." He kissed his cheek. "Let's go shower really quick and then take a nap before the next round." He quirked a corner of his lips.

"Sounds perfect."

With closed eyes, Kai sniffed at the air. *Is that bacon?* He sniffed again. *Yep, bacon.* He fluttered his eyes open, focusing on the empty spot in the bed next to him, light filtering in through the white draperies covering the bedroom window. Conner must be making him breakfast. *How lucky am I?* He thought back to last night. Who would have thought Conner had been gay this whole time? It was still hard to believe. His mind drifted to their lovemaking. He smirked and raked a hand through his hair. After sex had been blowjobs, followed by more sex. Damn, he'd never had a night like that before. He was pretty sure there'd be more. A lot more. He sighed and climbed out of bed, skimmed his jeans up his legs and stepped out of the bedroom, through the main room and into the kitchen.

Conner stood at the stove in his blue button-down shirt, partially buttoned at the bottom, showing his muscled chest, and a pair of black boxer briefs, his thigh muscles pulling the fabric snug.

Kai did a double take and pointed at Conner. "Is that my underwear?"

Conner turned around, spatula in hand. "Mine was dirty." He lifted his brows.

"You're going to stretch out the legs." But damn, did he look hot like that. Kai shook his head and walked to Conner, then wound his arms around his waist.

Conner huffed. "They'll be fine after I wash them."

Kai swayed him. "That's okay. You look great in them." He kissed his lips. "What are you making?"

"Pancakes and bacon." Conner grinned at him.

"I love it when you cook me breakfast, you know." Kai released him and looked into the frying pan. A fat pancake rested in it, the top bubbling. "You better turn that."

Conner waved the spatula at him. "Go and sit down."

"Sure." Kai waltzed to the glass and rattan dinette, all set up with plates, orange juice and coffee for three. "You want me to wake Bryce?"

"No, I think he needs to sleep. He was pretty drunk when he came home last night." Conner placed the pancake on the top of a stack on a plate, then set the spatula down on the white counter.

"Really? I didn't even hear him come in." Kai sat down. It was unusual for Bryce to get fucked up on a work night. Maybe he had today off?

Conner placed the plate of pancakes and a plate of bacon on the table, then sat down next to him. "He was slurring and falling down. I actually helped him to bed." Conner flipped a pancake onto his plate and poured syrup over it from a brown bottle.

"You did?" He thought back. How did he not hear any of that? He must have been really wiped out from the week and all the damn worrying. *Wait*... He looked Conner over. "What were you wearing?"

Conner smirked and swallowed a bite of bacon. "I put on my jeans and a shirt." He glanced at him, raising his brows.

"What are you worried about? I thought Bryce wasn't gay." He lifted his chin at him.

As he pursed his lips, he set a pancake on his plate, the memory of Conner wearing only his shirt last night flashing through his head. "He's not, but that doesn't mean I want him seeing you . . . you know." He faced Conner. "In that get up you wore to bed last night."

Conner sniggered. "Kai Nez, you mean you're jealous of Bryce seeing me with only a shirt on?"

Kai harrumphed. "Nobody needs to see that but me." He ate a slice of bacon, washed it down with orange juice, then smiled. "And that's something I'd like to see every day." He cut into his pancake.

Conner placed his hand on Kai's forearm. "Kai."

His gaze met Conner's. "Yeah?" Why did he look so serious all of a sudden?

"I want to see *you* every day. I want to wake up with *you* every morning and go to bed with *you* every night." Conner gnawed on his lower lip.

Kai narrowed his eyes. Was Conner saying what he thought he was saying? "Are you asking me to move in with you? For real?"

Conner nodded. "When your lease is up here, of course." He lowered his brows. "I-I want to give Bryce time to figure out a new living situation, too."

"Um . . ." Kai stared at his plate, thinking. He'd been living with Bryce since they'd graduated high school. Was it too soon to move in with Conner? He stole a peek at him. They'd seemed to do fine together while the chindi thing was going on. Maybe it *was* time. He couldn't really think of a reason not to at this point.

"Kai?" Conner wrinkled his forehead.

"Yeah . . ." Kai gave a slow nod of his head. *Why not?* "Yeah, I think that could work."

Conner freed a held breath and relaxed his shoulders. "Oh, thank God. I thought you were going to turn me down for a minute." He let a wide smile roll over his lips. "So, when is your lease up exactly?"

Kai ate a bit of pancake, then swallowed it down. "About six weeks."

Conner sipped his coffee. "Okay, then we have six weeks to plan." He set his coffee down. "There's something else I want you to know."

"What's that?" Kai gulped some orange juice, then focused on Conner. This sounded serious, too.

"I'm going to talk to my parents tonight." Conner sighed. "I want to get this over with, now that I've started it."

Kai chuckled. "Going all in, huh?" He studied Conner. "Don't you want me with you when you do this?"

Conner twisted his mouth. "I don't think so. You've never met them, and I don't want you to have a bad first impression."

Kai placed his hand over Conner's, resting on the table. "I'm sure they'll handle it much better than my mother did. I'm sure there's not much they could throw at me that would make me not like them. I mean, they did give me you." He squeezed Conner's hand. "If you want me to be there, I will."

Conner gave him a faint smile. "Thanks. But I'm going over tonight, after you go to work. I've already thought about everything I want to say. I'll start out slow and if I think it's going to turn ugly, then maybe I'll bring you with me to finish it another time."

Kai released Conner's hand and offered him a quick grin. "Okay, but know that I'm here if you need me."

"I know." Conner smirked. "I'll come to the bar after and fill you in." He wrinkled his nose. "And to be sure fucking Brandon doesn't try to hit on you tonight." He scowled.

"You don't have to worry about Brandon. You are way

better than he could ever be." Kai chuckled. There was no comparison *at all*.

Chapter Twenty-one

Kai, dressed in his black restaurant t-shirt and jeans, dried a wine glass with a white towel and scanned the groups of people sitting at the bar. Everyone was almost done and probably needed checks. He set down the glass on the cooler and walked to an elderly couple. "How are you doing?"

The man smiled at him. "We're ready for our check."

He stepped to the POS system at the island and rang them up, staring off at the fake brick wall, the machine spitting out their invoice. He caught motion out of his periphery vision and glanced at Beth.

Beth let a wide smile spread over her lips and waved a pointed finger out into the restaurant, cocking her head, her short, blunt-cut, blonde hair swinging over her shoulders.

He twisted around.

Conner, wearing a thin black V-neck sweater and jeans, sided up to bar and slid over a metal, slatted bar chair. "Hey." He skimmed his hand through his bangs and released a long sigh.

Kai's heart skipped. Maybe things hadn't gone so well with his parents. "Hey." He brought the invoice to the elderly couple, then stepped to stand in front of Conner. "Drink?"

"Yeah, just a beer." Conner offered him a quick smile, then stared at his hands, entwined on the bar top.

Kai poured his beer and set it in front of him. "You okay? You don't look so good."

"I'm okay. It was just hard." He rubbed his eyes. "I feel like I broke my mother's heart tonight."

Kai placed his hand on the back bar. What should he say to that? "I'm sorry. That sucks." He pressed his lips together. "So, she's not happy about you being gay?"

Conner gave his head a slow shake, wrapping his hands around the beer. "No, she's fine with it. She just wanted to know why I didn't trust her enough to tell her a long time ago." He turned to Kai. "She wanted to know what she did to make me think that she wouldn't support me."

Kai lifted his brows. "Well, that's a different reaction than I expected." Pretty damn different than how his mother had reacted. He glanced down the bar, making sure no one else needed him for anything. "So, but she's okay with it. With us?"

Conner freed a soft scowl. "Yeah. She wants to meet you. She thinks she remembers being a classroom helper in your class back in middle school and you being this cute little thing." He released a sharp laugh and took Kai in. "That's exactly what she called you, too, a *cute little thing*."

Kai's face flushed and he shook his head, then wiped the bar. "Seriously? She might have been. I remember moms coming in as helpers, but I wouldn't have known it was your mom." He wasn't sure what to think now. He leaned forward. "I hope you told her I'm not like that anymore." He chuckled. This was a ridiculous conversation. Under his breath, he said, "God . . ."

"You were, really." Conner smirked. "I remember how you were in middle school." He took a deep breath and sighed. "My dad was . . . quiet."

"Yeah?" Kai focused on him. "And?"

As Conner shrugged, he sipped his beer. "And so, I don't know what he thinks. My dad is a person who believes that if you don't have something nice to say, don't say anything at all. Well, he didn't say much."

Kai chewed his lower lip. "So, but no one blew up at you

or said anything nasty?" *Like my mother did.* He wouldn't even entertain remembering that day.

"Nope." He gulped his beer, then focused on it as he brought it to the bar top. "Which I think makes me feel even worse when you consider how I behaved. Especially what I did to you back in high school and to Paige all those years." He wrinkled his brows. "I don't even have a very good excuse for it." He looked at him. "Except that my best friend was a homophobic asshole. I mean, most people are closeted because their family doesn't agree with it, right?"

Kai sighed. "Yeah, I guess so." The only real reference he had was his own mother. *Not exactly a typical mother...* He'd never talked about things like this with the guys he'd hooked up with. He'd never cared enough. He glanced at Conner. He needed to help him. "Conner, whatever your reasons were for doing what you did, they were your own. I don't think you can compare your situation with anyone else's. For whatever reason, you didn't want to be gay."

Conner widened his eyes. "Yeah, you're right. I hated the idea of it. I couldn't believe that someone like me could be that way." He furrowed his brows. "*I* was homophobic, but I didn't take it out on anyone else. Just myself." He straightened and looked around him. "Fuck. I never thought about it like that before."

Kai placed his hand palm-up on the bar. "That'll be twenty dollars please." He smirked at Conner, wiggling his fingers.

"For what?" Conner let a wry grin creep over his lips.

"Therapy. You know, bartenders are pretty good at it. We hear all kinds of shit." He burst out a sharp laugh and withdrew his hand.

Beth edged up beside him. "So?" She smiled from Conner to Kai.

"So, what?" He looked her up and down.

She flung a white towel at him. "Everything good now

The Haunting Crush

---

between you two?"

Kai placed his hand on his hip. "Yeah, why?"

She glanced at Conner, then grinned at Kai. "Bryce said you two broke up or something." She raised her brows.

"Oh, my God. Bryce and his big, fucking mouth." Kai shook his head. "We're fine. Right, Conner?"

Conner offered her a charming smile. "Yes, very much in love and very much together."

"Good, because I think you two are really cute together." She winked at Kai and sauntered away.

"Well, everyone in this whole restaurant knows everything. I guarantee it." *Fucking Bryce.* Kai grabbed a wine glass from the dishwasher.

"Kai."

His heart skipped. Damn, Conner could still get to him like that. "Yeah?" He turned to Conner.

"Come meet my parents tomorrow, okay?" Conner wiggled his brows. "My mom wants to make her *cute little thing* some dinner." He snickered.

Kai grit his teeth inside a grin. "Jesus, fine." *I see that comment is going to become a thing.* He wiped the wine glass, thinking on what Conner had told him. "What about your dad?"

"We'll see, won't we?" Conner sipped his beer. "I guess I'd like your help with him. Maybe we can talk to him alone tomorrow."

Fear pinched Kai's chest. It would be hard, but he'd do this. Conner needed him. "Sure. We can talk to him together."

"Thanks, baby." Conner smiled at him and drank his beer.

Wearing a white sweater and jeans, Kai sat in the passenger side of Conner's BMW M3 as Conner drove up the long winding driveway to his parent's house.

Conner, dressed in a gray fleece and black jeans, drove the car to the double side of the three-car garage, parked and shut off the engine. He faced Kai. "How are you doing?"

"Fine." Kai clenched his jaw. He wasn't really fine. He'd never met a boyfriend's family before. But then, he'd never had a boyfriend before.

"You look pale." Conner brushed his hand down Kai's cheek. "Why are you so scared? You already sort of know my mom."

Kai drew a deep inhale. "I guess I'm a little worried about your dad. I mean, I didn't grow up with one, so . . ." How could he explain this? He wasn't used to fathers. Bryce didn't even have one.

"Kai, just relax. You deal with all sorts of people behind the bar. Maybe just pretend you're behind the bar when you're talking to him." He came close and kissed Kai's cheek. "Do you think that would help?"

Kai nodded, thinking Conner had a point. "Yeah, I'll try that." He forced a smile at him. "Let's go." He opened the car door and stepped out, then waited for him, taking in the large beige Hacienda-style home. His gaze was drawn to the open balcony above the garage, the black iron railing, and the curves in the roofline. "This place is huge."

Conner took his hand. "My parents had this place built. They bought the land, had an architect draw it up, and then contracted with a builder."

"Yeah?" *Bet it cost a fortune.* Kai tightened the hold on his hand. "Ready?"

"Yeah." Conner led him to the side of the garage, up a long, curvy set of cement steps around desert landscaping lit up from below to the entryway. A lionhead fountain spat water into a basin from the wall on one side. The other side opened to the view of Four Peaks out in the distance, and above them was another balcony with precast columns.

Conner opened the right side of a set of immense wooden doors.

A woman with shoulder-length wavy brown hair walked into the entryway. Her eye shape and color matched Conner's. She wore a long-sleeve red blouse with a long, flowing black skirt. She offered them a wide smile. "Oh, hi, honey. Right on time." She stepped to Conner and hugged him, then kissed his cheek. She turned to Kai. "And you must be Kai?"

"Yes, ma'am." Kai bit his lip and held out his hand to her.

She glanced at his hand, then held her arms wide. "Can I get a hug?"

"Uh, yeah." Kai gave her a quick hug.

As they parted, she grabbed Kai's hands, focusing on him. "You can call me Judy." She looked him up and down. "My, you've become quite a handsome young man since you've grown up." She gave his hands a shake. "You were such a cute little boy with those big brown eyes. I'm not surprised Conner fell for you."

"Uh . . ." Heat rushed to his face and he glanced at Conner.

"Mom, stop embarrassing him." Conner chuckled and tapped his mother's shoulder. "What are you making for dinner?"

She freed Kai's hands and turned to walk inside the house. "Oh, your father insisted on cooking steaks. So I made salad and some baked potatoes."

As Kai followed her into the entryway, he took in the high ceiling with a chandelier centering it, the curved stairway leading up to Conner's old bedroom, then the travertine tile floor. The memory of that night flashed through his mind. It seemed so long ago now, when he'd walked up those stairs.

Conner seized his hand and led him through the hallway, past a wet bar and into the large family room with a modern brown leather sectional wrapped around a fireplace. The room was open to the kitchen, with high-end stainless-steel appliances, dark, alder wood cabinetry and black granite counters. A long island angled out from the kitchen.

"Sit on the couch, Kai, and I'll grab you a beer." Conner waved his hand at the couch.

Kai took a seat at one end and surveyed the room, the tall ceiling and the balcony hovering over it all with the bookshelves. His gaze travelled to a sliding glass pocket door, partially opened to the flagstone patio with arched stucco Grecian columns, and red draperies. He'd stood right there, watching his classmates play beer pong. He'd seen Conner with Paige's arms wrapped around him just before he'd left. And now, five years later, he was here with Conner. Was this really happening?

Conner sat next to Kai and handed him a beer in a brown bottle. "You look like you've seen a ghost, and not the one in your place." He wrinkled his forehead.

Kai blinked a few times, then focused on him. "Sorry, it's just sort of weird being here after the last time, you know."

Conner sipped his beer. "Guess I was more concerned about you helping me with my dad than how you'd feel coming here."

Kai lifted a corner of his mouth. "It's not bad, it's just weird. Like I remember that night so clearly. Where everyone was standing, the beer pong table, everything."

Conner leaned in. "Everything? Like my bedroom?" He arched a brow.

Kai flushed and freed a sharp chuckle. "Yeah. That's something I'll never forget."

Conner brushed his lips against his cheek and whispered, "We should sneak up there later."

Kai flashed his eyes at him. "Stop it. Your parents are home." Was he always thinking about sex?

"They go to bed early." As Conner wiggled his brows, he adjusted his jeans.

Kai glanced at Conner's groin and narrowed his eyes. Under his breath, he said, "Are you getting hard thinking about it?"

Conner raked his teeth over his lower lip. "Yes. Fuck, I want you now."

"Stop it. We have to talk to your father." Kai searched the room. "Where are your parents, anyway?"

"Dad is outside grilling and Mom is . . ." Conner looked around him. "I don't know. She's around."

Conner's father, wearing a white polo shirt and khaki pants, walked in through the sliding glass doors from the patio, a plate stacked high with steaming steaks in his hand. "Oh, hello." He stepped to the couch and stopped. "You must be Kai."

Kai set his beer down on a square, dark wood coffee table and stood, wiping his hands on his jeans. "Yes, I am. Nice to meet you, Dr. Mitchell." He looked him over, the salt and pepper hair, the blue eyes, the generous lips, so much like Conner's.

Dr. Mitchell smiled at Kai. "You can call me Jeff." He lifted the plate of steaks. "Sorry, I'd shake your hand, but . . ." He peered toward the kitchen. "Where is your mother at, Conner?"

"Not sure."

Conner's mother walked out from the hallway. "I'm here, I'm here." She smiled at them. "I've set the table in the dining room. Bring the steaks, dear, and we can get started."

They followed Jeff through the kitchen and into the dining room, then sat down at a long dark wood table with cream cushions on the high-backed chairs. The table was set with white and gold china, white linen napkins with gold holders, silverware, and stemmed glasses. Conner sat next to Kai, and Conner's parents sat across from them.

Kai scanned the room. These formal rooms were pretty fancy. Behind Conner's parents, a set of French doors opened to the balcony over the garage, and a large window centered the end of the room. Built-in shelves and cabinets lined either side of the window and a buffet cabinet rested behind him against the wall. "This house is so beautiful."

"Oh, thanks, honey." Judy bent over the table, piling steak and baked potatoes on everyone's plates, then took her seat. "Can you pass the salad around, Conner?"

"Sure, Mom." Conner dished salad onto his plate, then passed it to Kai.

"So, how's business, Conner?" Jeff cut into his steak.

"Good, Dad. Got a nice commission check coming this month." Conner prepared his potato with butter and sour cream.

Kai took some salad, then passed it to Jeff. "Here you go."

Jeff took the salad bowl and set it down. "Kai, I hear you tend bar at the Fountain Bar and Grill?"

He peeked over at Jeff. "Yes. I've been working there since high school." What would someone like Dr. Mitchell think about his profession?

Jeff gave him a warm smile. "Some of my golf buddies at Firerock tell me there's an amazing bartender over there who twirls bottles in the air and makes incredible drinks. Is that you?" He tented his fingers on the table.

Kai let his lips curl in a shy smile. "Uh, yeah, that's me." He squirmed in his seat. Was he really so famous in town that people talked about him at Firerock Country Club?

"We'll have to go in sometime when you're working and see it." Jeff put a forkful of steak in his mouth.

"Sure, I usually work nights." He glanced at Conner, smirking. This was going all right.

"But he's switching to days, so we can spend more time together." Conner bumped Kai with his elbow. "Right?"

"I didn't say I'd switch to all days. Just a few." What was Conner going on about? They hadn't even talked about his schedule since they'd gotten back together. He furrowed his brows.

Judy poured red wine into a wine glass, giggling. "Just like Conner to try and dictate to you when you can and can't work."

"Mom." As Conner chewed, he flashed his eyes at her.

"He's an only child, Kai, so he's used to getting whatever he wants." She shook her head with a sigh, grinning. "I suppose I spoiled him a little."

Kai looked at him, a grin spreading over his lips. "Yeah, he does like telling me what to do sometimes."

Conner shook his head, smirking. Under his breath, he said, "Sometimes, you need a little push."

Kai sent him a mock glare. "Sure."

Kai sat on a resin wicker outdoor chair on the front balcony over the garage of the house, looking out at the lights of the town and the outline of Four Peaks lit up by the moon, hovering over the Mazatzal Mountain range.

Conner dropped down in a chair next to him and handed him a low-ball glass with bourbon in it. "My dad will be out in a minute."

Kai nodded. So far, meeting his parents had been pretty easy. Now was the real test, spending some alone time with his father.

Jeff stepped out of a French door and took a seat in a chair beside Conner, then picked up a glass with bourbon in it from a round outdoor table in front of them. "So, you two do this every night, huh?" He held his glass out to them.

Conner clinked his glass on his father's. "Yep, great way to end the day."

Kai tapped his glass to Jeff's, then took a sip. "It was nice of Judy to take care of the dishes."

"Yes, she thinks we need to talk." Jeff glanced at Conner, then sipped his drink. "Your mother and I spoke about your situation after you left last night."

Conner pursed his lips, then faced his father. "Dad, you didn't say much to me last night."

"What was there to say? Your mind was pretty much made up." Jeff focused on Kai. "It was a shock, to say the least, but it's the twenty-first century. Parents aren't supposed to be angry with their kids for being gay anymore, right?" He released a quick breath and focused on Conner. "I know I set some pretty high expectations for you, and maybe that's a big part of why you thought you had to hide this from us. All I really want now is for you to be happy and if this is who you are, then who am I say any different?"

Conner smirked. "So, you're okay with it?"

His father pursed his lips, then grinned. "If you're happy, then I'm okay with it. Yes." He cocked his head. "I'm just trying to make sure everyone's happy now, including your mother." He freed a sharp laugh.

Kai watched the exchange, taking sips of his bourbon. How easy the two of them looked together. How much had he missed in his life not growing up with a father?

"So, Kai, what are your plans with my son?" Jeff gave Kai a coy grin.

Kai widened his eyes. "Uh, what?"

Jeff chuckled. "You know, are you going to make an honest man of him?"

Conner dropped his mouth open. "Dad, it's a little soon to be talking like that."

Jeff gave his head a shake. "I'm just joking with him. But your mother has been looking forward to seeing you get married for a while now. In fact, we figured it would have happened by now." He drank his bourbon. "You two can do that now, you know." He lowered his brows. "And haven't you two already known each other forever?"

"I know, but . . ." As Conner glanced at Kai, a shy grin

crept over his face. He grabbed his hand and rested them on his knee. "We have to move in together first."

"When is that happening?" Jeff glanced at Kai.

Kai straightened in his seat. This was serious. Conner's dad must really like him to be talking this way. *But marriage already?* He had to admit, he didn't hate the idea. Someday. "My lease is up in a month or so. I'll move in with Conner then."

"Okay, good." Jeff rocked once. "So, you'll be over here for the holidays, I assume?"

"Sure." Kai gave Jeff his most charming grin.

Jeff focused on Conner. "Guess your mother will have to get a new stocking for the fireplace for Kai."

Conner laughed. "Yeah, I forgot about that."

Kai's gaze darted from Conner to Jeff. "Stocking?" With all that had happened, he hadn't even thought about the holidays coming up. He squeezed Conner's hand. How awesome would they be this year with Conner and his family?

Conner smiled at Kai. "My mom hangs stockings for all of us, including my uh, significant other. We get all sorts of fun little things in them and candy. It's like she's still treating us like we're kids."

"She's not entirely happy that Conner actually grew up. I think she wants to treat him like a little boy as much as she can." Jeff snickered and sipped his bourbon, then leaned toward Kai. "She calls him baby Conner when no one's around." He lifted his brows.

"What?" Kai erupted in a belly laugh.

"Dad." Conner glared at his father. "Don't tell him that."

"Oh, please, tell me more." As Kai's laughter slowed, he glanced at Conner and smiled. "I'm going to have to use that."

Conner pursed his lips. "No, you're not. Ever." A grin spread over his face. "You cute little thing." He smirked at him.

"Guess we *both* have funny nicknames from your mom." He shook his head and sipped his bourbon. Seemed he might finally have a father figure in his life.

"Anyhow, boys, I'm tired and heading to bed. I have an early procedure in the morning. You two can finish up here." Jeff stood and smiled at Kai. "I really enjoyed meeting you, Kai."

Kai stood up and stepped to Jeff with his hand out. "Pleasure to meet you, sir."

Jeff shook Kai's hand, then came in for a quick side-hug and a pat on the back. "Goodnight, son." He walked off through the French doors and into the house.

Kai's heart swelled. *He called me son.* He sat in his chair, tears stinging his eyes. He rubbed them away.

Conner peeked at him and lifted his brows, then whispered, "Kai."

He focused on Conner. "What?"

Conner rose from the chair and held out his hand. "Come with me."

Conner is up to something. He could see it on his face. Kai took his hand.

Conner led him through the French door, the front room and to the circular stairs. He stopped and turned, placing his fingers over his mouth. "Ssh."

Kai shook his head. Damn Conner was bringing him to his old bedroom, he knew it.

The clanking of Conner's mother working in the kitchen sounded out through the house.

Conner guided Kai up the green Berber-carpeted stairs, then to the hallway with the three doors. He shoved Kai up against the wall, bringing his hands up over his head, and crushed his mouth in deep kisses, pressing his hardening cock against Kai's hip, releasing soft moans.

Holy shit. He's really doing it. Kai opened his mouth and

tangled his tongue with Conner's, the memory of the graduation party coming to life in his mind. He ground against Conner's thigh, heat filling his shaft.

Conner broke the kisses. Inside a breath, he said, "Fuck, Kai, I can't stop." He thrust against Kai, his breath coming in quick pants.

"I don't want to stop either." Sensitivity lit up his cock, making it pulse. He bit back a groan.

Conner shoved him into his old bedroom, quietly shut the door and pushed Kai onto the bed, lying down over him. He thrust his hard shaft against Kai's hip, seizing his mouth with penetrating kisses.

Kai roamed his hands down to Conner's buttocks and pressed their hips closer still, winding a leg around Conner's. Pleasure rippled up his spine and coiled in his gut. "Fuck, this feels too good."

Conner ground his solid cock over his thigh through their jeans. "We have to hurry." He snuck a hand up under Kai's sweater and kneaded his nipple into a hard nub.

As a shock of sensation tore through Kai, he gasped. He moved his hand between them and unfastened both of their jeans, then worked their cocks out and held them together, thrusting his hips.

Conner's face tensed. His head arced back, and he slid his shaft against Kai's, through his hand. "Fuck, I'm coming."

"Shit, me, too." Sensation surged in Kai's groin, sending wave after wave of intense pleasure coursing through him. As it slowed, he laid his head on the bed, catching his breath. "Jesus, Conner. That was—"

"Exactly what we needed after all these years." Conner lifted his head and gazed down on him. "Fuck, I love you. So much." He brushed his hand over Kai's forehead. "This time, it was done for the right reason and I'm not going to be a dick after."

"Good. I love you." Kai looked around the dark room, a nightlight giving off ambient light. "I can't believe I'm here right now with you, doing this again. Guess I don't have to fantasize about it anymore. I can have it whenever I want."

"Fantasize? You fantasized about this, too?" Conner lifted a brow.

"Of course I did."

"What, when you, uh . . ." He glanced down. "Jerked off?"

"Yeah." He bit his lip. "Now, get off me and let's get cleaned up before your mom comes looking for us."

"Shit, thinking about you doing that is making me hard again." He lifted off the bed and raked a hand through his bangs.

"Stop." He snickered and placed a quick kiss on Conner's lips. "Think about it later."

Chapter Twenty-Two

One Year Later

Kai, dressed in a thin, gray sweater and black jeans, sat at a low-top table for four on a patio, looking out over the red rock cliffs of Sedona, the setting sun making changing patterns in the crags. He picked up his white wine and sipped it, then smiled at Conner. "One year, huh?"

"Yeah, we came here one year ago today." Conner, wearing a white fleece and jeans, grinned, then bit his lip. "So, did you get the scholarship applications done before we left?"

He lifted his chin at Conner. "Yes. Don't worry." He glanced down at his now empty plate of food and the bill Conner had paid. Conner was such a nag when he wanted something.

"And so, did you decide what you wanted to study?" Conner drank his wine.

Kai placed his fingers on his chin. "I was thinking something with chemistry, I don't know, maybe biochemistry or chemical engineering. Not sure which." He'd stick with what he knew he was good at.

Conner set his hand on Kai's thigh. "You have time. I'm just happy you finally decided to go to college."

"I know. If I didn't, I'd never hear the end of it." Kai rolled his eyes. Conner had started in on him shortly after he'd moved into his apartment. Ten months of nagging was enough.

"You know, you don't have to worry about money, Kai. If

you need to work less hours at the bar, you can." Conner squeezed his thigh.

"I know . . ." He let a smile creep over his face. Conner had insisted on supporting him through all of this. If it were up to Conner, he'd quit working completely. That was not going to happen.

Conner came close to Kai. "So, you remember what happened a year ago, right in the hallway back there?" He pointed into the restaurant, toward the bar area.

Heat flushed Kai's face. "Yeah." Conner would never let him forget it. Not that he wanted to.

Conner took his hand. "You told me you loved me." He chewed his lip, taking Kai in. "I want you to know that I love you more now than I ever thought possible."

Kai's heart swelled with emotion. "Conner, I never thought I'd ever be with you like this. Back in high school, I figured you could only be my crush." He freed a short chuckle. "Hell, even when you moved back to Fountain Hills, I thought the same thing. I was pissed at myself for still having a crush on you after all those years. But I did. It took a while for me to realize that I wasn't dreaming the whole time when we were first together."

Conner placed a hand on Kai's cheek and kissed his lips. "You're not dreaming. This is real. And we're going to go to that bar back there and order dirty martinis." He kissed Kai again.

"Are we now." Kai smirked. "You like reliving things, don't you?"

"Yeah, you could say that. If something was good once, it's even better the second time." Conner stood up. "Come on, let's go to the bar."

Kai rose from the table. "What about the rest of the wine?" Damn, he hated to leave good wine like that go to waste.

Conner lifted his wine glass to his lips and gulped the rest down. "There."

Kai snickered and did the same. "No blowjob involved this time?"

"Oh, there will be blowjobs, be certain of that." Conner licked his lips, then adjusted his jeans. "Damn it, Kai, why did you have to bring that up?"

Kai glanced at Conner's groin, then whispered in his ear. "You getting hard for me?" It was still so easy to get Conner going.

"When am I not?" Conner offered him a coy grin. "Come on." He tugged Kai's hand and guided him through the restaurant of gold walls lined with brown booths, then took a seat at the wrap-around bar in wood with the blue light glowing underneath.

Kai sat down and looked over the liquor bottles on a wood shelf on the back wall. "So, dirty martini, right?"

A male bartender stepped to them, wearing black. "Dirty martini? Preference on vodka?"

"Tito's, please, and make one for both of us." Kai smiled at the bartender. This bartender was on it. He liked that.

"Sure thing." The bartender made their drinks and set them down. "Here you go."

Conner picked up his drink and sipped it. "That's good, thanks." He scanned the area. "Not many people in the bar yet. Guess we won't get hit on."

Kai gave his head a shake. "Who's going to hit on us when we're obviously a couple? You've been holding my hand and kissing me all night." Apparently, Conner was doing his best to reenact the entire night.

"Oh yeah, right." Conner lifted their still entwined hands and set them on the table. "No need to hide it anymore."

Kai sipped his drink. "No, thank God." He looked him over, his stunning face, the ice-blue eyes, and the scar on his cheek. With a grin, he kissed his scar.

Conner narrowed his eyes. "Why do you always kiss me there?"

"It's, I don't know, sexy. It's a part of you that makes you unique." Kai shrugged his shoulders. "You took a bad sack that day. I remember it. I was in the stands, watching."

Conner lifted his brows. "Yeah, no shit. I got a cleat to my face. Five stitches. My mom was not happy."

Kai smirked. "Why, her baby Conner got a boo-boo?" He burst out a belly laugh.

"You shut up." Conner shook his head, biting his lip, then focused on Kai. "You're a real fucker sometimes, you know that?"

"Yeah, but I'm a lovable fucker." Kai placed a long kiss on his lips. It was time for something a bit more intimate. "Let's drink up and go back to our couch on the porch and bourbon before the sun sets all the way."

"Yeah, all right." Conner drank his martini.

Kai sat on the wicker couch on the porch of their cabin overlooking the creek, the water gurgling over rocks and clashing with boulders. He looked up at the colorful leaves swinging in a gentle breeze on the cottonwood trees lining the shore. How did he ever get here? His life had changed so much in the last year. He had so much to look forward to. He wasn't just living day to day anymore.

Conner sat down next to him and set two low-ball glasses on the glass and wicker table along with a clear, rounded bourbon bottle. He poured the bourbon, then handed it to Kai. "Here, baby."

Kai's heart skipped. He was *almost* getting used to being called *baby* by Conner. He held up his glass to Conner. "Toast."

Conner held his glass up, chewing his lip. "To what?"

"To you, bringing me here." Kai creased his brows. "To

you, giving me closure with my father. To you, showing me how to love instead of just crush on someone. To you, teaching me how to handle my mother. To you, loving me enough to come out." He blinked. *Did I really say all that? This place must be getting to me.*

Conner's eyes glistened in the setting sunlight. "Damn, Kai, you're going to make me cry." He swiped his eyes and sniffled. "But you forgot something."

"What's that?" *I think I pretty much covered it.* Kai lowered his glass.

Conner set his glass on the table, then shifted back, fishing something out of his front pocket.

"What are you doing? I'm trying to toast." He furrowed his brows, studying Conner.

Conner knelt on the porch on one knee and held up his hand, his finger and thumb pinched together, an object glittering between his fingers. He creased his forehead, tears welling up in his eyes.

Kai's heart thumped in his ears. He widened his eyes. "What are you doing?" A lump formed in his throat. "Conner?"

With a thick voice, Conner said, "I love you, Kai. I want to spend the rest of my life loving you. Will you marry me?"

Kai blinked and hot tears tumbled down his cheeks. "Holy shit." His voice wavered. Did he hear him right? The porch spun around him. He focused on Conner, gazing deeply into his blue eyes, then swallowed hard.

"Kai?" Conner sniffled and a tear broke free to race down his cheek.

Conner asked me to marry him! "Fuck, yeah. Yes." He released a held breath.

"Yes?" Conner rose to sit next to Kai, wrapping an arm around his shoulders. "Yes?"

Kai wiped his face. "I said yes already." He peeked at Conner. There was so much to say, but damned if he could speak.

Conner devoured him in an intense kiss, winding both arms around him, then broke the kiss and placed his forehead on Kai's, smiling from ear to ear. "I'm so fucking happy right now."

Kai's heart ached with love and hope. "Me, too." He kissed Conner's scar, then held out his hand.

Conner straightened and placed a thin gold band around Kai's left ring finger. "I hope this fits."

"It does." He looked at his finger. "Holy shit, Conner." *I'm engaged to Conner fucking Mitchell. Not Paige, not anyone else. Me.* His attention flew to Conner's stunning face. He would have his whole life to admire that face.

Conner let a quick smirk curl his lips. "No one is going to hit on you at the bar anymore."

Kai huffed. "That better not be the only reason you're doing this."

"Of course not." Conner snickered and pulled out a second ring from his front pocket. "Here, put this one on me." He handed it to him.

Kai held the thin, gold band up, looking it over. "These are great, not too much, but just enough and very traditional with the gold." As he smiled at Conner, he slid the ring up his finger. "There."

Conner bit his lower lip. "I have something else to tell you."

"What?" He wasn't sure his heart could take much more. Kai drew a deep inhale, steadying himself.

"My mother has an engagement party all planned out for next weekend." Conner's gaze darted over his face.

Kai furrowed his brows. "How long have you been planning this?" He thought back on all the secret phone calls Conner had shared with his mother. Now he knew what they'd been doing.

"A few months." Conner stole a peek at him, then grabbed up his bourbon and took a gulp.

"What if I'd said no?"

He scoffed. "Fuck, you wouldn't say no." He sniggered.

Kai thought about it and let a wide grin spread over his face. "Yeah, there's no fucking way I'd have said no. I'm not stupid." He laughed.

"No, you are not." Conner picked up Kai's bourbon and handed it to him. "Okay, for that toast . . ."

"Yeah?" Kai held up his glass to Conner. Now he could speak again. "I'll add, to you, the love of my life and my husband to be."

"To you, the one who gave me the strength to be myself." Conner tapped his glass against Kai's, then sipped it.

Kai sipped his bourbon. "Damn, have I told you how much I love you?"

"All the time." Conner placed a tender kiss on his lips. "Keep it up."

The End

About the Author

Christie Gordon started writing gay and M/M romance fiction after becoming preoccupied with anime and in particular, the boys love and yaoi genres. She's always had stories in her head and always enjoyed writing, so she took up fiction writing classes at a local community college and published her first book with eXtasy Books back in 2009. Christie likes to write complicated characters with painful pasts that refuse to be ignored until the characters are forced to face them head on. Angst? Yes. Happily ever after? Always. It's the struggle to get there that counts.

Christie's day job is in the high-tech industry with a Bachelor of Science in Electrical Engineering and a Master's in Business Administration. She currently lives in the Phoenix, Arizona metro area and enjoyed eight years in the bay area of California but grew up in Minnesota. She shares a home with her partner of twelve years, a musician by night and a coder by day, who is currently in three bands, giving her plenty of time to keep writing. She is also a mother of two sons, one currently in college for engineering and the other preparing for nursing college. Her one-eyed rescue pug is always by her side, snoring the day away.

Printed in Great Britain
by Amazon